KARATE
FOR YOUNG PEOPLE

By
**RUSSELL
KOZUKI**

*With
photographs
by the author*

STERLING
PUBLISHING CO., INC. NEW YORK

Other Books of Interest

Growing Strong
Judo—Athletic Institute
Junior Karate
Mas Oyama's Essential
    Karate
Natural Body Building for
    Everyone

The author and publishers wish to thank the following for posing as models in this book: Dennis Cheng, John Cheng, Robert Cirina, Robert Gato, Raymond Lennon, Imogene E. Neogra, Anthony Sabato, and Arthur Sibbio.

Contents

BEFORE YOU BEGIN 5

STANCE AND BODY BALANCE 6
Natural or "Ready" Stance . . . Horse Stance . . .
Forward Stance . . . Back Stance . . . Cat Stance

PUNCHING TECHNIQUES 24
The Karate Fist . . . The Straight Punch . . .
Lunge Punch . . . Reverse Punch . . . Hook
Punch . . . "U" Punch

STRIKING TECHNIQUES 39
Back Fist Strike . . . Bottom Fist Strike . . . Knife-
hand Strike . . . Palm Heel Strike . . . Elbow
Strikes

BLOCKING TECHNIQUES 57
Low Block . . . Forearm Block . . . High Block . . .
Knifehand Block . . . "X" Block

KICKING TECHNIQUES 76
Front Kick . . . Side Kick . . . Roundhouse Kick
. . . Back Thrust Kick . . . Stamping Kick . . .
Flying Front Kick

COMBINATION TECHNIQUES 102

SPARRING 104
Basic Sparring . . . Spar 1 . . . Spar 2 . . . Spar 3
. . . Semi-Free Sparring . . . Spar 1 . . . Spar 2 . . .
Free-Style Sparring

SCORING IN SPORT KARATE 126

INDEX 127

Before You Begin

Not too long ago, karate was taught only for self-defence. Today it is widely played as a sport—an exciting game for both the players and the spectators.

In sport karate, you are not allowed to actually strike or kick your opponent. If you did, you might injure him seriously. Whenever the words "hit," "strike," "blow," "impact," etc. are used, they are meant in the figurative sense only.

With practice, you will be able to stop just short of hitting your opponent. Of course, he will do his best to block your blows just as you will try to block his. In a way, it is a contest of fighting skills—the first one breaking through the other's defence scores a point!

This book will show you how to practice and play karate safely. Boys, girls, and older persons can all safely participate if the rules of the sport are properly obeyed. A person who practices karate is called a *karateka*. A good karateka never loses his temper or displays poor sportsmanship. Always show respect for the rights of others.

Before you begin every practice session, be sure to "warm up" your muscles. Almost any sort of body exercises will do. Good examples are push-ups, sit-ups, and leg-stretching exercises, all of which not only loosen up your muscles, but also serve as excellent body conditioners.

Stance and Body Balance

It is impossible to perform karate techniques properly without a steady stance and good body balance. A strong stance and good balance depend mainly on correct posture.

The center of body balance is located in the area just below the navel. This is called your mid-point of balance. Keep your center of gravity low so that you cannot be easily pushed off balance. The upper part of your body should remain straight and upright when moving.

Natural or "Ready" Stance

The natural stance is almost like any everyday posture. Keep your feet about a shoulder width apart and hold your fists slightly in front of your body. In karate training, you must learn to move smoothly and quickly into a defensive or attacking posture from the everyday stance.

Illus. 1. Natural Stance

Horse Stance

Illus. 2—Plant your feet about two shoulder widths apart with your toes pointed straight ahead. Stay low, but with your back straight. Prevent your feet from sliding, and tense your legs outwards. Your knees should be in a straight line directly above your big toes. The horse stance is a strong defensive stance against attacks from the side.

Illus. 2

Illus. 3

Illus. 3—To move in either direction from the horse stance, first turn your head in the direction in which you want to move.

Illus. 4

Illus. 4—Bring your left leg across in front of your right, or vice versa, depending upon the direction of movement.

■ **Horse Stance**

Illus. 5—Then move your right (or left) leg out so that you are again in your original position with your feet two shoulder widths apart.

Illus. 5

Illus. 6

Forward Stance

Illus. 6—Side view. Illus. 7—Front view.

This stance is used for both attack and defence. Your strength is to the front, and 60 per cent of your body weight is on your front leg.

Keep both of your heels flat on the ground and your rear leg straight and rigid. When moving forward or backwards, stay as low as possible by keeping your knees bent.

Usually, the length of stride depends upon your height, but the width between your two feet should be about the width of your shoulders.

Illus. 7

Forward Stance ■ 13

Illus. 8—Begin your advance from the left forward stance.

Illus. 8

■ **Forward Stance**

Illus. 9—Bring your right foot up next to the left, keeping both knees bent, and continue to step forward with your right knee bent at a 30° angle. Barely lift your foot above the ground while moving.

Illus. 9

Illus. 10

Illus. 10—Keep your left knee bent until the right foot is placed on the ground. In that instant, straighten and extend your left leg. To move backwards, simply reverse the procedure.

To turn to the rear from the forward stance, place your back foot directly sideways about a shoulder's width past the heel of your front leg. Stay low, pivot on the balls of your feet, and face in the opposite direction, at the same time shifting your weight forward.

Back Stance

More flexible body movements are possible with the back stance than with the forward stance because a shorter stride is required. For this reason, many karate players prefer the back stance over the more rigid fighting stances. Seventy per cent of your body weight is on your rear leg with your upper body straight in a half-front-facing position.

Keep the toes of your front leg in a straight line with the heel of your rear foot. In other words, the toes of your front foot should be pointing in the direction of your opponent.

Illus. 11—This is a front view of the back stance.

Illus. 11

Illus. 12

Illus. 12—This is a side view of the back stance.

You must take care not to allow the toes of your back foot to turn towards the rear. This would make it difficult to tense your rear leg properly when moving forward or backwards. Your entire body weight must shift naturally in the direction of the movement.

Illus. 13—Advancing from the back stance. Shift your weight to your front leg, keeping your knees bent, back straight, and body low.

Illus. 13

Illus. 14—When you bring your back leg forward next to your front leg, do not raise your foot. Make it glide across the ground.

Illus. 15—Continue moving your back leg forward past your front leg until *it* becomes the front leg. Shift your weight onto the rear leg. You should end up in the same position as before, but reversed.

To turn in the opposite direction, pivot round on the balls of your feet, shifting your body weight at the same time.

Cat Stance

Illus. 16—In this stance, used mostly for defence, the karateka faces his opponent in a half-front-facing posture with his rear knee bent and leg kept tense.

Illus. 16

Illus. 17

Illus. 17—To move into the cat stance from the natural position, bring your left foot about 6 inches behind the heel of your right foot.

Illus. 18—Raise the heel of your right foot, and point your toes straight ahead. The toes of your left foot should now be pointing sideways in relation to your front-facing position.

Punching Techniques

The Karate Fist

Illus. 19, 20, 21—The karate fist can be employed in many different ways for both attack and defence, so it is important that you learn how to form it properly. Extend your hand out, fingers together, roll all four fingers tightly into your palm, and press your thumb against the rolled-up index and middle fingers. (See title page photo.)

Illus. 19

Illus. 20

Illus. 21

The Straight Punch

The knuckles of the middle and forefinger are used as the striking surface in the straight punch.

Illus. 22—Stand in the natural stance with your left arm extended, and your right fist cocked at your hip with the palm side turned upwards. The punch is delivered in a straight line to the target.

Illus. 22

Illus. 23—As you extend your right arm, begin to twist your right wrist counter-clockwise as your elbow passes beyond your stomach. Also start to pull back your extended left hand at the start of the punch. Your fist should strike the target with the palm facing downwards, and your left hand pulled back in a cocked position on your left hip.

Illus. 24—At the moment of impact, the sudden tensing of your body muscles, the reaction force of the withdrawing arm, plus the speed of the twisting blow, all combine to add power to the punch. This sudden concentration of one's full power is called the point of "focus" in karate. Immediately relax your muscles so that you can make the next move quickly.

Illus. 24

Lunge Punch

Illus. 25—The lunge punch is frequently used when closing in on an opponent. The punching hand is on the same side as the advancing foot. Keep your back straight and avoid lifting your foot too much when moving. The punch is focused just as the advancing foot touches the ground.

Illus. 25

Illus. 26

Reverse Punch

Illus. 26—This is probably the karateka's most powerful punch. The punching hand is on the same side as the rear leg. The added power of the reverse punch comes from the forward-twisting motion of the hips as the punch is thrown. At this instant the body muscles are fully tensed.

Reverse Punch ■ 29

Illus. 27

Illus. 27—Start your reverse punch from a forward stance with your left arm extended. Hold your right fist close to the top of your hip. Keep your hips at a 45° angle.

■ **Reverse Punch**

Illus. 28

Illus. 28—Shoot your right fist forward, at the same time drawing your left hand back. Twist your right hip forward. Keep your arms close to your body and your back straight throughout the entire punch.

Illus. 29—Twist your wrist as your arm thrusts forward. Thrust back on your rear foot. You should be facing directly towards the front as you deliver the blow.

Illus. 29

Hook Punch

The hook punch is an adaptation of the basic straight punch. It can be used to good advantage when your opponent moves in close to you.

Illus. 30—The punching hand is hooked sharply to the inside when the elbow passes the stomach. Keep the punching arm tight against your body.

Illus. 31

Illus. 31—Keep your back straight as you deliver the hook punch. This punch can be directed at your opponent's head, neck or side. Remember, speed is important in all punches, but do not sacrifice control for speed or you might injure your opponent accidentally.

"U" Punch

Illus. 32—Here the punching arms form the letter "U". The double blow can be delivered to your opponent's face and stomach at the same time.

Illus. 32

Illus. 33—Assume the forward stance and place both fists over your right hip. Do not lift the shoulder of the upper punching arm. This would prevent proper tensing of the chest muscles and make the punch weak.

Illus. 34—Thrust your weight forward and move both arms forward in a "U" shape.

Illus. 35—Punch simultaneously with both fists, the right fist to the face and the left fist (facing up) to the stomach or groin.

Striking Techniques

Back Fist Strike

Illus. 36—The back fist strike is a very effective technique utilizing a snapping motion of the wrist and forearm. It can be aimed in a sidewards or downwards direction against your opponent's head and body. The first two knuckles on the back of your fist are employed as the striking surface.

Illus. 36

Illus. 37

Illus. 37—Begin the back fist strike by crossing your arms in front of your chest with your striking fist on the bottom. Instead of the blow travelling in a straight line, it will follow a half-circle course to the target.

Illus. 38—With a quick snapping motion from the elbow, start to deliver the strike, returning your other hand to a position close to your hip. This blow is most effective against the face or stomach.

Illus. 38

Back Fist Strike ■

Illus. 39

Illus. 39—At the moment of impact, keep your elbow slightly bent to avoid injuring it. The position of your fist at the end of the strike depends upon how you struck the target with the first two knuckles.

Bottom Fist Strike

Illus. 40—Usually used against the hard, bony parts of the body, the bottom fist strike can be directed at the softer targets such as the face and neck as well. This powerful technique utilizes the bottom of the fist as the striking surface. You can deliver it straight down or sideways. Begin the bottom fist strike in the same way as the back fist strike.

Illus. 40

Knifehand Strike

Illus. 41—Open-hand techniques are used effectively in attack and defence, with the palm, the back of the hand, the fingertips, and the outside edges of the hand all used as striking surfaces. The little-finger side of the hand is the striking edge in this blow.

Illus. 41

Illus. 42

Illus. 42—To form the knifehand, flatten out your hand and bend your thumb. Keep your fingers pressed together. Place your striking hand behind your ear without raising your shoulder. Extend your other arm straight in front of you.

Illus. 43

Illus. 43—Bring your striking arm round in a circular whiplike movement aimed at your opponent's neck or temple.

Illus. 44

Illus. 44—Withdraw your other hand to your hip as you deliver the strike. Your palm should be facing up and your wrist should be bent.

Palm Heel Strike

This is essentially a self-defence technique, although it can be used to distract your opponent in sport karate.

Illus. 45—Deliver the blow upwards at a 45° angle in a straight line to your opponent's nose. Be careful when working on this technique with an opponent!

Illus. 45

Illus. 46—Begin in the natural stance. Extend your left arm forward, opening your fist as you do so. At the same time, extend your right arm forward, opening your fist and twisting your wrist so that your fingers are pointed upwards.

Palm Heel Strike ■ 49

Illus. 47

Illus. 47—Thrust your right arm at your opponent with the palm of your hand straight up, and snap your left arm back into a fist position at the hip.

Elbow Strikes

Illus. 48—There are five variations of the powerful elbow-strike technique—forward, backwards, upwards, sidewards, and downwards. Elbow strikes are especially effective in close fighting, and are very easy to learn.

Illus. 48

Illus. 49—In the *forward* elbow strike, swing the point of your elbow sharply round and forward to the target (usually the ribs or solar plexus). Begin with your relaxed arm swinging out. Then thrust the elbow forward towards the target, tensing your arm and turning your wrist over.

Illus. 49

Illus. 50

Illus. 50—In the *backwards* elbow strike, your elbow moves back in a straight line. Keep the elbow close to your body. Begin this strike by quickly lowering your body slightly and thrusting your striking elbow forcefully towards the chest or solar plexus. Immediately repeat the procedure with your other arm in the event your opponent has shifted his body to the other side.

Illus. 51

Illus. 51—In the *upwards* elbow strike, you thrust your elbow straight up in a direct line to the jaw. Begin with your fist at your hip. Your target is the middle of your opponent's chin. As you move your arm upwards, turn your wrist so that your palm is facing your ear at the moment of impact.

Illus. 52

Illus. 52—In the *sidewards* elbow strike, keep your forearm close to your body and thrust your elbow sidewards in a straight line. Your target is your opponent's chest. Assume a natural stance and cross your arms high in front of your chest, elbows pointed towards each side. Thrust sidewards with your striking elbow, at the same time moving into a horse stance.

Illus. 53

Illus. 53—In the *downwards* elbow strike, aim the point of your elbow directly down on your opponent's spine or neck. Assume a forward stance as you are delivering the strike.

Blocking Techniques

In karate, "blocking" means striking aside or deflecting your opponent's attack with your hands, arms, or feet.

Low Block

Illus. 54—The low block serves as an effective defence against attacks to the stomach and groin areas. The outer edge of your wrist and fist are used to deflect your opponent's kicks and blows.

Illus. 54

Illus. 55—Practice the low block in the natural stance. Bring your fist across your chest and up to the ear on the opposite side of your head. Extend your other arm straight in front of you, palm down.

Illus. 55

Illus. 56—Drive your blocking arm downwards and across your chest, focusing the block about 6 inches in front of your thigh. Always execute the block with the arm on the same side as your forward foot for extra power.

Illus. 56

Illus. 57

Illus. 57—As your blocking arm approaches its final position, withdraw your other arm sharply to the hip position. The blocking surface is the outside edge of your wrist and fist. The low block can be executed from either the horse stance or the forward stance.

Forearm Block

This block is usually performed from the forward stance to protect the chest and the stomach area. It can, however, also be used effectively against kicks and blows to the face and neck.

Illus. 58—In this block, you use the inside edge of your forearm to block your opponent's blow or kick. As in all blocks, the forward leg should be on the same side as the blocking arm. This prevents you from losing your balance at the moment of impact.

Illus. 58

Illus. 59

Illus. 59—Practice the forearm block in the natural stance. Bring your closed fist up to the ear on the same side of your body with the palm side facing your opponent. Extend your other arm forward.

Illus. 60—Swing your blocking arm round and forward sharply, at the same time withdrawing your other arm. Begin to twist your blocking fist in a circle.

Illus. 61

Illus. 61—Focus strongly at the point of contact, and twist your fist inwards and up so that the knuckles are facing upwards. Snap your other arm back into hip position. Your blocking fist should be at about shoulder level.

High Block

Illus. 62—The high block is usually used to deflect blows to the face and head. The blocking arm is swung sharply upwards with an inwards twist of the forearm.

Illus. 62

Illus. 63

Illus. 63—To practice the high block, extend one arm straight in front of you and cock the fist of your other hand at your hip, facing upwards. Keep the bent elbow of the blocking arm close to the body at the start of the block.

Illus. 64—Cross both hands in front of your chest. Be careful not to raise the shoulder of your blocking arm nor lift your elbow higher than the blocking hand.

Illus. 64

Illus. 65

Illus. 65—Thrust the blocking hand upwards with an inwards twist of your forearm, at the same time withdrawing your other hand to your hip. The palm of your blocking hand should be facing your opponent.

Knifehand Block

Illus. 66—You can employ the knifehand block from almost any stance, although it is most frequently used from the back stance or the cat stance. To form the knifehand, see Illus. 42 on page 45.

Illus. 66

Illus. 67—Extend one arm straight in front of you and bring your blocking hand across your chest and up to the ear on the opposite side of your body. Your open palm should be facing the ear.

Illus. 67

Illus. 68—Using your elbow as the pivot point, slash your knifehand downwards at an angle across your chest. Twist your forearm strongly counter-clockwise while keeping your wrist straight and rigid.

Knifehand Block ▬ **71**

Illus. 69—At the same time that you are bringing the knifehand down, pull back the other hand to your chest with the open palm turned upwards. Avoid raising your shoulder, which would prevent you from tensing your chest muscles and thus weaken the block.

Illus. 69

Illus. 70

"X" Block

Illus. 70—This is an excellent, speedy block against attacks to the head and face. Very little strength is needed. After the block, your open hands are used to pull your opponent off balance while you counter-attack with a front kick or a back fist to the face.

Illus. 71

Illus. 71—Assume the ready stance to practice your "X" block. Cross your open hands directly in front of your chest.

Illus. 72

Illus. 72—Thrust your crossed hands sharply upwards. Do not spread your elbows—keep them in line with your body. Spreading your elbows will make your block weak and ineffective.

Kicking Techniques

With diligent training, your feet can become very effective weapons. There are four major types of karate foot attacks—front, side, back, and the roundhouse kick—and a number of variations.

Front Kick

Illus. 73—This kick may be performed in two different ways. In one, the kick depends on the upwards snapping action of the knee; in the other, the ball of the kicking foot is thrust forward directly at the target. In both kicks, the kicking foot should be brought high with the ankle flexed upwards. Keep your back straight, and withdraw your kicking foot quickly after the kick to prevent capture by your opponent.

Illus. 73

Illus. 74

Illus. 74—From the natural stance, bring the knee of your kicking leg up high.

Front Kick ■ 77

Illus. 75—In one motion, carry out the kick by making full use of the rising, snapping action of your knee and the forward thrust of your hip.

Illus. 75

Illus. 76—Withdraw your kicking foot quickly to knee level of the supporting leg. If you hesitate, your opponent might grab your foot and throw you off balance.

Illus. 76

Illus. 77

Side Kick

Illus. 77—The side kick is normally made from a side stance. However, regardless of the stance used, the heel of the kicking foot should be brought up to the knee of the supporting leg, which is kept slightly bent and tensed outwards as in the horse stance. The kick can be thrust outwards strongly at the target in a straight line as shown here, or the edge of the kicking foot brought up quickly in a rising arc to attack the softer targets, such as the chin or solar plexus.

Illus. 78—From a sideways position in relation to your opponent, raise your kicking foot quickly to the level of the knee of your supporting leg. Keep your head turned towards your opponent.

Illus. 78

Illus. 79

Illus. 79—Thrust your kicking leg out in a straight line at your target. Use either your heel or the edge of your foot as the striking surface.

Illus. 80

Illus. 80—Quickly withdraw your kicking foot back to the cocked position before lowering it to the ground. Keep your eye on your opponent.

Roundhouse Kick

Illus. 81—In this kick, your target can be either the head or the rib area of your opponent. The ball of your foot is the striking surface. The kicking leg is brought up directly sideways and whipped forward to the target in a circular movement. Your supporting leg is very important in all kicks—you must not only maintain your balance on it, but it must absorb the shock of the impact of your kicking leg.

Illus. 81

Illus. 82

Illus. 82—To practice the roundhouse kick, assume a modified forward stance, both knees bent slightly, and hold your hands in front of your body.

Illus. 83—Raise your kicking leg sideways, keeping your knee and ankle tense. The calf of your leg should be as close as possible to the back of your upper leg.

Illus. 84

Illus. 84—Swing your hip forward in a circular movement, and use the snapping action of your knee to strike
the target directly in front of your body. Withdraw the
kicking leg quickly back to a cocked position before
returning it to the ground.

Back Thrust Kick

This is an effective defence against an attack by your opponent from the rear.

Illus. 85—In this kick, the heel is the striking surface, and you thrust it back in a straight line to the target. The chest, stomach, or groin are the target areas in the back thrust kick.

Illus. 86—From the ready stance, bring up your kicking foot to the knee level of the supporting leg, and turn your head back towards your opponent.

Illus. 86

Back Thrust Kick ■

Illus. 87—Thrust your heel back in a straight line directly towards the target.

90 ▪ **Back Thrust Kick**

Illus. 88

Illus. 88—Quickly withdraw your kicking foot back to the knee of the supporting leg. Speed is important to maintain balance as well as to avoid capture of the leg.

Stamping Kick

Illus. 89—This is an excellent defence technique against an opponent who attempts to grab you from behind. The heel of your kicking foot is thrust downwards strongly on the shin or instep of your opponent.

Illus. 89

Illus. 90

Illus. 90—Assume the ready stance, raise the heel of your kicking foot to the knee of the supporting leg, and look back and down at the target.

Illus. 91

Illus. 91—Thrust your heel downwards in a direct line to the target. Focus the stamping as close to the ground as possible.

Illus. 92

Illus. 92—The stamping kick can also be delivered to the shin of an opponent, in which case the inside edge of the foot, as well as the heel, is the striking surface.

Illus. 93

Illus. 93—Here, the stamping kick is being delivered to the back of the knee, utilizing the outside edge of the foot as the striking surface.

Flying Front Kick

In karate, a jump kick is often employed as a surprise weapon. This type of kick may be done by jumping off the ground on one foot and kicking with the other, or jumping up and kicking with the same foot.

Illus. 94—Begin in the natural stance. Bring one leg up sharply to the level of the other leg.

Illus. 94

Illus. 95

Illus. 95—Spring up in the air, pushing off hard with the supporting leg.

Illus. 96

Illus. 96—Here the push-off leg is used to deliver the kick in mid-air.

Illus. 97

Illus. 97—Withdraw your kicking leg quickly so that you will descend with both feet on the ground.

Illus. 98—Be sure you land in as balanced a posture as possible to guard against your opponent's inevitable counter-attack.

Illus. 98

Combination Techniques

Many hours of practice are required before you will be able to move quickly from one technique to another while maintaining good balance and a strong defence at the same time. The ability to shift smoothly from one stance to the next depends largely on good posture and body balance. The upper body should remain straight, and the supporting leg placed solidly on the ground. Dozens of different technique combinations are possible.

Illus. 99, 100, and 101 illustrate a typical reverse-punch, front-kick, roundhouse-kick attack combination. It is important to bear in mind that your hands must always be kept ready to block any possible counter-attack.

Illus. 99

Illus. 100

Illus. 101

Sparring

One of the end results of sport karate training is developing skill in free-style sparring. There are three types of sparring—basic sparring, semi-free sparring, and free-style sparring. In basic sparring, and to a limited degree in semi-free sparring, the opponents face each other at a set distance, and take turns practicing an agreed set of techniques on each other. However, in free-style sparring, nothing is pre-determined, and each participant tries to score on the other with a "killing" blow, stopped just short of actual contact.

Many different attack and defence techniques must be practiced by the karateka on this road to proficiency. For obvious reasons, as a beginner, you should be well trained in basic karate blocking and attacking techniques first. After that you can move on to formal basic sparring, then progress to semi-free sparring, and finally to free-style fighting.

Basic Sparring

In basic sparring sessions, the two opponents are expected to face each other in a natural, or "ready," stance, and then bow to each other as a sign of mutual respect, just as boxers touch gloves before a bout. At the end of the practice session, the two karatekas again exchange bows. On the following pages are some examples of formal basic sparring.

Illus. 102—After the bow, Defender waits for Attacker
to get into attacking position.

SPAR 1

Illus. 103—Attacker drops back into a low-block, forward-stance attacking position, while Defender remains in his natural, or "ready," stance.

Illus. 104—Defender drops back into the forward stance and executes a low block to deflect Attacker's front kick.

Illus. 105

Illus. 105—Defender counters with a reverse punch to the body.

Illus. 106

SPAR 2

Illus. 106—Attacker assumes a low-block attack position.

Illus. 107

Illus. 107—Defender steps back into the horse stance and uses an outside forearm block to stop Attacker's punch.

Illus. 108

Illus. 108—In the same motion, Defender counter-attacks with a back fist strike to the face.

Illus. 109

SPAR 3

Illus. 109—Attacker assumes a low-block attacking position.

Illus. 110—Defender stops Attacker's lunge punch with a high block.

Illus. 111—Defender counter-attacks with a reverse punch to the body.

Illus. 110

Illus. 111

Illus. 112

Illus. 112—An attacker moves in, trying to find an opening.

Semi-Free Sparring

After the formal basic sparring, the karateka moves on to a more advanced type of training. Semi-free sparring is very much like basic sparring except that the participants work in a more relaxed stance, and are permitted to move about freely. The attacker attempts to find an opening and score while the defender tries his best to block or dodge the attack, and to counter.

As in basic sparring, the karatekas bow to each other before they begin.

SPAR 1

Illus. 113—Both Attacker's and Defender's forward feet are in a direct line and on the same side.

Illus. 114—Attacker aims a roundhouse kick to the head. Defender withdraws his forward leg while blocking the kick with his knifehand.

Illus. 115—Defender counter-attacks with a front kick to the groin.

Illus. 115

Semi-Free Sparring ■ 117

Illus. 116

SPAR 2

Illus. 116—Defender senses his opponent's kicking attack and executes a side kick to the knee to disturb Attacker's balance.

Illus. 117 and 118—Defender follows through with a roundhouse kick to the head.

Semi-Free Sparring ■ 119

Free-Style Sparring

There are no pre-arranged attacks or moves in free-style sparring. On the other hand, any action which might endanger your opponent is strictly prohibited. Good sportsmanship and control of one's temper is expected of every player. The skilled karateka can deliver a "focused killing blow" just short of actual contact with his opponent's body.

In free-style sparring, the two opponents move about at will, exchanging blows, blocks, and kicks until one scores with a strongly focused kick or a blow to a vital area. Because there remains the possibility of a serious injury if karate techniques are carelessly employed, only the more experienced karatekas are permitted to engage in free-style sparring.

Illus. 119

Illus. 120—Two karatekas assume fighting stances waiting for the command to start their free-style sparring practice under the watchful eyes of their instructor who is acting as the referee.

Illus. 121

Illus. 121—Will the flying opponent kick in mid-air, or attack with his fists when he lands?

Illus. 122

Illus. 122—Blocking a back fist blow to the face.

Illus. 123—A lightning-fast front kick scores a clean point!

Illus. 124—A smashing back kick stops an opponent dead in his tracks!

Illus. 125

Illus. 125—A leaping front kick scores a point — an example of controlled power!

Scoring in Sport Karate

In sport karate, all blows and kicks are stopped just short of actual contact, and unsportsmanlike conduct or any action endangering one's opponent are strictly prohibited. It is a test of individual fighting capabilities with built-in safeguards.

Point scoring is based on theory. For an example, was a given blow executed with enough skill and power to disable your opponent had it actually struck him? Normally, the referee in the ring with the contestants calls the point, although the assistant judges, placed in the four corners of the ring, may call the point even if the referee does not see the scoring point himself. In such cases, the majority rule must prevail.

A point may be scored by executing a fully "focused" karate kick, strike, or blow just an inch short of the target! Actual contact to the opponent's face or body is not permitted. This rule is strictly enforced to prevent serious injury to the participants. However, a scoring point may be allowed even if there was "light" contact, should the referee and the judges agree that contact was unintentional, the technique well executed, and there was no injury to the opponent. In the event these officials decide otherwise, no point would be allowed, and the guilty party warned of immediate disqualification and forfeiture of the match to his opponent should he commit another infraction of the rules.

Most matches run for three minutes, with the karateka first scoring two half points or one full point being declared the winner. A full point is awarded only on a perfectly executed technique. The length of the matches and the scoring method may vary somewhat in some contests, depending on the size and the importance of the tournament. Because sport karate is relatively new, it is not unreasonable to expect some future rules' changes and other innovations in order to create a safer and more exciting sport.

Index

advancing
    back stance, 19–20
    forward stance, 12–16
back fist strike, 39–42
back stance, 17–20
back thrust kick, 88–91
backwards elbow strike, 53
balance, 6, 84, 91
basic sparring, 104–113
blocking techniques
    forearm, 61–64
    high, 65–68
    knifehand, 69–72
    low, 57–60
    "X", 73–75
bottom fist strike, 43
bowing, 104
cat stance, 21–23

combination techniques, 102–103
downwards elbow strike, 56
elbow strikes
    backwards, 53
    downwards, 56
    forward, 52
    sidewards, 55
    upwards, 54
exercises, 5
facing position, 17, 21
fist, 24
fist strikes
    back, 39–42
    bottom, 43
flying front kick, 97–101
focus, 27, 64
focused killing blow, 120

forearm block, 61–64
forward elbow strike, 52
forward stance, 12–15, 56
free-style sparring, 120–125
front kick, 76–79
half-front facing position,
   17, 21
high block, 65–68
hook punch, 33–34
horse stance, 8–11
jump kick, 97–101
karate fist, 24
karateka, 5
kicking techniques
   back thrust, 88–91
   flying front, 97–101
   front, 76–79
   roundhouse, 84–87
   side, 80–83
   stamping, 92–96
knifehand block, 69–72
knifehand strike, 44–47
low block, 57–60
lunge punch, 28
natural stance, 6–7
open-hand techniques, 44
palm heel strike, 48–50
pivot point, 71
point of focus, 27, 64
punching techniques
   hook, 33–34
   lunge, 28
   reverse, 29–32
   straight, 25–27
   "U", 35–38

"ready" stance, 6–7
rear attack, 88
reverse punch, 29–32
roundhouse kick, 84–87
scoring in sport karate, 126
semi-free sparring, 114–119
side kick, 80–83
sidewards elbow strike, 55
sparring
   basic, 104–113
   free-style, 120–125
   semi-free, 114–119
sport karate, 126
stamping kick, 92–96
stance
   back, 17–20
   cat, 21–23
   forward, 12–16
   horse, 8–11
   natural or "ready" stance,
   6–7
straight punch, 25–27
striking techniques
   back fist, 39–42
   bottom fist, 43
   elbow, 51–56
   knifehand, 44–47
   palm heel, 48–50
"U" punch, 35–38
upwards elbow strike, 54
warm up, 5
"X" block, 73–75

THE RAG PICKERS

THE RAG PICKERS

By H. Vernor Dixon

DAVID McKAY COMPANY, INC.
New York

67-212

THE RAG PICKERS

Copyright © 1966 by H. Vernor Dixon

Library of Congress Catalog Card Number: 66-19260

Manufactured in the United States of America

Van Rees Press • NEW YORK

Dedicated to
Bob Wackerman
Thanks for your help
H.V.D.

Author's Note

BECAUSE of the nature and background of this book, because it is written about the department store business, and because it is pinpointed geographically in the City of San Francisco, some people may think they see themselves or others in the fictional characters used herein. If that mistake should occur, it will be highly gratifying and flattering to the author for having drawn characters so true to life. But let us not be misunderstood. No living person has an actual counterpart in this story. All characters are strictly fictional and exist only in the imagination of the author.

On the other side of the coin, however, it is equally true that the writer has spent considerable time in researching department stores that do exist, such as Saks Fifth Avenue, Roos/Atkins, Bullock and Jones, Macy's, the Emporium, and so on. Merritt-Wilson is not fashioned after any one of these stores; it is, rather, a composite. After all, if a person is writing about the steel business, it necessarily follows that the best place for research is the steel mills themselves. Yet it does not also follow that the writer would have any particular steel mill in mind. The same is true here. There is no such department store chain as Merritt-Wilson, nor is it fashioned in any way after any particular chain. Let us be kind and concede that the writer may have an imagination of his own.

H. VERNOR DIXON

THE RAG PICKERS

I

Joe Haley came home that morning at a little after four A.M. He opened the front door quietly and closed it softly, then tiptoed up the carpeted stairs to the bedroom floor of the house. Normally, he would not have bothered to exercise caution, but this was not a night he was supposed to have out. He hadn't even bothered to call home to say he was detained by business, or some other alibi. Mary might be a little perturbed on this night, even though it had happened many times before during their marriage. So he exercised due care. He went noiselessly into the bedroom, saw that Mary was asleep, and got out of his clothes in the dark. When he was in the raw, which was the state in which he always slept, he went to the bed, pulled the covers back slowly and gradually lowered himself into the bed at Mary's side. Then he pulled the covers up to his chin, turned on his side, grinned and winked at nothing, and went instantly to sleep.

Mary awakened him in the morning by shaking his arm. He yawned and stretched and blinked his eyes and sat up just as Mary disappeared out the door in her nightgown, slippers, and the old flannel robe she so adored. Joe yawned again and chuckled softly. Thank God, they hadn't had a row, though maybe it would come during breakfast. Well, he thought, all in due time. Sometimes it didn't even happen. Maybe this would be such a lucky morning.

He slipped his lean shanks out of bed, stood on the floor and stretched his whole body. He leaned over to touch his toes with his fingertips a few times, then walked to the front windows where he pulled back the curtains. It was a cold, gray morning, with billows and puffs of fog trailing their skirts down the street.

Even the automobiles parked at the curbs looked cold and gray. A typical San Francisco summer morning. What was it that some great muckimuck had had to say about San Francisco? Oh, yes. W. Somerset Maugham had once said something like, "One of the most miserable winters I ever spent in my life was one summer in San Francisco." And so true. But not for a San Franciscan. The old boy hadn't been properly acclimatized. San Franciscans loved their fog. Nature's built-in air-conditioner. Three days of summer weather in the seventies or eighties and San Franciscans started yearning for the fog to return. Four days of hot weather and they cursed aloud and whispered to each other, "This is earthquake weather. Mark my words. Unseasonable." Anything slightly out of the usual was always earthquake weather. The year '06 was never far from their minds, even though they always referred to that catastrophe as "the great fire." Only strangers, and in bad taste at that, ever mentioned the "earthquake" of 1906. To San Franciscans it was always "the big fire." Yet they talked forever about earthquakes.

Joe turned away from the windows and blinked at the bedroom. Everything was in white and gold. The big studio-type bed had a white spread and white padded headboards. The thick carpet was white, but alongside the bed was a gold throw rug. The chaise longue and all the rest of the furniture were painted white with tiny traces of gold running through. Even the mirrors on the walls had gold etchings in their borders. Joe thought, Like a really high class whorehouse. It was odd, but Mary, who was the most virtuous of all the women he had ever known, did have the taste of an expensive whorehouse madam. He chuckled, scratched his scalp, and headed for the bathroom.

He shaved and took a shower, then stood before the big, full-length mirror in the wall to towel himself. Many times he had tried to induce Mary to do it with him on the polar bear rug before the big mirror, but had never succeeded. She liked her sex almost as well as Joe, but not that well. To her, any sexual act out of bed was sheer folly and exhibitionism. He remembered one time he had tried to do it to her before a roaring fire in the living room fireplace. She had finally become angry enough with him to slap his face and call him a rapist. He had never gone that far again. Yet, he sighed, it would be fun before that big mirror.

He finished drying himself, then cocked his head to one side to appraise his image in the mirror. He raised his arms and flexed

2

his powerful muscles. He liked and approved of all he saw. His hair was coal black, with a small wave on the right side, his eyes were deep green that varied from light to dark depending on his mood, his nose was thin and highly arched, his lips were sensuous, there was a slight dimple in his square chin, and the olive skin of his face was almost baby smooth. No woman could resist looking after him as he walked down the street. His body, too, complemented his features perfectly. He was six feet two inches tall, at one hundred and ninety pounds; his shoulders were square, his chest like a barrel, his hips thin, his stomach ridged and flat, and his legs were long, lean, and lithe. There was a certain rugged look about him that prevented him from being too handsome. Very few men had ever made the mistake of thinking he would be easy to take in a fight. Joe had never in his life been knocked off his feet and had the scarred knuckles to prove how well he could defend himself.

He went back into the bedroom and got dressed. When he had finished, he looked like a fashion-plate model with black shoes, custom-made shirt, tailored tie, and a tailored lightweight black mohair suit. As a department manager for Merritt's, one of California's best-known department stores, he was supposed to wear Merritt clothing, but had never done so. His bosses simply looked aside when he turned up in expensively tailored clothes. He would rather quit his job than wear a Merritt suit.

He left the upstairs, which had four bedrooms, his and Mary's, two for the three boys, and a guest room, and went downstairs. He paused to peek into the overly large living room and shuddered, as usual. It was all done in the Louis XIV period, just a bit after the Trianon. All the ornamentation of the Louis XIV period was there—panels of carved plaster in eggs and darts, grapes and acanthus leaves, fluted columns, two bronze doors, French damask coverings on the walls, and parquet floors over which were scattered silk rugs. The big sofas, too, were covered with heavy Chinese silk. In a palace or a mansion it would have been at least acceptable, but in a home in San Francisco it was unbelievable.

He walked to the doorway of the breakfast room and saw that, except for Mrs. M., Mary was alone. He wondered where the boys might be. He looked beyond to the empty kitchen and at last nodded his approval. The kitchen was very modern, with white painted walls and deep yellow doors on all the storage cabinets. For Joe, that was the one cheerful and right room in the whole house. But, of course, it had been lifted entirely out of a page in *Good Housekeeping*.

He tiptoed into the breakfast room and put his arms about the ample waist of Mrs. M., who had her back to him. He squeezed her tight and bit the back of her neck. She giggled and squealed her delight. Mrs. Moriority, twice his age, was more than a little in love with him. She was a tall bosomy woman in a white tailored skirt and blouse, with gray hair that was almost white surrounding a full rather reddish face. The old man had brought her around right after Joe and Mary were married, and she had been with them ever since. Joe had a hunch that she and the old man had probably been hitting the sack together over the years, and that he finally had to get rid of her. However, she was a damned good housekeeper and loved the children almost as well as did their mother.

When he released her she turned around to face him, still giggling. "I swear, Mr. Joe," she said, "you'll be the death of me yet. Now, you keep your hands off me, you hear?"

He said soberly, "But I just can't help myself, Mrs. M. Passion overcomes me, lust comes creeping out of its hiding place—"

"Oh, go along with you, now."

She winked at him, slapped his shoulder, and went to the kitchen.

Joe dropped into his place at the table in front of orange juice, buttered toast with jam on the side, ham and potato pancakes, basted eggs, and a silver pot of coffee. He swallowed the orange juice and looked across at Mary. She had already enjoyed her quota of juice, toast and marmalade, and was drinking her coffee. He noticed she was half through the morning paper.

She was staring at him levelly over the edge of the newspaper, and at last she asked, "Where were you last night?"

Ignoring her question, he asked, "Where are the boys?"

She settled back and said, "Mrs. M. is giving them breakfast in the solarium. She set up a card table. I didn't think you should be bothered by them on this particular morning."

He was about to ask, "Why not?" but then remembered what day this was and said instead, "Damned thoughtful of you, Mary. I guess this is the big day. This is the day of total takeover."

He leaned over to eat his ham and eggs, and she asked him thoughtfully, "Just why is today so important? After all, the Wilson outfit bought in months ago."

"Today," he said, between mouthfuls, "we start out with our

4

left foot forward as a combined outfit, Merritt-Wilson. We got sixteen stores. Wilson's has four stores. It's like the mouse buying out the elephant, but that's the way it is. How the hell Lew Kane ever swung the deal I'll never figure out, but he did it. He is now God himself."

She asked quietly, "Is he Jewish? Many Jews take the name of Kane."

Joe shook his head. "I thought so at first, then I found out. Lew Kane is Scotch, Irish, and English, with maybe a little Greek thrown in. No Jewish blood that I know about, although I guess all of us have some of it. I guess you could call him a straight Anglo-Saxon, maybe. He's a big man, damned near my size and, from how he looks to me, in mighty good shape. Anyway, some-how or other, he bought out the Merritt outfit. You know as well as I do that mama Anna Merritt was anxious to get out ever since old man Merritt died. She's a good woman and shrewd and raised in the business, but I think that somehow she got tired of it." He spread his hands. "The fact remains, she did sell out to Lew Kane. And, of course, today is the first day he takes total control."

"I thought he had that for months."

"Sure. Sure. I mean it differently. The deal itself started cook-ing maybe six or seven months ago. It was signed, sealed and delivered about three months back. Ever since then the Wilson outfit has been moving in gradually. First, the assistant store-manager was changed, then the assistant controller, then a couple of buyers were shifted around and a couple of department heads, and so on. Then new furniture began appearing in the executive offices, and a week ago the new name was put over the entire chain, Merritt-Wilson. Everyone has been pissing in their pants—"

"Please, Joe."

"Sorry, but I mean it. They're all scared to death. Almost anyone's job can go down the drain. So they all walk scared. Day before yesterday Kane had a meeting of the executive staff of the whole chain. We met at the Palace Hotel. After that meeting I'll bet there were two dozen new drunks on the streets of San Francisco. Who wouldn't be scared, for God's sake? But now comes the big day and that's today."

"I know."

"Yeah." He polished off the last crumb in his plate and looked at her. "Today is it. This is the day we start officially as a new chain, the Merritt-Wilson chain. Most of the personnel changes have been made, the new furniture is in, and today all the new executives inhabit all their new offices."

She asked anxiously, "How about you?"

He shoved his chair back and got to his feet and grinned at her. "Baby," he said, "any time I start worrying about a job you can crap in my hat and I'll wear it."

"Please, Joe."

"So I'm vulgar. But I'm not even too sure I'll stay with this outfit. If it doesn't go my way I'll walk out."

"You're so sure, so confident."

"Honey," he chuckled, "I'm the best damned sales manager on the entire Pacific Coast, and everyone knows it."

"I know you are good, but—"

"No buts about it."

She said musingly, "I've always liked you being with Merritt's. It always had a certain sort of prestige."

"Sure," he laughed, "old-fashioned and easy going. But things will be different now. Kane won't hold still for any of the old Merritt's techniques. Mark my words. You'll see plenty of changes."

He walked around the table to kiss her cheek, then stepped back to look at her. Even in the morning her beauty was almost breathtaking. Mary was as Irish as she could be, but she was the gorgeous Irish. Her hair, which she wore shoulder length and turned under in a pageboy, was as raven black as Joe's, her eyes and lashes and thick brows were just as black, her chin was smoothly rounded, and her lips were full and seductive against skin that was creamy white.

Joe loved to caress her skin, any part of her body. But what truly amazed him was her figure. Even after having three boys, her body and her breasts, particularly, were still those of a virginal young woman. Her neck was fairly long and willowy, her shoulders were narrow and sloping and her firm breasts were about medium size. Joe remembered, however, how brown the nipples of those breasts were and how they tasted in his mouth. Her waist was as narrow as that of a young girl, her slim hips were pear shaped, and her long legs were beautifully contoured. No matter what Mary wore, and sometimes she could put horrible combinations together, she always looked well groomed.

Joe stared at her, then went back to the solarium. He kissed the three boys "Good morning," and they crowded around him.

The eldest was very much like Joe. His hair was always in

6

place, his shoes were always shined, he was dressed neatly and in the best of fashion at all times, and he had Joe's engaging smile. The middle boy was just the opposite. Regardless of how well Mary dressed him, he always managed to look a little sloppy and rumpled, but he had a direct stare that was disconcerting to adults. He was the one who hid frogs and lizards in his bureau drawers. The youngest boy was the love of Joe's life. He was extremely sensitive, he idolized his parents, and he could be reduced to tears with just a scowl. Joe told Mary quite often, "He's the one who'll grow up to be an artist or a writer." Mary did not argue the subject. She believed the same way. All three of them looked like their father. There was no doubt they would be just as big and just as handsome.

Joe kidded with the boys and punched them gently in the ribs, then left them to join Mary. She walked with him out to the front door, one arm in his. There she paused and again asked, "Where were you last night?"

He had had time to think about it and came up with a ready answer and a rueful smile. "I'm sorry," he said, "it was all my fault. Two of the managers from the Fresno store stayed over, and I ran into them after work. Well, it was only decent of me to have a couple of cocktails with them. One thing led to another and first thing I knew it was past the dinner hour, so I took them out on a tour of the town." He remembered quickly that young Patrick usually got on the telephone right after dinner and was as bad as a teen-age girl. So he added, "I did try to call a few times, but the line was always busy. Who were you talking to?" he asked accusingly.

"Not me," she sighed. "That was Patrick. Honestly, Joe, he hangs on that telephone for hours. I don't think it's healthy in a young ten-year-old boy. Do you?"

He shrugged. "I'll have a talk with him."

"Yes, I wish you would." She kissed his cheek. "Good luck today."

"Thanks."

He patted her fanny, then went out through the door.

What was her name? he was wondering. Charlotte. That was it. Probably a phony. She had come into the store for some exchange or other just before the closing hour. Joe had to initial all exchanges, so a salesman had brought her to him. She had looked into Joe's sea-green eyes and suddenly her fingers were shaking faintly. From there the next step was to dinner in a little out-of-the-way spot in North Beach. After that, to a motel room on Lombard was a breeze. He thought, with a grin, that it had been worth it, too. She had been damned good in bed. Those wiry babes usually were.

He turned into his garage under the house whistling under his breath.

Joe drove away from his home in the new Thunderbird in a thoughtful frame of mind. He also drove slowly and cautiously. The streets were wet and the fog was so thick that he had to use the windshield wipers. This was when most accidents happened, on a mid-summer day when the streets were slick.

But he was not thinking of the weather. He was thinking of Harold Drury. Drury had been controller of the Merritt chain for sixteen years and was now controller of the whole works. The controller of a retail chain was almost on equal standing with the president, sometimes even had more power. Controllers rarely had anything to do with the lower echelons. Joe was not that high in the chain for Drury to bother about him.

Yet the day before, just as Joe had been leaving the store for his date with Charlotte, Drury had stopped him as he was getting on the elevator. He had asked Joe if he drove to work, and Joe had replied that he did. He had then asked Joe to pick him up at his home in Pacific Heights the following morning on his way to work. Normally Joe would have been stunned, but he had Charlotte on his mind and in a moment had forgotten about Drury.

Now he had ample time to think about it and could not make heads or tails of the situation. Drury probably made fifty or sixty thousand a year, so even if his car was being repaired he could certainly afford a taxi. It was also a fact that big executives did not like being obligated to lesser people. So, it would seem to boil down to one thing: Drury wanted something from him. Men like Drury always had reasons, and usually good ones, for what they were doing. But what the devil could the reason be?

Joe cut across the city, then turned up Fillmore Street until he reached the big ridge overlooking the Golden Gate and the Marin hills to the north known as Pacific Heights.

Drury was waiting on the curb before the address he had given to Joe. It was a three-story brick house set back from the side-walk with white fluted columns at the entrance. It was quiet,

8

conservative, and expensive. Joe looked at Drury as he held the door open for him. Drury was a small, thin man not much over five feet six inches tall and probably weighed not more than a hundred and twenty pounds. He was bald, his nose and lips were thin and tiny, but shrewd eyes blinked from behind rimless spectacles. He always wore dark colors. This morning he looked rather like an undertaker on the job.

He dropped into the right-hand bucket seat, closed the door softly and mumbled to Joe, "Nice of you to pick me up."

"No trouble at all, Mr. Drury. Having car trouble or something?"

Drury glanced at him sideways and sucked at his lower lip and shook his head. "Not at all."

Well, Joe thought, I tried.

Joe wheeled the Thunderbird away from the curb as Drury commented, "That's a nice house you got, Haley."

Joe was surprised, but noncommittal. "Oh?" He hadn't even known that Drury knew where he lived.

"Yes, indeed. The missus and I were at a cocktail party in St. Francis Woods recently. I happened to admire the house across the street, and the host told me that it was yours." Drury again looked at him from the corners of his eyes. "Looked damned expensive to me. Not at all what I would have expected a department manager to live in."

Joe was about to be angry, but exploded with laughter instead. "Believe me," he said, "I haven't been tapping the till, Mr. Drury. That house was built for me and Mrs. Haley as a wedding present from my father."

"Hmmmmm. I surmise, then, that the big contractor, Patrick Haley, must be your father."

"Didn't you know before?"

"No."

"That's the old man, all right. I guess he is the biggest in the business."

"As I said before, the house looked expensive to me."

"I suppose everything in it is the very best. When it was built, about ten years ago, it would have cost somewhere around fifty thousand dollars. But now, with the boom of land prices in California, it's worth better than a hundred grand. As you also said before, it's quite a place for a department manager to live in. My wife loves it."

They lapsed into silence for a few blocks and Joe was wonder-

9

ing again what was on Drury's mind. Suddenly the older man said, "I was just thinking of something that Anna, I mean Mrs. Merritt, was telling me not too long ago. We were talking about you, and I was telling her that I thought you were one of the most talented young men to come along in the retail business in many a year. She agreed with me. But then she said something else. She said that you were also talented in another direction."

"Oh?"

"Yes. She said that you had another, more secretive and more disturbing talent. She said you were head man of the underground."

Joe glanced at him without understanding. "The underground?"

Drury nodded. "She meant it figuratively, of course. What she meant was that whatever happened in the main store, or even in the chain, all information and gossip eventually reached you and was sifted through your brain."

Joe shook his head. "I still don't get it."

"Maybe you aren't even aware of it. But I have been watching you recently, and I realize, too, that it is true. You are a very handsome man, Haley."

"Thanks for the compliment."

"It's no compliment. Anyway, the fact remains you attract all the female employees to you like bees to fresh blossoms. They seek your favors. They want you to think kindly of them. So they pass on to you all the morsels of gossip they know about the business."

Joe started to smile. "Now I follow you. Cripes, you'd think I was some sort of father confessor."

"Precisely. And some of those women, of course, occupy confidential positions, such as secretary to the store manager, or stenographers of certain departments, or secretary to the president, or even my own secretary, for that matter. I've seen her talking and laughing with you more than once."

"Julie? Nice gal."

"Of course. But the point I wish to make is this, and Anna made it before me, you probably know more about what is going on in the main store or the other stores than anyone else in the chain."

Joe reached Van Ness Avenue and turned to the right. Now they were getting somewhere, and they were getting there in a hurry. Also, what Drury had had to say was correct. Joe had known it for some time. Whatever gossip there was in the chain inevitably came to his ears. The controller, however, did not have the whole answer for it. He had only half of it. What he did not know was the other side of that same coin. Quite aside from his good looks and quite aside from the fact that the gals thought they were doing him favors, there was another reason, and a big one, why they passed everything on to him. He kept his mouth shut! At no time had he ever violated any of their confidences, and he had no intentions of starting now, even for such a big wheel as Drury.

"Well," he said, "that's an exaggeration. They gossip with me, sure, but that doesn't mean I know everything going on."

"I think it does."

"No, Mr. Drury, you're wrong there. Let's take the biggest thing that has happened recently—the merger. Wilson's has four outlets. We have sixteen. Yet it's Wilson's, or Lew Kane I mean, who has bought us out. It's the tail swinging the dog. So I'm curious? You're damned right I'm curious. Who wouldn't be? So you claim I have unusual sources of information. All right. Granted. So I've pried and pried, and I've asked hundreds of questions, and I've talked with dozens of different gals in high positions, and not one of them has ever come up with the answer of how it was done. In other words, Mr. Drury, I probably know most of the little things going on, but nothing of any importance." He paused, then again glanced briefly at the controller. "But you," he said, "I'll bet you know that particular answer."

Whether or not Drury knew the answer, it was obvious that he was not going to say anything about it. He ignored the last sentence completely. But he did put a knee up on the seat and twist about so that he was facing Joe. He studied him for a long time and finally he nodded.

"Let's not quibble," he said. "What you say is probably true. There are some things about which you know nothing. Yet you do have sources of information no one else in the chain has, and there are many things you do know about. For example, I've seen you talking with Mr. Kane's secretary many times. I've also seen her laughing with you."

"Susie? Nice gal."

"They're all nice gals to you. Part of your charm, my boy. Incidentally, no one else would dare call her Susie."

"Oh, we're buddies." Joe chuckled.

"Of that I am sure. So now we get to the point, and I'll put it right out on the table. There is certain information I want from you, for which I am willing to pay."

"Pay?"

"That is correct. I also understand something else about you. You never open your mouth about any gossip you hear. The women seem to think that is a virtue. I do, too, but I also think that virtue can be bought."

Joe frowned. "You think I'll sell out?"

"As I said, I've been watching you. You fool me not at all, Mr. Haley. You are a man without morals, without conscience, and without principles."

"Hey, what the hell—"

"Let me finish, please. I think I know you quite well and I believe you will sell out if the price is right. What is your next step up? Are you after a buyer's job?"

Joe said thinly, "I make more money already than any of the buyers."

"But that is the next step in ascendancy beyond department manager."

"That is one step I'll bypass. I'm aiming at merchandising."

"Hmmmmm. You do aim high. It is even possible you could handle it. You are talented, after all. Very well. So what if I should offer you the position of assistant merchandiser? What would you say to that?"

Joe swallowed, but shook his head. "You can't do it. It has to go through Kane."

"I can do it, Haley, believe me. I still have a bat to wield. It may not be easy, but I can do it. Do you believe me?"

Joe chewed at his lower lip for a long while, then slowly nodded. "I guess you could, at that. And what do I sell you for this job?"

"Information. That's all." He fell silent for a minute as Joe left Van Ness and turned left onto O'Farrell, toward the hub of the city.

Then Drury said, "About a month ago, as you know, Kane moved my assistant into another department, head of Credit, and made Mr. Jackson, who used to be head controller of Wilson's, my assistant. Jackson is a much younger man than I, about in his mid-forties, I would venture, and quite competent. I have given a lot of thought to that move. It could be that Kane moved Jackson under me so that he could learn the business and soak up what I know and move into my shoes on my retirement."

Joe knew better, but he said, "Seems logical."

12

"Or," Drury continued, "he could have put Jackson under me for another reason. Jackson has only handled the finances of four stores. Now it is necessary to handle the finances of twenty. I, on the other hand, have been handling the problems of sixteen stores. It is simple for me to add another four but not so simple for Jackson. You see what I mean?"

"I follow you."

"Good. So it could be that Kane has put Jackson under me until, let's say, he gets the feel of the ground and knows his way about. Then there comes the day that Jackson tells Kane he knows how to handle all twenty of the stores, and I am out on my ear. Do you follow that, too?"

"Perfectly." He lied by saying, "However, I don't accept the latter."

Drury looked pleased for a moment, even vain, but then he was again as sober faced as ever. "You may wonder," he said, "why I worry about which way it will go. I am quite well off, and I could easily retire right now. However, I think I have another good nine or ten years in me—"

Joe interrupted by saying, "You said you were putting it all out on the table, Mr. Drury. Let's not lie to each other now."

Drury said stiffly, "I was not conscious—"

"Please, Mr. Drury. I didn't go to school just to eat lunch. You aren't a damned bit worried about retiring now or in ten years from now. All you're interested in is which way the wind is blowing right now."

"W-e-l-l—"

So, Joe thought, his hunch had been correct. He said, "If things remain the way they are right now for the next ten years, you'd be content and have no squawks with anyone. But if anyone steps on your corns, meanwhile, you damned well mean to fight back. Is that right?"

Drury looked at him almost with admiration, then quickly veiled the lights in his eyes and admitted, "Could be."

"Like hell. It's stronger than that. I got a hunch you know where the body is buried. In fact, I'd be willing to bet a hundred to one on it. So, okay. You don't mind if they treat you right. But if anyone intends shoving you around, you're going to throw a monkey wrench into the works. And that, when you come right down to it, is why you're bribing me. Am I right or wrong?"

"I didn't say—"

"You don't have to. I can add up the score."

13

Joe pulled to the far left of O'Farrell Street, then turned sharply into the drive-in garage at the corner of Mason Street. He went up the winding concrete ramp to the third floor, where the signs told him vacancies were available. He drove down a lane and pulled the Thunderbird into a parking space, locked the car, put the keys in his pocket, and started walking with Drury toward the elevators.

While they were waiting for the elevator, Joe said, "A couple of the gals were talking one day. Don't ask me who because I won't tell you. Anyway, I overheard one of them say, 'Tie your kite onto Mr. Drury, baby. Now that this is a stock deal they're setting up a board of directors.'"

"Yes, that's true."

"So," Joe continued lying, "this one gal said to the other, 'I've even heard they're considering Mr. Drury as chairman of the board.' That's about it, sir. That's all I know at this moment."

Mr. Drury coughed and smiled and his lips were twitching. "Thank you," he said. "And if you hear anything else, of course—"

"Naturally, I'll pass it on."

"Thank you again. You're a fine young man, Haley."

Also, Joe thought, no morals, no conscience, and no principles. Why, you old bastard.

He almost had to laugh out loud. How easy it was to make a big wheel feel good. And how easy it was to keep him that way until he hit the skids.

What Joe had actually heard was the reverse. He had been talking to Susie one day, Kane's private secretary, when Drury had strolled by toward the elevators. Joe had remarked to Susie, "There goes a guy with a lot of brains."

Susie had remarked simply, after laughing, "Brains, yes, but no future."

It hadn't been necessary for her to say anything more.

And Joe was thinking, Never tie your kite to a falling star. I'll make the merchandising office on my own. In fact, it's better that way. If I make it under Drury, I'll be out the same day they grease the chute for him.

2

Joe and Mr. Drury walked north up Mason, then turned east on Geary. When they reached the corner of Powell and Geary they had to wait for a red light. The fog was not so thick downtown and was beginning to lift and thin out a bit. Joe figured it would be burnt away by about eleven; then they would have clear skies and perhaps even a hot afternoon. You could expect almost anything during a San Francisco summer.

Joe watched a cable car going by, loaded as usual with laughing tourists who, also as usual, were dressed much too lightly for the cool foggy weather. He let his attention wander over Union Square, which occupied the whole block before him. The square was crisscrossed with cement walks, patches of grass, shrubs and trees, and dozens of slatted benches for the idlers. The whole block west of the square was occupied by the St. Francis Hotel, Macy's took up a good portion of the block to the south, and around the rest of the square, facing it, were many specialty shops and literally a dozen or more airline offices.

Joe looked across the square to the east. The stately old building of Merritt's took up half of the block to the east of the square. It was five stories tall, of white marble and huge glass windows. It ran all the way from Maiden Lane to Post Street, then about halfway down Post Street toward Grant Avenue. It looked expensive, conservative, and secure; almost like a bank.

A Merritt label on anything was a badge of quality and good taste. Joe doubted that the latter would hold true from here on out. Wilson's had always gone in for quantity rather than quality.

What the hell, he thought. It's no skin off my nose. They can turn it into a high class five-and-dime if they want. Or, he grinned, they can even turn it into a brothel and hire Sally Stanford as merchandiser.

The light changed and the two men started across the street. When they reached the curb, Mr. Drury turned his head and blinked at Joe.

"If you don't mind," he said quickly, "I'll hurry on ahead of you. I'm a bit late as it is. See you at the meeting."

Joe watched him walk away with a deep frown. Now, what

15

was that all about? Then a light dawned and he shook his head. Drury did not want to be seen walking into the building with him.

Joe had to laugh.

Ten minutes later, at nine A.M. on the nose, he was standing in back of the old board room that had never really known a true board of directors. Merritt's had always been a family affair. All the male executives, minor and major, were leaning against the walls. The female executives were seated. They were dressed in their Sunday-go-to-meeting best, even though they had been told that Kane's talk this morning would not last more than fifteen minutes. Somehow, they all knew that it was to be an important fifteen minutes. This meeting was restricted to main store personnel and the top executives. No one from the chain was present. That meant something.

Kane was standing at the head of the room and had already started his talk, but Joe was only half listening. He was wondering again about the merger. Word had got around about a year ago that Anna Merritt might consider stepping aside. She had been immediately besieged by offers from every direction. The biggest offer, as Joe understood it, had been from Garfield's, the enormously powerful New York outfit. They wanted a Pacific Coast outlet. Their many offers had been more than generous. Yet she had settled with Kane, whose four Wilson stores put together would not be the size of one store in the Garfield chain. Furthermore, Garfield's was a top quality organization. Every dictate of logic, therefore, indicated Garfield's. Yet it was Kane who won out.

Mrs. Merritt had made one public statement and that was all. She had said simply, "Merritt's has been in my family for three generations. Garfield's would have to change the name, and I did not care to see that happen. The name of Merritt is almost a tradition in this state, and I wish it to remain that way." Joe had felt at the time that she was lying through her teeth. After all, she was a Merritt only through marriage. What the hell did she mean by "my family"?

The original store had been started in Sacramento during the declining years of the gold rush by the grandfather of Mrs. Merritt's late and lamented husband. Grandpa had then opened another store in Stockton, which was also a success. So he had decided to try his wings in the big city. The first store there had been on Market Street. When that was destroyed during the fire, the old boy built the present edifice at Stockton and Post.

Then his son had taken over and enlarged the chain to eleven stores. He was the exact opposite of his father. He died one day of a heart attack while passing the plate in church. Then it was the turn of his son, Anna's husband. He turned out to be a better merchandiser than either of his two ancestors and enlarged the chain to sixteen stores.

The sky seemed to be the limit with him, but suddenly, when only fifty years old and apparently in his full prime, he lost interest in practically everything and became a recluse in the big Hillsborough mansion down the Peninsula. He died not long after that. Rumor had it that he blew out his brains one night, but if he did it was certainly well covered. Then Anna, who had been a buyer at the Emporium when she first met her husband and was well trained in the business, took over in her husband's place. Now it was Kane's turn.

Most peculiar, Joe thought. None of it made sense; not recently, anyway.

He looked at Kane and finally gave him his complete attention. He was a damned prepossessing man. He was just as tall as Joe, but much thinner, with a wiry, tight body that seemed to be in excellent shape. His straight hair, which was thinning, was dark brown and quite gray at the temples. His skin was well tanned, with tiny wind lines at the corners of his eyes and lips. Joe had heard that he played a lot of golf and was still good at tennis. His nose had been broken at some time or other and was still a little crooked, and he had a thin white scar on the bony ridge of his left cheek. His face seemed to be made of bones and hollows, with hardly any flesh. His gray eyes were kindly and humorous, yet shrewd, and there always seemed to be laughter playing about his thin lips. He was wearing dark cordovan moccasins, brown slacks, a deep gold virgin wool sport coat, an off-color almost canary-yellow shirt and a thick woollen tie. If anyone else in his organization tried to wear such a costume, he would have been fired on the spot. Everyone, from salesmen all the way to top executives, must wear business suits at all times.

Then Joe's attention was fully aroused, because Kane was saying, "You people facing me are the heart of this organization. And you are the brains. I am speaking confidentially, naturally, but it goes without saying that whatever happens takes place first in this store, then later echoes throughout the entire chain.

It is from this point that everything else emanates. This is the hub. And because this store is the most important store in the whole chain, it goes without saying that the people collected here are the most intelligent, the most knowledgeable, and the most talented in the whole chain. Otherwise, you would not be here. This is where all the top echelon executives are located and this is where all the buyers are located.

"But it goes deeper than that. Department managers in this store are not like department managers elsewhere. It is from this store that the other stores draw their merchandise, so department managers here also act somewhat like wholesalers. Practically all of you do double duty. That is not true out in the chain. There they have local conditions only to surmount. Here you have yourselves to think about and nineteen other stores as well. You are the elite."

Joe blinked and laughed inwardly. The big fraud! Sure, it made sense, but what did he tell the people out in the chain? "You are the shock troops. You are the people manning the front line trenches." And so on in the same vein.

He went on following the same thought, so Joe's attention again wandered. He looked to the wall on his right and saw one woman standing. She was a stranger, yet she looked faintly familiar to Joe, so he appraised her. What he saw was very good. She was perhaps in her mid-twenties, maybe five feet six inches tall and about a hundred and fifteen pounds. Joe guessed her size at somewhere around an eight. She had deep auburn hair, which she wore rather close-cropped about a small head so that it seemed almost like feathers. She did not wear a hat, but she had a broad bow of ribbon tied in her hair just above her forehead. On her it was unusually attractive. Very few other women could get away with it.

Then Joe realized that everything about her was a bit unusual and his eyes opened wider. She was wearing an orange sheath that fitted her body as if she had been poured into it, with a tiny belt at the waist. Over one shoulder was draped casually a woolly orange half-jacket. And on her feet were pointed shoes of a faint blue shade. He balanced it all in his mind: orange dress, auburn hair, and blue shoes. It didn't sound right, but on her it was perfection. This babe knew color, and she had fabulous taste. She also seemed to have a sharp and rather attractive profile, what he could see of it. Then she turned her head to look across the room, and he knew who it was.

Her name was Betty Parker. Joe had heard of her more than once during the past year or two, and had met her briefly the week before. Wilson's biggest store was on Market at Seventh. At that store she was department manager of the women's fashion floor, approximately the same position Joe held at Merritt's in the men's division. She was a ball of fire. She had come from Los Angeles about two years ago. Her first year at Wilson's she jumped the quota of her floor better than twenty percent. But during the second year she did a fantastic job of jumping the quota almost seventy percent over her previous year. Everyone who knew anything in the business had been talking about her.

Joe looked at her admiringly, then turned his attention back to Kane.

The big wheel was saying, "So I expect more out of you than anyone else in the chain. That is the true purpose of this little meeting, to let you know. We are going to do things in this Merritt-Wilson chain that have probably never been heard of before. We're going to experiment, you and I, and, if you'll pardon the vernacular, we're going to work our tails off. Forget the traditions of Merritt's. Forget the history of Wilson's. We're all of us starting out brand new today. And this," he said harshly, "I demand of all of you. I demand and expect your loyalty, especially the people in this room, every step of the way. No half measure will be acceptable. Or," he said, and his features contorted fiercely for a moment, "believe me, you're right out on your fannies. Can I put it any simpler than that?"

The meeting was over and there was shocked silence in the room. Almost no one present made under a thousand dollars a month. Drury made fifty or sixty thousand a year; the merchandiser, about whom everything really revolved, was in the same class, and there were a half-dozen or so others not too far under those figures. The room, in other words, was loaded with big money people who would be in the same bracket no matter in what industry they found themselves. You simply did not tell people of that calibre that they could be kicked out on their behinds. And never, never did you threaten them. What Kane had said was unbelievable, and it registered on every face present. Most of those in the room could walk out and get jobs just as good somewhere else, or maybe even better. What the devil had got into the man? His first day really on the job, and he had made an enemy of practically everyone in the room.

Joe squinted narrowly and leaned back against the wall to

think about it. He could come to only one conclusion. Kane actually wanted and welcomed their antagonism. What he had said was deliberate. He had known precisely what he was saying and had thought it out beforehand. Now, why the devil would he want people to hate him? This was not a football team. There you dealt with a bunch of apes. Here he was dealing with intelligent people. What was on his mind?

Joe remained leaning against the wall and watched the others as they turned on their heels and walked angrily out of the room, or went reluctantly forward to shake hands with Kane. Even the ones who went forward had little to say to him. Joe waited. He wanted to see who would be the last people left.

He was whistling a silent tune through his teeth when he felt his elbow nudged. He turned around and was facing Julie, Drury's private secretary. She was looking at him with an odd smile. He grinned back at her. She was a tall, skinny, rawboned sort of a woman, perhaps in her mid-thirties, with a bony face and mouse-brown hair piled high on top of her head.

She whispered in Joe's ear, "Kick you in the pants where it hurts, Junior?"

"Not me, baby. Never me."

"Jees, I wish I had your nerve. Comes a day of reckoning, though, and there is always one question: How is it on your floor?"

"You'd like to know, really?"

"Isn't it almost the same as telling God, or one of His disciples?"

"Comes close, I guess. So I'll tell you how it is. Half of the jerks working for me are make-ups."

"Same complaint everywhere."

"Because it's true, that's why. Then about twenty-five percent manage to haul their weight. I have no squawk about them. Then, thank God, I got about twenty-five percent who are in the high bonus class. I could kiss their feet every day of the week. They're the ones who make the day for me." He paused, then chuckled and said, "You know, I got a guy on my floor who is never a swapper?"

"What's a swapper?"

"He swaps a customer for zero. In other words, no sale. He's on call and he has to take his turn, so he comes up with some character who was just looking and walks out on him. That's a swap.

"Anyway, this guy is never a swapper. You know what he is? Another Markey Cohen."

"Honey, you keep losing me. Now, what is a Markey Cohen?"

Joe was happy to explain, "At one time there was a character named E. Cohen who worked as a salesman on a men's floor somewhere, so the story goes. Anyway, this guy Cohen never left a customer empty handed. Even when somebody walked out on him, he always picked up a suit and took it back to Hold and told the floor manager, 'Mark it E. Cohen. The man says he'll be back to pick it up later.' Well, what the hell, in no time at all, half the suits in stock were in Hold. So whenever another salesman needed a 38 or a 36 or something, he'd go back to the floor manager and tell him, 'Pull it out of marked E. Cohen.' Eventually, the whole thing became shortened to a Markey Cohen suit. And that's what this character is working for me, another Markey Cohen. On the other hand, he's not a bad salesman. So I let him get away with it. Also, get a load of this, now. I got a wanderer."

"Hmmmmm. So he keeps hitting the water faucet."

Joe laughed. "Hell, no. This guy is a fairy and he's really not very good on his own. So you know what he does? He just wanders around the store and watches customers when they leave other salesmen. He seems to have a knack of knowing when they have changed their minds about just looking and have finally decided to buy. Then he moves in and makes a quick sale. He's a wanderer."

Julie chewed on her gum for a moment, then said, "I must mingle with you peasants more often. Good God, the things I learn!"

"Stick around with me, honey, and you'll learn it's much too good for the peasants."

She said admiringly, "That ain't no lie, Buster." Then she followed the direction of his eyes and saw that he was watching Betty Parker. "Met her yet?"

"Miss Parker? Yes, about a week ago. But why is she here? This was just supposed to be for the big wheels of the main store."

"Which is where she belongs now."

Joe blinked at her. "Come again?"

"The great man moves fast, my boy. Yesterday he pulled Nancy off the women's fashion floor, told her to collect her salary and an extra two months, and fondly bade her good-bye."

Joe frowned and pulled at an ear lobe. "That's no great loss.

That floor needs somebody strong, and Nancy was far from fitting into that category."

"So now Miss Parker has the job. She takes over as of right now."

Joe's frown deepened. "No good," he said. "So, okay, I hear she's dynamite over at Wilson's, but this is not Market Street. Besides, that floor calls for an older woman. Hell's bells, there are only two or three gals on that floor who are under fifty. You gotta be an older woman to run that mob."

"Tell it to God."

"Not me, honey. Let him find out for himself." Then he smiled. "So now she's with us, huh? Well, well."

Julie said teasingly, "Single, too. She's never been married."

"Oh, really?"

"Also, I hear tell, she's a virgin."

"In this business?" Joe burst out laughing. "Knock it off, please. One thing I've found out, this business is as bad as show business."

"No complaints from you, of course."

"God made women, and He also made Joe Haley. It makes a nice combination. Who am I to kick?"

She raised her eyes to the ceiling. "Oh, brother." But she was chuckling to herself as she walked away.

Joe's eyes swung back to Betty Parker. She had left her position against the wall and was walking forward toward Kane. He was in the front of the room, surrounded by Drury, the store manager, three of the buyers, all the merchandisers, the head security officer, head of credit, two department managers, and the head of personnel. He seemed to be talking to everyone at the same time, yet Joe noticed that as Betty approached him his eyes found her, he stopped talking and a thin suggestion of a smile tugged at his lips. She paused uncertainly at the edge of the group, but Kane shoved some people aside, reached through two of the buyers, took Betty's hand in his and pulled her into the inner circle. Then he went on talking again, while she stood quietly at his side, looking at him curiously.

Joe thought wryly, A virgin, huh? Not for long, baby.

Joe left the board room and took the elevator downstairs to the basement. He walked back over a concrete floor, between rows and aisles of boxed merchandise, to the semi-enclosed shipping office. Peter Stack was behind the counter going through a number of yellow forms. He looked up and grinned at Joe.

He was young, about Joe's age, with brown hair, blue eyes, harassed features, big shoulders, and uneven teeth. He rarely ever got out of the basement, so he was wearing corduroys, a faded green sweater, and a Levi jacket.

He said pleasantly, "Hi, Haley."

Joe frowned at him and asked, "How about those cashmere jackets?"

Pete went through his papers, then said, "Not in yet."

"What the hell do you mean they aren't in? What kind of a joint are you running down here?"

Pete said reasonably, "Look, Haley, it's not my fault and you know it. What the hell do I have to do with what comes in and when it comes in? All I know is when it's here."

"I know. I know. But you're sure they're not here."

"Positive. I've had my eye out for them ever since you mentioned it."

Joe said disgustedly, "Then it's the damned buyers. They're lying to me again. For the last two weeks those jackets have been selling in every store on the square, and we still don't have them. Aw, nuts. I should get a job driving a truck."

"Not at the money you make."

Joe started to turn away, but Pete said, "Hey, wait a minute." There was a slight leer twisting his lips as he half-whispered, "It just so happens that last night I'm tooling down Lombard and I see this Thunderbird turning into a motel. So I look and, lo and behold, there's my old buddy Haley heading in with a strange doll. Man, you make that scene more than anybody I know."

Joe smiled with his eyes only. He was still mad about the jackets. "A man has to have some sort of a hobby, chum."

"You got a beauty, no doubt of that. But seriously, though, I'd be worried in your shoes. You got a wife and three kids. What happens some day when an accident falls on your head and you got some babe knocked-up and she decides to make a stink about it? What happens then?"

"Nothing. Because it can't happen. After the last boy was born I had myself sterilized."

Pete's eyes opened wide. "No kidding! And you a Catholic?"

"I don't practice it."

"But how about the wife? I hear she's a real candle burner."

Joe laughed shortly. "Do you think I'm crazy enough to tell her?"

23

"I hear tell that sometimes a job like that increases a man's sexual capacity."

Joe shook his head. "I wouldn't know," he chuckled. "That was never one of my worries."

He walked away leaving Pete laughing behind him.

Joe stopped before the elevators, pushed the button and waited. He looked at his watch. It was exactly nine thirty, so the outer doors would be open and the customers would be coming in. For a minute or two, anyway, the elevators would all be going up.

Joe stepped back and lit a cigarette and thought of the big store above him. The first floor was divided in half. On one side were men's accessories such as shirts, ties, underwear, shoes, hats, and so on. To the rear of that department was luggage, gifts, and some jewelry. The other half was occupied by women's accessories: blouses, skirts, sweaters, hosiery, and so on. Back of that was the Misses department and another smaller department for children's wear. The second floor was strictly for men, featuring slacks, sport coats, robes, car coats, and every possible variety of sports wear for men. The third floor, which was Joe's floor, featured suits, overcoats, raincoats, tuxedoes, and a small but colorful department known as the Mixed Grill, which was quite popular with the younger men. The fourth floor was the women's fashion floor, where suits, dresses, millinery, coats, and all the better and more costly female habiliments were sold. On that same floor, to the rear, were all the executive and buyers' offices, as well as the board room. The fifth floor was taken over entirely by the cafeteria, credit, personnel, and clerical offices.

Merritt-Wilson was not a true department store. There were no household furnishings, kitchenware, appliances, or things of that sort. Almost one hundred percent of the job of Merritt-Wilson was devoted to selling what men and women wore on their backs. In the trade it was known as a specialty chain—one of the best in the business.

Joe thought of it and could almost taste what it would be like to run such an enterprise. He hungered for such an elevation so badly that sometimes at night it was an actual pain in his groin. He knew he was handsome and used it to the hilt. But he was sick and tired of the appellation of "pretty boy." It was difficult to convince anyone to take him seriously. He had, therefore, been forced to learn more and perform more than others on his same level. He had always to be head and shoulders above them, and

24

usually succeeded. He was going up and he was going up fast. Some day, he thought, I'll stand in Kane's shoes.

An elevator finally arrived. He got aboard and punched the third floor button. Why, he wondered, had he wasted time going down to the basement? Joe was always supposed to be on his own floor when the outside doors opened. It was an unwritten rule amongst all department managers.

As Joe stepped off at the third floor, he found himself facing Kane and Miss Parker. They were about to get aboard the elevator he was leaving, but Kane obviously changed his mind when he saw Joe.

He told Miss Parker, "Wait a moment, please," then he took Joe by the arm and walked him about twenty feet away.

He asked quietly, "Where have you been? Aren't you supposed to be here at nine thirty?"

Joe wondered, What the hell? Was this teacher asking some kid why he was late to class? That's the way it looked.

He managed to smile, however, as he explained, "I was down in the basement checking to see if some cashmeres had come in."

"I see." Kane looked into his eyes on the same level and said, "There is something I have been meaning to bring up with you, but I thought it better to wait until the ship was under full sails. I have, of course, been going through all the books, especially pertaining to personnel income. As far as I can see, practically everyone in the old Merritt chain is working on an income that is eminently suitable to whatever level on which he finds himself. You, however, seem to be the one exception."

Joe felt a knot tighten in his stomach. "Is that so?"

"Yes, indeed. Adding together your salary, the percentage you take on the gross—incidentally, I have never before heard of a department manager taking a percentage on the gross—and the percentage you take on the plus-quota, you average pretty close to sixteen hundred a month. I can tell you quite frankly that that is a slight bit better than any of the buyers make. It would be no problem at all for me to hire, let us say, an average department manager to take over your job at half of what you earn."

Joe's teeth flashed whitely, though he was really not smiling. "That is right, Mr. Kane. But you put your finger right on it when you said 'average.' I like to believe I left that average status behind me long ago."

"Oh, no doubt of that. No doubt at all. I am not arguing that point. But would you mind telling me how come Mrs. Merritt decided on that sort of income?"

Joe gritted his teeth and thought a moment before replying. Was he deliberately trying to antagonize him as he had everyone in the board room? Kane knew damned well why he got the income he received.

But he forced down the temper that was rising within him and said, "It's simple enough. I came here three years ago, as department manager. I instituted a number of reforms that jumped the gross of this floor eighteen percent in eight months and the following year the gross rose even higher. But then I got a real brainstorm, wardrobe selling."

"I know all about it."

Joe almost snapped at him, "Who doesn't? Everyone in the retail business is talking about it and a lot of them are imitating it. All it amounted to was selling a man a complete wardrobe at the same time, a couple of slacks, some sport coats, a suit, and a topcoat, all of them interchangeable, for a slight reduction in price. Everyone fought me over the idea. Even Mrs. Merritt. But at last she did give in and agreed to give it a short try. You have no idea what happened that first month we advertised it. We were swamped. And the idea has been selling like hotcakes ever since then."

His anger was rising again as he continued, "So, all right. When I took over this floor it was running about a million a year, maybe a bit better than that. It is now running three and a half million a year. Mrs. Merritt was decent enough to think that I should share in the profits a bit." He paused, then asked harshly, "Does that answer your question?"

Kane said musingly, "But now that the operation is under way, I could get someone to take your place at considerably less money."

Joe's eyes narrowed and his temper was hot in his throat. He took a deep breath and said, "Okay, Mr. Kane. You get your man. I'm going to my office for my hat right now, and then I'm walking out of here. Anyone with any intelligence knows I am not a single-idea man. If I can come up with one good one, I'll come up with others just as good."

Kane's lips were thin, but his eyes were smiling. He said softly, "Forget your hat. You're just so damned handsome that I got wondering about it. You've got guts. That's all I wanted to find out." He held out his hand and asked, "Shake on it?"

Joe stood there staring at him, then his anger slowly died and at last he was smiling. He reached out and shook hands with Kane. "Okay," he said. Then he laughed and added, "You sure made me hot under the collar there for a minute."

"That's what I was hoping to see. You and I are going to get along fine. You told me something that's damned important. You don't intend resting on past glories. You're thinking of the future and other good ideas. And if you come up with any other good ideas you'll find I am just as generous as Mrs. Merritt."

"Don't worry about that, Mr. Kane. Any time I produce anything I expect to get paid for it. I'm not in this business for my health."

Kane grinned. "That makes two of us. Be seeing you."

Joe watched him walk away and frowned thoughtfully. Then suddenly he understood. This was a hell of a good way to separate the men from the boys. The wolves would come out into the open and tell Kane off. Then it would be up to Kane to placate them, and get them to stay on the job. The rabbits, of course, would keep their mouths shut and try to hide, and Kane would know who they were.

By God, Joe thought, he's quite a guy at that.

3

WHILE the two men were talking, Betty Parker had walked away to a table just beyond the elevators. It was stacked high with trade magazines and newspapers waiting to be distributed throughout the store. She went through them and found what she was after, the Bible of the women's fashion world, *Women's Wear Daily*.

She turned immediately to a small box on the last page, which read:

PARIS FLASHES
Cable Fairchild News Services
PARIS—New midcalf length for day at Cardin.
Soft feathered chemises at Cardin.
Evening feathered bathing belle hats at Cardin.
Wraparound pantskirts with spotted or plaid wool stock-
   ings at Castillo.

Silver-buckled black patent balmoral shoes at Castillo.
Full bell sleeves on coats at Venet.
Softened-up tops over trousers at Courreges.
The all-black look for after-dark everywhere.

Then she turned to inventories and read the San Francisco section on the next to the last page: "——down 2 or 3 percent below July 31 last year but store officials say they are still within plan. Ready-to-wear inventories are down slightly more—4 to 5 percent. Sales trends upward, new branch stores going ahead of volume quotas." That was what she wanted. She skipped a few sentences and read, "One inventory problem has been shrinkages, with teenagers the chief offenders."

Always they are with us, she thought. Those kids would steal the gold out of your teeth if you closed your eyes. What was the matter with them?

She saw Kane turning away from Joe, so she walked quickly back to the elevators. She watched Kane narrowly as he approached with his usual smile for her, and her brain was racing. What was with him, anyway?

She would never forget the time when he had walked into Ohrbach's in Los Angeles, a little over two years ago, and had introduced himself. He was president of the San Francisco Wilson chain. It was only four stores and she had never heard of it. But she pretended she had. He had taken her to lunch and the following day had taken her to dinner at Chasen's, an expensive restaurant. She expected then that he would make a play for her, but it had not materialized. The following day he telephoned the store and asked her to meet him in the Beverly Hills Hotel. Now it comes, she thought. But, no. He met her in the lobby where they sat and talked.

Then he made the big offer. She could hardly believe it. She was already a department manager at Ohrbach's and doing a bang-up job of it. She was making three-fifty a month and had been promised a raise of another twenty-five. But Kane offered her six hundred a month to start and a free hand running the women's fashion floor in his Market Street store. Her reason told her there was not that much difference between Los Angeles and San Francisco. Even in the Bay City she doubted very much if department managers made that kind of money. There could only be one reason for the offer.

She thought it over. She was tired of Los Angeles. Also, she

had an independent income, so she did not have to worry about losing a job, no matter where she might be. She accepted the offer.

Nothing turned out as she had imagined it would. It was Kane who found a beautiful apartment for her in the Marina District, and it was Kane who helped her select and buy the furniture. That figured, but nothing else followed the pattern. He seemed genuinely glad to be in her company, anything that pleased her seemed to please him. He was never harsh with her. He gave her his advice any time she asked for it, but never at any time did he make the big play. She did a good job at Wilson's, became really enthused about her work, and did a truly fabulous job. During the last week of April, at the end of the fiscal year, she had expected a raise of twenty-five or fifty dollars a month, in addition to the generous bonuses she was getting. Instead of that, her salary was jumped to seven hundred and fifty dollars a month. At last, she thought, now comes the big play. Maybe it took a man like him two years to get around to it.

And still nothing happened.

Now she was being moved into the women's fashion floor of the much bigger Merritt store, and Kane was just as kind and as decent as ever. However, she had done some investigating and had learned that the top woman department manager in the San Francisco store received six hundred a month, and she had been battling her way up to that level a good twenty years or more. What in God's name, she wondered, went on with the man?

And there was still no answer.

Kane came up to her, smiled, and took her arm and said pleasantly, "Sorry I kept you waiting, my dear. Now, let us go up to the snake pit." He reached around her to punch the elevator button.

"Snake pit?" she asked.

He nodded. "That's what the girls on the floor call it. No one has ever made a success of the women's fashion floor. That is why it is called the snake pit, and that is also why I present you with this challenge."

They stepped into an empty elevator to go to the fourth floor and Betty shuddered. "You expect me to lift up this department by its bootstraps?"

He nodded. "I do. I have absolute blind faith in your ability. I checked you very closely at Ohrbach's, in case you didn't know. They were about to make you a buyer when you left."

"They made the offer when I told them I was leaving." Then

she added honestly, "But your dollar was bigger, and I wanted to come to San Francisco."

"I know. The point I make, though, is that you are a young, rising star in this business." As they got off the elevator at the fourth floor he said, "You may have wondered more than once why I pay you so well. Now and then, not very often, but it does occur, someone comes along who is head and shoulders above everyone else around them. I have a talent for spotting that sort of person, and when I do I grab them and pay them so well I know they will never leave." He chuckled and squeezed her arm. "That's about all there is to it."

She smiled at him, but inwardly she was shaking her head. She knew Kane was not an overly generous person. The mystery was still as deep as ever.

When the elevator doors closed behind them Betty looked to her left and saw a number of large rooms with some clothing on display. To her right were also a number of open rooms with a few things on display. But the huge room in which she was standing had lounges, sofas, enormous windows, one small desk, and absolutely nothing on display—not even a mirror. It was quite chic. The carpet under her feet felt as if it were six inches deep.

Yet there seemed to be a great deal of business being transacted. Saleswomen were going back and forth, different-toned bells chimed everywhere, and a number of customers were walking about, some listlessly and some sharp-eyed and with purpose. The subdued color scheme was predominantly beige, with some gold and a splash of pastel pink here and there. For better than two weeks now, the Merritt-Wilson chain had been running a change-of-name sale, and it was still going on. At this point, however, it would be remnants only that would be selling.

Kane took her arm and walked her toward the small desk in the middle of the room. A woman about forty years of age was behind the desk. She got quickly to her feet as she saw Kane approaching. She was wearing a severe black sheath dress and a string of pearls about her neck. Her black hair was beautifully coiffed, she was thin and rather tall, her dark eyes looked harassed, her face was lined, her thin lips smeared broadly with lipstick and her eyebrows were plucked too finely.

"Mr. Kane," she trilled. "What a happy surprise."

"Thank you, Miss Togliatti. I would like to introduce you to Miss Betty Parker. Miss Parker, Miss Marie Togliatti."

30

"Oh, my goodness," she trilled again. "Miss Parker, of course. I hear you're just a ball of fire over at Wilson's."

"That's very kind of you."

Then she turned back to Kane, and told him, "I'm sorry you find me so upset this morning. And I can't imagine what on earth could have happened. Nancy is always so prompt, at least in the mornings. And now she hasn't shown up and I am absolutely in a tizzy. Of course, I do have a signature, but you know the old saying about when the cat is away—"

Kane hid a smile and nodded. "Yes," he said, "I know." He told Betty, "Miss Togliatti is assistant department-manager. A very loyal employee."

Miss Togliatti continued trilling, "I do try, Mr. Kane."

"Of course. And don't think we don't know it. But I believe I have some news for you, Miss Togliatti. Miss Nancy won't be here this morning, or at any time. We—ah—we felt we had to let her go and that it would be best to do it quickly, painlessly, and silently. I would appreciate it if you would get all of her personal belongings together and mail them to her. Would you mind?"

"Oh, no, not at all."

Then she realized just what he had said and her features underwent a change. Betty was watching her closely and saw tiny pinpoints of steel-like hardness appear in her eyes. "You—ah—you say you had to let her go? Does that mean that she is discharged?"

"Let's just say that we took her resignation."

"Well then—in that case—" She looked hard into Kane's eyes and waited.

Kane missed completely what was in her expression. He smiled and said, "So now you have a new boss. Miss Parker is now the manager of this department. She takes over immediately. If you will be so good as—"

Whatever else he had to say was not heard by either Miss Parker or Miss Togliatti. The latter turned her stricken gaze to Betty and the light slowly went out of her eyes. The lines deepened in her face, her shoulders sagged, and she suddenly had sagging jowls. Oh, God, Betty thought, deliver me from this. Miss Togliatti was an old maid fighting for her place in the sun, and now that sun was eclipsed. She had worked her fingers to the bone—and for what?—to be the next department manager. Always she had been fighting to be the manager. This had probably happened to her many times before. Betty's heart bled for her, and for one of the few times in her life she was incapable of looking another woman in the eye. She had to turn away.

Kane had missed the little play between them and was looking at his watch. "I'm sorry," he said, "but I do have to run. Betty, you can have Miss Togliatti introduce you around and show you the ropes. The store manager was supposed to be here to welcome you, so I imagine he will be along in a minute or two. Take your time and get the feel of the floor, and I'm sure you will make out like a champ. I'll drop by some time during the afternoon."

He waved at the two of them and was gone.

Betty looked back at the assistant, and the two stood there facing each other for a long moment. There was nothing in Miss Togliatti's eyes and features but sheer hate. Betty felt sorry for her, but she did not feel responsible for it. She shrugged her shoulders slightly, and in a moment all sympathy was drained out of her. She looked Miss Togliatti straight in the eyes so firmly and for so long that at last the assistant had to look away.

As soon as Miss Togliatti's eyes slid away, Betty said, "I know exactly how you feel, Miss Togliatti, but believe me it will never be mentioned again. Now, shall we see what the floor is all about? I understand I have an office somewhere."

Miss Togliatti's mind was off in some private world of its own for a minute or two, so Betty waited patiently. Then the assistant looked at her briefly, still with hatred in her eyes, and said hoarsely, "Sorry, but I can't leave the floor. I have the only signature. But right directly behind you there's a narrow hallway between two rows of offices. Yours is the third office on the left. You'll find Miss Dexter in there. She can spare the time to show you around."

"Who is Miss Dexter?"

"She is your detail girl."

Betty turned around and saw the hallway at the other end of the room and started walking toward it. She looked back over her shoulder and had to smile. Three of the sales ladies were already clustered about the assistant, and all were chattering excitedly. So typical of a sales floor; news traveled fast.

Betty continued on back to the hallway and walked between the rows of offices. It was all women working in the rooms. She recognized a few of them and realized that this was the buyers' chain of offices. Heaven forbid, she thought. With the buyers right here at my back I'll have them on my neck every day of the week. She much preferred having the buyers ten miles away from her. She knew how vicious they could be when anything slumped in one of their departments. And now she had them practically in her lap.

She stopped at the third door on her left, which was actually doorless like the other rooms, and looked in. It was a small room, about eight by ten feet, with no decorations anywhere except for a calendar on one wall. There were two desks, two chairs, a typewriter on a stand, and some coat hooks on the wall. Except for the one window out over Union Square, there was nothing else.

A young woman was at the desk nearest the door going over some reports. She looked up and blinked uncertainly at Betty. She had brown hair that was already tangled, her features were very ordinary, except that her lower lip protruded in somewhat of a pout, she wore heavy glasses, and the suit she was wearing, though well tailored, was bagging about a thick-waisted body. Betty knew well why she was a detail girl. She would be completely lost on a sales floor.

"Miss Dexter?" she asked, as she stepped into the room.

"Uh-huh. Something I can do for you?"

Betty smiled. "Quite a bit, I am Betty Parker, the new department manager here."

Miss Dexter grinned. "Who you kidding? We got a manager."

Betty practically had to draw a blueprint of why and how she was there, and at last the detail girl understood. Then her hand flew to her mouth to smother an outburst of laughter.

"My God," she gasped, "does Marie know?"

"Yes."

"Jees, Miss Parker, why didn't you come to me first? I'd of given a million dollars to be there when Marie got the word. Oh, brother!"

Betty said shrewdly, "You two aren't exactly in love with each other?"

Miss Dexter suddenly realized this was "the boss" she was talking to and clammed up. "Oh," she simpered, "we get along. Boy, I don't envy you. Every one of those old bags out there will have a knife in your back before the day's out."

Betty nodded at the desk under the window. "Is that my desk?"

"Yes, ma'am. This one I'm at is really Marie's. We sort of share it."

"What does she have to do with a desk?"

"Well, naturally, when she isn't replacing the manager on the floor, she's back here at her desk."

"Doesn't she sell with the others?"

Miss Dexter blinked at her. "Marie? I've never seen her sell anything."

That, Betty thought, will be changed almost instantly. Everyone on any floor she managed had to sell. There would be some big changes made for Miss Dexter, as well.

She knew that Miss Nancy still had her personal belongings in the other desk, so she walked beyond Miss Dexter and hung her bag on a coat hook by its strap. Then she turned about and faced a man standing in the doorway. He looked at her and grinned and said, "Hi, Betty."

She returned the smile with warmth. She liked Fred Maloney, the new store manager. She had met him the week before and each had instantly felt a certain friendliness about the other. He was in his early forties, his dark hair was thinning a bit, and usually he had the worried look in his eyes of any store manager. He had a solid build, somewhat like a medium-sized football player. He dressed well, of course, and at all times he seemed as if he had just stepped from a shower. There was a well-scrubbed look about him that Betty liked. The only facts she really knew about him, however, were that he had a nice home, a lovely wife, and a growing son and daughter. Except for the interlude of the big war, when he had been a paratrooper in the ETO, he had worked for Merritt's ever since leaving high school. Until two weeks ago he had been assistant store-manager. At that time the manager had been moved upstairs to personnel, and Maloney had taken over in his place.

He looked at the detail girl and said, "Hi, Irene," then his eyes went back to Betty. "Sorry I wasn't here to welcome you. I got hung up with Drury."

"Mr. Kane brought me in."

He said dryly, "So I heard. Anyway, I'm here now. I'll take you on a tour of the floor and introduce you to all your hatchet women. Incidentally, how do you like your office?"

She laughed lightly and said, "I won't be using it, except for a place to put my coat and purse. I'm a floor gal, Mr. Maloney. I like to be where all the action is going on and where all the money is being made. I also like to direct traffic. Which reminds me. I have a request for you already."

"Name it."

"Take that little desk out on the floor and lose it. Then see if you can get me a desk about counter high, one I can stand at. I don't want a stool or a chair. Never use them. Then place it right smack in the middle of the floor facing the elevators. That, Mr. Maloney, is where I'll be doing business."

But he was not smiling as he said, "That's where you intend taking your stand, out in the middle of that floor?"

"Eight hours a day."

He shook his head. "The gals aren't going to like it. They don't mind having a signature on the floor, but they resent close supervision."

"They'll get used to me, in time. You see, Mr. Maloney, I also happen to be a hell of a sales person myself. I can probably outsell any top girl you got out there."

"Now, now," he smiled. "Four of them are the best in the business."

She said stubbornly, "And I can still outsell them. If I didn't believe it I wouldn't have the nerve to walk out on that floor."

He said mildly, "I don't think you realize what you're up against. But you try it your own way. You know, don't you, that I am your immediate boss?"

"Oh, yes."

"And the assistant manager, too, until one gets hired. You don't have anything to do with merchandising."

"Same as at Wilson's. What you're really trying to tell me is that any time I have a beef with the buyers I must go through the proper chain of command, and that's you."

He chuckled and nodded. "You got it right. Let's go out on the floor."

Betty took a deep breath, let it out slowly, and walked out with him.

The moment they disappeared through the doorway, Irene dialed the telephone number of her closest friend on the first floor and said breathlessly, "My God, Alice, wait'll you hear."

One hour later, after Maloney had gone, Betty went to the employee's lounge and dropped onto a sofa. She wanted a little while alone to sort things out in her mind. She was lucky. There were no sales personnel around at the moment.

The floor was considerably larger than she had at first thought. Suits and coats were one department, dresses another, Juniors another, millinery another, and so on. Then there were the lounges for the employees and the customers, the two dozen fitting rooms, and, of course, the big stock rooms. Betty's immediate impression was that the floor was overly large, overly staffed, and very badly run. About the only thing she agreed with at this moment was that Merritt's did not believe in having women's merchandise on display. It was always much smarter to have a customer ask for what she wanted, then have a saleswoman display it for her. Clothing displayed on racks was cheap.

She had also met all of the saleswomen. Most of them were over fifty, which was necessary on a high fashion floor. They were very well groomed and most of them seemed to be sharp and knew what they were about. Maloney had told her, in brief asides, which were the top sales people. She remembered the names of two of them, Miss Snider and Miss Hall. It had also been apparent to Betty that they were intense competitors and hated each other's guts. Nothing wrong with that, however. That was normal in the rag business.

All well-run retail floors had a certain rhythmic flow about them. It was disconcerting to Betty that she had detected no pattern whatever while out on the floor. Business seemed to be done in a haphazard manner. Snider and Hall probably put on pressure to sell, but no one else did. They took their customers as they came up on-call, and if the customer happened to wish to buy, they wrote it down in their books. That was about the way it went. She had seen few double sales, and not once had she seen a saleswoman try to show a coat or a hat to a customer who had just bought a suit or a dress.

There were two reasons for this. Merritt's was well known, well established, and well liked. There was no real problem selling Merritt's merchandise. The second reason was that at no time had any manager tried to put pressure on the sales staff. Even Maloney was fooled. He, too, thought that the floor did better without too much interference. Not from now on, she thought. All hell is going to break loose in this joint.

And there was no better time to start than the present.

As she walked out on the floor two janitors came along from the service elevator. They were trundling a tall counter between them. A third janitor was directing them. They paused and looked about for someone in authority as Betty approached them.

She pointed and told them, "Put the counter over there in the middle of the floor, facing the elevators and about twenty feet away from them."

They put the counter where she wanted it, then wasted another ten minutes while they moved it one inch one way, then another inch another way. But at last it was settled to their satisfaction.

They were about to walk away when she told them, "Get that little desk at the side and move it down to the basement, or somewhere. I don't want it."

Betty helped them clean the papers and pencils out of the small desk and placed them all on top of the counter. She was glad that Miss Togliatti was not around at the moment—she had gone on a distress call to one of the fitting rooms. The porters put the desk on a dolly and took it away.

Betty stood back and looked over the counter. It was about three and a half feet tall—she could stand and lean comfortably behind it. It was two feet deep and four feet wide. Plenty of working space on top. It was a good-looking counter, which was all to the good since it would be the first thing seen by anyone leaving the elevators.

Miss Togliatti came rushing over just as she was putting the papers, pencils, and other stationery equipment into the shelves behind the counter.

The assistant gasped, "What—what happened to the little desk?"

Betty said flatly, "I had it removed. We don't need it."

"We don't? But this—this—this thing—"

"This is the control desk of this floor from now on."

"You mean this is what we use?" She blinked and said, "We don't have a chair or a stool?"

"That's right. This is a standing job we're doing out here. There's one thing I've learned, Miss Togliatti; when you're sitting down you hate to get up and move, but when you are already standing up you don't mind moving at all."

"You mean we have to stand all the time? But that's inhuman."

A slight smile tugged at Betty's lips. "This is the way I like it, Miss Togliatti. This is the way I have always worked."

"Oh, I couldn't use anything like this."

"You won't have to for very long." She leaned an elbow on the counter and said, "You are going to run the floor for the next three days from behind this counter. I don't even know the numbers of the departments yet, and I have no idea what's in stock. There's a lot I have to find out. I give myself three days.

Then I will be at this desk and the only time you will be here is when you relieve me.'

Miss Togliatti said stiffly, "I should certainly hope not."

Betty looked up and saw three women getting off the elevator. "Look," she said, "we have to forget this last name business. From now on you're Marie and I'm Betty. Okay? See these three women coming off the elevator? Normally, now, would they walk toward the little desk that used to be over there?"

"Oh, no. There was no reason for that. The girl on-call always took them."

"But now watch them walk toward this counter. They see it already."

"What's the purpose?"

"Simple. They see the counter and they see me. I greet them and find out what they want and turn them over to the on-call girl. That way they think they're getting a little something extra. But if they ask me a question now I wouldn't know how to answer. You take them."

Betty walked quickly away from the counter, just as a tall, slim, attractive woman stepped to the elevators and pushed the Down button. Betty saw that she had nothing under her arms. She stopped before the woman and said pleasantly, "I trust you were happy with your purchase."

The woman looked down her nose at Betty. "And who are you?"

"I am the department manager. You found what you wanted, of course?"

"No," she snapped, "I did not. So you are the manager? Do you know something? I used to think so, but now I am convinced—your girls here are all indolent."

"Oh, really?"

"Yes. I asked to see a certain suit, and they showed me one that was four sizes too small. I like the suit, mind you, but when I wanted to see my size they said it wasn't in stock. The girl even walked away."

Betty said, "That could easily be true. We have just merged with another chain, you know. This change-of-name sale has just about depleted all of our stocks. I can well imagine that the suit she showed you was the only one we had to show."

"But she was rude."

"I apologize for her. You know how it is in a big sale. They are all worn out." But then she stepped back a bit and looked the woman up and down and her mind was racing frantically. She had to show the saleswomen on this floor what it was really like to sell. She remembered a dress she had seen and admired while going through the floor with Maloney and told the woman, "When you were walking across the floor a minute ago I was watching you and I was thinking of a certain dress. It's a blue sheath with just a suggestion of flair at the hips, which you could use, because of your slimness. As I watched you walking I thought, 'Good Lord, that dress was made for her.' Would you mind if I showed it to you? I would just like to see if perhaps we think the same."

The woman was reluctant, she glanced at her watch, but she was also flattered. "If it won't take more than a moment."

Betty looked around and saw Miss Snider watching them. Someone had to learn something and now was the time. She called Miss Snider over and asked her, "Would you mind showing the customer the—ah—it was a blue sheath."

Miss Snider nodded, "I know the dress."

Betty walked away, with a sigh of relief, to the side of the floor where she could watch the fitting rooms and waited. Fifteen minutes later the customer came onto the floor and Miss Snider was following her with the dress over her arms. She was removing tags, so it was a sale.

Betty hurried over and intercepted them. She smiled broadly. "I see we do think the same."

The customer was obviously happy. "Thanks for telling me," she said. "And such a buy."

"I knew you would like it. Did you know that there is a coat that goes with it?"

"No, I didn't."

This time Betty went back to the stock room. She hadn't any idea of what she was looking for, but she could always depend on her good taste. Very quickly she found a coat that would go perfectly with the blue dress, and it was the right size. It was not, however, on sale. The price was $199.95, but she brought it out and turned it over to Miss Snider. Again a sale was consummated. Then Betty took them to the millinery department where she knew of a hat that would fit the dress and coat perfectly. Miss Snider wrote up a tag for $309.18.

But when the customer left Miss Snider leaned over the counter and looked Betty in the eyes. Miss Snider was a woman in her sixties, with a big bosom, piercing eyes, hanging jowls, blue-gray hair, and a commanding manner.

"Miss Parker," she said, "I was selling before you were born. Who do you think you are, Jesus H. Christ? Were you trying to teach me how to sell?"

Betty looked directly back into her eyes. "Yes," she said, "and I think I succeeded. I intercepted a customer who was dissatisfied and was leaving and managed to write up three hundred and nine dollars. Now, who do you think knows more about selling, you or me?"

"Why, you—" Betty looked around and saw that others were listening to the irate Miss Snider. Good. The saleswoman continued, "I don't like interference, and I don't like fresh department managers. If it came right down to it, baby, and one of us had to leave, I don't think it would be me. So I'll tell you right now, don't try to do my selling for me from now on."

Betty had difficulty controlling a smile. Miss Snider was playing directly into her hand. "Very well," she said, "If that's the way you feel about it. Then let's have it understood here and now. I happen to be a pretty good sales person myself, and my job on this floor is to help everyone sell. But from now on I won't step on your toes again. Anything I manage to sell I'll turn over to the other books. Is that agreed?"

Miss Snider sensed some sort of victory and smiled grimly. "Good enough. You run your department and I'll do my own selling and we'll get along."

"Very good. Then that is the way it will be. Anything I sell, or help to sell, will go in someone else's book. That is all, Miss Snider."

The older woman turned away with a proud smirk, but after she had walked a few steps she paused and blinked and looked back at Betty. She was no fool. She realized she had been trapped by her own words. But then her back stiffened and she thought, I'll show her, the little bitch.

Betty was young, but she had learned a few lessons well. If there were fifteen people on a sales floor and one of them was top-dog, the other fourteen either disliked or hated the top-dog. Word would spread of what had happened. Now she would have fourteen people who would at least be partially sympathetic to her. Of course, she did run the risk of losing the top-dog.

Marie Togliatti was also gambling. She was watching Betty

with hate dancing in her black eyes. For the first time that morning, Marie was smiling. The redhead had challenged the wrong person. How stupid could she get?

4

BETTY was appalled with how the floor was run. The girls did about as they pleased and cheated on each other. She noticed one little trick that most of them got away with repeatedly. A girl would take a customer into a fitting room. While the customer was changing, she would come out and tell Marie, "Put me down, please." She would then go back to take care of her customer. When she was on-down it meant she would get back on the call-board much faster than she was supposed to. That, too, would be changed.

Lack of discipline was most noticeable when the girls were far down on the call-board. When they were down they were supposed to go into another room, telephone customers, write cards, or even check their stock. Most of them simply went into the lounge and smoked and gossiped.

By the time the noon hour was over with, however, Betty had changed her mind on one point. It would not be possible to institute reforms on that floor in a hurry. She realized it was going to take time. If these girls had ever known discipline, it would be possible to change things around rather quickly; but they had never known it. If she tried to move too fast she would have rebellion on her hands. Kane and Maloney would not expect that of her. She sighed. Kane was right. The floor was a snake pit. And it was up to her to tame the snakes without getting bitten.

Maloney dropped by and asked how she was doing. She said flatly, "I'm sinking in a bed of quicksand."

He had to laugh. "You'll get hold, in time."

"You can bet your life on that."

"I will. Chin up."

Maloney went by her and walked on down the long hallway leading to the executive offices. Good kid, he was thinking, and dropped her almost instantly from his mind. He had his own problems. For two solid weeks he had been running the store on his own with no help from anyone. It meant that he could not take his normal day off, and it also meant that he had to be in the store on Mondays and Thursdays, when it stayed open at night, from before nine in the morning until better than nine thirty at night. He was feeling a little worn out.

The store could not be run by one person. He was grateful for being moved up to the managership—normally, it would have taken another three or four years—but something had to be done to give him some relief.

He stopped at the open doorway of Julie's office and jerked his head at her. She smiled and said, "He's in."

He moved on to the open doorway of Drury's office and looked inside. The older man was just settling himself behind his big desk after a very satisfying lunch. He was remembering what Joe Haley had told him. When he saw Maloney, he called, "Come in, Fred."

Fred walked in and dropped into a chair opposite Drury. He looked around and nodded with satisfaction. It was a beautiful office, not quite as grand as Kane's, of course, but very nice.

Drury asked cheerfully, "Well, how's it going? I imagine for you, at this point, it's a bit of a rat race."

"That's what I came to talk to you about, Mr. Drury. I'm beginning to sag in the middle."

"Think you can keep going another week?"

Fred looked at him with heightened interest. "Sure."

"Then I have good news for you. You know Chet Baker at Wilson's Burlingame store?"

Fred pursed his lips. "I don't know him, but I have heard of him. Isn't he the store manager down there?"

"Uh-huh. We tried about a week ago to get him for your assistant, but he turned us down even though he knew he would still be getting the same money. He changed his mind a few hours ago. He called up and said he'd take the position. So you'll have a man working for you in a week."

Fred asked curiously, "Why did he change his mind? He's already a store manager. Why would he be interested in stepping down to assistant?"

"Well, hell, Fred, this store is about twenty times bigger, for one thing. There are plenty of reasons why he should move in here."

"I don't know. In his shoes, I wouldn't do it. On the other hand, I'm glad I have someone coming."

Drury looked at him narrowly. "You're not overly elated."

Fred nodded. "I have to be honest. Once a manager always a manager. He'll be trying to make my decisions for me."

"Kane wants it that way."

"Oh. Well, then, God has spoken."

Drury was feeling good about Kane at that moment and snapped, "Don't be so damned irreverent."

"Sorry." Fred shrugged and walked out of the room. Since when had Drury fallen in love with the new boss?

He paused in the hallway for a moment and wondered if he should call Ellen. There seemed to be some sort of crisis in their marriage lately. It had him worried. So far it was just a lot of little things, but he was used to dealing with women in the store and he could see danger signals beginning to fly. She no longer liked their home in Westlake and complained bitterly about being almost constantly in fog. The children themselves also seemed to be getting on her nerves. She snapped at them constantly.

The biggest warning, though, was when they were in bed at night. Fred was no longer as sexually powerful as he had been in his twenties, but he felt he was doing very well for his age. He enjoyed his sex as much as he ever had, though not quite as often. Ellen was definitely not yet going through the change of life, yet for months now she had not seemed to enjoy sex and quite often succeeded in putting him off. He remembered something his wise father had once said, "Marriage is cemented or it becomes unglued in bed. Don't ever forget it, my boy." He was remembering it now only too well, and he felt a slight touch of fear in the pit of his stomach.

For years, though, he had made a definite point of never calling home during the business hours as so many men did. There was something about it that, to him, was less than manly. So he pondered the question for a moment, then discarded it. Hell, he thought, what will it gain?

He turned to go down the hallway and ran into Sam Kuller coming out of the merchandising offices. Sam had a sheaf of papers in one hand and his florid face was unusually red with anger. Sam was head merchandiser of all the men's departments, and a good one. He was a little smaller than Fred and waspishly thin, his unruly sandy hair always needed a comb, his emotions were written on his bony face for anyone to see, and he was one of the few executives allowed to go about in his shirt sleeves.

43

Sam was close to sixty and had been doing it all his life. He wouldn't know how to work with his coat on.

Sam grabbed Fred by the arm and almost shook him. "Maybe you can tell me," he half shouted. "What the hell goes on with that goddamned Joe Haley? He's raising hell with my buyers again. Just a little while ago he called Burke a silly, stupid, shithead nincompoop. Frankly, I agree with him, mind you, but you can't tell a buyer that to his face. Now, can you?"

Fred smothered a smile and said, "It isn't quite proper. But what's Joe mad about?"

"Oh, it's got something or other to do with some cashmeres Burke promised him, and they aren't in yet."

"Isn't it always the same thing? The buyers promise everything and you get nothing. Cripes, Sam, how often have you and I gone around and around over this very same thing?"

Sam's sandy eyebrows arched. "Oh, oh. Protecting your boy already, huh? I should've known. Step on one of your fairheaded kids and I'm stepping on your toes. I wonder if they really know how loyal you are where they're concerned?"

Fred grinned. "I doubt it. I don't make a display of holding their hands."

"You're sure a hell of a lot different than your former bossman. I'm tickled silly they moved him out and gave you the job. Now we'll get things done in this rag house."

"You and I always worked well together, Sam."

"That we have, my boy." He had forgotten what he was angry about and started smiling. "And from now on it will be even better. Give you another ten years in this woman's womb they call a store and you'll be signing my checks, if I'm still alive, that is. Goddamn but I get a lot of aches and pains lately. A pint of booze every night doesn't seem to help much any more."

"You drink that much, or are you bragging?"

"Hell's bells, boy, not too many years back they used to call me quart-a-day-Sam. How do you think I stayed on in this business as long as I have? There are only three ways you can make it in retail: you gotta be a fairy, or insane, or a drunk. I chose the latter."

"I guess I fall in the insane category."

Sam winked at him. "Or maybe a latent fairy?"

Fred laughed. "Speaking of fairies," he said, "I have to go talk to one right now, down on one."

Sam almost split with laughter. When he had calmed down

44

he gasped, "The way you just said it. My God! Wait'll I pass this one around."

Fred was mystified. "What did I say?"

"You said—oh, my God—you said that you had to go talk to a fairy now down on one."

"I mean on the first floor, of course." Then he realized what Sam was laughing about and burst out laughing himself. "Jees," he gasped. "Damn it all Sam, you're a dirty-minded old man. I'm leaving your company right now."

He walked down to the fourth floor elevators and punched the button. He looked around the floor for Betty, but she was not in sight. He glanced over at the new counter and saw Marie and Miss Snider watching him with their heads close together. He smiled and nodded. They smiled and waved.

Marie whispered, "There he is now." That was when they waved. Then she said, "You aren't going to believe this, but I saw it with my own eyes. On my way back from lunch I stopped in his office. I was just going to put it right out on the table and find out just how much authority this new Miss Parker has. Well, I went into his office and it was empty. Then I saw some papers on his desk and, not that I was snooping, mind you, but I couldn't help but see what they were."

"It's always that way about papers on a desk in empty offices."

"Oh, stop being catty. However, I did see what the papers were all about. Miss Parker, you know, came from Wilson's. Well, I guess any time a change is made they have to sign new papers and all. These new papers were there for Miss Parker to sign. Her salary was on the top page."

"Which means that you saw the other pages under it. But go on. What about her salary?"

Marie paused significantly, her black eyes fairly snapping. "You would never guess what that salary is."

"Hell," Miss Snider snorted, "no manager on this floor ever made over five hundred a month. That's why I can always tell 'em off. With my bonuses and commissions I average seven-fifty to eight hundred a month."

Marie said tiredly, "I know, I know. But this little redhead has got you topped."

"Oh, stop kidding."

"I'm not. Honestly. I saw it with my own eyes." Then she announced triumphantly, "The redhead draws down seven hundred and fifty a month AND bonuses. How do you like that?"

Miss Snider said uncertainly, "Aw."

"It's true. Cross my heart and hope to die." Then her voice lowered even more. "But you know what it means, don't you?"

Miss Snider was in a bit of a daze. "No, what?"

"Oh, now, use your head." She looked about, then whispered hoarsely, "It means she's sleeping with Mr. Kane, that's what it means."

It was as if she had hit Miss Snider in the stomach. She suddenly felt each and every one of her sixty-two years. And for a moment she looked it. She knew now that she could never win in any contest with Miss Parker. It was a pitiful knowledge for her to swallow.

Fred got off at the first floor and walked back through shirts and ties to gifts and luggage. The department manager, Paul Francis Atwater, did not see Fred coming. He was busy arranging some gifts on a table. Fred stopped and watched him for a moment with a light smile. Paul was as queer as a three-dollar bill, yet Fred and everyone else in the store liked him. Paul was an obvious homosexual. Normally they tried to weed out obvious homosexuals, but not Paul. He was in a class by himself. He was in his late thirties, tall and wiry, with fairly decent shoulders, a flat stomach, and narrow hips. As with so many homosexuals, Paul kept himself fit with barbells and in gymnasiums. He was actually a rather distinguished looking person and dressed the part to the hilt, going in heavily for custom-made shirts and ties and special handkerchiefs from Rome, Paris, and London. He had a rather quick grace in the way he moved, and his hands were as demonstrative as those of a woman.

He turned about after a moment and saw Fred and was delighted. "Freddie-boy," he said. "How nice. Don't you think these new crystal ashtrays are the loveliest things? God, my dear, what a terrible time I had getting them away from that horrible wholesaler." He shuddered. "What a brute."

He walked over to join Fred and was suddenly concerned. "You look tired. Goddamn it all, why do these bastards have to load everything on you?"

"I'm okay."

"My ass! You're tired and it shows." Then his eyes were dancing as he said, "Why don't you come up to Mother's some night and let me massage you?"

"Oh, you go to hell."

"You know how I would just love to stroke that powerful body of yours."

Fred had to laugh. "Shove it."

"Hmmmm. That IS an idea." Then suddenly he looked over Fred's shoulder and said, "Isn't that your wife?"

Fred spun about and saw his wife coming down the few steps from the main entrance. She was smiling and was looking straight ahead. She would never see him so far in the back. Fred watched her proudly as she crossed the first floor toward the elevators. By God, at a distance, she did look like a twenty-five-year-old woman. Ellen was forty-one, but she still had a slim figure, about which she was very careful when it came to eating and drinking, and her legs were truly beautiful, slim, long and well contoured. Her blond hair was cut and turned under in a long pageboy. Her features were fairly even, her chin was pointed, and her hazel eyes—her most prominent feature—were widely set. She dressed youthfully and with style, and she had a certain switch of her hips as she moved steadily forward on three-inch spike heels.

Paul said, "Aren't you going to say hello?"

Fred shook his head. "She's probably here to do some shopping, which means she has to look me up before she leaves. She needs my signature for that twenty percent discount, you know. I'll be seeing her."

He watched her as she went into an elevator and wanted to tell the whole world that this was his wife.

Ellen stepped into the elevator and punched the button for the fourth floor. A loudspeaker in a high corner of the elevator was playing some sort of music softly. She began humming to it. She got off at the fourth floor and ran into some of the girls whom she knew well. Then she also met Betty. They eyed each other up and down and neither liked or disliked what they saw. Each of them reserved judgment. Then Ellen went about the floor by herself for fifteen minutes or so, seemingly appraising what was left of the sale merchandise. Gradually she worked her way down to the far end of the floor.

When she was sure that no one was looking she ducked through a door and went down an angular stairway to the floor below. She came out in a short hallway and walked out into the open area of the third floor. She looked quickly about and saw Joe at once. He was standing before a desk, talking on a telephone. She walked over and stood behind him.

Joe said finally into the telephone, "You got until tomorrow morning, Burke, or I'm going over your head to Kane himself. I'm tired of the crap you been handing out," and slammed the phone.

"Hello, Joe."

He turned slowly about and blinked at her. The boss's wife. How many bosses do I have? he wondered. One thing for sure was that Fred Maloney was his most immediate boss. And this was his wife, and she was in love with Joe.

He had known it, now, for a couple of months. Fred bought his own clothes with no help from his wife, so Joe had never had an occasion to run into Ellen. About six months ago, though, he had been in Fred's office for some reason or other when she came in. She took one look at Joe and then a second look and that was it. Since then she came back at least a couple of times a week, and she always found some excuse for dropping by the third floor.

He grinned and displayed snow-white teeth, though he was not smiling inwardly. "Hi, Mrs. Maloney."

"Ellen," she pouted. "I've told you before."

"Oh, sure. I keep forgetting." He looked slyly around the floor. All of his staff seemed to be busy, but he was positive that each and every one of them was watching from the corners of their eyes. What the hell! They had to be idiots not to know what was going on. "What can I do for you, Ellen?"

"Nothing, really," she said, in what she figured was her most fetching manner. "I just thought I'd drop by, just for fun, and get your quota for now. You know how Fred is about quotas. That new girl on the fourth floor," she lied, "gave me her's."

"Oh? Sure." He thought quickly and made up a figure and said, "As of this moment it's five thousand, two hundred and eighty. He'll be happy to know, I'm sure." In my hat, he thought. Fred wasn't interested in quotas until the day was far gone.

"Thanks," she said. "And how is the wife and family?"

"Very well. I might ask the same about yours."

"Oh, they do nicely. Well—" She paused indecisively and did not quite know how to break off. Her eyes slid away. Oh, God, she thought, how could a man be so damned beautiful and still be alive? Then she said quickly, "I'll tell Fred and surprise him."

"Yes. Do that."

"Well, good-bye."

"Sure. Good-bye."

She looked into his eyes and her own seemed to melt, then she spun about on her spike heels and walked away.

At the elevators, she turned and smiled and waved to him, using her fingers only. Joe nodded. It's coming to a head, he thought. God only knows, it's coming to a head. Then what did a man do? She would probably be good in bed. After all, she had logged a lot of hours in some bed or other. That age was usually the best kind. He knew from experience.

But then he thought of something else more important. Fred Maloney had backed Joe Haley all the way, even when he had only been assistant manager, and many times when it could have cost him his job. No man had more loyalty than Fred Maloney, and he never asked for it in return. Joe had never run into anyone quite like him before. If there was any one man in this world for whom he had deep and abiding respect, it was Fred Maloney.

Cripes, he thought, what's a man to do?

Joe was tired at the end of the day. He was always tired at the day's end. He had an amazing amount of enery that he could tap at will, but when he got through toting up the day's receipts when all the sales staff was gone he always felt as if he had just taken a beating. No matter how important people might think they were behind the scenes, the rag business paid off at one end only, on the sales floor. And that was where Joe was talented.

He took his final quota, picked up the telephone and called the store office. "Fred? This is Joe. It's eighteen thousand, two hundred and seventy-five and a few pennies. Got it? Okay. I am going home and soak in a hot bath. You can go soak your head. Good-bye, you bastard."

He turned off the light over his desk, picked up his hat and walked out of the office. He walked through the now empty floor and punched the down elevator key. There was a soft swish and the doors opened. He stepped inside and found himself facing Lew Kane, who was also going down.

"Well," he said, a little taken back, "I didn't expect to run into you, sir. I heard you were out of the store most of the day."

Kane nodded. "I was. Lawyers. Have a good day?"

"I think so, yes. About two thousand over the quota."

"Sounds good. Mind telling me, Haley, what you're aiming at?"

"Merchandising, of course."

"I have a hunch you don't mean to go up the chain through the buyers' offices on your way."

"I don't. Buying can be skipped."

Kane nodded. "It's been done before."

Joe looked into Kane's eyes and saw that the older man was interested in their conversation, so he said boldly, "I hope you don't mind my asking, Mr. Kane, but there is something I have never been able to figure out."

"What's that?"

"Just how the devil you managed to put this deal together?"

Kane laughed and lightly squeezed his arm. "You're not the only one who wonders about that." The doors opened then and he said, "Here's the first floor."

They stepped out and Joe figured that was the end of the conversation. They walked across the main floor to the doors, where a security guard let them out on the street. But then Kane paused at the curb and looked at Joe.

"Did you ever know," he asked, "that I once worked for Merritt's?"

Joe blinked his surprise. "Hell, no. I've never heard that."

"It was a long time ago. I got my training as stock boy at the Emporium, then I went with Hastings as a salesman. From there I moved over here, also as a salesman. Drury was here then and Sam Kuller and a few others, but they have no reason to remember me. I was here about a year and a half down on the first floor. Incidentally, I was a damned good-looking young man myself during those years."

"You still are."

"Thanks. Anyway, I always liked this store, and I promised myself that some day I would own it." He chuckled and added, "Sometimes dreams do come true."

"They sure did with you. And you still haven't told me how you put it together."

Kane was thoughtfully silent for a long moment, then he said, "I'm not about to, my boy. It's strictly between me and my God."

"I understand that Mrs. Merritt pledged all of her stock for you."

"Oh, yes, that's common knowledge. Now, if you don't mind, I must hie myself home."

They heard the store doors open and close behind them, and the two of them turned around. Betty crossed the sidewalk toward them with a tired smile. "My feet," she said, "are killing me." Then she looked up at the two of them and giggled. "Standing with you two is almost like being in the company of a couple of Watutsis. You make me feel like a pygmy."

Kane said gallantly, "No pygmy ever looked like you. Could I give you a lift home? I didn't take the car today. You can share a taxi with me."

"Thanks," she said, "I'd love to, but I'm meeting a friend. Damn friends, anyway. Sometimes they make more demands than your enemies."

Joe said quickly, "In that case, how about letting me buy you a drink? There's a nice cocktail lounge right around the corner."

Betty looked at him levelly out of her green eyes and was indecisive for a second or two. She would like a drink, and she did have about twenty minutes to kill. However, she had heard a great deal about Joe Haley. Family man or not, he was the biggest tomcat in the city. She liked him, but she had no desire to get involved with him in any way.

"No time," she said. "I'll take a raincheck on that."

"Okay. Some other time."

The two men stood silently and watched Betty until she disappeared around the corner. Joe was remembering the wonderful sway of her fanny as she went around the corner and turned back to Kane with a broad grin. He was on the verge of saying something about it, but Kane was looking at him narrowly, his lips pressed thinly together.

Kane cleared his throat and said thickly, "I wouldn't follow that up, if I were you. Because, you see, I wouldn't like it one damned bit."

Joe stared at him as if he had lost his mind and anger was again welling up within him. But before he had a chance to say anything, Kane turned and walked away.

Kane walked down to the corner and flagged a cab. He got in the back seat and gave the driver his address on Russian Hill. He thought through the events of the day and was satisfied with the way everything had gone. Of course, there were dozens of loose strings hanging about, but they would be picked up in time. He thought of his biggest problem. He had to go at least two years, and possibly three, without drawing any money out of the chain for his personal use. Otherwise, the whole house of cards would collapse. Except for the bankers and Anna, no one else knew that the big chain of Merritt-Wilson had damned little cash. Hell, he thought, we'll manage somehow.

His second biggest problem was Drury. The controller had been buying Merritt stock throughout the years, as had other employees. But they had all sold out to Kane when he had put on pressure. But not Drury. He had owned a little better than twenty percent of Merritt stock and when the merger had been made had insisted on the same percentage in Merritt-Wilson. There was nothing for Kane to do but give it to him. The sonofabitch, he thought. He had me by the balls and he knew it.

Drury was a special problem. Any controller of a retail chain exercised tremendous authority. He not only ran the financial picture, but he was also in charge of all mark-downs, budgets for the merchandisers and buyers, and advertising (this was the important point).

Drury had been a good man for Merritt's, but he was the worst possible man for the new setup. Kane was thinking bigger now and Drury just had to go. He was an almost insurmountable barrier in the way of Kane's idea of progress. Kane had to chisel on the advertising dollar without the bank knowing. Drury would never hold still for such chicanery, nor would he take the chance. Jackson would go along, but not Drury, which was why Jackson had been placed in the office. On the other hand, how the devil did you get rid of a man who owned twenty percent of the stock? That was really more than Kane himself owned. He had pledged Anna's stock (which he did not own, except under a five-year option to buy), he had pledged his four stores, and he was four million in hock, besides. If Drury only knew it, and if the bank cared to go along with him, he could come pretty close to edging Kane out and taking over himself. Thank God, Kane thought, he hasn't even the inkling of such an idea! No one had.

The cab stopped before the eighteen-story apartment building on the crest of Russian Hill and Kane got out. He paid the driver and looked up at the building, which was less than two years old. A little over a year ago, when Anna had said that she might be willing to sell, he had bought the penthouse of this building. That and the new Rolls-Royce and, of course, all the new furnishings for the penthouse had come to about a quarter of a million dollars. Kane was a moderately wealthy man, but he did not have that kind of money. Nevertheless, he splurged. This was the big gamble of his life and he had decided to take it. And, he was quite sure, it had helped swing the deal with the bank. He looked successful.

He nodded at the doorman who grinned broadly (Ain't he the biggest owner? Yeah, man!) and took the elevator up to the penthouse. He let himself in and walked down a short hallway into the big living room. Bessie was not about, so he walked on to the huge windows looking out over the Golden Gate, the Marin hills to the north, Richardson's Bay, the San Rafael Bridge, the Golden Gate Bridge and, to the east, Richmond and even part of Berkeley on the east shore. It was a spectacular view. In another hour or so the sun would be sinking. That was the best time of the day, when the sun set. He promised himself to watch it.

He turned away from the windows and looked at the living room and had to smile. Bessie, of course, had hired an interior decorator. She would never trust her own judgment. The room was done in soft greens and gold, with a few splashes of rose here and there and a touch of white to highlight the other colors. There were deep sofas and luxurious chairs and teakwood tables and abstract paintings on the walls and break-front bookcases and, in the long dining alcove, a dining set of expensive Danish modern. Besides the living room and dining alcove, the penthouse had also a kitchen, butler's pantry, master bedroom, two guest rooms, library, maid's room, a workroom that Kane used, a small laundry room and two terraces. Give me time, he thought, and I'll have what I want, either a French Normandy manor, or old-English Regency with mullioned windows.

He took his coat off and threw it over a chair as Bessie came bustling from the kitchen. She kissed his cheek and beamed at him. In the kitchen again, he thought. They had a housekeeper who was an excellent cook, but Bessie preferred doing her own cooking. She said softly, "You look wonderful, Lew. The first day, too." He hid a smile and rubbed the scar on his cheek.

She was the one who was wonderful. When he married her she had been the equal of a dozen Betty Parker's. A twenty-one inch waist, weight a hundred and eight pounds, legs that made any man spin his head around, and blond hair that looked as if it had been taken out of a gold mine. At that time, she had been the glamour queen of San Francisco, and he had been lucky even to make her notice him. That she had wound up marrying him had been a miracle. Then slowly the change had taken place. He thought he had married Princess Moon Beam herself only to discover that she was actually a hausfrau at heart. Giving

53

birth to the two boys, of course, had a lot to do with her change, but it went deeper than that. She was a woman who loved her husband, her children, her home (wherever it happened to be), and everything about her life. She just simply loved. And she didn't give a damn about being beautiful.

He looked at her now and had to grin inwardly. She was big-bosomed, she had no waist at all, her hips had spread (she still had good legs, though), and her hair was pure gray. She always dressed well, occasionally even in high-fashion, and she still looked good, but she made no attempt whatever to hide her age. "Lew," she had said more than once, "I can't keep up with you. You're a handsome brute. I'm just the housewife." And she meant it.

He remembered sadly, for himself, that is, when she had first started to change. It had not been long after their marriage. She was pregnant almost at once, and she never did seem to quite get over the largeness. It had distressed Lew. He had even thought of divorcing her. At that time, he had been almost as handsome as Joe Haley and had women running after him. Instead of divorcing her, however, he began stepping out at nights. It went on for almost ten years and at no time did she ever suspect. Same as Haley, he thought. Then, after he began to slow down a bit, he realized that he had the most perfect wife a man could ask for. How could anyone ask for more than pure, undiluted, blind love? For a while he hated himself. But he got over that, too, and finally settled down with Bessie. Today he loved her with every cell of his body.

He put his big hands on her shoulders and said, "Damn it, you get more like a Yiddish wife every day."

"Maybe I got a little of it in me?"

"No," he laughed. "You louse up your charge accounts too much for that."

"We got a letter from Frank today."

"Oh?" Lew was not too fond of his older son, but asked, "What's on his mind?"

"Oh, he's having a good time in Europe, I guess."

"Damn it, Bessie, don't you think it's time he settled down?"

"But he's just a boy."

"A boy!" he roared. "He's twenty-eight years old, goddamn it. You call that a boy? You know something? I couldn't even put him in one of the stores as a stock boy. He's hasn't enough brains."

She was aghast. "He has a fine university education."

"Learning what, I ask you? All he did at college was learn how

54

to use the good manners you taught him at home. He took all the cinch courses. He didn't learn a damned thing that would be useful to him." He said disgustedly, "Write him and tell him to come home." He did not dare tell her that he could no longer afford to keep Frank in Europe—she would not understand—so he said, "I think maybe I got a spot where I can place him. And, for God's sake, tell him to fly tourist class. I should put out another five hundred dollars so he can eat lobster and have free champagne? Tell him to get his tail home."

Bessie bit her lip. It was very rare for Lew to become angry with her, and when he did she listened. "Very well, dear."

"What's in the pot?"

"Your favorite," she smiled. "Chicken paprika with noodles, German style."

"Ah. Mit noodles, yet."

They ate in the dining alcove, where they were served by the housekeeper. Bessie chatted away and Lew ate and thought. Bessie hardly ever seemed to need a reply from him, so at the dinner hour he could do considerable thinking. It was Drury who was still on his mind.

When they had finished dinner Lew was a bit perturbed. Because Bessie had been talking and because he had been thinking about Drury, he had missed the sunset. It was still twilight, but that was not the same as watching the sun go down. He got up and turned on a few lights. Then he walked into the library and stood pensively before his gun cabinet, wondering if he would get in any big game hunting that year. He doubted it, and it made him feel a little sad. It would be the first year he had missed hunting since his father had bought him his first single shot .22.

Bessie came into the library and said, "Oh, yes, Bill called today. He intended dropping by this evening, but he can't make it."

"Oh?" Lew thought of Bill and grinned.

The two boys were a year apart, so Bill was twenty-seven. He and Frank were the exact opposites of each other. Bill was a hustler. He looked very much like his father and had his father's drive. He had graduated from college at twenty, had spent another year on his Master's, then, of all places, had gone to work for a big trucking outfit. Lew had almost begged him to come into the store, but Bill was independent and wanted no favors from his father. At twenty-three he borrowed some money from a bank, though his father would have been glad to lend it to him, and started his own trucking company. He suffered and sweat it out and almost went bankrupt a few times, but at last he got going. Now, still a bachelor ("I'm looking around now, Dad"), he had a fleet of sixteen or seventeen trucks. Lew was so proud of him it hurt. Yet, he and Bill were never very close. Lew knew why. Bill did not care to walk in his father's shadow and intended surpassing him in every way. By God, Lew thought, he might just do it, too.

Lew asked Bessie, "Why can't he come by?"

Bessie laughed and replied, "He says he's having dinner tonight with a living doll. Says she works for you, too, though he didn't tell me her name."

The food he had eaten was suddenly sour in Lew's stomach and he looked positively ill. But it couldn't be. Not Betty Parker. That was simply too much of a coincidence. God, no, he thought. Oh, God, not a cruel joke like that!

5

KANE was exceedingly busy during the following week. He was making a personal tour of the entire chain and was on the move from morning until night. There were four Merritt-Wilson stores in downtown San Francisco and another in Stonestown, out toward the beach. Then, down the Peninsula, they had stores in San Mateo, Burlingame, Redwood City, Palo Alto, and two stores in San Jose, a big one downtown and a brand new one in the shopping center of Valley Fair. There were also stores across the bay in Oakland, Berkeley, and Walnut Creek. The other stores were in Sacramento, Stockton, Modesto, Fresno, Bakersfield, and one far north near the Oregon line in Redding. Kane put in an appearance at each and every one of them.

When he returned from Redding to the big store at Union Square the change-of-name sale was all over with and new merchandise was flooding in. The merchandising and buyers' offices were in an uproar. Kane walked into his office on a Thursday morning, hung up his hat, and sat behind his desk. He looked tanned and very fit. Actually, he thrived on hard work.

Susie came in from her office, tilted her head to one side to

56

appraise him critically, then nodded her approval. Susie was a bit hippy, with the secretarial spread, her legs were long and quite thin and her figure left much to be desired, but she had a nice face of even features, intelligent, sharp, shrewd, and humorous blue eyes, and mousey blond hair that she tied in a bun at the back of her head. She was thirty-seven years old, she had been married three times, and she had one loyalty, Lew Kane.

She sat down and told him sharply, "You could have called now and then. When God is gone I am not exactly Christ, you know. The sex is all wrong."

"Busy," he said.

"You probably been shacking up with every female department manager in the whole chain."

"Only fourteen or fifteen."

"Sure," she smiled. "Anyway, where do you want me to start?"

He leaned his elbows on the desk and pressed his fingertips together. "I'll tell you something, Susie. Ninety percent of all the urgent calls you've received you can forget. Whatever crisis was involved is now all resolved."

"Naturally. Why do you think you hire me, because I'm stupid?"

"I hire you because you're gorgeous, yet you're probably a lousy lay. Three husbands?"

"I can get testimonials from each one of them, signed, sealed, and delivered. Right now I got a fourth one in mind, if Mr. Paul Francis Atwater doesn't get to him first. Damn, but it's getting tough to compete with these fairies."

Kane laughed and leaned back in his chair. "Okay, Susie. What's problem number one?"

"Joe Haley, Burke, and Kuller are going around and around."

"That's a problem for the store manager and merchandising."

"Not any more it isn't. Now it's serious. Now it's up to you."

"That bad, huh?"

"Yes. Want my opinion?"

"I'd appreciate it, if you don't mind."

"All right. Seems that Burke has been shorting Haley too many times, and now Joe is fighting mad. Their last tussle was over some cashmere jackets that never did get here, but now it's even worse. Now that the big sale is over with, Joe wants his stock filled out. He is doing fine with all the other buyers except Burke. Burke has failed to deliver in a big gabardine suit deal and also in Daks slacks. That latter could be important, you know."

57

"They're always in demand. And they aren't here?"

"Not one."

Kane picked up the telephone and dialed Kuller's number in merchandising. "Sam?" he asked. "Okay. Give me one quick reason why Burke shorted Haley in cashmeres, and why he is now shorting him in gabardine suits and Daks."

There was a long pause, then Sam said, "The quickest reason I can come up with is that Burke went over his budget in top-coats, and we've had some pretty good weather this summer."

"Why did he go over?"

"Well, I think he got talked into it back in New York by the Garfinkle outfit."

Kane drummed his fingers on the desk for a moment, then said, "I don't know Burke very well. Can't even place him. He must be a Merritt man."

"He is."

Then Kane asked bluntly, "How do you like him?"

"Well—"

"You've given me the answer. Can his assistant move in?"

"No. Needs at least another year of training. I follow you, though. Okay. I'll look around and see who I can come up with."

"Pass the word to Haley and tell him to keep his mouth shut and sit tight."

"Will do."

He hung up and grimaced. "It's a dirty business," he said. "Actually, I know Burke very well. I was just waiting for an opportunity to get rid of him. He's one of Merritt's weak ones. Oh, well. And next on the list?"

She looked him in the eyes and said harshly, "Mr. Jack Harrison. Really, you must do something about that wonderful old man."

"You worried about him?" he laughed. "Let me tell you something. He's seventy-one years old, and he knocks off sixty thousand dollars a year. He is in charge of all merchandising, men's and women's, and he is in charge of all the buyers. He is one of the greatest men this business has ever known. And you worry about him?"

She said stubbornly, "Yes, I do. Ever since you've taken over you've had him dangling on a string. He was in here talking to me every day you were gone. He looks lost."

"Why?"

"He can't make up his mind whether you need him or not.

He's worried about it. And you know his pride. If he thought he wasn't needed, he would walk out of here in one minute flat."

Kane frowned and stared off into space for a moment. "Really? I wasn't aware of how he felt. I've just been so busy. And he figures I've had him dangling on a string? I'll be damned."

He was silent for a long while, thinking, then he said, "I'll tell you something about the old boy. A month ago I took the whole merchandising office and all the buyers, as well as Mr. Harrison, back to New York. The change-of-name sale was coming up. I needed money for advertising. If you put on enough pressure the wholesalers will come through also."

"I know."

He said ruefully, "They didn't for me. As far as they were concerned, I was a small-time operator. Many of them hadn't heard of me. I needed over a hundred thousand dollars pledged in advertising for that sale. You know what I came up with? Two thousand.

"Man! Anyway, that's where Jack came in. He came up to see me at the Waldorf-Astoria and told me he would see what he could do. I had no idea what a power that old man was. He went out and fought with those wholesalers, and got every last dime of that hundred grand I needed."

Susie grinned. "You can't beat him."

"You're telling me! But that's not all of it. He had a schedule of calls to make. I don't think you know how those wholesalers are with little people. You keep your appointment on the minute or you're canceled out. Jack, of course, knows that. So one day he got through talking with one wholesaler and thirty minutes later had to be across town to talk with another. It was pouring. You couldn't get a taxi for love or money. Jack didn't even have an umbrella. But, by God, he set out and walked all the way across town and kept that appointment, soaking wet. And he got the money. Imagine that old man?"

"He's grand."

Kane grinned. "You love him, too, don't you? So do I. So, between us, let's see what we can do about him."

Kane left his desk and walked out of the room. The next office to his, on the right, with an open door, was Harrison's. Kane stepped to the door and looked in. The old man was seated behind his desk, seriously going through some papers. His thick hair was pure white, he had a round, florid face, with hanging jowls, hazel eyes that never missed a trick, and he dressed like a mortician—white shirt, black tie, black suit, and black shoes. He was about five feet ten and almost as round as he was tall. He was a heavy boozer (it was known all over the store that every night he went home he went to bed dead drunk), but he was also a heavy eater and that was what kept him alive.

He looked up and saw Kane and got instantly to his feet. "Come in," he smiled. "Come in and sit down."

Kane went in saying, "I just had my ears boxed."

The old man chuckled. "By whom?"

"Susie. She's says I've been ignoring you." He paused a moment, then said seriously, "I hadn't been aware of it, Jack."

The old man snorted, "Nonsense. You've been as busy as the proverbial one-armed paperhanger. I didn't expect you to come around holding my hand."

"Nevertheless, let's put it out on the table." He rarely smoked inside the store, but now he put a cigar in his mouth and touched a lighter to it. When it was drawing well, he said, "We've had a lot of changes and you know there will be more to come."

"Sure. It's expected."

"Except in one department, and on this you have my word. As long as you feel capable of holding down your job this office is yours."

"Oh, now—"

"I mean every word of it. So I brought a good merchandiser over here with me, but he isn't in your league, and I did not bring him here to step on your heels. I want you to know that."

Harrison said sharply, "A lot of heels around here are getting callouses on them already."

"But not yours. I'd like to have you understand this. This job is yours as long as you care to run it." Then he grinned and asked, "How do you feel, you old goat?"

Harrison leaned back and smiled. "Not bad, Lew. The usual sore points for a man my age, but that's about it. I got another year or two left in me."

"Better make it more than that. It's going to take time for me to get out of the woods, and I need you to chop down some of those trees." He stood up and leaned on the desk. "You know I'm telling you this from the heart?"

"I know it. And—well—thanks. I appreciate it."

"Okay, Jack. Drop in my office after lunch. I'd like to go over the Garfinkle statements with you."

"Something wrong?"

"Burke apparently went too heavily on topcoats and cut Haley's water off elsewhere, and now Haley is raising hell."

"That Burke is an idiot."

"Seems to be a commonly accepted view around here. So you drop in later and we'll talk it over. Maybe we'll shift some funds away from one of the other buyers and boost Haley's department. We'll see."

"Sure."

As soon as Kane left, Harrison leaned forward on his forearms and looked off into space with a sharp twinkle in his eyes. Kane had apparently thought he was worried. Hell, he chuckled, it was the other way around. Harrison knew well that at least for the next few years he was the one indispensable man in the business. If he walked out tomorrow the whole chain would run a definite risk of collapsing. Kane had learned that himself when it came to getting money out of the New York wholesalers. They were not fools, those wholesalers. Every one of them knew that the only things holding the Merritt-Wilson chain together were chewing gum and saliva and pure, undiluted guts. None of them would budge an inch for Kane.

Harrison's position was entirely different. He had been head merchandiser of Merritt's for almost forty years and knew every wholesaler in the business, and they all knew him. Jack Harrison was a name that was almost legendary in New York. He was also liked and trusted, and his opinions were listened to with attention. Without Harrison, Kane would run out of credit in New York in three or four months. The old man was the glue that held everything together, and he knew it and knew it well. For that matter, though, so did Kane.

He pulled some clipped papers toward him and saw that they were from advertising. It was a mimeographed copy of a Paris letter reprinted from Harper's Bazaar. He read:

> PARIS . . . A time for decision. Hurry. This is no time for brinkmanship. Here and now, you've got to make your choice between a dozen alluring opposites. Your line: bulked up or arrow narrow? Your furs: a heavy fall, settling on hems, wrists, the whole length of a Tartar coat—or simply a flattering frame. You've got to face the tunic: to pick clipped curls, take a gamble on gai gaiters, or risk a zany stocking. And, this is the day

for the big decision: WHO WILL WEAR THE PANTS?
If Paris has her way, it must be you.

He laughed and shoved the papers aside. So much abracadabra.
When would these fool women ever learn that you did not need
esoteric language to sell clothes? Probably never. They had their
little world of their own and they meant to keep it inviolate.

He closed his eyes and pressed fingertips against the lids. That
damned pain again. Seemed to be getting worse. Maybe he really
should see a doctor. But, he admitted frankly to himself, he was
afraid to.

He thought of his own private little hell. His only son dead of
a heart attack, and his only daughter killed in a stupid automobile accident. And no grandchildren. And Lucretia, poor
Lucretia, poor, beautiful, loving Lucretia, living in an insane
asylum completely out of her mind.

He opened his eyes and wryly laughed at himself. Why, he
wondered, don't I just deny His existence? No, that wouldn't
do at all. By doing that he would have no one to blame it on.

He sent into the merchandising offices for Burke's file for the
past month and went to work. Kane would want answers.

He worked well into the noon hour and was just closing his
books when Joe Haley stepped into his office. Harrison cocked
an eyebrow at him and a light smile tugged at his lips. God, he
was a handsome brute. Big and powerful, too, which was unusual.
Joe would be no patsy in a fight with anyone. With his looks,
he had probably had more than his share, too.

"So?" he asked. "Something on your mind?"

"Yes, there is."

"I haven't heard from management."

"Maloney told me to talk to you. I'm not going over his head.
Actually," he grinned, "I mean to go over your head to the great
man himself."

"You're a presumptuous sort of bastard, aren't you?'

"I don't ever remember getting any medals for shyness."

"I'll take odds on that. Look, Joe, right now I'm hungry. I
need to feed my face. So suppose we get to the point. You're here
about Burke."

Joe's thick black eyebrows raised a fraction. "That's right.
But how—"

"Word does get around, my boy." He got to his feet and placed
a narrow brim hat rakishly on the side of his head. He took

Joe's arm and walked him to the door. "Take my advice," he said. "Forget it."

Joe said angrily, "Oh, no. I'm not getting the brush-off."

"I don't mean it that way. What I mean is—call it a hunch—but I don't think your problem is going to be with you very long. I've been talking to Kane, and about an hour ago I was talking with Sam. He says to pass the word along to you and tell you to keep your big fat mouth shut. Good enough?"

Joe laughed. "Perfect," he said. "That Burke asshole has been driving me nuts ever since I've been here."

"Well, Anna kind of liked him, but I guess now things are out of her hands—" His words came to a halt, his eyes got wide, all color drained from his face, and he dug his fingers viciously into the pit of his stomach. Joe grabbed him by both arms to keep him from falling down. His own eyes, too, got big.

"Jees, Mr. Harrison—"

Jack gasped and sucked in huge lungfuls of air. After a long time some color returned to his face, and he leaned back against the wall. He said weakly, "Just a—a little attack."

"Cripes, you scared me. What was it?"

The old man swallowed hard and lied, "Nothing, really. Just a small attack of acute indigestion."

"But you haven't eaten yet."

"No matter. Happens any time, according to the doctors." He continued lying, "They got me on a kind of diet now, so it should go away in a week or so." He managed to smile and shoved himself away from the wall. "Be seeing you."

He squared his shoulders and walked away, but Joe could see that his legs were far from being steady. Joe watched him narrowly until he had disappeared. He was thinking of what Sam Kuller had told him.

"Any one of us," he had said, "could be booted out of here on our skinny asses and the chain would still go on. But there is one man none of us can do without, and that's old man Harrison. The plays are all called from New York and that's where the old boy has his fingers in every pie on the table. Lose him and the whole works goes down the drain."

Joe thought about it. He knew an attack of indigestion when he saw one. What had hit Harrison was worse than that. Heart trouble?

He walked away chewing at his lower lip, wondering if he

should tell Kane, but decided against it. That was almost as bad as being a stool pigeon.

Joe left the hallway of the executive offices and walked out to the fourth floor elevators on the women's fashion floor. Before punching the button, he turned and looked toward Betty Parker's counter. Marie was behind the counter talking to a customer, but Betty was standing at one side talking to Chet Baker, Maloney's new assistant.

Joe had met him when he had arrived the day before and had not yet made up his mind whether to like him or not. Baker was a little above the average height, but under six feet. His build was about average, he dressed well, as everyone had to, and he seemed to be a very well-poised young man. His face was hard, so that Joe knew he went in for athletics of some sort, and he had a way of walking that spelled muscles. His skin was tanned, his light blond hair sun streaked (surfing, maybe?), and his blue eyes were candid but shrewd. His chin was rounded, and he had a rather thick neck. Joe thought, he can't be a bar-bell boy. What the devil does he do?

Whatever he had been talking about with Betty had come to an amiable end. The two of them smiled and Baker walked away. Joe looked at Betty, who seemed to be watching him curiously. He had been burning ever since Kane had practically told him to stay away from her. His jaw set stubbornly and he walked over to the counter to join her.

"Hi," he said. "Remember that drink you put on the cuff?"

"Yes"

"How about making it lunch, instead? I'm leaving right now."

She turned to Marie and told her, "Hold the fort until I get back."

Marie complained instantly and bitterly, "I've only been relieved twice today."

Betty snapped, "Very well. Then get Irene to relieve you. She has a signature. I'm leaving right now."

She turned to Joe and mumbled under her breath, "That bitch," and walked on back to her office. Joe thought he heard a slight accent in her speech and wondered about it. She returned with her makeup freshened and carrying her bag. Joe was still more than a little surprised and overcome. He had not expected her to accept. Just whose toes am I stepping on now? he wondered. Kane's?

He walked her down to the Old Poodle Dog, where they were lucky to get a table for two against the wall. The Old Poodle Dog was one of the finest restaurants in San Francisco. He was especially fond of their frog's legs. They ordered, then sat back and looked at each other.

Joe laughed and said, "So now we're together, and you're wondering why you came out with a character with my reputation."

"Something like that," she smiled. "I haven't heard anyone yet say you would make a good choir boy."

He tilted his head back and looked at her from under slitted lids. "I detect a touch of an accent. I noticed it before. Can't put my finger on it, though."

She laughed again. "No wonder. It's compounded of French, Italian-Swiss, and German."

"Really?" he smiled. "That's quite an order. How come?"

"I was raised in those countries."

"Oh?" He looked at her with heightened interest. "But I thought you were an American. Parker, after all—"

"Is American," she completed for him. "It's a long story."

"No time like the present, and I would like to know about you. But don't get me wrong. This isn't a pitch. I just happen to like you, is all."

Their food arrived and they were silent for a while, but after a moment she said, "It's a simple story, yet rather difficult to tell. I have lived with it all my life, yet I have never really got used to it."

"Very mysterious."

"Not really. Well, to begin in the beginning, my parents were traveling in Europe when my mother was pregnant. Apparently, they expected to be back in the States when I was born, but sometimes those things happen prematurely. I suppose that is what happened."

Joe frowned. "You mean you don't know?"

"Yes. I don't know. There is so much I don't know. My father was detained in Paris on business, but my mother went on. She was in a little village just outside Dijon, in eastern France, when it happened. I was born in a hotel off the civic square. Since my father was not present, his name was not signed. This is when the difficulties started. The year was 1939."

He blinked at her and his frown deepened. "Isn't that the year Germany invaded Poland?"

"Yes. I was born in November, just two months after that. That was the year when the world turned upside down. You can imagine. Anyway, my mother returned to Paris with me and we joined my father. When I was two months old the two of them were killed."

Joe stopped eating and stared at her. "No!"

"It was an accident. I've been told I was with a nursemaid when it happened. The details are, naturally, vague, but they died in a taxi that went over the bank of the Seine."

"Cripes! And you a baby."

"So now," she smiled, "it becomes more complicated. My birth was clouded because of the absence of my father. The authorities were not sure whether I was French or American, and there were no relatives to claim me."

"There must have been someone."

She shook her head. "Not a soul. My parents were both the last of their lines. But my parents had left an estate, and I was in the protective care of a nursemaid; so no one was unduly worried. Then, as the debate dragged out, France was suddenly at war, and I was completely forgotten."

She nibbled at a frog's leg and was silent for a moment, then said, "I lived with a nursemaid in a suburb just outside of Paris during the war years. Then, after the war ended, I suddenly had another nursemaid who took me to Switzerland. Whether that was a good move or not I have never been able to figure out. If we had stayed in France, things might have been settled much sooner. On the other hand, who could possibly be interested in a small child who seemed to be doing all right when millions of dispossessed people were hungry and frantic and trying to get back home?"

"You seem to take it all rather philosophically."

She shrugged. "What other way is there? I was raised for a while in Switzerland. By this time, the war being over, some attorneys in America had established contact, and I was still in funds. It's a funny thing," she smiled, "but wherever I was I was always known as 'That American girl.' And I was proud of it. Which is why, no matter what school I attended, I always majored in English. Thank God for that. Also, I always sought out Englishmen and Americans to talk to." She said proudly, "Very few people notice the accent."

"It's still there, though. But how about Germany?"

She sat back and rubbed the side of her nose with a finger. "Well, by this time I was sixteen and going to college. The American attorneys were Goldsmith and Klein. Their office is right here in San Francisco, and Mr. Klein is still alive. He wrote to me and told me to go to Germany, that it would be easier to get me out of there. He was right. When I was eighteen I left Germany on a quota for the United States. Would you like to know," she laughed, "why I went to Los Angeles?"

"Why?"

"Because all the American movies I had seen were made in Hollywood, and that was about all I knew about the United States, Hollywood."

He chuckled. "It figures. So then?"

She shrugged. "Two years in UCLA to finish school, and then to work."

"Because you had to?"

"Oh, no. Not at all." She figured that perhaps she was saying too much, but she told him, "I still have an independent income from the Parker estate which I could live on if I wanted to."

"Your parents must have been quite wealthy."

"No," she said, shaking her head, "I don't think so. But they invested well, and I suppose I gather the fruits of their investments."

"You mean reap."

"Yes," she laughed. "Reap. I guess what it all amounts to is I have a certain drive that compels me to do something and make something of myself."

He tilted his head to one side and appraised her. "Strange girl," he said. "Strange life. Did you ever look up your parents' background?"

"There was nothing to look up. They were rootless. My father was an importer and exporter. He traveled all over the world."

"You have nothing to remember them by?"

"Not a single, solitary thing. Only the estate. Whatever they had that belonged to them personally was lost during the war years. If there was anything of value, I have no doubt that my various nursemaids pawned it. There is nothing. That is somehow tragic, isn't it?"

"Yes, it is."

They were lost in thought as they finished their lunch. Over coffee, however, she asked him suddenly, "Do you know Mr. Kane very well?"

"Kane?" he laughed. "Hell, no. Who does?"

"Do you know his son, Bill?"

"I've seen him around a few times. Looks a lot like the old man. They tell me he has a lot of drive, too."

She said eagerly, "Oh, yes."

"You know him?"

"Yes." She was silent for a long while, then said, "It is because of him I accepted this engagement with you. I hope you don't mind?"

"Well, it does rather kick the hell out of my conceit. But what's on your mind?"

"It is complicated, you know. Always there are complications. You see, I owe a great deal to Mr. Kane, but perhaps," she said, looking him levelly in the eyes, "not quite what you think. So I have been wondering."

His interest was fully aroused as he asked, "About what?"

"Well, I met Bill in Wilson's about a month or so ago. I have been seeing him now and then. But now I wonder about something. I am, after all, an employee of Mr. Kane. It might not be seemly for me to be going out with his son. Bill and I have had a rather tacit agreement not to say anything about it. Yet I wonder. I am not one to hide things. It bothers me. So, I ask you. What would you say?"

His first thought was, I'll be damned. She was not only not involved with Kane, but she did not even expect to be. How naive could a redhead get? Yet she meant it, that was obvious. He had heard, too, about her salary and bonuses, and there was only one answer to that. Yet here she was indirectly telling him that Kane had never made a play for her, and she never expected one to be made. Was she daff? Was she off her rocker? Kane had to have plans for her, of that he was sure. She did not seem to know that, and here she was talking about his son. And she meant it. What she had asked him was asked seriously.

He asked dryly, "Are you in love with Bill?"

She stared at him, then shook her head and laughed. "Heavens, no. I hardly know him." Then she said seriously, "All I know is that he is a nice young man and I like him, but he is Mr. Kane's son and it bothers me. What do you think I should do?"

Joe was angry with himself. He did not figure that he had let himself in for this, yet he found himself in it and it made him mad. He paid the bill and took her by the arm and walked her outside. He had her so tightly by the arm that as they were going up the street he almost lifted her off the sidewalk.

"Okay," he said, "I'll tell you. You got a cute fanny and your figure leaves nothing to be desired and—well—you just got what it takes. So Kane is setting you up for a target."

"Now, please—"

"I've seen this before. A man like Kane is in no hurry. He knows you're not easy to be had, and if he plays it wrong you'll walk out on him. So he wraps you around with a good income, power, authority and so on and after a time you get used to it and you'd be lost without it. That, my friend, is when he makes his big play. And that is when you succumb—I'd bet my life on it. Now, is there anything else you would like to know?"

She looked at him and said viciously, "Yes, damn it. How come you cheat on your wife?"

6

BETTY returned to her counter on the fourth floor still raging inwardly at the nerve of Joe Haley. At that moment two salesgirls went walking by and Betty overheard one say angrily to the other, "Oh, fuck Balenciaga!" Betty stared after them and suddenly burst out laughing. She laughed so hard tears came to her eyes. Not that there was anything particularly humorous about the crudity. Men and women in the rag business talked crudely amongst themselves at all times. Betty was used to that. It was simply that the four letter word put matters back in their proper perspective.

She had no reason to be angry with Joe. He had said simply and to the point what she had thought about many times. Yet he had to be wrong. If Kane was going to make a move in her direction, it should have happened a year or so back. She had no idea what was in his mind, yet she doubted that he was at all interested in her body.

She was about to leave her counter when a woman of about sixty, well-groomed, with beautifully coiffed hair and a perky little hat perched on the back of her head, approached her and put a small package on the desk. She smiled at Betty and unwrapped the package, exposing a tweed skirt of checked plaids.

"My dear," she said, "I am afraid I have difficulties. This skirt is part of a suit I bought here about six months ago. The jacket fits perfectly, which is why I haven't brought it along, but the waist of this skirt is much, much too tight. It must be let out."

Betty lifted the skirt and looked at it, and asked, "Cash or credit?"

"Credit, of course. The name is Mrs. Milton Alexander."

Betty picked up the telephone, dialed Credit and spoke to one of the girls. After a few moments the girl was back on the wire saying, "Mrs. Alexander has unlimited credit and, I might add, is one of our best customers."

Betty put the phone back in its cradle, smiled at Mrs. Alexander, and said, "If you'll wait a moment, I'll call one of the fitters—"

Mrs. Alexander chuckled and gasped, "I'm sorry, but I don't have the time. Even now I am late for an appointment. But I have already taken the proper measurements. So just tell your fitter that I need another inch and a half about the waist. She will know how to take care of it. And thank you very much."

She rushed off toward the elevators. Betty stared after her, then shrugged and called for a fitter. When the fitter came to the counter Betty handed her the skirt and told her the brief history. The fitter turned the skirt inside out, looked at the seams and laughed as she shook her head.

"Miss Parker," she said, "this is ridiculous. I know Mrs. Alexander and I remember when she bought this suit. I let the seams of the skirt out as far as they would go and it fit her very good. I guess, though, she's put on some weight meanwhile, and now it's too tight. Too bad."

"Why do you say, 'Too bad?' "

The fitter held the skirt toward her and showed her the two seams. "Look for yourself. No cloth left. There isn't even enough there to let the waist out half an inch, let alone what she wants."

Betty examined the seams and smiled. "Of course not," she said. "Well, okay, I'll put it aside and give it back to her."

She was busy making out some tickets for a carload of new Kimberleys that had arrived on the floor when she rather sensed an electric pulse in the air. She looked up from the counter just as Mrs. Anna Merritt left the elevator and came walking toward her. Every salesgirl in sight dropped whatever she was doing and hurried over to greet Mrs. Merritt. It took her almost five minutes to smilingly dismiss all of them and at last arrive at Betty's side.

There she touched cheeks with Betty and hugged her and asked, "How do you like your new job?"

"Well, it's going to be a lot of work, but I like it."

"I'm glad. You belong here in Merritt's."

Betty laughed. "You always did say that."

"And I always meant it, too."

She stepped back a bit for a moment and they appraised each other, as women always do. Betty was glad she was wearing the new green dress today with the narrow belt and the perfectly matching shoes. She reached up subconsciously to pat her deep auburn hair into place. You always had to look your best around Mrs. Merritt because at all times she, herself, looked as if she had just stepped from a page of *Vogue* or *Harper's Bazaar*. Mrs. Merritt knew clothes from A to Z, and she knew how to wear them. She had style.

She was in her fifties and no one would doubt her age, except for possibly a few years. Yet, somehow she had an aura of youth about her. She was tiny, hardly over five feet tall, but her small body was perfectly proportioned and her legs were long and slim for her height. Her delicate features looked almost as if they were done in Dresden china, and her white skin seemed to have a translucent quality about it. The color of her wide eyes was not too far removed from Betty's, a rather yellowish-green, almost chartreuse. She, too, had at one time been a redhead, though now her short-cut hair was a beautiful silver gray that shimmered in the light.

She had met Betty, while on a business shopping tour for Merritt's, when Betty had first arrived at Wilson's from Los Angeles. She had exclaimed then about the color and tone of Betty's hair and two days later returned with a lock of her own hair that had been cut many years before. They compared it with Betty's hair. The two were remarkably similar. They had been friends ever since. In spite of the difference in age, Betty liked her about as well as anyone she had ever known, and it seemed that the affection was reciprocated.

Shortly after her husband George had passed on, Mrs. Merritt sold the big mansion in Hillsborough and built an exquisite French Normandy country house on four acres of estate grounds in the Peninsula's fabulously expensive Woodside. Betty had spent many a happy weekend on that estate. It was almost like home to her. Mrs. Merritt even had one guest room designed especially for her that no one else could use.

She looked at Betty with wide eyes, she was a trifle nearsighted, as she asked, "When are you going to move out of that apartment?"

Betty pouted. "I like it there. It's convenient, it's just the right size and it's furnished the way I want it."

"But just three rooms, my dear! You told me yourself that every month you get a check from your estate for five hundred dollars. With the seven fifty you make that comes out twelve fifty a month. You could afford something much grander than that."

"But I like it."

"Nonsense. You're going up the ladder, young lady. You need a place where you can entertain important people. I give you a year or so on this floor. Then I'll wager that Mr. Kane moves you into buying."

"If he doesn't, I'll demand it. I'm just about ready for that step."

"Of course you are. And, you know, I still pack a lot of weight around here."

This was one of the things that Betty disliked about their relationship. Mrs. Merritt was always trying to do something for her, and Betty disliked it intensely. With her background, she had had to stand on her own two feet most of her life and make most of her own decisions. She did not like people "doing things" for her.

She said, "Please, Mrs. Merritt—"

"Damn it all, why do you constantly refuse to call me Anna?"

"I'm sorry, I just can't. It would be like my calling Mr. Kane Lew."

"Well, sure, that old billy-goat."

"But, please, let me do things on my own. I'm doing all right. You just said so yourself."

Mrs. Merritt smiled and patted her cheek lightly. "Of course, dear. I do know how you feel. I guess I just get a little carried away at times. I promise you, I shall keep my big mouth closed. Don't fret. Now," she sighed, "I had better go see the hired help. I'll see you on my way out."

Betty nodded and smiled to herself. By hired help she had meant, of course, the executives.

She went back the long hallway to the executive offices and the whole area was immediately in an uproar. Everyone poured out of the offices to greet her. Then Kane came out of his office and took both her hands in his. "How's my best girl?"

"Oh, fair to middling," she laughed. "Let's go in your office. I have something to talk to you about." When they stepped into the room she told him, "Close the door."

He dropped into his chair behind the desk, and she lowered herself to a deep leather chair near his elbow. She took a cigarette from her purse and he hastened to light it for her.

As he dropped back to his chair he asked, "Did you see Betty?"

She looked at him with some surprise. "Well, naturally. I think I'll ask her down to the house for this Sunday and get a young crowd around."

"Ask her, but forget the other guests. Her tail is dragging. This floor she's running now is three times bigger and ten times tougher than the one she ran for me on Market."

Mrs. Merritt said sharply, "I told you that before."

"Hell's bells, don't worry about it. Give her time and she'll be running it with her left hand."

"Does she have any new boy friends I don't know about?"

Kane shrugged. "She always has a few dozen in tow." Then he frowned and tapped a pencil on the desk and said, "A few minutes ago Marie Togliatti told me casually—ha!—that Betty had lunch with Joe Haley today."

Mrs. Merritt's expression was suddenly vicious. "That sonofa-bitch!"

"I thought you liked him."

"I do, in spite of what he is. But, Lew, that girl really is a virgin. And I'm damned if I'd like to see that bastard get into her pants."

"It's going to happen sometime."

"When she gets married. Not before." She was silent a moment, then looked at him shrewdly. "You shouldn't have any trouble handling that situation."

He rubbed the scar on his cheek and looked into her eyes. "You can't tell about Haley. However, I think I can handle it. He does like his job."

"Of course. Now then." She sat up straighter in her chair and was suddenly all business. "I just got back from New York a few days ago."

"Cripes. I didn't even know you had left town."

"Oh, yes. I had a hunch about something, so I flew back to New

73

York. I went around and made a canvas of all the wholesalers. I used to be a buyer, you know, before I married George."

"I know."

"So I've known that gang back there for a long time. Most of them, at some time or other, have tried their best to get me in a hotel bed. They don't hold it against me because they didn't succeed. We get along." Her eyes narrowed a degree. "I ran into something that startled me."

He sighed and sat back wearily in his chair. "Hell," he said, "I can spell it out for you. Lew Kane doesn't pack any weight back there. I know it."

"Now I know it, too. I didn't before. How come, Lew?"

"Well, I figure it's because, in their books, I've just been a little guy running a small chain of four stores. Now, suddenly, I take over sixteen more stores from the most established outfit in the West. Unfortunately, they still see me through the wrong end of the telescope. I know how they're thinking, like a lot of the people around here, that it's the tail wagging the dog."

"I was even told that."

"Of course. They don't see how I can possibly make it. They all expect me to fall flat on my face."

"Believe me, Lew, I don't want this chain dumped back in my lap."

He snapped at her angrily, "It damned well isn't going to happen, except over my dead body. You're looking at the boy who is going to be the biggest man in this business on the entire Pacific Coast, or I'll eat my hat."

She got to her feet and sighed. "All right. It did shake me up, though, when I learned how they were talking back there."

He got up and walked with her to the door, where he said, "I still have Jack Harrison, you know."

"And thank your lucky stars. He pulled me out of a few tight spots, too, after George died. They told me what he did for you back there on advertising. He always comes through. I hope you aren't working him very hard?"

Kane had to laugh. "He's just sitting here for the big deals, that's all. I wouldn't dream of working that old man."

"You do have a little sense," she smiled. "Well, I'll go see Betty about the weekend. Be good, Lew."

He opened the door and watched her walk down the hallway until she had disappeared. He was about to go into Susie's office when he saw a burly, barrel-chested man coming down the hallway toward him. He smiled and held out his hand. He was Halbert Johnson, one of the biggest building contractors on the Coast. He looked like one of his own buildings, square, squat, and powerful, with white hair, wind-swept features, and eyes that disappeared when he smiled, which was not too often.

"Hi, Hal. Come on in."

He stepped aside and nodded toward his office. He and Johnson both belonged to the Bohemian Club and the Olympic Club. They had sometimes had a few drinks together and were on first name terms, but that was about as far as it had ever gone. Johnson was known as a rugged character who got drunk and liked to break up the joint. Nevertheless, he was a top man in his business.

Kane got out a bottle of Jack Daniels and poured him a hefty snort. Johnson tossed it off in one gulp, then dropped into the chair Mrs. Merritt had just vacated. Kane sat behind his desk.

Johnson looked at him and said, "Okay, so for once this is a business call. I've been reading over that spec. you sent me. Frankly, Lew, it doesn't make much sense. So let's go over it. Okay?"

"Okay. What is it you'd like to know?"

"Well, you want me to buy five pieces of property in specified locations, build five stores on them, and then lease them to you. Right?"

"So far."

"Good. As I see it, I am to lay out all the dough, and you just sign the leases. I couldn't get any more out of it than that, so I must be wrong, or the spec. is wrong."

"No. The spec. is correct. Can you imagine what it would mean to have five stores under lease to Merritt-Wilson—"

"Oh, shove that crap, Lew. So I build these stores for you and all of a sudden you cave in. Where do I stand?"

Lew smiled. "You have the buildings. You could always lease them to someone else."

"That's a crock of shit and you know it. If you fell on your ass, the only way I could lease these stores to someone else would be by laying out a lot of that long green to make modifications." He leaned over the desk and said angrily, "You know how it stacks up? If you went down the drain, I would go right down it with you. Now, why in God's name did you ever offer me a proposition like that?"

Lew explained, "There are a lot of people in New York I have to make sit up and take notice. They don't think I can swing this thing. So instead of holding still, suppose I start enlarging the chain with five more stores? Do you see what that would do in New York? It would set them right on their ear."

Johnson almost smiled and his eyes were practically closed. "What's my guarantee I don't go broke?"

"I have some stock of my own, you know."

"You can take that stock and shove it. If you fall on your face it isn't worth the paper it's written on. Besides," he said, shrewdly, "the bank would get it. You'll have to do better than that, Lew. Anything like real money?

"Well—" He hesitated.

Johnson snorted and got to his feet. "I'll be damned," he said. "I always thought you had your share of brains. Now I'm not so sure. The kind of contractor you need is a bastard like Patrick Haley. But you know what you've done to me? You've just insulted what little intelligence I have. Good day to you, Mr. Lew Kane."

He stalked angrily out of the office and slammed the door behind him. Kane sighed. He hadn't really expected the deal to go through, anyway. So what was lost? But then he thought of what Johnson had said about Patrick Haley. He was even bigger than Johnson. He was probably the largest contractor on the Coast and had recently finished constructing one of the new federal buildings. Unfortunately, Kane did not know him personally.

But then he thought, Haley? Couldn't be. Too much of a coincidence. Still, you never knew. Wilder things did happen.

He reached for the telephone and dialed Joe Haley's department. He got one of the salesmen, then after a moment Joe was on the wire. "Yes, Mr. Kane?"

"Joe? How are you?"

"Fine, sir. What's on your mind?"

Kane said slowly, "Well, I was just talking to a friend of mine and your name happened to come up. Now, I don't know much about you yet. But this friend of mine said that he thought the big contractor, Patrick Haley, was your father. I told him I was blamed if I knew."

Joe laughed and said, "He was right, Mr. Kane. The old man has been plundering this city and state for a good many years now."

"So he really is your father."

"Very much so."

"Well, well. I'll have to tell my friend he was right."

"Sure."

"Thanks, Joe."

Kane hung up and sat back and started thinking.

When Halbert Johnson left Kane's office he walked to the fourth floor elevators and punched a button, then turned about to look at the good-looking redhead behind a counter. Jees, if he were only twenty years younger! The elevator arrived and he took it down to the third floor. A salesman approached him, but he waved the man aside and said that he was looking for Haley. Joe was back in his office, but came out and shook hands with Johnson.

"How are you doing, Hal?"

"Oh, not much. And how's that old man of yours?"

Joe laughed. Well, you've known that Irishman longer than I have. You know how he does, at all times."

"And the family?"

"As usual. All healthy," Joe squinted at him. "Look, Hal, I've known you ever since I was a kid. You just didn't drop by to say hello."

Johnson chuckled. "I guess you do know me, at that. No, Joe, I was just up talking with your boss, and I got wondering what kind of a jerk he was. Maybe you'll know the answers. Let me tell you about it."

He explained the whole setup. When he had finished Joe looked off into space for a moment and whistled softly under his breath. "Five new stores," he breathed. "I'll be damned. He hardly has a foot in the door here and already he's thinking of expansion. By God, you do have to hand it to him."

"But the sonofabitch has no dough to swing it with. He literally asked me to take all the risks. Who the hell does he think he is?"

Joe looked Johnson in the eyes. "Let me put it this way. Suppose it was Saks, or Roos/Atkins, or Macy's that asked you to build these stores and lease them back to them. Would you do it?"

Johnson lifted his hat from his head, ran his thick fingers back through white hair and nodded. "For them, yes. They're all solid, going-ahead firms. It would be a good deal. I could make plenty loot off of leases like that. And if I didn't care for leasing, I'd have no trouble selling out to a bank, or a realty combine. But with this boss of yours I have to have some kind of a guarantee, and he's about to give nothing."

77

Joe said, "Nevertheless, I'll bet you all the tea in China he swings it with someone. He has to."

"Why?"

"Like he was telling you. He has to make the big boys back in New York sit up and take notice. They think he's penny ante. But if he starts expanding with five more stores, right on top of taking over the chain, they'll realize they're doing business with a big-time operator. And a guy who thinks like that is well worth doing business with. See what I mean?"

Johnson said patiently, "You're missing the whole point. I can understand his angle with no problem at all. But, and I ask you again, why the hell did he expect me to back him? I'm not pulling his chestnuts out of the fire."

Joe nodded. "I see what you mean."

"Anyway, that's the story. I gotta get going. I'll have the old lady call Mary soon, and we'll get together for dinner."

"Fine. Be seeing you, Hal."

He watched Johnson walk away and leaned back against his floor desk. Undoubtedly, he would be the only other man in the whole organization who would know what Kane was thinking. But then he remembered Kane's call and laughed quietly to himself. So Kane was inquiring about the old man? Now he knew why. Maybe, he thought, I'd better tout the old man onto what's cooking.

He picked up the phone and dialed his father's office.

The elder Haley's offices were on Geary St. between Seventh and Eighth Avenues. It was a three-story building, rather wide and quite deep. The executives all had their offices on the first floor. The floor above was given over to architects, engineers, and estimators. The third floor was all filing and clerical offices. About a hundred and twenty people worked in the building. Haley, of course, had warehouses, storage yards, and other buildings scattered elsewhere about the city.

Patrick Aloysius Haley was a wizened Irishman who was still amazed that he had begat a son so big and powerful and good looking from his skinny loins. He was about five feet nine inches tall, and he could not have weighed over a hundred and forty pounds. His face was deeply lined, his eyes were snapping brown, he had Joe's beautiful teeth and he, too, had a deep cleft in his chin. His face was strictly shanty-Irish, with the usual pug nose and the long upper lip. His black hair was thinning badly and he had a bald spot on the top and back of his head, which he tried to cover by brushing over it. His hair was also turning quite gray. The fingers and knuckles of his hands were gnarled from time spent as a bricklayer and a carpenter before becoming a contractor.

When Joe called he was behind the big desk in his private office going over some estimates for another Lake Merritt apartment building in Oakland. Mae, his private secretary, a rather faded blonde with huge breasts, came into the room and stood at his side to place more papers on the desk. Patrick reached out absent-mindedly, lifted the hem of her skirt, ran his hand up her legs and began stroking the smooth skin of her bare behind. Mae had learned the first month with him that if she ever wore panties she could kiss her job good-bye. She was always obliging, in every way possible. She stood patiently where she was, but when his hand dropped she walked quietly out of the room.

When the phone rang he picked it up and barked, "Yeah?"

"Dad? This is Joe."

"Oh. Hiya, boy?" He leaned back in the chair and asked, "And how is it with you this fine day?"

"Can't complain. Listen: I have something to talk to you about."

Joe explained his entire conversation with Halbert Johnson. When he had finished, Patrick snorted and said, "That Johnson never did have a lick of brains. For the life o' me, I can't figure out how he got where he is."

"He's a pretty big man."

"Any jackass can get fat if he sticks his head in the right bundle of hay. Right now, even without using me brain, I can think of three different angles for swinging a deal like that. Number one, you build all five stores at the same time and all alike. So you save money on architects, materials, and everything else. Number two, you design and build 'em in such a way that you can convert 'em any way you want. And number three," he chuckled, "you jack up your rent on the leases. If the guy wants 'em bad enough, and your man sounds like he does, then he'll pay."

"You mean you could do it?"

"With me left hand. I could put about five million in a deal like that and come out owning County Cork and the church to go with it."

Joe laughed. "You're an old bastard."

"Admitted. But a smart old bastard, you might add. So you think maybe I should get in touch with your Mr. Kane?"

"No, no. Not so fast." He then told his father about Kane's telephone call and said, "I have a hunch he'll be getting in touch with you."

"That's even better. Very well, then, I'll wait for his lordship. Thanks for the tip, Joseph."

"I'm always willing to help you get fatter and fatter. After all, you're leaving it all to me one of these days."

"By God, though," Patrick roared, "you'd still better be married to that woman o' yours or you get not a red penny. You ever leave her, or she ever leaves you, and you wind up sitting on your fat ass with nothing."

Joe said wearily, "Jees, you tell me that at least once a month."

"Because I want you to listen and understand it, that's why. I know how the girls roll on their backs and spread their legs for you. Seems to me, all you are is a walking hard-on. Ain't Mary ever enough for you?"

"You know better than that. Like father like son. Who are you to preach?"

Patrick sighed. "I guess you're right. I can't keep me own pants closed. Well, boy, thanks again."

"Sure. So long."

Patrick dropped the phone in its cradle and his little eyes narrowed. Merely talking about sex had begun to arouse him. He called the switchboard operator and told her he was not to be bothered with any calls unless they were important. Then he pushed Mae's buzzer on the desk. She came to his office and stepped inside the door. She stood there looking at him and knew from his expression exactly what was in his mind. She turned, closed the door, and locked it. Then she walked around the desk and settled onto his lap with a giggle.

Patrick pressed his lips to her soft neck and she giggled. He started loosening the buttons of the blouse over her huge breasts, and at that moment the telephone rang.

"That bitch," he growled. "I told her— But then it must be important."

He lifted the telephone and snapped, "Haley here."

A man asked, "Mr. Haley?"

"That's what I just said, isn't it?"

"Oh?" There was a moment of silence, then the man said, "I

am not sure I have the right Haley. This is Mr. Lew Kane, president of Merritt-Wilson. I was calling for—"

Patrick said, "You got the right Haley. Ain't you me son's new boss?"

Kane chuckled and said, "That's right. I just learned today, much to my surprise, that the biggest contractor in town is Joe's father."

Patrick managed a weak laugh. "If I ain't, Mr. Kane, I'm damned if I know who is."

Kane said uncertainly, "Yes, of course."

Mae bit the lobe of Patrick's ear and he almost yelped, but he managed to ask, "What's on your mind, Mr. Kane?"

"Well, sir, I have a rather big construction project in mind—" He paused, then said, "You realize this is confidential, of course?"

"Sure."

"Good. I was thinking of having five new stores constructed in different cities. I would then take them into the Merritt-Wilson chain on a lease basis. No use wasting your time, so I'll put it out on the table. The contractor would have to lay out anywhere from four to five million. Could you handle a deal of that sort?"

Mae was now squirming actively on Patrick's lap, but he replied, "No problem there."

"Well, well. Would you be interested in talking it over with me?"

"Yes, sir, I would be. I'm always interested in new deals. When would you like to get together? You name it."

"Well, let me see. I do have some free time tomorrow. Why don't you drop by my office sometime between three and four?"

"Good enough for me. See you tomorrow, Mr. Kane."

He put the phone in its cradle and squeezed his arms about Mae.

Kane leaned back in his office chair, but he was wondering. Haley had seemed a little abrupt. He had also been very short of breath. Heart trouble, he wondered, or perhaps too much smoking? It had been a very brief, very odd, and unsatisfactory conversation, considering the millions involved. But then, he thought, these big contractors were a different breed of cats, anyway.

He wondered about Joe, if he would be as circumspect as his father. Probably, yet perhaps not. His father, though, would tell him all about it.

Kane picked up the telephone and called Joe's department. "Joe?" he said. "I've been talking over certain information with your father. I imagine he will tell you all about it. So when he does I want you to do me a favor."

Joe asked innocently, "What's that, Mr. Kane?"

"Just keep your mouth shut, is all. This is a big deal and I don't want it out. I don't want anybody to know about it. Do you understand?"

"Of course."

"Thanks, Joe. I depend on you."

"No reason why not."

Joe put down the telephone and was thoughtful for a long while. The old man had said he could handle it. That was all Joe needed to know. So now Kane had got in touch with the old man and the ball was rolling. Joe knew his father. If there was a fat profit in the deal, the old man would close it. Kane was on a spot. He did need to push the deal through to impress the New Yorkers. Joe thought of his father's proposition number three. That would be the crux of the whole thing. If Kane came through with a rental-lease a bit above normal, and he probably would, Patrick would start building.

Joe wondered, in that case, what his own relations would be with Kane. It would certainly be different, that was for sure. If the old man put up anywhere near five million dollars, Kane would be tremendously obligated to him. It also followed that he would be somewhat obligated to the son, or at least he would have to walk a bit differently where the son was concerned. He might even have to think about boosting the son out of his present elevation, and that would be a great deal different than Drury doing it.

Joe's heart started beating just a bit faster. Somehow or other, he thought, the big man seemed to be moving right into his hands.

7

JOE had Sundays and Wednesdays off, but he worked on the late Thursday schedule from twelve noon until nine at night. Everyone had to put in at least one late night out of the two. Joe liked the Thursday schedule because on Tuesday night, in the summer, he and Mary and the kids could take off for the Russian River, or somewhere, spend Tuesday night and all of Wednesday, and drive back Thursday morning in time to be to work at noon. Then he usually had Sunday just to lie around the house while Mary went to church.

Also, there was a sort of tacit agreement that Thursday night was Joe's night off, domestically speaking. He would not be home until late, anyway, so it was only reasonable that he might go out for some drinks with the boys and kick around with them for awhile. Thursday was Joe's night to prowl, and he did not go out with the boys.

Joe walked across the empty floor, he was always the last to leave, and took the elevator to the fourth floor. Joe walked back to Betty's office. She looked up and smiled wanly as he stood in the doorway

"Trouble," she said.

"Oh?"

She leaned back, rapped a pencil against her teeth and said, "I learn more every day. Now I learn that all the other department managers of all the other stores in the chain come up here and rob the main store for stock."

"That's been going on for years."

"I just found it out. So it happened today, a gal from Fresno and another from Oakland, and I'm all fouled up with Findex."

"Straighten it out in the morning. How about kicking around North Beach for a few hours? Should be very pleasant."

She squinted at him, chewed her lower lip between her teeth, and after a moment she said, "I am glad you stopped by. I owe you an apology for what I said after lunch. What goes on with you and your wife is certainly no business of mine. I'm sorry."

"Forget it," he laughed. "I was getting pretty rough, too."

"I asked for that. You didn't ask for me to get nasty. I am sorry."

"You're quite a gal."

She stood up and smiled into his eyes. "That's right, only I'm not the kind of a gal you think I am. Sorry, Joe, but I do not go out with married men."

"I can't persuade you to change your mind?"

"Absolutely not. I like you, Joe, and I hope you and I become friends, but it will never go beyond that, believe me."

He looked at her from under lowered lids, then shrugged and

said, "I'll remember you tonight when I'm drinking champagne out of a slipper."

"Oh, get out of here, you clown."

"Good night, fair one."

Joe took off. He was not about to waste too much time with any one woman. He left the store and walked across the square to the St. Francis Hotel. He went into the Oak Room, the men's bar, and had a screwdriver. He did not feel like going home, so he thought of all the places he could go that night and all of them seemed good to him. He would pick up a babe somewhere. He hadn't failed yet. He got the Thunderbird out of the garage and drove down to a bar called the Pierce Street Annex in the Marina District. He had a drink at the bar and concentrated on the action. Nothing there that he cared about, so he drove away and went to the Drawing Room on Van Ness, a smaller and more intimate bar.

He had one drink and drove from there to the Buena Vista, at the foot of Hyde Street, overlooking the bay. Action had just started at the Buena Vista. It would get better around midnight. He looked over the negroes, fairies, lesbians, and normal people, and saw a girl sitting at one of the window tables with a beatnik who was sporting a beard and a mustache, khaki clothes and sandals, and the rest of the scenery. The beatnik looked big, but the girl had already spotted Joe and was watching him. She was no beatnik and seemed fed up with her partner. She was a blonde with a cute round face and beautiful figure. She was wearing expensive clothes and a mink stole was draped over her shoulders. Nothing cheap about this broad. She was slumming and she was bored. The beatnik, too, was beginning to watch Joe. He was at least intelligent. He could sense that his water was about to be cut off.

Joe grinned and swallowed his drink, shoved his empty glass across the bar and stood up. He walked over to the table and leaned over the blonde. "My goodness," he said. "Six months ago in Cannes. How is the pater?"

The blonde swallowed a laugh and looked him up and down and liked every inch of what she saw. "Delicious," she purred. "You know the pater."

"Yes, indeed. I'll never forget the grouse in Scotland. I think we bagged four hundred that day. Your father is a wonderful wing-shot. And you, my dear?"

"Oh, I manage to get around."

The beatnik said, "Look, bud—"

Joe ignored him. He said to the blonde, "You have a very bad memory. The mater told me where you had gone, so I tracked you down. You and I had a date tonight. My goodness, don't you remember?"

Her hand flew to her mouth in mock agony. "Oh, my God. You're right. You called from London, didn't you?"

It was Joe's turn to swallow a laugh. "Yes, indeedy. And now I find you with this—this unwashed character."

The beatnik growled more deeply, "Look, Mac—"

Joe continued to ignore him. "Then shall we be off? You can tell your—ah—your unpleasant escort goodnight. I shall wait for you outside."

He turned away from them and went through the doors and waited outside on the sidewalk. He was almost doubled up with laughter. Suddenly, someone tapped Joe on the shoulder. He turned around and faced the beatnik and just managed to duck a quick left and a hard right. The beatnik, Joe realized, now that he was standing up, was bigger than himself. He also seemed to have a lot of muscle. Joe punched him in the stomach and clipped him on the side of the head with a right, and the beatnik backed away for a moment. Joe was able to look the situation over. The blonde was standing to one side and a few other people had poured out of the bar to watch the fight. The blonde looked amused. She probably thought Joe would be the one to go down. Joe was worried not at all. He had trained under professionals and fought like one. The beatnik, he knew, was a wild swinger.

The beatnik moved in with his arms cocked to start swinging. Joe moved in under the first blow and smashed a hard right over the other man's heart. As he stepped back he hit him in the mouth with a left. Blood started to pour. The beatnik looked more than a little surprised. Then his temper went wild and he moved in swinging from every direction. Joe was delighted. He simply kept a bit out of range and zeroed in on the target of the other man's chin. The beatnik began to tire and wear down. But he was big and he did not go down easily. Joe had his chin and mouth practically cut to ribbons before the beatnik's knees finally buckled and he pitched forward on the sidewalk on his face. He was not exactly unconscious, but it was impossible for him to get back to his feet.

Joe grabbed the arm of the blonde and hurried her around

the corner to his car. He started the engine, backed away from the sidewalk, and burned rubber pulling away.

The blonde swung her slim knees up on the seat, twisted about and leaned back against the door to smile at him. She put a cigarette between pink lips and got it going with the dashboard lighter. She blew out a puff of smoke and laughed and said, "You were magnificent. I don't think Bert even touched you."

"Nothing that hurts. Where did you pick him up?"

"In North Beach. I'd heard about beatniks. I wanted to meet one."

"Didn't last very long, did it?"

"Not when you came along, big, bad, and beautiful."

"Joe's the name."

"Italian or Irish?"

"Irish as Paddy's pig."

"I'm Marilyn."

"Okay. I know a bar over at Union and Fillmore—called the Rainbow. We'll drop in there for one drink so I can wash the blood off my knuckles. All right with you?"

She shrugged. "Whatever you say. You know, you're a vicious person for being so gorgeous." Her shoulders quivered. "Mmmmmm."

He glanced at her from the corners of his eyes. "On the other hand, you'll find out that I can also be kind, tender, and gentle."

She laughed at him. "We'll see."

Joe parked in the red zone of a bus stop and escorted Marilyn through the doors of the Rainbow bar. He took her to a couple of vacant stools at the piano-bar, then went to the men's room to wash.

In a short time, he rejoined Marilyn and ordered two vodkas and tonic. He noticed that half the other men in the room were slyly watching Marilyn and was pleased. She was a living doll, all right. The blond color of her hair was real, she had a pleasantly rounded face with a small rounded chin to match, laughing blue eyes, and a generous mouth that looked as if it would be as good for loving as it was for laughing. Her legs were beautiful, her figure left nothing to be desired, and her high breasts seemed firm and apparently free of padding. Joe was an expert on that subject. If any padding had been present he would have known it. He was also an expert on clothing. The narrow shoes she was wearing cost at least fifty dollars, the golden sheath dress, which was probably from Europe or New York (he had seen nothing like it in San

Francisco), could go for another four or five hundred, and the stole was easily worth a few thousand. She was also wearing a diamond ring and a narrow diamond wristwatch. Joe was not sure of their value, but guessed another few thousand. The gal was a walking bank.

"Visitor to San Francisco?" he asked.

"The answer," she smiled, "is yes, but again, no." She laughed at his puzzled frown. "It's quite simple, really. I live with my mother on Long Island and go to finishing schools back east. Mother and Father—"

Joe's heart sank as he interrupted, "Are you twenty-one?"

"Of course. I can prove it." She took a driving license from a beaded bag and handed it to him. According to the date of birth, she was twenty-one and a few months over. He handed it back to her. "You see?"

It was a fake and he knew it, but he didn't care. She was probably nineteen or twenty. Otherwise, why would she bother with a California driver's license when she should have a perfectly good New York State license? But as long as she could produce proper identification if asked, why worry?

He asked, "You were saying?"

"Well, let me see. Oh, yes. We used to live here when I was quite young, but then Mother and Father were divorced and she took me back east with her. My father always came back once a year to visit me, but this summer I decided to visit him out here. And that is the plain, simple truth, so help me, your honor. And you?" she asked. "You're a married man, of course."

"Well, I—ah—"

"Don't lie. There is no need for it. It's just that tonight I don't really care."

The waitress returned with their drinks and Joe took out a pocketbook to extract a few bills. Before he could put the pocketbook away, Marilyn lifted it from his fingers, flipped it open and looked at his driver's license, which was always on top. She handed it back to him.

"Haley," she said. "Joseph Haley. Sorry, but I had to know. You would have told me some other name and I hate lying."

"You're a queer little character. For your information, though, I never lie about my name. But you said something about not really caring tonight. What did you mean by that?"

She was thoughtfully silent for a moment, her eyes downcast, her expression quite sober. She said softly, "You wouldn't understand. It's just that I reached a big decision today that concerns me alone." Then she looked up at him and was laughing again. "I like you, Mr. Haley. Shall we paint the town maybe a little pink?"

"You can go all out for solid red, if you want."

Joe was always cautious about one thing. Whenever he was out with a strange woman he made sure that he took her to places where Mary was not known, where he was not likely to run into any of their friends, and where he would not meet any of his business associates, or anyone else who knew him well.

Therefore, when he and Marilyn left the Rainbow, Joe drove over the Golden Gate Bridge and continued the few miles north to San Rafael, where he knew an out-of-the-way bar. They had a few drinks and moved on to a bar in Fairfax, where they were able to dance to a juke box. Marilyn's body felt very firm and young in his arms. But he noticed that she was beginning to drink a little too fast. He dropped a word to the bartender and from there on her drinks were watered. Even so, she was a bit too gay. They doubled back to a bar in Mill Valley and again Marilyn's drinks were watered. If there was anything Joe hated, it was going to bed with a drunken woman. Marilyn was still rather high and chattered away endlessly. Joe knew women. He knew she was summoning up her courage to go to bed with him. But why? he wondered. She was not married, and she was not going to cheat on anyone. Why would she need false courage?

At two A.M. the bar closed. They went out to the Thunderbird and Joe helped Marilyn in her side and slammed the door. He went around to the left door and slid in under the wheel. Marilyn was instantly in his arms, the first time they had kissed. She pressed her body to his and crushed her lips down on his and held him by the back of the neck with one hand. It was the "hottest" kiss Joe had experienced in years. He responded by becoming instantly aroused and squeezing her breasts in his hand. He forgot all of his earlier suspicions as she whispered in his ear, "Hurry. Please hurry."

He left Mill Valley and roared over the Golden Gate Bridge, slowing down only to pay the toll. Soon they were back in the city. He took the ramp leading down to Lombard St. and drove five blocks, where he pulled in quickly to a motel he had used before. He went into the office, pushed the night bell, and signed the register before a sleepy-eyed clerk. He got the room key and drove the car into a stall under a porch. He led Marilyn to a second-story, open porch, found the right door and unlocked it. The two of them stepped inside.

When he reached for the light switch Marilyn grabbed his arm. "Please," she whispered, "no light."

"Now, look—"

"Please," she pleaded. "I couldn't face it if you turned on a light."

His organ was throbbing and without conscience, so he got undressed quickly and simply dropped his clothes to the floor. When he was naked he ripped back the covers from the bed and sat down on a cold sheet. He waited and listened and could hear nothing. He waited a while longer, then asked, "Marilyn?"

Her voice came out of the darkness, close by; "Yes?"

"Where are you?"

"By the—the side of the bed."

"Are you undressed?"

There was a long silence, then she whispered, "Yes."

He rolled over to the other side of the bed and reached out into the darkness and suddenly felt her hot skin under his fingers. He closed his hands about her body. She was quivering a bit. He pulled against her, and after a moment she fell to the bed and was in his arms. Her body was so very, very firm and her skin was so smooth. A bell rang in his mind that she must also be so very, very young, but by this time he was beyond caring.

He started to make love to her and ran into difficulties. Her fingers dug into his flesh and she moaned softly. He tried again, and she cried out in pain. But now he was feeling the full fury of his own passion and entered her brutishly, without tenderness or compassion. The whole performance was completely unsatisfactory. Joe had tried to make love to her properly, he prided himself on satisfying the woman, but this time he was hardly better than an animal.

He rolled away from her at last and lay on his back and blinked into the dark. Then he sat up suddenly and reached about until he felt a lamp by the side of the bed and turned it on. He looked down at Marilyn. Her body was indeed beautiful and so very young. She was tanned, except for a narrow strip of white over her breasts and another about her hips. Her eyes were closed tightly and she was crying, the tears trickling slowly down her cheeks. Joe then looked down at the white sheet and found what he was afraid would be there.

"God!" he breathed. He lifted her hand and held it in his

powerful fingers. "Jees," he whispered, "why didn't you say something, baby? Why didn't you say something?"

She gasped, "I—I couldn't. Then you—you wouldn't do it." She opened her eyes and looked at him. "Would you?"

He shook his head. "Hell, no. I wanted one virgin in my life and that was enough. I have never wanted another. Aw, hell, baby, why did you do it?"

"I—I had to."

Then he asked bluntly and harshly, "Tell me the truth. How old are you, really?"

She stammered, "S-s-s-s-seventeen."

He closed his eyes and swore softly under his breath, but then he dropped her hand and gently smoothed her hair back from her forehead. "I should have known," he said. "This is my fault. Damn it, I'm old enough to know. I can't forgive myself for this. I'll never forgive myself."

She tried to smile, but failed. "I'm glad it was you."

He said shrewdly, "In other words, baby, you made up your mind to go to bed with a man tonight, and it had to be some stranger."

"Y—yes."

"That figures." He kissed her forehead and wiped the tears gently from her eyes and asked, "Why did you do it? Tell me. I think I have a right to know."

"I—I had a fight with my father." She cried suddenly, "I hate him. You hear me? I hate him. It's a terrible thing to say, but he's a despicable man." Her voice grated as she continued, "He was always accusing me. Always. He said that the way I was raised, with my mother and all, that I was probably a little tramp. You know?"

Joe's hands clenched into fists. "Yes."

"He accused me of everything, of things I have never done. I guess he hated my mother, but he was taking it out on me. I tried to tell him I had never known a man, and he just laughed and sneered at me. And so—and so—"

Joe said wearily, "And so you got even with your father. That is all it amounts to. Now you are no longer a virgin and now, I suppose, you will throw it in his face."

"No! I hadn't thought of telling him."

"Do me a favor and don't, or you may involve me."

"Oh," she cried, "I would never do that." She tried to sit up but dropped back to the pillow. There was sudden pain in her eyes. She looked at Joe, wide-eyed and afraid and whispered, "I hurt. I—I'm afraid you hurt me."

"Oh, fine."

"I—I think so. I feel on fire. Joe," she gasped, "take me home. Please. I—I'm going to be sick."

"Jees."

He picked her up in his arms and told her hoarsely, "Get dressed. I'll have you home in a few minutes."

Joe dressed quickly, but he had difficulty helping Marilyn dress. She was hurting badly and every minute or so she wilted in his arms. At last, however, he had her clothed. He carried her downstairs and to the automobile, where he put her in the right hand seat. He drove away from the motel, but slowly. Marilyn was beginning to hurt worse than ever and the tears were thick in her eyes. She gave him an address and he drove down to Marina Boulevard, to the big homes overlooking the St. Francis Yacht Club, the yacht harbor, and the Golden Gate beyond. Her home was the biggest mansion on the street.

Joe helped her out of the car, through a passageway lined with flowers, and to the front door of the house. There he held her by the shoulders and told her, "I probably hurt you more than you realize. If you don't care to walk into the house by yourself, honey, I'll carry you in."

She brushed her fingertips against his cheek and smiled wanly into his eyes. "I'm so terribly glad it was you," she said. "But I'll make it on my own. Just let me go. I'll be all right. And thanks, Joe. I love you."

Her lips touched his cheek and she turned away from him and unlocked the front door. She slipped inside and softly closed the door. Joe stood a moment, scratching his chin, but then he sighed and turned away. He went out to the curb and started the Thunderbird and looked up at the black windows of the house, then shrugged and drove away.

Jees, he thought, you never knew what was going to happen. But then he felt strangely exhilarated. That was all part of the fun, wasn't it?

Joe was restless and nervous the following day. Marilyn had probably been hurt rather badly. He knew how big he was and how small she was and what a passion he had been in at the time. He hoped that she had made it safely to her own bedroom.

Give her a day or so and she would be all right. Female organs had an astonishing rate of recovery.

At a little after four o'clock he saw his father step out of the elevator. Patrick's narrow-brim hat was tilted cockily on the side of his head, as usual. As he walked toward Joe he looked about at all the cabinets loaded with suits and coats. Clothing was not displayed on the women's fashion floor, but the opposite was true of the men's floor. If men could not see what they were selecting, they would not buy.

Patrick paused to light a cigarette, then joined his son. "Let's go in your office," he said.

He followed Joe into the small manager's office. Joe closed the door, and the two sat together on the edge of the desk.

Joe said, "Mary told me this morning that you called last night and said you had a date with Mr. Kane. Have you seen him yet?"

Patrick blew out a puff of smoke and nodded. "I just left him. He knows what he's about, that man."

"I think so. Did he tell you the deal?"

Patrick rubbed his Irish button-nose and nodded. "We went all through it, as well as you can expect in an hour or so."

"Where does he want the stores?"

"San Rafael, Santa Rosa, San Leandro, North Sacramento, and Vallejo. Close as I can figure right now it would run me maybe four and a half million, including the land."

"Can you swing that?"

Patrick gave him a look of surprise. "Begorra, me lad, I could swing a couple more just like it. Howsomever, I might let the banks in on it. I'll take anywhere from six and a half to eight percent, depending on what your Mr. Kane will hold still for, so I could give four percent to the banks and still come out smelling sweet and purty."

"In other words, you think it will go through."

"Joe, I've told you before nothing ever goes through until someone swings that pick in the ground. Looks like it, though. He's anxious to get it going, and I don't know anyone else big enough to handle it, unless you go out of the state. We did have one argument, though."

"What was that?"

"I told him all the stores had to be identical, and he blew his top. He wants 'em all different. But when I got through explaining to him that that was the only way I could make money on it he calmed down." Patrick chuckled. "You see, lad, he's killing two birds with one stone."

"I know. His big object is really to impress the New Yorkers."

"Uh-huh. It's good figuring, too. He's got my respect just for thinking that way. Anyone else in his shoes would sit tight and consolidate the merger before looking around. Not this lad. He's all for branching out immediately. And I think he's right. I'm always willing to go along with a man like that, especially," he laughed, "if there's plenty in it for me. And I think there is."

He shoved himself away from the desk and told Joe, "But the reason I dropped by is to tell you to keep your mouth shut."

"I've already been warned."

Patrick winked at him. "You're a good lad, even if you can't keep that zipper closed. Well, boy, give Mary me love."

"You bet."

Joe sat there for a moment, after his father had gone, thinking of the gamble Kane was taking and admiring him for it.

Kane, too, was thinking of the big gamble. He was looking across the big desk at his assistant controller with exultant lights dancing in his eyes. Maxwell Jackson said, "So you got one foot in the door," and returned his smile, although on his face it was a bit frozen.

Jackson had the brain of an adding machine and usually the expression of one. He was in his mid-forties, a bit over the average height, with sloping shoulders and a rather heavy build. He had never exercised a day in his adult life and wouldn't know what to do with a muscle if he had one. The skin of his bald head and face was pale, his narrow eyes were gray-blue, his lips were thin, his jowls were pink-shaven, and he had a thick double chin. He dressed well, although his ties never seemed to quite match anything else he was wearing. He looked like a well-to-do Montgomery Street broker, which was almost true.

Jackson had a talent for playing the stock market. Besides having the brain for it, he was also lucky. He had also done extraordinarily well in real estate.

He had very few friends and kept to himself most of the time. The few friends he did have had never been able to figure out why he kept on working for Lew Kane. Only Jackson knew why he did it. He knew and knew it well that he was not capable of exercising discipline over his own nature. Even on vacation he was generally lost. He was a man who needed the discipline of a daily job. So he kept on with Kane and made ten times more money on the side.

Kane said with smug satisfaction, "I think he's our man. Haley's crude, of course, but then, so are most contractors, generally speaking. When I was talking to him on the telephone yesterday he seemed a bit abrupt and only vaguely interested. So I asked him about it today. You know what he said? He laughed and said, 'Laddie-boy, for the first time in your life you're in a deal involving millions of dollars.' Then he said, 'Every deal I touch is in the millions, and I usually got two or three going every year. So how are you going to impress this Irishman, boy?' " Kane laughed. "Imagine? And, you know, he's right."

Jackson pursed his lips and nodded. "In other words, he can handle the whole thing himself."

"That's right. You get together with him in his offices Monday morning. Incidentally," he asked, "you didn't show up until noon today. Anything wrong?"

Jackson's eyes narrowed to slits and he looked off into space. "Sorry," he said. "It couldn't be helped. There was a family crisis this morning."

Kane frowned. "Family? Oh, yes, I forgot. You have your daughter with you this summer. Any place I can help?"

"No, thank you. It's rather intimate. I would not care to discuss it."

Kane cocked one eyebrow high and looked at him searchingly. He was thinking that he wouldn't care to be in Jackson's shoes no matter how many millions he made. He was a dead, dry fish, and his friends you could lose. They were as humorless as Jackson. Yet, in his way, he was the best right-hand man Kane had ever known. It would be pretty hard getting along without him.

Kane leaned back in his chair and said, "Very well. Now then, how are you making out under Drury and when will you be able to take over? As you can see, Max, things are moving fast. I can't have Drury in my way much longer."

Jackson turned his attention away from what was on his mind and said, "It won't be long now. His job isn't much more difficult than the one I was doing for you at Wilson's. What's the difference, when you're counting hundred dollar bills instead of ten dollar bills? The difference is just in quantity. You still have to count the bills."

"Of course. You figure you're pretty well caught up?"

"Very much so. At this point, I know every move Drury makes

and why he makes it. All that I am working out now is the Findex system."

Kane grunted, "I don't understand it very well, myself."

"Naturally. We didn't need it at Wilson's. Too small. But any time you get seven, eight, or more stores, Lew, you have to have something like Findex. You know how it works, of course. Say a manager in Fresno has a customer for a certain woman's suit in size eight, but they're out of it down there. So she calls Findex in San Francisco and wants to know who has an eight. The clerk looks it up and tells her there are two eights in the Sacramento store. So one of them gets sent down to Fresno and a sale is made. Findex here lists all big merchandise and everything that moves fast. In that respect, we know where everything is in every store of the chain. Slow-moving items, however, are not on Findex. Department managers keep track of things like that on their own. It's an excellent system. All I am learning now is how information is fed into it."

"I see. The ground up angle."

"That's right. As soon as I have that figured out to my satisfaction I'll be able to step into Drury's shoes. Incidentally," he asked slyly, "have you figured out a way yet to get rid of him?"

Kane growled, "We'll figure that out when the time comes." He dropped his hands down to the top of the desk. "Well, okay, Max, I guess that's it."

Jackson left the room and walked into Drury's office, where he had a desk against a far wall. Drury was arguing with one of the women buyers about a mark-down in some women's dresses on the fashion floor. The discussion seemed rather heated. The dresses had been moving slowly and Drury wanted the mark-down to get rid of them, but the buyer was against the idea. It would look bad on her books. They were going at it hammer-and-tongs.

Jackson went to his desk, hardly noticed, and started going through some reports. His telephone rang and he picked it up. His personal attorney was on the wire. Jackson could not transfer the call elsewhere, so kept his voice low. He took a card from his pocket and referred to it as he said, "That's right. California license plate CVC–198. The car was a black Thunderbird. Oh?" he asked. "You already have the information? Let me have it."

He listened and his jaw dropped and his face became paler than ever. When the attorney had finished talking, he replaced the phone slowly and leaned his elbows on the desk to punch his fists into his eyes. He remained that way for a long while, but at last he straightened and stared out the window. Then he pulled a telephone book toward him and his finger went slowly down the Haleys.

He picked up the telephone again, took a deep breath and dialed the telephone number of Joe Haley's home.

Joe was glad when the day came to an end. He had had only an hour or two of sleep the night before and was tired. He left the store and went to a bar, where he had a couple of quick straight shots. They might help to pick him up. Then he got his car out of the garage and drove slowly west, home.

The boys had heard his car arriving and were waiting to greet him. They threw themselves at him almost as one person. Patrick was the oldest at ten, Michael was next at eight, and Joseph Jr. was last at six. They looked like well-scrubbed boys almost anywhere, except that each one had his parents' black hair and Joe's green eyes. It was also obvious that each would be as big as his father, if not bigger. It was also just as obvious that they loved their father with all their hearts.

Joe was never at a loss for affection where the boys were concerned. He gave it as well as received it. His time was their time. Regardless of where he and Mary went, the boys were always with them and particularly with their father. He played baseball with them and taught them how to fight, how to handle a football, how to hunt, how to fish, and everything else a young boy loved. He was a stern disciplinarian, but the boys did not mind that. His discipline gave them a sense of security. As far as they were concerned, he was everything a father should be.

He roughed the three of them about and banged their heads together and laughed at and with them, then he asked Pat, "Where's the old bag?"

Pat frowned and said, "She's upstairs. What's the matter with Mom, Dad? She was on the phone—then all of a sudden she ran upstairs crying."

"Oh?"

Joe shoved the boys away from him and frowned. What, indeed, could be wrong? Mary did not cry very often. She was emotionally a tough person. Maybe she had received bad news from someone.

"You characters go out in the kitchen," he said. "We'll be down in a minute."

He went up to the master bedroom, opened the door, stepped inside and closed it behind him. It was still light outside, but the curtains had been drawn and the room was in semi-gloom. Mary was dressed, but was lying face down on the bed. She had heard the door open and close. She rolled to her side and looked at him, then shoved herself upright and slowly got to her feet. She faced him with a rigid body, almost as if it had been frozen. In spite of the gloom, she looked very desirable to Joe. He could not see her expression or her eyes, so he moved closer.

He asked worriedly, "Something wrong?"

"Not with me," she said. Then she asked harshly, "Joseph Haley, where were you last night?"

Oh, oh, he thought. Joseph Haley. That was always bad news. He asked innocently, "Why? It was Thursday night, wasn't it?"

He started to move closer and raised his hands to put on her shoulders, but she screamed, "Don't you dare touch me, you monster!"

He paused and instantly his mind was flooded with Marilyn. He did not need to reason from cause to effect. Every nerve end in his body told him that it was Marilyn. He felt a chill settling in his spine.

But he managed to ask, still innocently, "What, in God's name, is wrong with you?"

"I had a telephone call a little while ago."

"Oh?"

"Yes. It was a man. He wouldn't give his name. But he said that he was a father and that he had a daughter by the name of Marilyn." She asked nastily, "Do you know anyone by the name of Marilyn?"

Joe's eyes closed and his teeth gritted together. Oh, God, he thought, I guess it had to happen one of these days. He opened his eyes and looked at Mary and asked, "Am I supposed to?"

She stepped toward him and her nose was not far from his own. She looked up and glared into his eyes. "This man called. He said that last night you were out with his daughter. He said that you raped her."

"So now I'm a rapist? A family man—?"

"Don't tell me," she screamed, almost like an Irish fishwife. "Married men do it, too. I know. I read it in the papers all the time. But it wasn't rape," she said. "It was statutory rape."

"There is a considerable difference."

"In degree, yes. But it means the same to me. He said his daughter is only seventeen. He said you had her out and that you took her to bed." She choked up for a moment, but then asked him, "Do you have anything to say?"

"I don't know," he said, "what there is to say. You have me completely confused. You say he wouldn't give his name?"

"No. But he said he was thinking of going down to the district attorney's office to have you arrested on a charge of statutory rape."

Joe's mind was racing wildly and he could come up with nothing. It was better to keep lying, however, until he was trapped.

"Look," he said, "there are forty-eight different Haleys in the telephone book. This character may have made a mistake, you know."

She shook her head violently. "He had the right Haley. Black Thunderbird, CVC–198. He said that he was awake when his daughter came home, and he got your license number as you were driving away. He said that when his daughter came in the house she collapsed on the floor." She closed her eyes and her shoulders trembled. "Oh, Heavenly Father!"

Joe said softly, "Mary."

She looked at him and screamed, "Don't Mary me, you cheater."

He stood stiffly before her and said, "Haven't you stopped to think that anyone could get the license number of my car and that anyone could find out my name? Cripes, Mary, use your head. Why would he bother to call you if he was interested in having me arrested? He wouldn't bother with either of us. He would simply call the police. Now, stop to think about it. Wouldn't he?"

Mary thought for a moment, then said, "All right. Then you tell me just where you were last night."

He realized that he would have to tell the truth, at least partly, so he said, "Well, I went to the Pierce Street Annex and—"

"Who were you with? I can check, you know."

Again he knew he would have to tell the truth. "No one," he said. "I wanted to be alone last night, to think over this merger deal."

"You've been thinking about it for months."

"There are still a lot of loose ends I wanted to think about. So I went where I said, then I went to the Drawing Room on Van Ness, then to the Top O' the Mark, and I wound up at Vesuvio's in North Beach. Why don't you call them up and ask if

I was there and who I was with? They wouldn't know me at the last places I was talking about, but they know me at the Annex and the Drawing Room. Give them a call."

"I certainly shall."

She got a telephone book and dialed both the Pierce Street Annex and the Drawing Room and talked to the bartenders. Then she looked at Joe and said, "They said you were there."

"And who was I with?"

"You were alone."

He spread his hands and smiled. "You see?"

"But they also said you were there very early, before twelve. Now, what about the others?"

"Well, in the others, they wouldn't know me. Nevertheless, I was alone."

She stood up and faced him again. "Joe Haley," she said fiercely, "you are lying through your teeth. This man who was talking to me had tears in his voice. He knew you and he knew your car and he had the number. I'll tell you something, Joe. I have heard rumors about you before, but I refused to believe them. Anyone can lie about a good-looking man. This one, though, I believe."

Joe said desperately, "Then why the hell didn't he just call the police instead of calling you?"

"Because," she said shrewdly, "maybe he wants to make you sweat."

Cripes, Joe thought, she could be right. But he said, "I don't believe it. This is from some sort of a crank who hates me and would like to louse us up. That is exactly what it amounts to. Can't you see it?"

She was silent for a long while, looking levelly into his eyes. At last she said, "I can't condemn you without a trial. So I am going to investigate this thing, and I am going to investigate it very, very closely. Meanwhile," and she was screaming again, "you can get everything you own out of this room and sleep in the guest room. Do you hear me, damn it?"

She went to the closest bureau and started throwing his shirts out on the floor.

8

Joe did not go to work the following day, a Saturday. He called Fred Maloney and told him that he was quite ill. Fred seemed to accept it. Joe then spent the entire weekend trying to reason with Mary. He talked and talked and argued and argued, and he got nowhere. Mary had too much ammunition. She also remembered something else. The man who phoned had asked, "What if I tell Mr. Kane about this?" So he also knew where Joe worked and all about him.

Joe told her, "Goddamn it all, anyone would know that. It proves nothing. I have all sorts of people who hate me. It could be almost anyone who could be trying to foul us up."

He was worried, though, about the statement that Marilyn's father had made, that he might go to the district attorney and have Joe prosecuted for statutory rape. He rather doubted it, though. He remembered the mansion at which he had delivered Marilyn. People in that class rarely bothered with the police. He figured that it was a threat designed to make him suffer.

Mary had all of his clothes and belongings moved into the guest room, and that is where he stayed. The Haley home, during that weekend, was a mortuary.

Mary's Irish temper had taken over completely. No matter how he argued, her answer was always the same, "I am going to hire someone to find out every move you made Thursday night. There are people who are very clever at that sort of thing. And until I do know, you and I are no longer man and wife."

He could not move her even a fraction from that position. Yet there was at least a little hope in it. Tracking down his movements on the night in question could be a tough job indeed. The probabilities were in his favor that Mary would draw a blank.

He doubted, too, that Mary would ever hear again from Marilyn's father. He had probably made the one call in an extreme fit of anger, but that would cool off. Joe would almost bet that the man would not repeat his call.

He went back to work Monday feeling as if he had been pulled through a clothes wringer.

On Monday mornings the store manager always had a brief

meeting with all the department managers of the main store. The main object was to publicly air gripes and pass on word of policy from on high. The meeting was held in the old board room. Maloney addressed the meeting, and the new assistant sat at his side. Behind them, however, Maxwell Jackson stood leaning back against the wall. Joe wondered what the devil he was doing there. No one in that department had ever shown up before. Then Joe noticed that Jackson's eyes were quite often upon himself. Joe tried a trick. He looked away for a moment or so, then quickly looked back at Jackson and, sure enough, the man was watching him.

Joe was puzzled. He knew practically nothing about Jackson and doubted that the other man knew much more about Joe Haley. He was one of the executives Kane had brought in from Wilson's. Then Joe noticed something else. Every time Jackson looked at him there seemed to be hatred in his expression and his lips twitched. Joe then had to laugh at himself for imagining things. Cripes, he thought, we don't even know each other. He turned his attention back to Maloney.

Fred was saying, "For the benefit of Miss Parker, who is new here, and others of you who seem to forget now and then, I would like to restate one of the main points of Merritt-Wilson policy. The customer is always right. When you get a return, try to put out as little as possible, of course. But if the customer insists on going over your heads to the store manager, then go all out on an adjustment, regardless of what was asked."

Betty stood up and said, "I had one like that last Saturday, late. This woman came in with a coat that was practically in rags. She said she had just bought it a few months before. I had that looked up in Credit and proved her to be a liar. The coat was almost a year and a half old. It didn't bother her a bit. She insisted that the coat had never fit her well, that she didn't like it, and that she wanted to be credited in full. Why, that coat looked as if a dog had been sleeping on it. I argued and argued with her and got nowhere. She wanted full credit, and no matter what I offered she wouldn't accept it. So then she said she was going to the store manager, and I told her just exactly how to get to your office." She asked Fred, "What happened? Did she call on you?"

Fred smiled and nodded. "She did, and she got a total refund."

"You're kidding."

"No, I am not. That's why I brought this up. She lied to me

right to my face and she knew it and she knew I knew it, but my hands are tied. Any time a customer is willing to go as far as my office, it is our policy to give complete satisfaction. We have learned over the years, Miss Parker, that we actually lose very little with that policy and that quite often we gain a good deal in customer satisfaction. In other words, the dollar loss is negligible and you can reckon a profit in good will."

"But doesn't it burn you up when they lie like that?"

"Of course. Just as much as it does you. But that's our policy and it works." He looked around and said, "That's about all for the morning."

Joe glanced at Jackson and saw that the other man was again watching him. He shrugged and walked out to the sales area of the fourth floor with Betty.

"He's right," he said. "I get some beauties. Yet I have seen some damned good customers remain on our books because of that policy. On the other hand, I understand it's much worse on your floor."

"Well, you know women."

"Sure." He grinned and said, "Male customers at least do have a little streak of honesty. When they're lying about something they get pretty embarrassed. Sometimes you can even make them give ground and back down. But a woman can look you straight in the eyes and lie her head off."

"Don't tell me," she laughed.

Joe felt as if he were being watched and turned around. He found Jackson staring at him again. Joe shook his head and frowned. What was it with the man, anyway? Then he laughed to himself. Maybe he was a fairy?

"Well," he told Betty, "I had better be on my way. Be seeing you."

She watched him go and chewed thoughtfully at a corner of her lip. Joe was not his usual self. He had seemed a bit despondent. Even his laughter had had a hollow echo in it. Oh, well, she thought, no skin off my nose.

Today was the first day she meant to take over total control of her floor. There was no sense wasting any more time.

Yet she did feel a slight reluctance to take full command. The big store was a bit beyond her experience. The main problem, of course, was the sales staff. Betty had always before worked with women her own age, or at least close to it. Most of these women were old enough to be her mother. Miss Snider could almost be her grandmother. Each and every one of them was an old professional. Out of the twenty-seven saleswomen only three of them were make-ups, and they were part-time workers. Betty was used to having it the other way around. They were also top sales people, and because they were good they were quite independent. They knew every trick in the trade and undoubtedly a few that Betty had never heard about. They had to be handled with kid gloves. Betty had learned very quickly that they did not look upon her as "boss" at all. They regarded her more or less as a traffic manager and someone to run things behind the scenes.

Betty knew, however, that somehow or other she had to impress her authority upon them. No one else in the store seemed to realize it, but she knew already that the actual sales potential of the floor could be at least fifty percent greater than it was. She had the sales staff, she had the clothing, and she had the customers. All she had to do was combine the three in a much more efficient manner. On the other hand, it could not be rushed. She must move very, very slowly.

She figured she would make one very small change that morning, so had all the sales people gathered around her counter a minute or so before the customers would start pouring in.

"I have noticed," she said, "that when any of you take a customer to millinery you still retain your top position on the call list. Naturally, you would much rather handle a customer to whom you might make a sale of three or four hundred rather than something for thirty or forty dollars in hats. I don't blame you. But it does make for very sloppy handling in millinery. You aren't really interested at all in selling a hat. You're thinking of that call list, and you always have one eye on the elevators. That is now going to be changed."

Miss Hall, a rather waspish woman, frowned and said, "I don't see how you can change it."

Betty smiled sweetly and said, "It's quite simple. From now on, when you get a customer for millinery, you go off the call list and go on-down."

Miss Snider gasped, "Oh, no!"

"Oh, yes. In that way, as long as you're off-call, anyway, you'll damned well try to sell a hat. And as long as it applies to all of you no one gets hurt."

Miss Hall squinted at her. "Is this an order?"

Betty stared directly back into her eyes. "That is exactly correct, Miss Hall. I am the manager of this department, and any time I put out an order I mean every word of it."

"In that case, you won't mind if I leave the floor for a few minutes?"

"Why? The doors are just opening."

Miss Hall said slowly, "I wish to go down to the manager's office. I have something to talk about."

"You have my permission."

When Miss Hall walked away all the others smiled secretively and gradually dispersed, whispering amongst themselves. Customers started pouring in and Betty became busy. About twenty minutes later Miss Hall returned. Because she had been off the floor, Betty had put her name on the bottom of the call list. Miss Hall was furious, but had nothing to say for the moment. Ten minutes later Chet Baker showed up.

He leaned his elbows on the counter and winked at Betty. "We had a visit from Miss Hall," he said. "Maloney told me to handle it. Suppose you give me your angle."

Betty told him simply about the change and what it amounted to. When she had finished she said, "I assume you backed me up."

"Well, yes and no. We didn't tell Miss Hall our decision. Maloney told me that any time anything like this happens it is always necessary for one of us to go talk to the other party. Then, when we do make a decision, there is at least some appearance of fair play."

Betty's body tensed and her eyes narrowed. "That little change," she said, "was my first real order as department manager. If you don't back me up all the way, I'll walk out of here in one minute flat."

"Aren't you being a little arrogant?"

"No, I don't think so. Chet, it is absolutely necessary for the women on this floor to have some respect for me. If the front office lets me down, then I have no value here at all."

He nodded. "I see what you mean." He looked off into space for a moment, then swung his eyes back to hers. He nodded again. "You're probably right, anyway. Okay, it stands."

"Now," she said, "you wait a minute. Gradually, over a period of time, I am going to be making many changes on this floor. Am I compelled to fight every one of them through your office?"

He admitted honestly, "Just about, Betty. The women on this floor are not ordinary sales people, so Maloney was telling me.

So each of them must feel that she has as much representation in the front office as you have."

"Well," she sighed, "then that's the way it is. So now I have something else to worry about."

Miss Hall came by at that moment and smiled at Chet. "Well," she asked, "has the matter been settled?"

He looked at her and said, "It has. Miss Parker was hired by Mr. Kane to manage this department. That is precisely what she is doing."

"You mean—?"

"I mean that any order she gives has our full backing. Any time you feel you are being treated unfairly, however, you have the option of talking it over with Mr. Maloney or me any time you please."

She glared at the two of them. "I wonder," she asked, "how they settle these things at Saks?"

Betty said, "It would be easy to find out. Unfortunately, though, you would starve to death at Saks. They don't pay commission, as you well know."

Miss Hall's eyes blazed, but she was an old pro and she knew she had lost this round. She spun on her heel and stalked away from them.

Chet started away, but then turned and looked back at Betty, hopefully. "I was just thinking. The two of us are new here. Why don't you come out to luncheon with me, and we can talk things over?"

Betty had difficulty stifling her laughter. "Sorry," she said, "but I have a luncheon engagement. Some other time, perhaps. On the other hand, I really don't know you. Are you married, or divorced, or a bachelor, or what?"

He spread his hands in an open gesture. "It was an honest invitation. I have never been married, or divorced. Strictly a bachelor."

She looked at the top of his forehead, where the skin was flaking at the hairline. Obviously, he spent a lot of time in the sun. She asked curiously, "Do you play tennis, or golf, or—"

He interrupted, "I have a bicycle. Every morning before breakfast I take a fast ride for two or three miles through Golden Gate Park."

"Really?"

"Uh-huh. It gives me an excellent appetite and the exercise is good for me, considering the confinement of my job."

"Invite me along some morning. I love to bicycle."

"Then," he laughed, "you have a standing invitation from now on. Just let me know the morning, that's all."

"Don't worry, I will. Good-bye, Chet."

She watched him go and thought, Nice person. Looks like I have another boyfriend coming over the horizon. The more the merrier.

She knocked off at the late noon hour and turned the floor over to Marie Togliatti. She walked three blocks down Stockton and turned right on Ellis to Day's, a few stores from the corner. It was a huge barroom with an enormous elliptical bar, booths around the walls, and a quick-serve food counter at the front of the room. Bill met her just inside the front door, grinned, took her elbow and guided her to the waiting chef. She had soup and a turkey sandwich, he had a salad and roast beef. They took their food on trays and went to one of the booths.

When they sat down Bill said, "Why all the rush? We could've gone to something much nicer."

"Thirty minutes, Buster, is all I can spare. If I'm even ten minutes away from that floor all hell can break loose. So I eat and run."

She looked across the table at him and smiled warmly. He was so much like his father. Bill Kane was actually an inch taller than his father, but just as thin and spare. He had his father's gray eyes, cavernous cheeks, and amused mouth. But he was not dressed like his father. He was wearing khaki trousers, boots, a red checked plaid shirt, and a suede windbreaker. He looked like a tall truck driver. Betty wondered, How could he have taken me to a better place in an outfit like that? She had to laugh about it.

They ate their food, Bill wolfed his down with the appetite of a man who worked hard, then they sat back and looked at each other. Bill smiled softly and said, "You're quite a redhead. You know that?"

"Oh?"

"Yeah. I was looking out the window and watching you come down the street. Believe me, you've got a wiggle that's all your own. And with that hair and that face and that body, man, you could make Bardot take a back seat."

"Thank you, dear sir." Then she leaned forward and said, Bill, there is something I want to talk to you about seriously.

You know how I like your father. I think he's truly wonderful. But this business of seeing you on the side, like we're sneaking down back alleys—I don't like it. Why do we have to do it?"

Bill put a hand across the table and smothered her hand in his. "I'll tell you something," he said. "To put it crudely, Dad doesn't care where I play around, or who I play around with, as long as it isn't one of his employees. He has always felt that if I dated one of his employees, there was a possibility that the whole thing could blow up in his face and, of course, he is right."

She nodded. "I understand that."

"So, he has asked me not to do it and I never have. Except," he grinned broadly, "as of now. Shall we continue being honest with each other?"

"Please do."

"All right. You are easily one of the most beautiful and one of the most desirable women I have ever known. You do things to me, lots of things. I think you like me, too, or we wouldn't be here right now. But, honestly Betty, we don't really know each other very well. So all I want is to know you better and for you to know me better. We may than wind up spitting at each other. Or it may be quite the reverse. All I want is the chance to find out."

"Fair enough."

"Then, when that time comes, I will be very proud to tell Dad that I am squiring one of his employees. I don't think then that he will mind. You see my point?"

"Oh, you men. You always make everything sound so logical. However, I do have to agree with you. But I still don't like it."

They talked about matters of no consequence, then Betty had to run. Bill walked with her to the corner of Ellis and Stockton, but paused there and held her hand for a moment. "I understand," he said, "that you and Anna Merritt are quite thick."

Betty smiled warmly. "She's been wonderful to me. At one time, you know, she used to be a redhead, too. One day, right after we first met, she brought a lock of her hair which had been clipped years before and compared it with mine. The color was almost the same. We've been close friends ever since."

"Then it wasn't because of the similarity in names?"

She gave him a puzzled look. "What's similar between Parker and Merritt?"

"I didn't mean her married name. I meant her maiden name."

"Her maiden name?" Betty frowned. "I don't think I ever heard it."

It was his turn to look puzzled. "Funny she never told you. It's the same as yours."

"You're kidding."

"Hell, no. Ask anyone."

"Well, I'll be— And she has never mentioned it. Isn't that odd?"

"I guess so. Well, look, I have to get back to work, too. Remember, I'm seeing you tonight."

She squeezed his hand. "Okay. Good-bye, Bill."

She walked away from him and she was frowning again. It really was odd that Mrs. Merritt had never mentioned her maiden name. She was always bringing up other things they had in common. One would think that the very first thing she would mention would be the similarity in maiden names. Why hadn't she?

She was turning into the main entrance of Merritt-Wilson's when she ran into Joe, also coming back to work. She stopped him and asked him, "Do you know Mrs. Merritt very well?"

Joe had his mind on some other matter, but he said, "Like any other employee, I guess. We didn't exactly buddy around with each other. Why?"

"Do you know her maiden name?"

Joe scratched his scalp and thought a moment, then shook his head. "Damned if I know. She and Merritt got married twenty-seven or twenty-eight years ago. Cripes I was practically in diapers then. How would I know?"

"I was just told."

"Oh?"

"Yes. It's the same as mine—Parker."

"Really? In that case, baby, stick close and maybe she'll have you in her will. And that wouldn't be bad."

He took her elbow and turned her through the main door, and the two walked into the store together. Everyone who saw them, and many did, naturally assumed that they had been having lunch together.

Kane heard about it the moment he returned from lunch. Marie dropped the information, casually as usual, as he stepped off the elevator at the fourth floor. He walked back to his office in a thoughtful frame of mind.

Jackson had spent the entire morning with Patrick Haley, then had joined Kane for lunch. His preliminary report was very good. "It seems," he had said, "that Haley has already made up his mind to go along with you. All he wants now are the details: floor space, parking areas, the land you have in mind and what he can buy it for, the design of the buildings, and so on and so on. As soon as he has the complete financial picture, then he'll talk business with you. Incidentally, he doesn't give a damn about your financial position."

"Why not?"

"Because he intends building in such a manner that he can lease out or sell to anyone else. He says that the way California is booming he can't lose no matter what happens. However," and here Jackson had paused for a moment, "I have a hunch that you are going to pay through the nose for those leases."

"That I had always figured. No one ever does anything for nothing."

So it was going well with Haley. At least, he was interested. It might not be a good idea, therefore, to lower the boom on his son. Even so, he worried about Joe and Betty. But, damn it all, he hoped she had better sense than to get mixed up with a character like that!

He was still thinking about it when Sam Kuller came into his office, dropped into a chair and stared at him. He was chewing on the stem of a dead pipe. No one had ever actually seen him put tobacco in the pipe and light it. In one of the drawers of his desk were dozens of broken pipe stems. He chewed through them when he got excited, which was rather often.

"Mr. Kane," he said, "you're going to have to come up with more dough for men's wear."

Kane looked at him with a level frown. "Aren't you rather exceeding your authority?" he asked. "Aren't you supposed to go through Jack Harrison?"

Sam nodded. "Right. However, I think you can credit me with a little intelligence of my own. From where I sit and the way the ball is bouncing, all you mean to use Jack for is big deals. If I'm wrong, say so."

"Well—"

"So I'm not wrong. You aren't about to bother Jack anymore with the running of these stores, but I still have to run them, on the men's side, anyway. Our inventories are low. Even with all the new merchandise you've been buying, they're still low. I'll put it to you flatly, Mr. Kane, you're going to have to come up with at least another two hundred grand on this fall's buying for men. I don't have to teach you the fundamentals of this business. If you don't have it to sell you lose money. Can you do it, or can't you?"

Kane suppressed a smile and nodded. "I can. The money is in the bank. Perhaps I owe you an apology. It is still difficult for me to think in terms of twenty stores instead of four. I try to cut corners, you know?"

Sam relaxed a bit. "I understand. Okay. So my buyers can buy what they need when they go to New York next week. You don't mind if I pass the word?"

"Please do. Send in a statement and I'll check it through."

"Very good."

He stood up to go, but Kane said suddenly, "You know you're next in line for Jack's job, don't you?"

Sam squinted at him and rubbed a hand over his chin. At last he nodded. "I know, and I've been thinking about it. I've been giving it plenty thought. And you know something? I'm damned if I know if I want it."

Kane looked surprised. "You know what it pays."

"That no longer interests me. You can get a man from New York."

"Oh, no. It would never do. You practically grew up in this chain. It has to be you. I have never entertained thoughts of anyone else, believe me."

A wry smile twisted Sam's lips. "Thanks for your confidence, Mr. Kane, but I don't know. Let's say Jack has another two years to go. Well, I'm not getting any younger either. In two years from now I'd like to quit and retire. But if I took over Jack's job at the time, I'd have to start fighting the werewolves all over again. No, sir, I don't know."

Kane came close to bellowing, "Damn it all, it has to be you. I won't hear of anything else. Do you understand?"

Sam shrugged. "I'll think about it."

"You'll do a hell of a lot better than that. Okay, think about it. You think it over for a week, then come in and tell me your decision." He paused, then added, "It had better be the way I want it."

Sam nodded. "Okay. I'll let you know."

He walked out of the office laughing uproariously to himself. Of course he wanted Jack's job. But he had been worried that perhaps Kane might have someone else in mind. Now he had it from the horse's mouth that the job was his. Thank God, he thought. He knew what would happen if he ever retired. He would drink himself to death. That was a fate he did not want.

He went into the merchandising office feeling very pleased with himself. It was a fairly large room occupied by himself, as head of merchandising for men's wear, and his assistant Peterson. It was also occupied by Miss Bennett, head of merchandising for women, and her assistant, Miss Smythe.

Miss Bennett looked up as he entered and observed shrewdly, "You just swallowed a mouse."

"That's good thinking," he said, "for a cat. But mice don't rest well on my stomach."

He went to his desk and sat down and pulled some books toward him and pretended that he was busy. He was thinking, however, of a pleasurable way to celebrate the evening. Sam had been born and raised in San Francisco. He knew all the alleys and byways, and he knew the characters who frequented them. He picked up the telephone and made a few calls, and his night was all set for him. God Almighty, he laughed, I wonder what the grandkids would think?

As soon as he finished work he met the girl at the corner of Post and Grant Avenue. She was wearing a red rose on her left shoulder, as the pimp had said. She was rather tall and stately, she dressed well, she had good legs, her hair was black, her hips were beautiful, her waist was slim and she seemed to have gorgeous breasts. Her name was Ida. She smiled professionally at Sam.

He asked her about the price.

"Well," she said, resenting the fact that commercialism had intruded so soon, "it's fifty dollars if we just go to a hotel and a hundred dollars for the night. Is that all right with you?"

"Look," he said, "I'm damned near old enough to be your grandfather. Tonight, however, you're my girl. Now, if you carry it off successfully there's a fifty dollar bonus in it for you. Do you think you can do it?"

She looked him up and down, then smiled and said, "For you, baby, it's the limit. Where do we go from here?"

He had to laugh with her and said, "I know a nice spot for dinner. We'll step out after that."

He stopped a taxi and took her to La Strada, a dining spot on Broadway in North Beach. The food, as he knew it would be,

111

was excellent and the atmosphere was perfect. Then he took her to the Condor, where they watched a bare-breasted entertainer do The Swim and had some brandies. From there they went to Club 365 and watched a good floor show and drank gimlets on the rocks and danced a little. That, as far as Sam was concerned, was the end of the line.

"Now," he said, "to bed."

She went along with him happily. She had become rather fond of Sam and to herself was calling him "Old Foxy." She liked his easy laughter and his vivacious way of talking. Especially, she liked his treating her like a lady. So if he had any problems because of his age, she was perfectly willing to help him out. She knew a dozen different tricks.

They stopped at a liquor store, where Sam picked up two bottles of champagne and a bag of ice to chill it in, then the cab driver deposited them at an excellent motel on Van Ness. Sam registered and got the most expensive suite in the place. Ida was no longer surprised. He was obviously used to money, and this was a big night for him.

A bellboy brought up a champagne bucket and some glasses and Sam proceeded to chill the wine as Ida got a fire started and pulled down all the blinds. They sat on the sofa and drank their wine and listened to soft music over the radio. Ida was liking Sam more and more and wanted to kiss him, but was afraid to. Some men resented it because they knew of certain duties whores had to perform. She contented herself with smiling at him and squeezing his knee.

Sam looked at her and said, "How did you ever—" But then paused and shook his head.

Ida said, "You were just going to ask me how did I ever happen to become a prostitute. Weren't you?"

"Well—"

"The answer," she laughed, "is just good luck, I guess."

Sam laughed with her and dropped the subject. This gal was all right.

They finished the first bottle of wine and Ida placed a hand gently on Sam's knee and looked into his eyes. "Look," she said earnestly, "more wine isn't going to do the trick. Believe me, I know. Now, what I want you to do is just to relax and stop worrying. I know my business, Sam, and you have nothing to worry about."

He laughed shakily. "Money-back guarantee?"

"Well, I won't go that far, but I think you'll perform all right. At one time," she said, "I was a stripper. Not bad, either. So what we're going to do—you're the audience and I'm putting on a show for you."

Sam's eyes lit up. "Hey, that sounds all right."

"But first you get undressed. Then you sit on this sofa and watch me."

"That doesn't seem necessary—"

"It is. Either you get undressed or I won't do it." She felt that once he watched her performance, he would respond. However, considering his age, by the time he got into the bedroom and undressed all could again be lost. She knew all too well how it was with older men.

When Sam went into the bedroom she turned down all the lights except one standing lamp glowing softly in a corner of the room. Sam returned to the sitting room naked, but with a towel wrapped about his middle. Ida had to hide a smile. Cripes, she thought, here he is with a whore and he's still modest.

He dropped onto the sofa, but then he did remove the towel and throw it aside. As Ida had surmised, he was still in no condition for sex. She turned up the radio a bit and got a platter program on the air. It was all she needed.

She stood across the room from him and started dancing back and forth, throwing in an occasional small bump and grind. She was graceful, and because she was doing it all for Sam, he was grateful. He watched her every movement with a light smile playing about his lips. He even forgot that he was naked.

She pranced back and forth before him, then she loosened the belt at her waist and suggestively, while rolling her eyes, pulled down the zipper at the side of her dress. She lifted the hem of her skirt and pulled it all over her head just as she disappeared through the doorway into the bedroom. Sam had to laugh. She did it just the way he had seen it in burlesque. Then she was back again dancing before him in a black nylon slip. She spun about and did more bumps and grinds and while she danced she watched Sam. Not a quiver. He was too entranced to react. That would come to an end pretty soon, she hoped. She had made up her mind that he was going to enjoy himself or she would practically die trying.

She danced before him and her fingers went to the back of her head. She wore her hair in a rather bunlike effect, but now she pulled the pins out and let the thick hair cascade about her shoulders. Then she pulled down the left strap of her slip, then the right strap. She spun about and lowered the top of the slip until her breasts were exposed, covered only with a black lace brassiere. She danced toward the bedroom door still lowering her slip until it was down to her hips and Sam saw the beautiful ivory skin of her midriff. Suddenly she pulled the slip all the way down and stepped out of it and Sam was staring at black breasts, a white midriff, filmy black lace panties, and long legs covered with weblike hosiery. Then she was gone into the bedroom.

When she returned this time Sam was no longer smiling. He noticed, too, that she had removed her garter belt and stockings in the bedroom, but had put the shoes back on. Probably, he thought, she needed the shoes for dancing. Actually, she was smart enough to know that the spike heels enhanced the beauty of her legs. Again she was dancing before him and now her hands were behind her fumbling with the fastenings of the brassiere. When it was undone she held her hands by the sides of her breasts and danced sideways before him. She slowly lowered the left cup of the brassiere until a perfect milky white globe was bare. Sam gasped and stared and thought, though fleetingly, that she must have borne children to have nipples that large. She turned then to her right side and slowly exposed the right breast. Then she danced to the bedroom door, removed the brassiere entirely and threw it into the air.

She was back almost instantly in the middle of the room, now wearing only the black panties. She stood in one place before Sam and held out her arms and shimmied her shoulders and the beautiful breasts bobbed up and down and swayed back and forth before his eyes. Sam was almost holding his breath. She saw the intensity of his gaze and looked down and smiled to herself and hooked her thumbs in the tops of her panties. Slowly she lowered them over her hips until they were below her navel and the curvature of her stomach. Then suddenly she pulled the panties below her knees, stepped out of them and threw them aside. She was not disappearing into any bedroom this time. Sam was ready.

"Now," she whispered. "Here, before the fire."

Sam got up and came toward her.

When Sam was all through they lay on the floor, side by side, staring at the ceiling. He was breathing hard, almost as if he had run a race. Ida lay there quietly, waiting for his breathing to slow down.

Sam turned his head to blink at her, then he sat up to look down at what, at least for the moment, was the most beautiful female body he had ever seen.

He said softly, "I didn't think it could happen again like this. Not at my age."

Ida said tenderly, "I've seen much older men than you have a ball for themselves."

"Really? You know, young lady, a moment like that is worth ten thousand dollars to an older man."

She laughed. "Care to write out a check?" She sat up and nipped his ear and said, "Now for the other bottle of wine and to bed for the two of us."

"Look, honey, you don't have to spend the whole night with me. You've earned your bonus many times over. All I am going to do is sleep and back to work in the morning."

She smiled and shook her head. "Oh, no, we don't. I give payment for valued received. Who knows? We might have a matinee."

Sam had to laugh at her. "Good Lord, not me!"

"It's happened before. It could happen again. So I'm staying."

She was right, much to Sam's amazement. He was used to waking early in the morning and opened his eyes before Ida. She was lying on her side, facing him, her cheeks cradled against her hands. His eyes again swept lovingly and wonderingly up and down her body. He was completely flabbergasted and astonished when she moved into his arms and he was again able to perform. Sam thought, Jees, I wish I could brag about this to someone.

When they were getting dressed he told her, "That second time I would never believe."

She smiled at him over her shoulder while fixing the bun at the nape of her neck. "How old are you?" she asked. "In your sixties?"

"Just."

"Uh-huh. You aren't through yet, Mr. Sam. I know more about sex than you do. If you went just once a month, you could probably keep on going for years."

"Hell, no! You're talking to the wrong man. I've passed that point."

"Not the way you performed last night and this morning you haven't. Believe me, I know. I have a girl friend of mine who has a gentleman in his seventies who has a merry-go-round with her exactly once a month. Thirty days, you see, gives you time to recuperate. You could do it, too."

Sam tucked his shirt into his pants and pulled the buckle tight. He squinted at her thoughtfully. "You sound pretty confident."

"I am."

"Okay," he grinned, "let's give it a try. You give me your last name and telephone number and—"

She turned to face him, shaking her head. "To you I'm Ida and to me you're Sam. Let's leave it that way. You can always get in touch with me the way you did last night."

"I've heard that—ah—well—girls change pimps—"

She smiled with acid in her eyes. "Not this pimp," she said bitterly. "He's going to be around for a long while because, you see, the no-good bastard is my husband and I'm the one supporting him. He isn't about to take off. So you call him in a month from now and we'll give it a whirl again."

Sam hurried to finish dressing. He was embarrassed. The slight revelation of her true life was a pretty lousy way to wind up such a gorgeous night.

9

THEY had checked in together, so they left the motel together. When they were out on the sidewalk Sam asked Ida if she would have breakfast with him. She smiled and shook her head. "You've had what you paid for," she said. "Anything beyond this would be prolonging the agony." She was silent for a moment, then she put a hand on his arm and said, "Incidentally, I'm sorry what I said about my husband."

"Oh, it was okay."

"But it wasn't. I could tell by the expression in your eyes. Suddenly you saw what a whore's life was really like. I'm sorry I opened my mouth. Believe me, Mr. Sam, it won't happen again."

He grinned at her. "I believe you."

"Good. Then I'll be hearing from you?"

"That's a bet."

"One month from now?"

"On the nose. Be seeing you."

He doubted that he would ever get in touch with her again, yet subconsciously he knew that he would. He caught a taxicab going downtown and had breakfast in the St. Francis Hotel, facing Merritt-Wilson's across the square. He was a man who always had considerable vitality, but on this morning he felt better than he had in years. He grinned and thought, thanks to Ida.

After a good breakfast, Sam walked out to the middle of Union Square and settled himself on a bench to watch the mobs of pigeons. He looked about at the young girls hurrying toward their daily chores and was surprised to see Joe walking slowly in his direction—it was only eight thirty. Also, Joe was walking with his hands in his pockets and his head down. He seemed worried about something. With his looks, Sam thought, I should let anything worry me?

He called out. Joe spotted him, joined him on the bench, and asked, "What are you doing here?"

Sam laughed and replied, "I had a pretty big night last night. You wouldn't believe it."

"Try me."

"Oh, no. This is my secret. But maybe you can tell me something."

"Fire away."

"Okay." Then Sam asked earnestly, "Do you think a man my age really has any sex left in him?"

Joe blinked at him, then forgot his worries and burst out laughing. "Sam," he asked, "do you know my old man?"

"No, I don't think so.

"My father is your age, at least, or maybe even a few years older. But do you know something, Sam? He has more juice in him today than any young punk I know half his age."

Sam's eyebrows went up. "Really?"

"That's right. You should see the dolls he squires around and, believe me, it isn't just for show. They hit the hay with him when the night is over with, or else."

Sam started chuckling. "I'll be damned. But you're talking about a unique man."

Joe's expression sobered and he shook his head. "No, I don't think so. But there are two things that are unique about him. He has absolutely no inhibitions, and I've never known him to worry for more than five minutes at a stretch." He looked into Sam's eyes and he was grinning. "So you had a time for yourself last night, and you didn't think it was in you. Isn't that about it?"

Sam laughed and slapped his knee. "You hit the nail right on the head. Of course, she was a whore."

"Of course."

"Why do you say that?"

"Because it would take a whore to have the necessary patience with a man as repressed as you."

"You're quite a psychiatrist."

"On one subject only. And even on that I'm not so sure of myself any more."

Sam looked at Joe curiously. "I've often wondered about that, your family life, I mean, and your second life outside. Maybe you take after your father? Maybe you should have been a bachelor?"

Joe shrugged. "I have never figured out the answer to that question and I've really tried. How I've tried! In my home, Sam, with my family, I am strictly a fireside-and-slipper guy. On weekends, for example, whatever my family wants is what I want, too. I am a family man all the way, believe it or not, and the most contented guy in the world." He paused and thought for a moment. When he resumed, he was talking more to himself than to Sam. "On the outside, though, I am an entirely different person. I see a good-looking woman, and I wonder immediately what she would be like in bed. My second thought is how do I get into that bed. You see what I mean? No thought for my wife or kids. They never enter my mind. All I think about at that moment is the challenge. Other men start worrying about possible complications. Not me. All I worry about is how to get that babe into some bed. That's it. The Irish are a queer race of people, that's for sure, but I still can't blame it on my Irish blood. The Irish are probably the worst cheats in the world, if they have a chance, but I go far beyond that. No, that isn't it."

"Have you ever had any idea—?"

"Just dimly. Any psychiatrist will tell you that there is such an animal as the rogue male. That's me, all the way, and I know it. It's like being a CPI. You know what that is?"

Sam shook his head. "No."

"Congenital psychopathic inferior. That is a person who is born an inferior, where society is concerned, and nothing he or anyone else does will change him. The field of medicine is acknowledging now that such people do exist, and they are not uncommon. That's me, a rogue male." He paused thoughtfully, then said, "But why is it that if I am like that—why in God's name do I love my family so much?"

Sam was embarrassed for the second time that morning. A door had opened slightly on a man's soul, and he had to look away.

He said heartily, "Well, it's been an interesting talk, Joe. Now shall we wend our way to the salt mines?"

As they approached the front of the Merritt-Wilson building Sam said, "Well, here we are again, the woman's womb."

Joe looked at him sharply. "The what?"

"The woman's womb. Haven't you ever noticed, Joe, how soft the constant chimes inside a department store are and how very quietly the bells ring on desks and in the elevators? And haven't you ever noticed how softly everyone speaks? Never raise your voice, my boy. Never. Because then we shall disturb the foetus, and the foetus, of course, is the customer. And haven't you ever noticed how soft the atmosphere is and how even the temperature, and that there is even a sort of liquid feeling in the air?"

Joe snorted, "I'll be damned. You really got it figured out, haven't you?"

"Let's just say I don't like to kid myself."

They went through the main doors of the store and Sam was instantly collared by Fred Maloney. Joe went on to the elevators by himself.

He was deeply worried. He knew Mary and he knew her temper. Only God knew what she would do if she really blew her stack. Joe was counting heavily on her religion. Yet he knew that he could not rely on that entirely. He remembered two different occasions when she had blown up with him and had used a string of four letter words that would have turned a Marine sergeant green with envy. He remembered another time at a cocktail and swimming party when she had caught him with a little doll in his arms. She had proceeded to do a little necking on her own, until he had forcibly dragged her away. When Mary's temper took over she lost total control of herself. It was something to worry about.

There was also something new to worry about. When he had gone home for dinner the night before, Mary had not been there. Mrs. M. had told him that she had gone out about an hour before all dressed up. That was all she knew. Joe sat up until midnight, and still she had not come home. He went to bed finally, in the guest room, and fell asleep without hearing her come in. She was not down for breakfast in the morning. He was afraid to ask Mrs. M. whether or not Mary was at home. He left the house to go to work without knowing.

He wondered where she was at that moment.

Mary was lying on a bed in a downtown hotel room, not far from Merritt-Wilson's. Her cheeks were on fire and burning with shame. Her lips were pressed so tightly together that they were white. The knuckles of her fists were shoved deeply into the sockets of her eyes, as if she wanted to blind herself. She actually had been thinking of suicide.

Oh, God, she thought, dear God, how did it ever get started?

She thought back to the day before, and it was all too easy to remember.

Mary got out of bed after she heard Joe leave for work. Then she went into the bathroom and leaned close to look into a mirror. She backed away and dropped her nightgown to the floor—she would never sleep *au naturel*, as Joe always wanted—then looked into the big mirror, critically.

Her body had the soft creamy skin that some Irishwomen, if they are lucky, are born with. Her legs were slim and attractive, her waist was narrow, even after the three boys, her hips were pear-shaped, and her breasts still looked as firm as ever. She shook her head and watched the thick black hair dance about her bare shoulders. She looked down at the thick black V of love and almost blushed as she looked away. I still have it, she thought, or most of it, anyway. Then why, she almost screamed out loud, does he cheat on me?

She was ninety-nine and nine-tenths percent positive that he had done so. She would never forget the voice of The Man who had talked to her. He had been so positive, so reasonable, and so convincing, yet without ever raising his voice above a whisper.

She could understand Joe's objections, that it could be a crank or someone who hated him. With his looks, there were probably many people who hated him. Yet she knew it was not so. It was all too pat, too perfect. And the voice of The Man was too compelling to be denied. She knew intuitively that every word he had said was true. She had, in fact, unconsciously been dreading the day she would hear something similar from someone. She would have to be blind to deny Joe's beauty, his vitality, his overpowering maleness and the magnetic attraction he exerted toward most women. She would also have to be pretty stupid to overlook the occasional caustic and waspish hints dropped laughingly by other women. So she had lived with it, but she had lived with it far, far in the back of her mind. Now it was out in the open.

She wanted to cry again, but it was impossible. She turned on the taps in the tub and after awhile immersed her body in lukewarm water, which she gradually heated until it made her skin quite pink. She stayed there for half an hour, soaking herself, her mind going around and around. She was not concerning herself, however, with Joe's guilt or innocence. That had already been established. What she was concerned about was her own reaction.

What shall I do? That was the big question.

When she had toweled herself, she dressed in loafers, tight fitting slacks and a loose sweater. She combed her hair, then walked into the bedroom. She heard sounds below. Mrs. M. was taking the boys somewhere in the station wagon. Thank God for Mrs. M. She always knew what to do in a crisis.

She went downstairs and had some toast and marmalade and coffee and stared out the window at the high fog. Then she remembered the promise she had made to Joe that she would have his activities of last Thursday night tracked down. She got out the telephone book and looked up private investigators in the yellow pages. There were dozens upon dozens. She looked at the boxes and found one that seemed to fit her problem:

PHILLIPS, PHIL C.
Domestic matters
Twenty-four hour service.

She dialed the number, talked to a secretary for a moment, then was talking to Mr. Phillips. He asked her to drop by his office at her convenience. Mary wanted action right now. She told him with some asperity that if he was not by her house within the hour she would call someone else.

Mr. Phillips rang the doorbell about an hour and a half later, just as she was about to call another investigator. She led him into the living room and closed the door, in case Mrs. M. returned. Mr. Phillips was rather short and squat, with a potbelly, a sloppy way of wearing clothes, small eyes, and the expression of a church deacon. The beauty of Mr. Phillips, however, was that he could pass for a nonentity in any crowd anywhere.

He blinked at her and said one simple word, "So?"

Mary had a hard time beginning. She was not used to talking over problems with anyone, even close friends. She was that rare woman who kept her problems to herself and talked them over with her husband only—and even then not too often. But eventually she relaxed somewhat and began talking. She told him, haltingly, of what had occurred and what she wanted done. Finally, after much judicious questioning, he had the whole story.

He took a pad of paper from his pocket and made notes, then tilted his head on one side and squinted at her. "What you want," he said, "is for me to find out exactly where he was last Thursday night, and who he was with. Right?"

"Yes, sir."

"You have already called the Drawing Room and the Annex?"

"Yes. They said that he was there, but that he was alone."

"But he could have run into some babe later. Huh?"

"Yes."

"And her name?"

"Marilyn. But that's all I know about her."

"Okay, Mrs. Haley. I'll tell you the truth right now, because I want no misunderstanding. I'm no miracle man. I get results only through hard, plugging work. But if I get any break at all, I do get results. Now, you give me one picture of your husband, but I'm in this business a long time and I know guys like that better than you, meaning no offense, of course. You see him one way. I see him another. The way I see a man like that, the minute he picks up a doll he stays away from the places where he's known and hits the off-beat spots, maybe even out of town. I've seen too many of 'em not to know. So we got three directions he could travel, either east over to Oakland, or north across the Gate to Marin County, or south down the Peninsula. Either way, he wouldn't go very far, so that narrows it a little bit. I give myself a week."

She looked at him blankly. "A week?"

He smiled at her thinly, rather amused. "Yes, ma'am. I'm not interested in milking you for everything I can get. I like satisfied customers. So I'm being truthful with you. If I don't turn up anything in a week I quit. I might walk out of here and just by luck have the answer for you tomorrow. Or I might put in a year and never learn a thing. Like I said before, luck plays a big part. So I'll give it a week and we'll see what happens. Okay?"

"Well, I—yes, I guess so."

He got to his feet and looked at her sharply. He asked, "You believe everything this man told you over the telephone?"

She replied heatedly, "Of course."

"Hmmmmm. I'm just wondering, is all. It's peculiar."

"Why?"

"I'd say that man knows either you or your husband, or both."

"I have certainly never heard his voice before."

"Well, okay, but people aren't usually that vindictive unless they know you. Give it a thought, Mrs. Haley." Then he looked at her. "You want me on the job?"

"Naturally."

"Good. Then get me some pictures of your husband and let's get a little more detail about him. I can use everything you got."

He left about an hour later, and it was almost noontime. Mary paced back and forth in the kitchen, turning hundreds of questions over in her mind. Because she had no one to talk with, or no one to argue with, her brain began boiling in upon itself. She argued with herself. She went through whole dialogues between herself and Joe and each time she emerged the victor and each time he was blacker in her eyes.

He hadn't just cheated on her. He had fouled his nest and ruined the good names of his sons. Mrs. M. was the keeper of a brothel. The boys were bastards whom Joe hated. And she, Mary, his wife—he had made her out to be almost a whore. She stood in the kitchen and started screaming.

It was a moment or so before she heard the telephone ringing. She looked at the clock on the kitchen wall and saw that it was a few minutes after four. Good Lord, where had all the time gone? She was hardly conscious that she had stopped screaming.

Mary picked up the kitchen telephone and said, "Yes? Mrs. Haley here."

A man's voice said, "Hiya, doll-face."

"Hmmmmm?"

"Hiya, baby. Don't you recognize your old lover, Ernie Bates?"

"Oh. Hello, Ernie. Joe isn't home yet."

"I know. Look, here's what I'm calling about. The boys are still on vacation. Okay. So I got a few days off and I got thinking. Why don't I come by in the morning and pick up you and the kids and take you down to Carmel for the day? The boys would love that. How does it sound to you?"

A moment before she had been screaming hysterically, but now a smile twisted her lips. Poor Ernie. He was so obvious. He liked the children, no doubt of that, but that was not what he really wanted. All he wanted was to be near Mary. He would use any excuse just to be around her. She remembered one time when he had tried to kiss her, he had been high, and she had allowed it. There was no harm in it, after all, and it did afford him so much pleasure. Even Joe got a big kick out of Ernie. He had told her more than once, "That guy idolizes you like a saint. Thank God I don't have to worry about him." But maybe, she thought suddenly, you do have to worry about him, you two-timing bastard.

Her eyes narrowed dangerously and she caught her breath, then she exhaled slowly and said, "I have a better idea than that, Ernie. Mrs. M. has taken the children away for the day, and Joe isn't coming home tonight," she lied. "So that leaves me all alone and, frankly, I'm lonesome. So, if you aren't doing anything special, why don't we go out and have dinner together tonight? Would you mind that terribly?"

Ernie was silent for a moment, the silence of shocked surprise. Then he said, "Well—I—I—you see—cripes, I hadn't thought—" Then his voice vibrated with sudden and unalloyed pleasure. "You mean just the two of us?"

"Of course, if you care to bring someone else along—"

"No, no. That isn't what I meant. Jees. Just the two of us? Well, Mary, of course. I'd love having dinner with you. You just name the place."

She thought a moment. Mrs. M. would probably bring the boys home just before dinner time, about the time Joe would be getting home. It would be better to get away from the house before she ran into any of them. So she told Ernie, "I'll leave the house about five thirty."

"Hey, wait a minute. I'll pick you up."

"No, I'd rather not. Please. I'll take a cab and meet you in the lobby of the Fairmont between five thirty and six. Would that be convenient?"

He almost shouted, "Convenient? I'll be there with bells on."

Why, she wondered, does he always have to be so corny? But she said, "Very good, Ernie. Then I shall be seeing you at the Fairmont. Good-bye."

She hung up and thought, Now, all I have to do is not think. Concentrate on Joe and what he did and nothing else. And above all else, dear God, don't think about the boys.

She went to her bedroom, searched the closets and found what

124

she wanted. She was feeling like a *femme fatale,* so selected a seductive black dress with a plunging neckline that had even made Joe blink. In fact, he had told her, "Don't wear that again, baby. The boys will think I'm out with a strange woman." So now she put it on again, only this time she did not wear a brassiere under it. She wore her highest spike heels and sheerest lace hose and the most expensive perfume and her most valuable jewelry. Since it was still a foggy day, she draped a mink stole over her shoulders. Then she perched a tiny mink hat on the back of her head and was ready to go.

She left in a taxi just as Mrs. M. returned home with the boys. She saw Mrs. M. turn around and stare after her. But, after all, what was the difference?

She met Ernie in the lobby of the Fairmont. He kissed her cheek and beamed at her. His shoes were shining, his brown hair was shining and plastered with some mixture or other, and he was wearing a newly pressed suit of charcoal gray. Ernie was about six feet tall. He had a good, thin, whiplike body, square shoulders, and a round head settled firmly on a rather thick neck. Ernie was an amateur athlete. He kept himself in such good condition that his skin was always glowing a slight pink. He had good blue eyes and straight brows, a fine nose, and a rounded chin that looked strong and dominant, yet there was something weak about his mouth. The lower lip was a bit pendulous and moist and almost pouting. His mouth simply did not fit in with the rest of his features, yet it did indicate his character.

Ernie had been raised by a very wealthy, doting mother. Yet, regardless of his background, Ernie never ceased being the Babbitt of his crowd. At thirty-five years of age, he was all through, and he knew it. He sometimes cried himself to sleep at night.

He was absolutely flabbergasted that he was to have Mary all to himself for a whole evening. It had never happened before, or anything even remotely approaching it. He had met Joe and Mary at the cocktail party of a mutual friend. Joe, for some reason or other, had taken a liking to him and had invited Ernie to his home. On the third visit, Ernie had fallen completely and irrevocably in love with Mary. And after awhile it became obvious to everyone, including Joe and Mary. Yet he was always such a gentleman that no one could take offense, including Joe and Mary. His love for Mary became one of the skeletons in the family closet that she and Joe could giggle about late at night. Who, after all, could ever take Ernie seriously?

Mary was taking him seriously on this occasion. Her Irish temper was boiling wildly within her and taking her over completely. She looked him up and down and liked what she saw and linked her arm in his and whispered, "Let's go to the Crown Room first. I could use a few cocktails."

Ernie was almost overcome. But he took her to the cocktail room at the very peak of the building. It was a beautiful room with tremendous windows overlooking most of downtown San Francisco and the water surrounding it. Ernie blinked when Mary ordered a double gimlet. He decided to be reckless, too, and ordered a double bourbon.

They had their drinks and chatted about mutual friends and acquaintances and Mary made sure that her mink stole was draped coveringly over her bosom. They had more drinks. And they had more drinks.

It was dark when they left the Crown Room. When he asked where she would like to go for dinner she named Ernie's without hesitating. She wanted to be seen, though Ernie did not realize that. He thought she was merely interested in good food. They went to Ernie's on upper Montgomery Street and had a few more drinks at the bar before their table was ready. Ernie's was known for its excellent cuisine, as well as the modernized Victorian atmosphere and decor.

When they were seated at their table on the main floor beyond the bar, Ernie laughed and said, "I own this place, you know. It was named after me."

She blinked at him and said with surprise, "That's right. I hadn't thought of that. The name is the same." Then she laughed, too, and said, "You must be a very good cook."

"Hell, I can't even cook eggs. But what would you like to have?"

She wanted a medallion steak, and Ernie ordered frogs' legs. They talked lightly of matters of little consequence as they went through soup and salad. It was not until Mary was having her steak that she suddenly leaned back, removed the mink stole and placed it over the back of her chair. Then she leaned forward, rather far, to cut her steak. Suddenly Ernie's smile froze and his eyes popped. He could hardly believe what he was seeing. The V of Mary's dress bared a considerable amount of creamy flesh. Her unobstructed breasts were also better than half exposed. and as she cut her meat, because of the physical play involving her right arm, the reddish-brown nipple of her right breast

126

occasionally stole into view. Ernie stared and was incapable of movement or speech. Never had he ever seen anything like this. He picked up a frog's leg and nibbled at it but was not really conscious of eating at all. And Mary, of course, knew exactly how he was reacting.

When they left the restaurant Mary again draped the stole over her shoulders, but she no longer used it to cover her bosom. As the taxi pulled away from the curb she turned suddenly to say something to Ernie and her whole left breast was exposed in all its white, globular purity. She reached up casually and pulled a bit of cloth over the nipple. Ernie swallowed—hard. She smiled at him, but the lights dancing in her eyes, if he had only known it, were almost maniacal.

By now, it was almost ten o'clock. Ernie thought they should have some after-dinner brandies, but Mary remembered a place that Joe had mentioned more than once and said, "How about Irish coffee at the Buena Vista?" Ernie agreed with her. They went to the bar and eating place on Bay Street, which had once been a short-order counter until a small coterie of movie people found it and made it famous.

While they were sipping their Irish coffee, the man at Mary's left said to the bartender, "I hear you had a beauty of a fight outside last week."

The bartender leaned his elbows on the counter and grinned and replied, "Yeah. The guy who came off top dog you'd never believe."

"Why not?"

"Well, let's just say he was a beautiful-looking man. You know the kind I mean, like a movie star? I'm telling you, man, if I looked like him I'd have every good-looking doll in the city. But you wouldn't expect a guy that good looking would know how to handle his dukes."

"This boy did?"

"And how! And the guy he clobbered was even bigger, a beatnik type. I didn't see the beginning of the action, but I figured pretty boy started to move in on the beatnik's doll, who was a gorgeous young babe. So him and the beatnik tangled out on the sidewalk. I watched it all through the windows. Pretty boy just cut this other guy to pieces."

"Did you know the gal?"

The bartender shook his head. "I heard the beatnik call her Marilyn, but she's a stranger to me. Anyway, this pretty boy has lots of brains, too. As soon as he creamed the other guy, he grabs the blonde by the arm and hustles her around the corner and into his Thunderbird, and he roars away peeling rubber all the way. That's smart thinking."

"Ever seen him before?"

"Oh, yeah, plenty times. He's been in. And this ain't the first time he's walked out with the best-looking doll in the joint. Can't say I know him, though. One time I heard someone call him Joe and that's about it."

He moved away to serve another customer.

Mary's back was as rigid as a yardstick. She was remembering what Phil Phillips had told her, "That could be the easiest character in the world to track down, or the toughest. Frankly, it all depends on luck." And she had all the luck. Her temper had been boiling before, but now it was steaming. She turned and squeezed Ernie's knee, and he stared at her with his mouth open.

She leaned against him and whispered, "Let's get out of here."

He walked out with her—in a daze.

Mary took control of the situation from that moment on. When they got a taxi she told the driver where to go, a rather modest hotel on Geary Street about a block and a half away from the St. Francis. One of Mary's friends had once stopped there and she remembered it. When they walked up to the desk it was also Mary who signed Mr. and Mrs. Tom Jones. She told the clerk sweetly that they had just arrived from Chicago by plane and that there had been some mix-up concerning their baggage. The clerk looked into her eyes and believed her. He gave her the key and she handed it to Ernie and they went up to the fourth floor and into their room. Mary closed the door solidly after her and turned the night latch. Then she flicked on the light switch and looked at Ernie.

He was simply blinking at her, his mouth half open. Ernie was not too bright, but he was also no idiot. It was pretty obvious to him that everything that was happening this evening had been planned by Mary beforehand. At no time had he thought that he would ever really be close to Mary. And now here she was staring into his eyes in a strange hotel room and there was definitely only one thing she could possibly have in mind.

He blinked at her and swallowed hot saliva in his throat. He watched her take the mink from her shoulders and throw it over a chair, followed by the little hat, then saw her kick off her shoes, still with her eyes fixed on his.

"Ernie," she said, slowly and distinctly, "you and I are going to bed together and we are going to make love. Take off your clothes."

"But—but—"

"Take off your clothes."

"Well—yes—"

He started getting undressed, but his eyes never left Mary. His brain kept telling him he was dreaming, and what he saw was not really happening at all. She stood there looking at him until he was down to his underwear, then she undid some hooks below her shoulders and the dress fell to her hips and in a moment she had stepped out of it and draped it over a chair. Ernie almost choked. As he had surmised before, at the dinner table, she had been wearing nothing under the dress. All she had on now was a lacy black garter belt at her waist and the black hose. She blinked at him and unsnapped the garter belt and peeled off the hose and threw them all aside.

She stood before him as naked as the day she was born and threw her arms wide and told him crazily, "Love me, Ernie." Then she moved toward the bed, but still he did not perceive the wild light burning in her eyes.

He pulled off his underwear and turned off the lights and joined her on the bed and was instantly in her arms. But the moment he started making love to her her mind reeled, and she had to think of something else—of Joe and of how it had been the first week they were married, and she continued thinking of Joe and her mind flipped and it was Joe making love to her. Then she managed to respond, and Ernie was sure that he had found heaven at last.

Ernie was more virile on this night than he had ever been before in his life. At three in the morning, however, Mary was no longer able to concentrate on Joe. Her temper began to cool and slowly she came back to reality. She knew suddenly what was being done to her and what she was doing to herself.

Suddenly her temper flared wildly again and she turned on Ernie and clawed at his face, four of her fingernails raking his cheek badly. "You beast," she cried. "You fiend! What, in God's name, are you doing to me?"

She clawed and raked at his bare chest, and though he struggled with her, he could not contain her arms. He became alarmed and frightened, and simply as a matter of self-protection slapped her with a hard left and right. All the fight went out of her and she collapsed to the bed, sobbing wildly.

Ernie jumped out to the floor and stared at her white body in the dark room, and was more frightened than he had ever been. I should have known, he thought, she's lost her mind. He could think of only one thing to do and that was to get away. He grabbed his clothes, dressed as quickly as he could, and almost flew out of the room.

Mary was crying so wildly that she had not even known he had left. She cried out, "Get out of here, you bastard. Get out or I'll kill you." Then she jumped up and ran into the bathroom and slammed the door so hard she cracked the mirror. But when she opened it later on, the bedroom was empty. She threw herself onto the bed and started sobbing, although no tears would come. She was cried out.

She forgot about Joe and thought of how she had humiliated herself; and it was then that she thought about suicide. She ran to the bathroom for a razor blade with which to slash her wrists. There were no blades. She thought about sleeping pills, but had none. Then she went to the window and looked down and thought of jumping. She was three floors above the street. It might work, but it might not. She could easily wind up not being dead—just a cripple. She shuddered and turned away from the window. There was no certain, sure way she could do it. She threw herself back on the bed and sobbing dryly thought about what a fool she had been. At last she fell asleep.

It was worse in the morning. When she awakened at a little after nine she lay in the bed and stared at the ceiling and thought about what an idiot she had been. She thought of her religion and of Joe and the boys and she wanted to destroy herself. She could never face any of them again. Above all, she could never face her God.

Finally she got dressed and went downstairs and paid the bill, pulled the mink stole about her shoulders and went out on the sidewalk to flag down a taxicab. Now she was thinking of the boys and of Mrs. M. and of her home. She was no longer thinking of suicide. All in the world that she wanted at this moment was to get home.

It was then that she ran into Sam Kuller, walking away from Union Square. He paused and shook hands and beamed at her. "Mary," he said, "how delightful. I was just talking to Joe, only this morning."

"Oh? It's nice to see you, Mr. Kuller."

He looked at the dress she was wearing and frowned and doubted that she had anything under it. What the hell was this? he thought. Were the two Haleys the same breed of cat?

A taxi came and she clambered aboard and waved at him. He called after her, "Be seeing you, I hope." He watched her drive away and thought about what a lucky guy was Haley. But then he wondered again about her dress and that she seemed to be wearing nothing under it and walked away with a puzzled frown.

10

SAM continued on down Geary Street until he came to the small, third-rate hotel called the Moby Dick. He went through the doors and turned into the lobby. Seated on one of the sofas was a tall young man who looked discerningly at Sam, tossed his newspaper aside and got up to approach Sam with his hand held out.

He smiled and asked, "Mr. Kuller?"

"That's right. Are you really John Garfield?"

Garfield's smile broadened. "There are three of us, Mr. Kuller, three brothers; Harry, Daryl, and I. We run Garfield's today. Are you perhaps surprised by my youth?"

"No, not necessarily. It's just pretty surprising to meet one of the fabulous Garfields, that's all. When you telephoned me a little while ago I thought someone was pulling my leg. But I had to find out."

"Glad you did. Let's sit down and talk a little."

As they moved toward the sofa Sam looked Garfield up and down. He was perhaps in his mid-thirties, tall and rather thin, and dressed by the most expensive tailors in New York. His face was thin with high cheekbones, his brown hair was thinning, and his eyes were narrow, sharp, and penetrating, yet they had the saving grace of humor. Sam rather liked him, even though he was supposed to be The Enemy.

They sat on the leather sofa and Garfield asked pleasantly, "You didn't tell anyone I had called, as I asked you not to?"

Sam had to laugh. "No," he said, "I didn't, but not because you asked. I didn't really believe it was you who had called me and I do hate to make a sucker out of myself."

Garfield laughed with him. "I see. Well, Mr. Kuller, I have gone to some effort to meet you. I flew in from New York last night and checked into this flea-bag under an assumed name. As soon as I am through talking to you I will be flying right out again. I don't wish to have anyone know I am in town, especially Mr. Kane or Mrs. Merritt.

"As you know, Mr. Kuller, Garfield's has over three hundred stores scattered all over the nation. We're big, mighty big. Your outfit of M. and W. is very small fry on our books. Yet we wanted a prestige name. Kane, however, beat us out, and I'm still damned if I know how he did it. So now Wilson's is in with Merritt's. So much the better. We could take over both."

Sam shook his head. "You don't stand a prayer. I've gotten to know Kane lately. That man's riding a rocket, and he knows exactly where it is going."

Garfield smothered a smile. "I admit," he said, "that your Mr. Kane is quite an operator. We admire him. But he is in our way, and when you get in the way of a steamroller, Mr. Kuller, you usually get crushed. I wouldn't gamble very heavily on Mr. Kane's life expectancy in this business."

Sam frowned and squinted off into space. He had become quite fond of Kane and was hoping he would make good. But it was true what the other man had said. Kane was just so much macadam for Garfield's steamroller.

But he said stubbornly, "I don't know. You can't discount Kane."

"I am not trying to. As I said before, he has a lot on the ball. Unfortunately for him, it isn't enough. Now, let's get down to cases. We have had you people examined pretty thoroughly. Under Kane, of course, we have come up with four top names; yours, Mrs. Bennett, Mr. Harrison, and Mr. Drury. You are the four people who count. Jack Harrison can't go any higher because he is too old, so he is out of the picture. Mrs. Bennett can't go any higher because she is a woman, so she also is out of the picture. Drury can't go any higher because he is strictly a controller. If he tried to run the business it would go smash." He looked sideways at Sam and said, "That leaves just you."

"I see." Sam looked at him and wondered, What's coming up, a bribe? So he said, "Before you offer me a bribe, Mr. Garfield, the answer is No. I wouldn't leave San Francisco to be president of Garfield's. My children are here and my grandchildren and my roots. This is where I expect to die."

Garfield smiled at him, a smile as cold as snow. "That wasn't what I had in mind," he said. "Suppose we managed to take over the M. and W. chain. That would mean that we would have an auxiliary chain of twenty stores. It would also mean that we would have to set up a vice-president to run that auxiliary chain. In other words, the man would have to step into Mr. Kane's shoes, but with the fabulous backing of Garfield's behind him. You do see what I'm driving at?"

Sam snorted, "You don't have to draw pictures."

Garfield added, almost casually, "The salary would be one hundred thousand a year."

Sam swallowed hard. Cripes, he thought, these big outfits really went all the way. But he sat back and thought it over. He had been in business long enough, all of his life, to know that the first loyalty you owed was always to yourself. If you ever allowed that special loyalty to be superseded by something else, you went nowhere, because then everyone would use you. The Big Shot always talked about playing ball and being on the team and so on, but what he really meant was his team and his ball and his bat. He owed loyalty to no one.

"Your offer," he said, "is very tempting."

"It was designed to be so. We don't often pay that high for vice-presidents."

Sam said dryly, "I don't imagine. It is only when you want something badly enough that you are willing to pay for it."

"Precisely. So we see eye to eye, Mr. Kuller." Assuming that his offer had already been accepted, he continued, "You are on the inside. That is exactly what we need. We can't figure out just how this Merritt-Wilson deal was put together. It doesn't make sense. Our attorneys have gone over it again and again and come up with nothing. The glue that holds it together, in other words, is not visible to the naked eye. So we need someone on the inside who can find out for us just how the whole thing was manipulated. We think the big weakness lies somewhere behind the scenes. When we know exactly what it is, our attorneys and brokers can take over from there, and we will wind up owning Merritt-Wilson's. So," he smiled at Sam, "we need you."

Sam slapped his hands on his knees and got to his feet. "I'll think it over, of course."

Garfield said sharply, "We're paying awfully high for information."

"I realize that." He thought a moment, then chuckled and said, "Too bad Drury's out of the picture."

"Why do you say that?"

"Because he's the only one left who owns stock in the outfit."

Garfield lied as he said slowly, "Of course, we know that."

"I figured you would. There's no great secret about it. Harold owned twenty-two or twenty-three percent or something like that of the old Merritt's stock, and he refused to sell to Kane. So when the big take-over arrived they had to give him twenty percent of the stock of the whole chain. Frankly, I doubt if Kane has much more than that himself."

Garfield said smoothly, "He took over Mrs. Merritt's stock."

Sam laughed and said, "Hell's bells, he doesn't own that. She just gave him an option to vote it for the next five years, that's all. All he owns in the old Merritt's stock is what he managed to pick up on the side."

Garfield closed his eyes and thought, Holy Mary, Mother of God, what suckers these westerners are. Sam had already given him all the information he needed gratis. Now he had enough to wreck the whole damned waterworks. He opened his eyes and smiled at Sam.

"You'll think over my offer?"

"Of course. I'm no idiot."

That, Garfield thought, could be questioned, but he shook hands and said, "Very good. I shall look forward to hearing from you."

It was then that Sam threw him for a loop and forced him to revise all of his estimates of westerners. Sam looked him in the eyes and said coldly, "I didn't say I had accepted your offer, Mr. Garfield. I just said I would think about it. I never cut another man's throat, Mr. Garfield, until he sees the knife in my hand. If and when that deed is done, of course, I shall consider your offer. Good day to you, sir."

Sam walked away leaving him in a state of shock. But then Garfield began to smile. He had all the information he wanted, anyway. Already he was thinking of firing the attorneys who had not learned about it.

Sam walked slowly back to the store, bemused, bewildered, and bedamned. A man like Garfield, he knew, was a man of his word, when it suited his convenience and when it made business sense. He would back up his offer, all right, of that Sam was sure. For one year. He would pay Sam one hundred thousand dollars for one year, then he would drop him like a sack of hot potatoes. What the hell! Kane was the best bet. He might even survive the steamroller. And no matter how you looked at the arithmetic involved, sixty thousand a year for the rest of his life was better than a hundred grand for a year or two at the most.

But then he thought back over the conversation with Garfield and realized it had been extremely brief. Why? Because of something that he, Sam Kuller, had said?

He was walking back through Union Square when he finally came up with the answer. It was well known amongst the executives of the chain that Lew Kane owned very little stock of his own, that what he had received from Anna Merritt was voting stock only for a certain period of years, and that Harold Drury still owned twenty percent of the works. But was it known outside of that limited circle? Sam realized suddenly that it was not and that he had innocently given Garfield the very information that he needed. Jee-zuss, he thought, what a dope! How stupid could a man get?

When he got back to the store he went directly into Kane's office. He closed the door and locked it, at which Kane raised his eyebrows, and dropped into a chair opposite the president of the firm. Leaning his elbows on the desk he cupped his chin in his knuckles and looked into Kane's eyes.

"You and I," he said, "got a little something to talk about. Prepare yourself for a shock."

He told Kane about his meeting with Garfield. He spared nothing, including the fact that he had been tempted. He then told Kane about his suspicions.

When he had finished, he said, "That's how it stands. The Garfields still mean to take over this outfit, and I seem to have given them ammunition. I felt sure he knew already about the stock. After all, it's common gossip around here. But then I realized that what was gossip with us could be a secret on the outside. I doubt very much, now, that he knew anything about it. Don't you?"

Kane nodded. "It's no secret, but not too many know it. I don't imagine that anyone back in New York knew it."

Kane sat back in his chair and placed his fingertips together and stared up at the ceiling. He was lost in thought for quite awhile. He was thinking it out exactly as he would think out a game of chess, a game at which he happened to be a master. So now the Garfields knew about his weakness—Harold Drury. No one could out-vote Lew Kane, he had voting control of eighty percent of the stock, so he was safe on that score, unless the bank turned against him, which was not likely. But conceivably the Garfields could buy out Drury and offer him a hell of a bonus for his stock. If that happened, it then followed that they could demand to be placed on the board of directors. Legally such a request could not be refused. And what would happen if a Garfield sat on the board? Plenty. He would be on the inside of every move the company made and would probably discover some way to move in even stronger. Having a Garfield on the board could be suicide for one Lew Kane.

But then he thought beyond that. Garfield's was one of the biggest department store chains in the nation, or in the whole world for that matter. The volume of business they did was astronomical. So how would the thinking go in New York if it were known that the Garfields had bought twenty percent of the stock of Merritt-Wilson? There was only one answer to that. Every wholesaler in the business could have only one thought, This is a very solid firm, indeed. If the Garfields buy in who am I to hold back?

In that respect, having the Garfields buy a small percentage of stock could be even more valuable than announcing the opening of five new stores. But how to keep from getting his own throat cut, meanwhile?

He leaned forward and asked, "The Garfields own the Westover Mills?"

Sam looked surprised. "Well, sure. It's the biggest wholesaler of men's suits in the nation."

"That's right. And the Garfields own Westover lock, stock, and barrel. But we don't handle those suits, do we?"

"Of course not. Westover supplies only to Garfield's."

"Yet they are wholesalers, and they could compete against the markets that supply us. Right?"

Kane was again leaning back in his chair, but now he was smiling. "Sam," he said, "you thought you screwed me this morning. I thought so, too, for a little while. But now I'm beginning to think maybe you did me a hell of a big favor. Yes, sir. A really big favor. Ask me to tell you about it some day."

Sam left the office shaking his head. Kane got up and paced the floor and thought over the checkmate he had in mind. He balanced knight against knight, bishop against bishop, castle against castle, and pawn against pawn, and moved his queen all over the board, and he could come up with but one answer. He had a checkmate solidly in the palm of his hand. There was no doubt about it.

He called his attorneys up to the office, however, to check with them what was in his mind. It did not take them long to run down the legal angles. They confirmed what he was thinking.

At four o'clock that afternoon he called Jackson into the office. He asked Jackson bluntly, "You got that Findex thing down?"

"A few more days."

"Suppose I asked you to take over Drury's office this minute, as of right now, could you do it?"

Jackson looked out the window for a few seconds, then shrugged and said, "I don't need him for Findex, and I don't need him for anything else. You can kiss him off, as far as I'm concerned. Is that all?"

"That's all, Max. Send Drury in to see me."

Kane was back of his desk when Drury came in. He dropped into his chair behind the desk and asked the other man to close the door, then waved him into a chair on the other side of the desk. They sat and looked at each other, quietly, with speculation.

Kane said at last, "You realize, Harold, that in this business it's strictly dog eat dog. The strong survive."

Drury nodded. "I've never known it to be any other way." He was thinking about his rise to eminence, so said, "I wouldn't have it any other way. If I can't take care of myself and the next guy, then to hell with the whole works."

"Yes, yes, of course. My sentiments exactly. However, there does come a time when a man has to do something he would rather not do. Yet it must be done, simply to strengthen the survival of all others concerned."

Drury was not smiling as easily as before. He looked at Kane and blinked. "I'm afraid I don't follow you."

"Well, Harold, it's this way." Kane had the courtesy to look away as he said, "Merritt-Wilson's is a new chain, a new idea, a new challenge. It is no longer Wilson's, and it is no longer Merritt's. What I am starting is an entirely new thing. So I am forced to balance out personnel to see who survives and who does not." God, he thought to himself distastefully, what corn, but he continued, "Some people I have brought with me and others of the old Merritt's chain also fit into the scheme of things. Others do not." He then had the courage to look Drury in the eyes as he said, "Unfortunately, Harold, and this is very hard for me to say, you do not fit into my planning. I thought it better to tell you now than drag it out. I'm sorry, but that's the way it is."

He sat back and waited quietly. For a moment Drury was frozen. After a lifetime in the business, he was given the boot. It was inconceivable. He was incapable of thinking coherently. His mind simply went around and around over the fact that he had been fired. He could not think beyond that.

It was a long time before he cleared his throat and said, "I hadn't been expecting this, Lew. It's quite a surprise."

"As I said before, I'm sorry. Naturally, I will accept your resignation."

Drury blinked at him sharply. That was the way Kane should have put it in the first place. Drury began to burn with anger, which was exactly what Kane wanted. He fired him and then said that he would take his resignation. Drury's anger increased and he exploded.

"Why, you two-bit mountebank," he sneered, "who the hell do you think you are, God? If the facts were only known, I sit in this firm a lot stronger than you do. I can have your hide for this."

Kane said piously, hating himself for it, "Please, Harold, I would rather we parted in a friendly manner."

"Oh, stuff that up your ass. You'll go down the drain just as sure as I'm sitting here. Cripes, man, don't you realize I can do it to you?"

Kane forced himself to look angry, when actually he was feeling elation. "There isn't a damned thing you can do," he snapped. "I vote eighty percent of this firm. You can't get around that."

"Don't worry, I'll be talking things over with the bankers."

"And you'll get nowhere. Better stop and think about it." He made his voice rise as he shouted, "And if you try to sell your stock to the Garfields I will—well—I'll find some way to pin your ears back, by God."

Drury stared at him as if he had lost his mind, then snickered, "The Garfields! You must be off your rocker. They bowed out when you took over. I can't imagine anyone less interested."

Kane was a very good actor. More than once he had thought he should have been in the profession. He suddenly assumed the expression of a guilty boy with his hand caught in the cookie jar. He stammered, with a great act of confusion, "Of course— what I meant—well— Naturally," he laughed hollowly, "the Garfields are no longer interested. I don't know what made me say that. Just forget it. Please?"

The telephone rang at that moment, for which Kane was truly grateful. He answered it, then placed his hand over the mouthpiece to tell Drury, "Come back at closing time, and we'll wind up the details. This is an important call, if you don't mind."

Actually, it was simply Fred Maloney calling to ask him a question of relatively little importance.

Drury sat there for a moment blinking at him. That remark about the Garfields, that had been a slip of the tongue. But what a stupid statement to make! Garfield's couldn't be interested any longer in Merritt-Wilson's. Or could they? Wait a minute, he thought, a great light suddenly dawning in his mind. Of course they could still be interested. If they bought his stock it would put them on the board of directors. And once they got on that board, who knew what damage they could do? He sucked in his breath sharply. Why hadn't he been smart enough to think of that before? He could probably sell his stock to them for at least fifty percent above its market value. Holy Mary, and Kane himself had put it right in his lap!

Drury got to his feet and nodded. "I'll be back at closing time."

Kane watched him leave the office and had difficulty hiding a smile. It was obvious to him that Drury had swallowed the bait hook, line, and sinker. He spoke into the telephone chuckling softly to himself.

Kane left the store rather late that day. He was feeling pleased with himself and pleased with the world and was equally pleased when he ran into Betty, also just leaving. He walked with her out to the sidewalk, then looked at his wristwatch.

"You're late," he said.

She sighed and nodded her head. "I know. I learned a big lesson today."

"What was that?"

"I found out why you're so quick to pay off a customer, even when you know she's lying to you."

"Oh?" He smiled and said, "Tell me about it."

"All right. This woman came in with a coat she'd bought

three months before in the Stonestown store. She said flatly that it had never been worn. She said also that it had been sold to her this spring as a winter coat. So I had her lying on two points already. It could never have been sold to her as a winter coat in the spring because we don't handle winter coats in the spring. And secondly, or firstly, it had been worn. You can always tell where a woman has been sitting in it. Then, too, when I held it up to the light I could see where she had tried to steam iron the lining. Other things, too. You know."

"Sure."

"You can't fool people in this business, but they try and try and try. On the other hand, you can't call a customer a liar, either. She said flatly it had never been worn, even though I pointed out to her the telltale signs. But she was adamant. So I said I would look into it and asked her to come back later. After she left, I called Pettibone, the Stonestown manager, and told him about it. He knew the whole story. She had tried to pass it back to him, but he had told her to take it downtown, which, incidentally, is a stinking thing for him to do. That means I have to take the credit on it."

Kane frowned. "He isn't supposed to do that. I'll have it looked into."

"Thanks. I don't try to pass my credits off on him. Anyway, this woman came back, and we went around and around again. I spent practically the whole afternoon with her. She had the gall to tell me that if the coat had been worn her roommates had sneaked it out of the closet when she wasn't looking. Oh, brother! So I turned her over to Marie. Finally, though, when she was back on my hands again I was about to give her full credit for the coat when I suddenly decided to look in the pockets. You know what I found?"

"No."

"A pass for the Republican convention at the Cow Palace, in her name." Betty laughed and said, "I handed her the pass and she just looked at it and picked up the coat and walked out of the store. There was nothing to be said. But do you know what that coat was worth?"

"No idea."

"Thirty-nine dollars and ninety-five cents. Maybe it cost you sixteen or seventeen dollars. So for that amount of money a good hundred dollars of the company's time was wasted."

Kane had to laugh. "You learned a good lesson."

"I know. Oh, I'll still give them an argument, I hate to see people get away with stuff like that, but I'll never let it go that far again."

"Good girl. Now, how about a ride home? I have the Rolls this evening."

"I'd love it. My feet are killing me."

"That, my dear, is the most common complaint in this business."

They walked down to the Ellis St. garage and the car was delivered almost instantly. The car was a Silver Dawn, four-door Rolls-Royce sedan, painted battleship-gray with dark brown leather upholstery. Kane was proud of the car. He had always thought that one day he would be a millionaire, yet he had never really thought of riding around in a Rolls-Royce.

As they headed out of the downtown section, he told her, "I know I should have a chauffeur for a car like this, but, damn it, I don't feel old enough to be sitting in solitary splendor in the back seat."

"And," she laughed, "you aren't. I'm glad you do your own driving. Chauffeurs are for old ladies."

They had nothing more to say until he came to Van Ness and turned down "automobile row" to head toward Lombard and the Marina district. Betty had been simply resting. But then she turned and looked at him. "How long," she asked, "have you known Mrs. Merritt?"

He kept his eyes straight ahead as he thought a moment, then replied slowly, "Oh, close to thirty years, I guess, or maybe a little less than that. I used to work for her husband, you know."

"I know. You told me that some time ago. Anyway, someone threw a slow curve at me today, and it just about bowled me off my feet. She and I are pretty close, you know, considering the difference in age."

"I know."

"I admire her very much and she seems to like me, unusually so. Makes it a little difficult at times."

He raised his eyebrows. "Oh?"

"Not that I mind, of course. But she does dictate to me at times almost as if she were my mother."

Kane pulled wide on passing another car and almost clipped a fender as he pulled back in again. He swallowed and asked, "Really?"

"Oh, yes. But, as I say, I like her so much I don't mind it. Yet something came up today that has me puzzled. She seems to delight on bringing up similarities between us, such as the fact that her hair was originally the same color as mine, our eyes are quite alike, we have the same bone structure, and so on. These things amuse her. But she has never mentioned the most obvious similarity of all, and by its very omission it staggers me."

"What is that, my dear?"

"My name," she said. "Parker. I just learned today that was also Mrs. Merritt's maiden name. Now, how do you like that?"

"Now you've thrown a curve at me. I have no idea why she wouldn't mention it to you."

"So you think it's strange, too."

He was thinking furiously as he replied, "In a way, yes. Yet it might have a very simple answer, after all." He paused a moment, then continued, "I might even know the answer, now that I think about it."

"You think so?"

"Yes. Anna always wanted children very badly, yet she went barren. Suddenly you came along, and you were exactly the daughter she has always dreamed about."

Betty nodded. "I've had that feeling at times."

"I have been quite sure of it. It has been obvious to me that she gives you all of her affection. As you say, there are so many similarities between the two of you. That is perhaps why she has never told you the greatest similarity of all."

"I don't follow you. Telling me her maiden name would seem to cement the bond between us."

Kane glanced at her briefly as he said, "Perhaps she doesn't want the bond cemented that closely?"

"Oh, oh. Now I see what you mean." She was silent a moment, then nodded and said, "You could be right. Not long after I was here, after we got to know each other well she mentioned, sort of half-jokingly, yet I think she meant it, that it might not be a bad idea if she adopted me."

Kane's hands were gripping the steering wheel so tightly that the knuckles were white. He had difficulty saying, "She did?"

"Oh, yes. Unfortunately, I reacted in the worst manner possible. I broke out laughing."

Kane groaned, "Oh, no."

"I'm afraid so. The idea that I, a full-grown woman, should need adopting by anybody was amusing, and it made me laugh. I apologized and explained what I meant, but she froze and just stared beyond me, and the subject has never been brought up again."

He turned on to Lombard Street, then asked, "Are you sorry?"

"If you're asking me if I'm sorry I laughed, the answer is yes. But if you're asking me if I'm sorry the subject has never been brought up again, the answer is no."

"How come? She is a tremendously wealthy woman. If she adopted you, you would come into her inheritance. Haven't you thought about that?"

Betty looked at him narrowly and said thinly, "Only to reject it, Mr. Kane. Maybe there is a perversion in my nature. If there is, I couldn't care less. But at this point in my life I do not wish anybody to give me anything just because they love me." She sucked in her breath sharply and said, "If you only knew what a great gift it is to me just to have their love—" Then she looked away and blinked her eyes.

He said softly, "In other words, you don't want them to pay for that love."

She nodded, but was not capable of saying anything at the moment. When they stopped in front of her apartment building, however, she turned about on the seat to face him and said, "I'd like to tell you something that has affected my life ever since it happened."

He switched off the ignition and nodded at her. "I'd like to hear it."

"You know my background. As you know, I was left with a French nursemaid when I was just a baby. To me, of course, she was my mother. And she lavished me with love and I thrived under it. She worked as a laundress during the occupation and kept the two of us alive. I think she also stole a great deal, wherever she could. Then, when I was six years old the war ended. I was old enough then to know that she was not my mother, a fact she never tried to hide, but to me she was everything that a mother should be. I was not old enough, of course, to know why she loved me so much. It was not me, naturally. It was the money."

"I don't understand."

"Oh, it took me years to finally piece it all together, but it did come whole circle. She was guarding what she thought was vast wealth. She figured that when peace came and she was able to get in touch with America and the proper authorities, the Parker estate would reward her with a tremendous sum of money.

But it was not easy to contact the right authorities, due to the confusion of the times. There were millions of displaced persons, in addition to one small child. After a year or so, though, she managed to get through to Goldsmith and Klein, the family attorneys. Mr. Klein finally arrived in Paris, and, I learned later, gave Yvette a check for two hundred dollars a month for all the years of my life she had taken care of me. Actually, the check was more than ample and did represent a small fortune to Yvette. But it was not what she had expected. From that moment on she hated me. I sensed it at first, and later I knew it. That was when I was transferred to another nursemaid and taken to Switzerland."

She was silent for a moment and Kane had nothing to say. Betty sighed, then said, "You can imagine what that would do to a small child. The one person in the world I loved hated me. Believe me, Mr. Kane, that was the end of the world." She drew in her breath, let it out slowly and said, "So, as I said before, no one can buy my love. I look all gift horses straight in the mouth. And when someone does love me, well—I can ask for nothing greater. It can't be balanced against any millions of dollars."

She was telling Bill Kane almost the same thing a few hours after talking with his father. They were dining at Sabella's, situated upstairs on a corner next to Fisherman's Wharf. Bill was dressed in a business suit, with a button-down collar and a conservative tie. Betty was wearing a flaming orange-red dress, tightly belted about her waist. Bill was sure that he had never seen anyone quite so beautiful. Betty rather felt that way herself.

They had enjoyed an excellent dinner of crab and shrimp salad, a meaty clam chowder, and a big Chiappino. That had been followed by rum pastries and slices of green apple with cheese. Now they were relaxing over coffee laced with rum, and Betty was doing most of the talking.

She was telling Bill, "It's all in the way I was raised, darling. I have a lot of the daring of the French, the caution of the Swiss, and the practicality of the German, as well as the economical brain of the American. It makes a queer mixture."

He laughed and said, "You ain't just whistling Dixie."

"I know. So, I do appreciate the fact that you have reserved a suite at the Mark, that you would like to go to bed with me, and that you would like to make love to me all night long. It

144

is even possible we might learn something about each other, as you suggest, though I doubt it."

He said earnestly, "I know we would."

She reached forward and placed her fingers lightly on his arm. "Bill," she said, "don't be such a child. Or, let's say, don't expect me to be such a child. What in God's name would we learn? That we both like sex? We can admit that now and get it over with."

"What do you know about sex? You've told me you're a virgin, and I'm damned if I don't believe it."

"Bill," she smiled, "have you ever been in China?"

"No."

"But you do know it exists, don't you?"

"Well, sure—"

"With me, the same is true about sex. I have not experienced it, except in a small way, but I do know it exists and I am quite sold on the idea that I am normal enough to love it when it does come along."

"On your terms."

"Exactly. With the proper ring on the proper finger. Not that I am hinting. You couldn't give me a ring right now for love or money. I don't know yet if I love you, and until I do I wouldn't even dream of marrying you, even if you wanted me." She added rather tensely, "I have to know, Bill.

"I could be wrong, of course, to prize virginity and love so highly, but no one has ever convinced me differently."

He mumbled in his coffee, "Now I feel a little ridiculous. I thought you felt the same way I do."

"Oh, but I do. My passion is the equal of yours any day. When I look at you I feel a small flame burning inside me, and it isn't easy to dampen it."

He looked at her hopefully. "You're not just kidding?"

"I never lie about such things. But there is a big difference between us. The end result in my mind is not the same as yours." She leaned back and ran her fingers through deep auburn-red hair and said thoughtfully, "People twist things around so much today. They seem to feel that a shared sexual experience, if it comes out right, is the surest indication that their marriage will have a happy start. I don't pretend to be an authority on psychology, but I do know better than that. Sex and love are not the same things at all. Anyone can have an extremely satisfactory

145

sexual experience, men do it with prostitutes, yet love doesn't have to enter the picture."

He leaned forward and looked intently into her eyes, as he said, "But you do have to admit that satisfactory sex is a necessary basis for love."

"Some of the greatest loves in the world," she laughed, "were never consummated physically. Sex is a biological function of the body. Love is of the heart and the head and the emotions." Then she met his eyes and said, "I do admit, though, that shared sex would naturally make for a deeper love and a better marriage. There is no doubt about it. What I take exception to is this everlasting desire to test sex before love itself has ever been put to the test."

He said bitterly, "You make me feel like a crumb."

She looked into his eyes and yellow lights were dancing in the green depths of her own wide eyes. "If I do," she said, "it isn't intentional. I would never do such a thing to you." Her expression sobered and the fires were banked in her eyes as she said, "You know as well as I do, Bill, that a virgin is never a sexually satisfactory partner for anyone."

He grinned at her and closed her two hands together on the table and wrapped his hands around them. His right eyebrow raised higher than the other and he said, "You know something? You're a kook. But I believe you."

She said softly, "Let's dance."

Once on the dance floor, she was in his arms and her head was resting in the crook of his shoulder. She could feel his long, lean, lithe body and the power of his muscles, and she shuddered a bit and wondered if perhaps she wasn't overly rationalizing things.

I I

WEDNESDAY was Betty's day off, in addition to Sunday, of course. She awakened a little after ten o'clock and yawned and stretched and got out of bed. She wore pajama tops only. She did not like anything binding her about the legs when she was in bed.

Thinking of what Mrs. Merritt had told her, Betty wandered

about the apartment and considered whether she should get a bigger place. She liked it where she was. She had a fair-sized living room, with a view down the street and out over a segment of the bay, a bedroom just as large, a decent kitchen and a dinette that could accommodate eight persons.

Whenever she had large dinner parties they sat on the floor and no one seemed to mind. She had a bullfight poster from Spain tacked on the bathroom door, bookshelves in the living room, filled with books, Chinese cooking equipment (a hobby of hers) in the kitchen, and personal photographs hung all over the walls of the dinette. The apartment was comfortable and she liked it. Why change? The hell with it.

She went into the kitchen and prepared breakfast. Betty had a good appetite and she liked good food well cooked. It was noontime when she had finished washing the dishes and cleaned up the kitchen and dinette.

She had a woman in once a week to clean house, so there was nothing really to do in the apartment. But she busied herself washing underwear and hosiery and hanging everything over the shower curtain railing. When the telephone rang she was wondering about Bill Kane. He had aroused her physically the night before more than any man she had met previously.

She walked to the telephone and answered it in her brief manner, "Parker here. Yes?"

It was Chet Baker, the new assistant manager of the store. "Hi," he said. "Wednesday is my day off, too."

"Oh?" she smiled. "I didn't know that."

"A happy coincidence, I think. What are you doing with yourself?"

She asked, "Why?" She was not about to give a direct answer. Obviously, he had called to make a date with her and she did not know whether or not she cared to go out with him.

"Well," he said, "it's such a nice day and I was just thinking— Remember me telling you I liked bicycle riding in the mornings?"

"Yes, I do."

"There is also nothing wrong with the afternoons. How does it sound to you? I can pick you up and we'll go riding through the park."

He waited and she thought furiously. Actually, it sounded like wonderful fun. She had not been on a bicycle in years. It would be a change. And, of course, if she did not care to pursue an off-hours relationship with Mr. Chet Baker, she knew precisely how to cut it off before it got very far.

"All right," she laughed. "Suppose you pick me up in an hour? That will give me time to dust off the minks."

He said happily, "Will do. Be seeing you."

When she opened the door to greet him, he took one look at her and gulped and blinked hard. My God, what she would do to the other men in the park! She was wearing ankle boots of soft leather, skin-tight stretch pants that made him wonder how she ever got into them, a wildly striped silk blouse that had been designed by one of the crazier Italians, a filmy scarf about her throat, and a beret with a tiny visor perched on one side of her auburn head. Vogue would applaud. But for everyday bicycling in Golden Gate Park? Jee-zuss!

The contrast with Chet Baker was almost laughable. He had on white tennis shoes, gray sweat pants, and a gray sweatshirt. He took his bicycling seriously, not just as a form of exercise, but also to keep down weight which was a bit of a problem for him. But he grinned and took her arm and helped her into his car, a powder-blue MG roadster with the top down. Two bicycles were strapped rather ingeniously on the back. They looked almost as big as the car. Betty settled in her bucket seat and looked ahead to a pleasant afternoon.

Chet left the car in front of the conservatory in Golden Gate Park and took the two bicycles off the back. Betty was awkward for a few moments and squealed with laughter, but in two minutes she was riding as well as Chet. During her years in Switzerland she had ridden a bicycle to school every day, and it was apparently something you never forgot. She pedaled along at his side, beaming proudly, and he chuckled and nodded and was as pleased as a young man could be, especially a man who had just discovered he was in love.

They cycled out the Main Drive and smelled the grass and the flowers and the shrubbery, and Betty was very happy. It was even more fun than she had thought it would be.

When they arrived at the beach Chet bought some small enchiladas on paper plates at the Hot House and they took them down to the sand to eat and watch the hard, angry surf pounding in from the vast reaches of the Pacific Ocean. Off to their right were the Seal Rocks below the Cliff House, but very little sea life seemed to be stirring except for circling, squawking birds.

148

They leaned back on their elbows and looked distantly out over the gray waters and Chet asked, "What are you thinking?"

"Well, I was just thinking what an exceedingly nice person you are. I had absolutely nothing to do today and here you come up with one of the most surprising afternoons I have ever put in. Most men, you know, would be impressing me by spending money, or something of that sort. You know how first dates usually go. But not you." She laughed and said, "We simply go riding on bicycles, and I can't think when I've had more fun."

He said huskily, "I'm glad. I was not, however, trying to impress you. I just thought that you might like something I enjoy."

"But that's what is so grand about it. I do enjoy it." She looked at him with her big green eyes very wide.

He lost himself in her eyes and had to look away. Lord, he thought, how did a woman ever get to be that beautiful? And what chance would he have with something like that? The answer was zero.

They drove slowly back through the park, this time on the South Drive. When they reached Stanyan, they reversed direction and found themselves at the MG. Chet strapped the bicycles on back and drove Betty back home.

When they stopped in front of her apartment he said, "It was really nice, Betty. Thanks for a wonderful day."

She looked at him and shook her head and had trouble hiding her laughter. "Mr. Chet Baker," she said, "you aren't escaping this easily. You go home and change clothes and come back and I will personally prepare you one of the damndest Chinese dinners you have ever eaten."

"Chinese? You learned this in Europe?"

"No. In Europe I learned continental cooking. But when I first arrived here and was going to UCLA my roommate was a Chinese girl. She taught me how to cook Canton style, and I've been learning a little more about it ever since." She frowned and asked, "You do like Chinese cooking?"

Chet broke into a broad grin. If she had said Mongolian he would have said he loved it. "You just get the chow mein and rice ready, that's all."

"Will do."

When Chet returned that evening, dressed in sports clothes, he found that Betty had changed to a Pucci original of yellow slacks and jacket, with wild lightning-like stripes of varying colors. She was, to him, even more beautiful than she had been that afternoon, and she could read it in his eyes. Her own eyes danced with delight as she led him into the living room, seated him on the over-size sofa and fixed a highball for him and a gimlet for herself.

They drank and listened to hi-fi records and talked about the store and Kane and life and love and flying and whatever else came to their minds. Then Betty served dinner in the dinette with candles glowing in the center of the table. They had clear soup served in melon halves, barbecued red pork with hot mustard, Steak Kow, chicken cooked with little hot peppers, bamboo sprouts, and crisp-cooked vegetables, and fried rice on the side. The meal ended with Chinese tea and almond cookies. Chet sat back and simply stared across at Betty. He had not left a scrap on any one of his dishes.

"You know," he said, "I've always been able to take Chinese food or leave it alone. But that is one of the finest meals I've ever had. I don't detect a slant in your eyes, though."

His praise did not mean too much to her. She knew she was a good cook, and she enjoyed astonishing people with her prowess in the kitchen.

They went into the living room and sat back with big snifters of brandy. Chet sipped at his drink, listened to the hi-fi, and looked about the apartment—and liked everything he saw. Chet was a good-looking young man and had dated many attractive women, as well as a few really beautiful women, but this red-head went beyond all of them. This was something you listed in the extraordinary category. She was beautiful, she had excellent taste, she knew good music, she knew how to talk, she was a smart business woman, she knew how to laugh, and she was a fabulous cook. What more could a man want? On the other hand, it didn't seem to make much difference how he listed her. He knew that he was already in love. Now, he wondered, how do I proceed from here?

He had, of course, heard a few rumors about Betty already, especially the one that the great man himself had her staked out.

He asked her, as casually as possible, what she thought about Kane. She shrugged and said, "He couldn't be nicer."

"How do you mean?"

"Well, he has done a great deal for me, really nice things. As far as I'm concerned, he's a sort of Santa Claus." Then she looked at him sharply and asked, "Why?"

Chet was not to be thrown by a simple question put bluntly. He grinned and said, "I was just wondering how the women got along with him."

"Oh. Same as the men, I suppose. He's rough and he's tough, but I think his treatment of the people who work for him, whether men or women, is pretty equable. I like him."

"So do I."

Then she looked at him and said, "Incidentally, you were a store manager down the Peninsula. Why did you step down to the job of an assistant in the city? Not that it's any of my business, but I am curious."

He wondered how far he should go, then decided that inasmuch as this girl was his target for life, he should go all the way. "I'll tell you," he said. "When the job was first offered to me I turned it down, even though I knew I would not have to step down in pay. That's one of the policies of this outfit, you know. Regardless of whatever job you take over, whether it's bigger or smaller, you still move on in the same pay bracket. You never get reduced."

"I know that." She smiled and asked, "Are you evading my question?"

He assured her, "No, I'm not. I'm going to tell you the truth. I started asking a few questions, and I got some surprising answers."

She said shrewdly, "About Maloney, I suspect."

"That's right. He's a good man and he can hold down the job he now has. But he will never go any higher. He has a very bad weakness. He is much too loyal toward the people working under him."

"I've noticed that already."

"So then you know what I'm talking about. Now, I don't mean to boast, but I do figure I have something on the ball, and I also figure I'm a little more coldblooded than Mr. Maloney. So, given a few years, if one of us gets moved ahead it will be me. That is precisely what I am gambling on."

She tilted her head to one side and appraised him closely. She realized something for the first time—Mr. Chet Baker meant to go places, and he probably had the drive to do it. She liked him already, but now she liked him a little more. She knew all about ambition.

"Well," she said, "I don't wish ill luck to Mr. Maloney, I have become very fond of him, but I do wish you luck, as well."

"Nicely put," he laughed, raising his glass to her. "Maybe the two of us will go a long way in this business."

"Let's hope so. Now, here is a record I would like you to hear—"

Betty was not due at work until Thursday noon, it was her late shift for the week, but Chet had to be there in the morning. He told her good night a little after one in the morning and drove home. It was a clear night, but he was in a bit of a fog all the way home. He let himself into his apartment whistling a popular tune considerably off-key. When he went to bed he was still thinking of Betty.

She was the first thing on his mind when he awakened in the morning. He thought of her again as he fixed his breakfast. Then he dressed and took a bus down the hill toward the center of town. When he arrived at the store he started immediately for the fourth floor but then realized that Betty was not due until noon. So he went on to his office and busied himself with the morning reports and mail.

He had the mail about all cleared out of the way when he realized that that there was a certain lack of hustle and bustle about him. He sat back and wondered about it, then had to laugh. Of course. All of the buyers and merchandisers, and most of the top executives had taken off that morning for New York. They would be gone for about two weeks.

He was supposed to be out on the floor, an assistant store-manager was always supposed to be out on the floor, but he skipped it that morning. When he finished with the mail he studied the files. Then he went through Maloney's desk, feeling like a criminal while doing it. But he knew he would learn things that Maloney would never tell him, and he did, especially some of the secrets of store policy. It was really weird, he thought, but one of the most difficult things to know was store policy. Sensibly and intelligently, one would think it would be spelled out for everyone, but it never was. Each executive jealously kept policy to himself. Chet learned a great deal that morning.

What he had learned was tested almost at once. Marie Togliatti came into his office and said, "Look, this character is way out on a limb. She brings me a dress that sold for ninety-eight ninety-five and wants her money back. She's from Fresno and claims she bought the dress down there. I had a hunch, I didn't think Fresno ever had that dress, so I checked with Findex and learned that the dress was never sold in Fresno. But this woman does have an account down there, and it's a good one. I can't call her a liar to her face now, can I?"

"Nope."

"So what do I do?

He leaned back and put his fingertips together and said, "In other words, you think the dress was stolen."

"Absolutely. What else? It's one of those heavy knits that would only sell in the bay area. We never carried it in the valley stores. Too hot. So she probably stole it either here, or in Oakland, or Stonestown. But damn it all, I can't accuse her of anything. It is one of our dresses. What do I do about it?"

"Give her back her money. But stall her and call Security to have a look at her before she leaves. They'll take it from there. Okay?"

Marie thought of it a moment, then shrugged. "It's not my money. I'll do as you say."

She turned to leave, then looked back at him and said coyly, "Oh, by the way, you don't mind if I tell you something?"

"Fire away."

"I don't think our new girl is going to be with us very long."

"You mean Miss Parker?"

"Yes. I know I shouldn't be saying this, but I overheard Miss Snider and Miss Hall talking together. You know who they are, don't you? They are the two top saleswomen, worth about a half-dozen of the others."

"So I've been told. And you heard what?"

Marie said triumphantly, "They were talking of switching over to the Emporium. How do you like that? If we lose them, then the others go too. And that will be the end of the fourth floor."

He stared at her and had difficulty hiding his anger. She was talking about the woman he loved. But he said coolly, "I'll keep it in mind. Thanks for telling me."

"You're welcome, Mr. Baker." She walked out giggling to herself. As far as she knew, she had damaged Miss Parker with the new assistant, for which she was grateful. Any little stone left unturned—

Actually, what she had told Chet was quite serious, and he knew it. If any department manager lost his two top sales persons he would be hauled onto the carpet instantly. It was the sales people, after all, who moved the merchandise and not the managers. To lose two top people at once was almost unpardonable. Even Betty could be in trouble over a thing like that.

He could hardly wait until Betty arrived. He called her down to his office immediately. Maloney had also arrived and sat in listening to them.

Chet told her of what he had learned, then he said, "A thing like that can't happen, Miss Parker. I haven't been here long, but I have learned that Snider and Hall are exceptional women. You simply cannot afford to lose them."

She said quietly, "I know that."

"But they are talking about leaving. What do you intend doing about that?"

Fred glanced at Chet and said, "Isn't this a matter that should be in my area?"

Chet said, "Most likely, but in this case I would like to carry it through. Do you mind?"

Maloney could hardly do anything else but shrug, but he did not like it. He felt that already his assistant was beginning to walk on his heels. He sat back and listened, but he was burning.

Betty said stiffly, "With your permission, of course, I would like the whole matter dropped here and now."

"How can we do that?"

"Because I think I have enough intelligence to handle the situation."

"What if they should leave?"

"They won't, believe me. I think I know women better than you do. They love to bitch, but when it comes to actually making a move and losing seniority and so on, they aren't about to do it. I would stake my job on it."

Chet saw her stiffness and his own spine became more rigid. He said gruffly, "You may have to stake your job on it."

"Then that is my affair, Mr. Baker. And I will stake my job on it."

Maloney looked from one to the other and said, "Well, now, let's just drop it for the present. I have faith in you, Betty, and I do believe you know your job. Work it out the best way you can, and I'll back you all the way."

"Thank you, Mr. Maloney. I wish others around here felt the same way."

She turned on a spike heel and walked stiffly out of the office. Chet sighed softly to himself. Put my foot in it then, he thought.

Betty went back to her floor. She was quite angry with Chet. One of the saleswomen, probably Marie, had tattled, so Chet had felt that it was incumbent to let her know that within the store, regardless of what went on during after-hours, he was her boss. He could have handled the whole thing in an amusing manner, but had chosen not to do so. All right, she thought. I'll fix your kite.

She went into one of the fitting rooms to help out a sale, then returned to her counter. A woman of about sixty years of age was waiting for her. She was beautifully dressed and spelled money. Betty recognized her just as the woman said, "Mrs. Alexander. I left a skirt here to be altered. Remember?"

Betty's eyes smiled at her. "Of course. I remember." She left the counter and returned after a few moments with the skirt in question. She turned it inside out and showed Mrs. Alexander the seams. "As you can see," she said, "there is no material left to let out. I understand that this suit was a size eight, but you had the skirt altered to a size ten."

Mrs. Alexander nodded. "That is correct. They didn't have any tens left. But I did want it so badly."

"I'm afraid there isn't anything that can be done. You have probably put on a little weight since you bought this suit."

Mrs. Alexander's eyes narrowed and she said angrily, "I haven't weighed over a hundred and twelve pounds in the last thirty years. I have certainly not put on any weight. The only thing I can think of is that in cleaning the skirt shrank."

Betty looked down at the skirt and knew it was the sort of material that would never shrink. She said, however, "That is possible. But we are not responsible for what cleaners do to your clothes. I am truly sorry, Mrs. Alexander, but there is absolutely nothing we can do about your skirt."

The older woman glared at her and said, "In other words, you do not intend doing anything about this."

"I didn't say that. I said that there was nothing we could do about it."

"You refuse to cooperate with me?"

Betty shook her head, holding on to her patience. "Mrs. Alexander, believe me, I would love to cooperate with you. But you simply can't stretch a twelve inch ruler to thirteen inches, can you?"

Mrs. Alexander looked her up and down, then asked frostily, "Who is the store manager now? I know you've had some changes under the new setup. Who is now the head man?"

Betty sighed and said, "Mr. Fred Maloney. You will find him—"

"I know where to look, thank you."

She stalked away and Betty said to herself, "Aw, nuts." They came in all sizes, shapes, and colors. You never knew what to expect.

About fifteen minutes later Maloney came by and leaned on the counter. "Okay," he grinned. "What gives with Mrs. Alexander?"

Betty showed him the skirt and explained everything to him. "She's just one of those people," she said, "who refuses to accept no for an answer."

"I know. Especially the better customers. And she has a damned good account, you know. We'd hate to lose someone like that. So what can you do?"

Betty picked up the skirt and twisted it about, then her eyes narrowed as she said, "Well, we could put in gussets. I don't think they would show too much. I would have to ask her about that, though."

"Good girl," he laughed. "You take care of it."

Betty laughed, "I'll beat her brains in."

"Now, now. Temper, temper."

He walked away and Betty chuckled and tucked the skirt away. She went back to work and was surprised when the day had completely drained away.

Marie had been relieving Betty on the floor all morning, before her noon arrival. She now came out of the inner office at precisely five thirty, which was her quitting time. She said, "Good night" to Betty and started on by.

Betty called after her, "Marie?"

She turned back and leaned against the front of the counter. "Yes?"

Betty said casually, "I think I told you and the others when I took over here that everyone on this floor had to sell. I haven't enforced it until now, because I had to find my own way around. Starting tomorrow, however, I expect you to carry your own book on this floor, and I expect to find sales in it. In other words," she smiled, "let's not waste time back in the office."

Marie was aghast. "Waste time!" she cried. "I've been back there working like a dog all afternoon."

Betty's cold smile broadened. "Then leave it for the dogs. Starting tomorrow you be out on this floor—selling. Irene can handle the office end. I want you selling, and eventually I want Irene out here, too."

Marie's face flushed a violent red. "I don't know about this. Maybe if I took it up with Mr. Maloney—"

Betty said cheerfully, "He would have to back me all the way, because, you see, if you read the fine print, it is strictly store policy. I want you selling, and that is definitely an order." She paused, then said, "One thing more. There is a rumor around that Snider and Hall are thinking of quitting."

Marie's shoulders twitched and her head came back, and Betty knew that she had hit the right person. Marie managed to smile and said sweetly, "Oh, really? That would be a terrible blow for this floor, wouldn't it?"

Betty shrugged. "Perhaps not. Anyone can be replaced, including yours truly. So I want you to do something. When you get here tomorrow morning tell Snider and Hall to make up their minds and let me know one way or the other so I can make arrangements to have them replaced. I know a couple of girls over in Wilson's who could probably fill their shoes very well."

Marie walked away from her on legs that were trembling. Betty leaned on the counter and chewed on her lower lip. She was taking a wild gamble, and she knew it. Losing Snider and Hall could even crack Kane's placid attitude. You simply did not lose sales people like that.

She was gambling on two factors. Both women had been with Merritt's for many years and she doubted that either of them would enjoy a change. They were undoubtedly just forcing a showdown with her, believing they would win. Then there was something else. Ever since she had had the run-in with Miss Snider, on her first day, she had been busily engaged in adding sales to the books of all the other saleswomen. She was able to do that quite easily, as she really was a top saleswoman. But she had avoided Snider as well as Hall. The two might hate each other's guts, which she knew, but they did hang together as a matter of policy. By now, they obviously knew how she helped out the other saleswomen. They were not stupid. Now that she had called the showdown for tomorrow morning, they would talk it over together and come to the inevitable conclusion that it was far better to go along with Miss Parker than to buck her—she hoped. It was a chance and she knew it, but it had to be taken.

Matters did not augur at all well the following morning. Both Snider and Hall avoided her. They took care of their customers, they kept to themselves, and they stayed away from the counter. Noontime came and went and Betty sighed and figured that she had lost the battle. She knew that Marie had passed on her words. Marie, herself, was trying to appear busy with customers on the floor, though she was disappearing into the office every half hour or so and coming out with eyes a bit more red than the previous occasion. It was obvious to Betty that Marie had talked with Maloney, and that he had backed Betty. Thank God for him, she thought.

She was wondering how she was going to explain things to Kane, when the big break came just before five o'clock. Miss Hall had a customer in a fitting room, but she came out and rather timidly approached Betty at the counter.

"Miss Parker?"

"Yes?"

Miss Hall did not look at her, but she said, "I have a customer in the fitting room who can't make up her mind between two different colors of the same dress. You have fabulous taste in color, so I was wondering—well—if you might just spare a moment—?"

Betty blinked and left the counter and walked with her to the fitting room. When she returned to the counter she found Miss Snider waiting for her. Miss Snider's lips were thinly pressed and her eyes were snapping but she said calmly enough, "Goddamn it all, Miss Parker, I need your help with a customer who thinks she's God's gift to the fashion world. Now, what she has in mind—"

Betty closed her eyes and her own lips were pressed together and she almost cried, and Miss Snider, being a much older and much wiser woman, knew it. She leaned over the counter and squeezed Betty's hand. "It's okay, dearie." Then Betty did cry and ran back to her office. She had won the battle.

Betty thought that the next two weeks were the finest she had ever known. She had won a battle, but she knew that it was only a minor skirmish. There were many other battles to be won before the fourth floor was ever running the way she wanted it, and she knew that she would have to fight all the way. Nevertheless, she felt good over winning the opening engagement, especially against two such old pro's as Snider and Hall. They came to her now, and she worked with them and they cooperated with her. They were not exactly friendly, but she figured she could build that up in time.

Chet Baker, of course, heard about the outcome through Maloney and was quite sheepish over his role in the little affair. He was even afraid to ask Betty for another date, the lack of which she did not even notice. She was too busy with Bill and other friends. She made a point, though, of seeing Bill twice a week only. He came on rather strongly and aroused her more than anyone else. It bothered her. So she spent considerable time with other young men from Montgomery Street and the industrial heart of the city. She did not yet wish to be involved too much with any one man.

She saw Joe Haley one morning, just before all the executives were due back in town. He came to her floor at about eleven and stood before her counter. His green eyes looked levelly into her own. "I got a favor to ask. Would you mind meeting me for lunch?"

She looked him up and down and was undecided for a moment. Then she noticed he looked a bit harassed. Her curiosity was aroused.

"Twelve thirty?" she asked.

He nodded. "Meet me at John's, across from Day's on Ellis. Cripes," he said bitterly, "don't ever walk out of here with me or you'll be ruined."

She met him at John's, a small, colorful bar and restaurant frequented by junior and senior executives. The food was good and the service excellent. Both had Salisbury steaks, French fries, and tiny new peas.

After they had finished eating, Joe sat back and sipped at his coffee and she thought, for the hundredth time, My God, what a hunk of man! Then he looked in her eyes and slowly, haltingly, started talking. He told her of what had happened to him, sparing no details, and she sat and listened quietly and somberly.

At the end he said, "Well, there it is. The reason I've told you is because I think you and I are a lot alike—same drive and attitude."

"You flatter me."

"Oh, stuff that manure. That isn't what I want out of you. What I want from you is what I think you can give, honesty.

So now I present you with the downfall of a guy named Joe Haley."

"Your wife had anything to do with you since then?"

"Jee-zuss, no! She has her room and I have mine. There was that freak accident at the Buena Vista, of course, when she overheard the bartender talking about me. So she has it all sewed up, and I can't deny it any longer."

"Did you try?"

He stared at her and burst out laughing. "Betty," he said, "I lied my head off. I happen to love my wife and my kids, believe it or not. I lied as hard as any man could, and then finally I broke down and told her the truth. Then I asked her forgiveness. No dice. She won't forgive me."

"How about the young girl, Marilyn? You don't even know her last name."

"Hell, I could find that out easily enough. I know where I left her off. All I have to do is go by and read the name on the mail box. But I'm afraid to. Her father has loused up my life so much that if I knew who he was and got a little too drunk, I might just look him up and break every goddamned bone in his body." He shook his head violently. "I would much rather not know who he is. I know how the Irish comes up in me when I get plastered."

"Hmmmmm." Betty sat back and stared at him and wondered about him and what she would do if she happened to be his wife, and she could not come up with an answer. "I don't know," she sighed. "You got in a beauty, that's for sure. But then, you've been asking for it for years, from what I've heard."

He nodded. "I know. Don't ask me to explain myself to you, though. I can't do it. At this particular moment, I can't even explain myself to myself, and that has always been such an easy job before. But there is something I want from you. You are a woman. Do you think you can tell me how long I can expect this torture from my wife?"

Betty thought it over and honestly shook her head. "I don't know, Joe. If you were my husband I would divorce you pronto. But you say your wife is very religious and a dedicated Catholic. That could make a big difference."

He asked eagerly, "Then you think she will forgive me eventually?"

Betty shook her head slowly. "No, Joe. I don't think that at all. I don't know your wife, but from what you have told me

I would say she will never divorce you, but she will also never again be your wife."

He blinked at her as if she had hit him in the face. "You're kidding!"

"No, I'm not." She looked into his eyes and was suddenly alarmed. She said, "Now, please, don't take anything I say seriously. What do I know about it?"

"That's all you need to know."

"No, believe me. These things always go much deeper than anything you can say. You couldn't possibly tell me the whole truth, and I couldn't grasp it if you did."

He looked down into his coffee and frowned and mumbled, "You're right, of course. What does anyone ever know about anyone else? Only what they are told and what they can see. And what they are told is generally a lie, and what they see is a photograph taken from the wrong angle." Then he looked up into her eyes and said, "I'm damned worried, Betty. I want my wife back. Is there anything you can think of—?"

She shook her head sadly. "Nothing."

"Well—" He sat back and was thoughtfully silent for a moment. Then he squinted at her and said, "You really think there is no hope for me at all."

"Joe," she said weakly, "there is only one answer and that lies with you and your wife. Don't ask me what it is because I don't know."

He closed one eye and looked at her with the other and said, "You know something? You're a pretty smart little apple. I'll tell you something else. You would probably be a hell of a romp in the hay, but you have my word for it that I will never make a play for you."

She laughed nervously and asked, "Why not?"

"Because," he said soberly, "at this particular moment I have more respect for you than anybody I know. Now, let's get the hell out of here."

They left John's and started back to the store. Betty took his arm as they were going up Stockton Street. He said musingly, "Even now, even considering the fix I'm in, if I ran into a gorgeous babe, I would think of what she would be like in bed. Even now." He turned and blinked at Betty. "How do you like that for a real psycho?"

Betty said, "Now I'll tell you something. I don't judge people. Some people I dislike and that's it. I never bother myself with the reasons. Other people I like, and I don't bother with the reasons for that, either. I know the weaknesses of the people I like, and I don't give a damn about them. In other words," she chuckled, "I happen to like you and I can't judge you. Is that all right with you?"

He smiled and reached over to pet her hand resting so lightly on his arm. "You and I," he said, "we'll get along."

They went back to the store and Joe got off the elevator at the third floor feeling a little better for having talked with Betty, but not much.

He went into his private office and sat at the desk and buried his face in his hands. Then he raised his head and looked at the opposite wall and thought, Okay, so that's it. That's the way it will go. He wondered, then, what he would do about it. He would not leave Mary, that was for sure. He was not the Catholic she was, but even so he did not believe in divorce and he did have three sons to raise. He also believed that it took a mother and father together to raise children properly, so he would not even consider a separation. A thing like this, he knew, happened many times in Catholic families. Maybe it worked out well eventually. So he and Mary would continue living together in the same house, though separately, but they would raise their children together. It could work that way.

12

JOE was on his floor on Saturday of the week when Kane, the executives, and the buyers returned from New York. He heard that they were back, and shortly after that Jack Harrison came down to his floor. He took Joe's arm and led him back to the small office. Joe glanced at him sharply. The old man looked worn and tired out, but his spirit was as high as ever.

Harrison told him, "I thought I had better see you first, before I hang up my hat. We've brought back a new man with us, Eric Jeffrey, a former Englishman."

Joe laughed and said, "There is no such thing as a former Englishman. They die that way."

"Well, this one happens to be an American citizen. Quite a background. He was one of the heroes of the R.A.F. during

162

World War II. I don't know how he happened to become an American citizen, but he did. I think he also married an American girl. Anyway, he was a buyer with Macy's in New York. Kane got him away, using his ordinary magic, I suppose. He'll be taking Burke's place."

Joe looked delighted. "Oh, oh. I could kiss you, Grandpa."

"Kane is making this change strictly because of you. So he will naturally be expecting you to get along with the new man. Understand?"

"You don't have to spell it out. I can see it."

"Bear it in mind and don't ever forget it."

"I will." Joe thought a moment, then cocked an eyebrow at Harrison. "How come, in this business, when anyone gets the sack they leave immediately? There's no two-week grace, or anything like that. You get the word, and you're out right now."

Harrison chuckled and said, "You know that in this business nothing can be kept secret. A person is fired and the word goes around as he comes out of the office. What happens then? The minute the fact is known he has lost total control of any sort of authority. He is no longer any good to himself or the firm. That's why it is always done this way."

"I guess it makes sense, at that. Sure."

Harrison slapped his arm. "Be good, my boy. I'll see you."

"Okay. And thanks for the advance warning."

Joe was out on the floor arguing with a customer when Burke stepped out of an elevator and approached him about forty-five minutes later. Joe turned the customer over to one of the salesmen and walked aside with Burke. The former buyer was a small man, slightly built, with a semi-bald head and the formidable strength of a twelve-year-old girl.

He looked Joe up and down and glowered at him, then said sharply between his teeth, "I wish I had guts enough to belt you right in the face."

"And," Joe amended, "the size to go with it."

"I know it was you who got my job."

Joe said flatly, "I've never made a secret of my dislike for you."

Burke's eyes lowered and he mumbled, "You kept pounding away—"

"Which would still do me no good if Kane thought you were a good man in your job. And if he thought you were a better man than I, and I made an issue out of it, then I would be the one sacked. You know that, too."

Burke's eyes came up and he blinked at Joe and seemed to be holding back tears. He almost whispered, "I have a family, you know, a wife and kids. I don't know what I'm going to do now. Jees, what does a man do when it comes at him out of the blue—like this—?"

Joe sucked in his breath and felt a sudden hot stab of pain in his stomach. Oh, no, he thought. Oh, God, Burke, don't crawl before me. Don't ask for my sympathy, not me, not Joe Haley, not the man who has always hated your guts. Please, please, don't crawl before me.

But Burke crawled and Joe knew precisely and blindingly why Kane had fired him. Joe had nothing whatever to do with it. Kane had simply wanted to get rid of a weakling, so he had partly used Joe as an excuse. Even Harrison was wrong.

Burke kept on babbling and Joe stared at him helplessly. A salesman, however, came over with a check for Joe to investigate—no checks were accepted on his floor without his signature—and he used that as an excuse to break it off with Burke. The former buyer actually shook hands with Joe, then took his leave. Joe stared after him and looked at his hand and slowly shook his head from side to side. Dear God, he prayed silently, if I should ever even think of crawling like that, hit me with a bolt of lightning first.

It was perhaps half an hour later when Kane stepped out of the elevator with another man. Joe appraised the stranger. It had to be the new man, the Englishman—he looked as British as Bond Street. He was wearing tweeds, a rough textured white shirt, a knit tie, and heavy brogans. He was at least six feet five inches tall and as thin as a beanstalk, his face was thin and hollow, his gray eyes sharp and penetrating, and his upper lip was graced with a salt and pepper mustache clipped in a military manner.

Kane introduced them and it was, indeed, Eric Jeffrey, the new buyer. Joe began to like him almost at once. He was not a man who threw out a big, fat smile of welcome. He looked at you soberly and appraised you closely, weighing you in the back of his mind, and then lights of interest appeared in his eyes.

Kane was saying, "You'll be working more closely with Mr. Haley, here, than anyone else in the chain. I might tell you now that he is not an ordinary department manager, as you may be used to the term back in New York."

Jeffrey said easily, "You told me that before, Mr. Kane."

"Oh, I did? Yes, I suppose I have. I did try to brief you on the flight out. Well, then—suppose you stay here and chat for a few minutes with Joe, then return to my office. You'll meet all the others before the day is over."

"I am sure I shall. Thank you very much."

Joe looked deeply into Kane's face and saw that he, too, seemed to be tired and worn. Apparently, it had gone rough in New York. Kane would not have been able to hide his good feelings if the trip east had been otherwise. Joe nodded at him and watched him disappear into an elevator, then turned his attention back to the Englishman.

Simply to break the ice, he said, "I've been told you were with the R.A.F. during the big war."

A slight smile tugged at Jeffrey's lips. "Word does get around. My, my. Yes, I may say I was fortunate to have been in the nest."

"Fighters or bombers?"

"Fighters. Hurricanes, to be exact."

Joe's eyes lighted as he asked, "Battle of Britain?"

Jeffrey hesitated a moment, then smiled and nodded and said, "Yes."

"Well, I'll be damned. Never has so much been owed by so many to so few, or something like that. So you were one of that outfit. I thought it was all Spitfires."

"Oh, no, not at all. The Spits took on the fighters while we, in the Hurricanes, took on the bombers."

"I see. I've read about it. Just how tight was it at the finish?"

Jeffrey had already added up his personal estimate of Joe Haley. He relaxed a bit and said, "Well, old boy, it was so tight that it was not even a squeak. The day we knew that we had broken the back of the Luftwaffe, when they failed to come over at their usual time, we had exactly eighteen operational aircraft to put up against them."

"No kidding!"

"Yes. It was that close. That was also a bad luck day for me. I made a sloppy landing that afternoon, wrapped up the machine, and lost my left leg."

"I didn't notice anything wrong with your walk."

"There isn't, if I can help it. Practice makes perfect, you know, and I do have a very fine artificial leg."

Joe felt embarrassed and said suddenly, "I wasn't thinking, Mr. Jeffrey. I'm sorry if I've said anything—"

Jeffrey interrupted with a slight laugh. "Think nothing of it.

Naturally, you are curious about me, just as I am about you. I've heard a devilish lot about you on the way out here. So let's get on with it, shall we? As soon as I could get around I was sent over here to America. I spent the war years in San Diego at the Consolidated Aircraft Corporation where I was a technical member of the British Air Commission. That is where I fell in love with this country." He smiled and said, "That is where I also fell in love with an American girl and was fortunate enough to marry her. So, when the war was all over with, and I had returned to England for a few years, I was lucky enough to get on your quota. I returned and went into the retail business, and here I am. Life's story in a—how do you say?—in a peanut."

Joe laughed and corrected him, "In a nutshell."

Jeffrey looked puzzled. "But a peanut is a nutshell."

Joe took his elbow. "Okay," he said, "let me show you around the floor. You may as well get to know the joint."

Joe showed him about and introduced him to the salesmen and his assistant and the detail men and showed him part of the stock. Jeffrey commented, "You're quite a few notches above Macy's."

"Well, we don't sell absolutely top quality, but we're not far under it. This is a specialty house, you know."

They were walking back to Joe's floor-desk when one of the elevator doors opened and Joe happened to glance in that direction. He looked inside and saw a gorgeous young blonde standing with some other people. It was Marilyn. He ran for the elevators just as the doors closed. He looked above at the red light and saw that the elevator was going down. He calculated his chances of intercepting it on the bottom floor and knew that she would be out of the store before he could get there down the stairs. She had probably been shopping on the fourth floor. Naturally. That was the fashion floor and she was high fashion all the way out. What a little doll, he thought. Even now, after everything that had happened, she still made his heart jump.

He went back to Jeffrey, and the Englishman asked him point-blank, "What's your biggest beef with the buyers?"

Joe looked away from him, then said soberly, "It's really two beefs. I know what this floor needs better than any buyer living. I meet the people day in and day out and I know what they want. But quite often when I try to pass that on to a buyer I get brushed off. I say we need a certain type of suit, for example, and the buyer comes up with something else that someone sold to him in New York. So it's a dog and it just hangs there, and then I get hell for not moving it. The second beef is sizes. Naturally, you run out of the more popular sizes first. So the buyer tries to get me to sell the other sizes before filling out the popular ones we need. I'm telling you, sometimes I see red."

"Don't blame you. I think I have been pretty well trained in that direction with Macy's."

"Then you might throw in a third beef. I know you're up against an office quota, and that you have to stay within it. But when something begins to get moving hot and I say that we need more of it and right now, I expect you to go to bat and put up a fight for me and see that we get it. To be honest with you," he grinned, "no one has ever done it for me."

"Not really?"

"No. But that's about it. Those are the big beefs that mean money for my department and, obviously, for the store. There are dozens of other squawks," he laughed, "but no need to go into them now."

"Very good. I'll get together with you later." He shook hands with Joe and said, "It has been a pleasure talking with you. But now I had better trot back to Mr. Kane's office."

"I'll be seeing you around."

Jeffrey said in his clipped fashion, "Right." Joe was glad he had not said, "Right-o." At least, a bit of America had worn off on him.

Joe watched him go, then got out his quota charts for the month. He was still a bit ahead of last year, but he was wondering how he could do better, when someone said, "Hiya, boy," and he turned around to face his father. The elder Haley stood rocking back on his heels, his hands on his hips, his hat pushed back and his eyes narrowed.

Joe said, "Oh, hiya, Dad. What's cooking with you?"

"I'm on me way to see your Mr. Kane."

"That deal is still going?"

"It is. But that is not why I stopped off to see me only favorite son." His eyes narrowed a fraction as he continued, "I had dinner with Mary last night. You weren't home. She didn't know where you were and didn't seem to care. I had the distinct impression that there is something wrong in the house of Haley."

Joe did not dare tell him the truth, so he lied, "Well, maybe it is a little more important than most quarrels we've had." He threw in a partial truth as he said, "It's got to do a little with how I bang around on my own."

"In other words," the old man said shrewdly, "you're gonna lie about it. But whatever is wrong is big, so I'll tell you something again, and you had better listen good. You ever get separated from Mary, Joseph Haley, and I'll cut you dead without a single dime. That's a promise. Good day to you."

Kane, at that moment, was in his office with Maxwell Jackson. He had the big merchandise book for the chain open but was looking across the desk at Jackson seated on the other side. Kane looked tired, and Jackson was a bit grim.

But Kane managed a slight smile as he asked, "That young blonde I saw you talking with in the hallway, was that your daughter?"

Jackson nodded. "Yes, it was."

"She's beautiful. So how did it go while I was gone?"

"Nothing to complain about. Every store in the chain is a bit over quota."

"That goes along with the growth of the state."

"Perhaps. But I think the chain is doing a little better than that. We aren't in bad shape at all, you know."

"I hope not. I expect growth and plenty of it. Now, Max, you and I haven't been able to get together. How does it go with Haley? The older Haley."

"He's due here almost any minute to talk to you. I don't think you can close with him."

"Why not?"

"He wants too much. Now he wants a percentage of the gross instead of paying rent for the five stores."

Kane's eyes opened a bit wider. "Say that again and more slowly?"

"I just said he wants a percentage of the gross, is all."

Kane leaned back and tapped his fingertips together and was finally smiling with unadulterated pleasure. "Is that so? You know something, Max, that character is a sharp Irishman, as shrewd and calculating as they come. And he wants a percentage instead of rent? How do you like that?"

Jackson said gruffly, "I can't see anything to be pleased about."

Kane leaned over the desk, as if lecturing to a small child. "Max, for God's sake, come alive. I just said he's a shrewd Irishman. All right. So if he figured I had any chance to lose my shirt he would demand a flat payment of rent, just to be on the safe side. But he isn't thinking that way. He's thinking that in me maybe he has found a winner. That's why he would rather risk everything on a cut of the percentage. You know something? That is the best damned news I've heard in two weeks."

Jackson still did not grasp it, though he did understand the economics involved. "Sure," he said, "but he could make much more money this way."

"Granted. But that isn't what I'm talking about. I don't say that I'll go along with him. All I say is that it makes me happy to know that he is thinking that way."

A sudden knock at the door interrupted their conversation. Kane called loudly, "Come in," and Patrick Haley walked into the room. He shoved his hat farther on the back of his head, shook hands with the two men, then went to stand at the windows looking out over Market Street.

He said musingly, over his shoulder, "One of these days, gentlemen, Market Street is going to be one of the most glamorous streets in the world. Right now, it's a little like Coney Island, but it's beginning to change. Big office buildings are going up at the lower end and at the farther upper end are deluxe apartments. The gap between is closing slowly but surely. Another ten years you won't recognize this street." He turned about then and cocked an eyebrow at Kane. "So how did it go in New York?"

Kane tilted back in his chair and shrugged. "So-so."

"Uh-huh. Them Jews ain't laying out the red carpet for you yet. Can't say I blame 'em. You got a lot of proving to do."

"Seems to me I've done a little proving with you even now. Mr. Jackson tells me you want a percentage on the five new buildings instead of a flat rental."

Haley walked toward them and leaned over the desk, resting on his palms. "I'm a gambler, Mr. Kane. Every job I do I gamble on it, one way or another. It makes me laugh to see people running up to Reno to gamble. Hell, I gamble more in five minutes than they do in their whole lives. Sure, I want a percentage. I got a hunch you're going places. You got style."

Kane laughed. "I have what?"

"Style, Mr. Kane. Just plain, simple style. It's something you can't define. You just know when you run into a person who has it, and you got it. You're a lot like my son, Joe. He has it, too.

You just know nothing is ever going to stop that boy, in spite of his good looks. He's going places, and I know it as well as I know I am standing here."

Jackson asked facetiously, "Would you say I have style?"

Haley ignored him and looked at Kane and said, "So let's get down to business. I've investigated the five pieces of property and my realty agents tell me they see no difficulties. My architects have also begun to draw up tentative plans, and my attorneys are looking into the legal angles. So I want you to hire an architectural firm and throw them in with my men. Then we'll set your attorneys up with mine. After that, Mr. Kane, you and I can sit down eyeball to eyeball and figure out how to come to terms."

Kane burst out laughing. "You certainly believe in the direct approach, Mr. Haley."

It was Haley's turn to shrug. "What's there to get excited about? Like I said before, this is a hell of a big thing for you, but I go through plenty deals like this every year. Once the whole deal is put together and you and I get through arguing about it, I'll bet you a hundred to one that we settle it one way or the other in fifteen minutes flat. I've never seen it to fail."

Kane nodded. "You're probably right."

"That's why I had to see you personally today. Do you want me to get the ball rolling, or not?"

Jackson said, "A point just came to my mind—"

Kane interrupted and said, "I like your approach, Haley. I think, too, that you and I can do business. All right, get the ball rolling."

Haley grinned and backed away from the desk. "Good. My hired help will get in touch with your hired help. After they finish beating each other's brains to pulp, you and I will have something to go on. Then we get together. Sound all right with you?"

"Sounds very good, indeed."

"Then that's how it will go. Good day, gentlemen."

He had hardly walked out of the office when Jackson protested, "My God, there are hundreds of things you should have talked over with him. I have a whole list of questions in my office I wanted you to ask him. How about land rights, how about liabilities, who signs the mortgages, does he want you to go partly on the notes, or not at all, and how about—"

Kane stopped him with a wave of the hand. He said patiently, "Max, we are doing business with a man so big he talks only on the summit and leaves everything else for his underlings. You can't do that in this business we're in, but I sure as hell wish we could. On the other hand, I'm going along with him. If I tried any other approach I think he would drop me like a hot potato. So we'll do it his way."

Jackson sighed and shook his head. "You're the boss. But, believe me, I would personally never do business this way."

"That," Kane said lightly, "is where you and I differ." He pulled the big merchandise book toward him and said, "Now, Max, if you don't mind—"

Max gathered his papers together and left. Kane pursed his lips together and frowned at the opposite wall. Matters had not gone too badly in New York, but they had not gone very well, either. No one had tried to shove him around. On the other hand, no one had gone beyond the book. One of the biggest things in the retail business, which could sometimes represent the difference between profit and loss, was to have the wholesaler pay a high percentage of what the retailer had to shell out on advertising the wholesaler's product in the local arena. All wholesalers expected to do this and did so without complaint. But there was a minimum and there was a maximum. Kane had been able to come up with nothing better than the minimum, or what the book said. Harrison had done a little better with some of the wholesalers, but the overall picture was nowhere as good as it would have been if Kane had been a well-established person. And he needed that maximum, or something close to it. He could get by on what he was getting, but that was it, just getting by. Kane's dreams and aspirations went far beyond merely getting by.

He wondered if five new stores would turn the trick, even if he had to pay for them through the nose. He turned it all over in his mind and came up with the same answer he had started with, it was a good possibility. Okay, he thought, it's worth the risk. He closed his mind on it and turned to other matters.

When he went home that night he was thoughtfully preoccupied, so Bessie did not bother him. She was, however, bubbling with some news or other, though he failed to notice it. Even at the dinner table, he chewed away thoughtfully on his food, almost like a steer, staring into space.

But she could not contain herself any longer and finally blurted out, while beaming at him, "Lew, I think our little boy Willie has finally fallen in love."

He paused with a forkful of food halfway to his mouth. "Our little boy?" he echoed. "Willie? Damn it all, Bessie, how many times must you stand corrected? He is no longer little and he is no longer a boy. He is a full-grown, adult man with a hell of a lot of muscle and a lot of size. I wish you would get over this notion of calling the boys—" Then he had to pause and laugh at his own mistake. "Okay," he said. "What's with Bill?"

"I think he's in love."

He lowered his fork then and stared at her. "You really mean it?"

"Yes."

"Hmmmmm. I remember him squiring around a lot of gals, but I don't ever remember him being in love before. He's never said anything to me."

Her eyes were dancing as she said, "He hasn't really said much to me, either. It's just the way he's been acting lately, and he has said he has a special girl. And his eyes kind of light up."

"Oh? You think she really is special?"

"There's no doubt about it in my mind. I think he's in love, for the first time. He dropped by last night, before you got back, and I kind of questioned him about this girl. He kind of grinned and said we'd be sure to like her when we met her. He even said that you knew her, but then he wouldn't say any more. Lew," she asked eagerly, "do you have any idea at all?"

He shoved his food aside and sat back and thought about it and there was a tiny chill in his heart. He did not know why. He remembered that once before he had been a little chilled about the possibility of some particular girl whom Bill might be out with but could not remember who it was. He tried to think of who the girl might be and could not come up with an answer.

He started eating again and chuckled and said, "Well, it could be somebody working for me in the Merritt-Wilson chain."

"Yes, Lew, I rather think it is."

"Did he give you a hint?"

"Only that she was very, very beautiful."

The word beautiful was synonymous with exactly one person— Betty Parker. Kane now remembered who the girl had been on the other occasion. No, he thought. It couldn't be. The coincidence was too wild. God, no. It had to be someone else. Not Betty, of all people. He was suddenly no longer hungry.

Kane spent a bad and virtually sleepless night. He tossed from side to side and even when he was asleep he groaned and sighed. Bessie got out of their bed and tiptoed into a guest room. Kane sat up, finally, and tried to work it out in his mind. He had thousands of people working for him in the chain. That Bill should become involved with the one person who was verboten, was unthinkable. Yet, as wild as the coincidence might seem, it was always possible—he had to consider it. Especially so in view of the fact that the girl was "very, very beautiful." It could be Betty.

When he got up in the morning he dressed in loafers, slacks, and a red-checked lumberman's shirt and told Bessie he was going down to the drugstore. Instead, he got out his car and drove to the Marina district and to Betty's apartment house. He saw Betty's Jaguar XKE parked at the curb and wondered about it. It was the one real luxury she allowed herself, and he knew that she used it only on her days off. Maybe she was going somewhere.

He rang her bell and in a moment the buzzer unlocked the front door. She was out of bed, anyway. Betty met him at the doorway of her apartment. She was wearing sandals, tight-fitting slacks, and a loose-fitting sweater. She blinked at him with considerable surprise, never having before seen him on a Sunday morning, then smiled and invited him in.

As he followed her into the dinette he said, "I hope I'm not upsetting anything."

"Oh, no. I was just having coffee, then I was going to drive down the Peninsula to spend the day with Mrs. Merritt. Would you join me in some coffee?"

"Glad to. I haven't had anything yet."

He sat at one end of the small table and she poured a cup of coffee for him, then dropped into a chair at the opposite end.

He took a swallow of hot coffee that almost scalded his throat, then looked at her and asked, "Who were you going down to the country with?"

She said noncommittally, "A friend."

"I see." He toyed with his coffee cup, then shoved it aside.

"Betty," he asked blindly, "how long have you been seeing my son, Bill?"

She was momentarily startled, then she was embarrassed and bit her lip and looked away from him. "I'm sorry," she said. "I never did agree with Bill's idea of keeping our relationship a secret. But he told me that you did not like the idea of him going around with any of your employees." She did not notice the sudden paleness that was creeping through the tan of his skin and continued, "I insisted just a few weeks ago that he tell you we were seeing each other, but he asked me to put it off a while longer. I'm afraid we put it off too long. You were bound to hear of it, after all. Things like that get around."

He cleared his throat and said hoarsely, "Yes, they do. I just learned about it last night."

"Oh?" She stared at him and the puzzle in her eyes began to deepen. "Is that why you dropped by this morning?"

"Yes, it is."

"I see." She stared at him more closely and made the natural mistake of thinking that the pain in his eyes was anger. Her own temper began bubbling and boiling dangerously close to the surface. "So," she said thinly, "you take exception to the sales girl and the boss's son. Is that it?"

"Is that what you think?"

She cried out fiercely, "That's the way it looks to me! What else am I to think? You drop by here early Sunday morning and start accusing me—"

He interrupted almost with a whisper, "Betty, my dear, I have accused you of nothing. I simply asked a question, and you start blowing your stack."

She said weakly, "I don't understand. You've dropped by to ask me if I've been seeing your son. Now that you know the answer to that you will next be asking me why."

"Not necessarily. He is quite a handsome young man, in a rugged way, he has a good background, and he is eminently eligible. No, Betty. It would never enter my head to ask you why you are seeing him."

"Are you going to tell me that you approve?"

He swallowed and said so softly she could hardly hear him, "No, I am not. I do not approve at all."

"Is it the sales girl angle, or the fact that I'm an orphan?"

"Neither."

She blew her breath out sharply, placed her hands flatly on

the table, and said, "Then that leaves just one thing, Mr. Kane. That leaves you and me. I've been wondering for a long while when the showdown would come, but, believe me, I never thought it would be this way."

"What showdown are talking about?"

"Ours. You and I. The two of us."

"Oh, that. I can well imagine that you have wondered many times about my attitude toward you."

"I have."

"It's understandable. I can say without fear of contradiction, however, that it isn't even remotely close to what you have been thinking."

"Oh, now, please—"

He raised his palm toward her. "Just listen. I had hoped I would never have to explain my attitude to you, but now it is vitally necessary."

"Because of Bill?"

"Partly, yes. The first time I saw you, Betty, which you don't know about, you rather took my breath away. It was almost like seeing Anna Merritt again in her younger days. I don't mind saying that when I was a young man I was halfway in love with her. So I sort of took you under my wing. It's been that way ever since."

She stirred restlessly and said, "Don't tell me that you looked upon me as a daughter, too."

He managed an abrupt laugh and replied, "Not exactly, though it is something like that. Have you been thinking otherwise?"

She was silent for some time, then nodded and said honestly, "Yes. I've wondered many times when you were going to make the big pitch."

"I see. Yes, I suppose you would think that way. Can't blame you. But I have never thought that way and that is the truth. I have a lot of faith in you. You do admit," he smiled, "that I usually know what I am doing?"

She returned his smile. "No doubt about that. I won't argue the point."

"Very good. You have no worries on the—ah—level you were thinking."

"Thanks." She was still not convinced.

"So now to get back to Bill. You understand how I feel about you. You must also understand that I love my son very much."

Her smile was warmer. "That I know."

"So we have two people whom I happen to love. Do you think that I would willingly hurt either of them?"

He waited and she saw that an answer was required. So she said, "No, I don't think you would."

"Very well. I would hate to see this tragedy happen to you. As a matter of fact, Betty, I would fight it every step of the way."

Her frown deepened and she sat up straight. "What are you talking about? What do you mean by a tragedy?"

His eyes dropped and he said softly, "That's what it would be, a tragedy."

"Oh, now, please—"

"I mean it, Betty." He looked at her and was able to simulate the pain he had felt in his eyes originally. He said slowly and distinctly, "Bill should never marry anyone at any time. This is very difficult for me to say, Betty, but I must be honest with you, regardless of what it costs."

He sat back and again waited for her reaction. His stomach was churning, his head aching badly, and he felt quite sick.

Betty stared at him and at last swallowed and said, "I don't follow you."

"No, I don't suppose you would. So I'll try to put it as simply as possible. Bill is in no fit condition to be married. It's something he doesn't know about, we have always kept it from him."

Betty laughed shakily. "Believe me, Mr. Kane, he hasn't talked seriously about marriage, and I don't even know yet if I'm in love with him. You seem to be jumping the gun."

"In that case," he sighed, "I've arrived at the right time. Bill," he lied, "has something badly wrong with him. I don't mean to tell you what it is. Mrs. Kane and I have never let it out of the family. But you can take my word for it that if you married him, it would be a tremendous tragedy."

"Physical or mental?" She thought a split-second and shook her head. "It can't be mental. There is certainly nothing wrong with his mind. Then it must be something physical."

He sighed again, but this time inwardly. It was finally going his way. He said stubbornly, "I can't tell you. It is something we have had to live with all of our lives, and we don't mean to be telling the world at this point."

"How about his brother, Frank?"

Kane blinked at her, then caught at the straw offered. "The same with Frank," he said. "Bill doesn't know, but unfortunately,

Frank found out some years back quite by accident. Do you know what the knowledge has done to him?"

"Bill tells me he is simply a playboy."

"That is correct. What Frank learned has ruined his life." He asked cautiously, "Would you care to have that happen to Bill?"

She threw her head back and snapped at him, "Naturally not."

"Then don't ask me to tell you what it is. I won't, because I don't trust even you to keep it to yourself. You simply have to take my word for it that something is badly wrong and that I don't wish to see you get hurt. That is why I came today, Betty. I had to warn you. I don't care how you do it, but you have to break off with Bill.

He was about to get to his feet when she looked straight into his eyes and said musingly, "You know, a thought just occurred to me. You are a very devious man. This tale of yours could easily be a way to get rid of your greatest opposition, namely your own son, and so keep me securely in your stable."

Then he got to his feet and leaned over the table to look down at her. His eyes were narrow and his voice was cold. "That," he said, "is smart thinking. It also happens to be too smart. So now it's up to you to figure out whether I was telling the truth or not. All I can say in conclusion, Betty—and this comes from my heart—is that it would be one of the greatest tragedies I can think of for you and Bill to fall in love with each other. Think it over."

He turned away from her and walked out of the apartment, and she stared after him. Then she exploded and said aloud, "Poppycock! What nonsense! Who the hell does he think he's fooling?" It wasn't even a very clever story. Did he think she was so stupid as to fall for something as simple as that? Good God, he wasn't half as smart as she had thought. She burst out laughing—but bitterly. It hurt her to think that he thought so little of her intelligence.

Suddenly impatient to be on her way she left the apartment in a hurry. She went down to the Jaguar and drove quickly to Bill's apartment house. He was waiting for her out on the sidewalk. She pulled up to the curb and slid over to the other seat and waved him around the car. He slid in behind the wheel and looked at her.

She said grimly, "When I go out with a man, the man does the driving."

He smiled and winked. "Now, you are what I call an eminently intelligent female. You're beginning to grow on me, honey. You are, indeed."

They roared away toward the freeway system going south down the Peninsula. It was a bit foggy in the city, but they ran into sunshine at San Bruno and from there down it became progressively warmer. They left the freeway at Redwood City and headed into the hills to the west and after a few minutes were in the exclusive section of Woodside. Bill swung up Hayward Road, then turned into a private circular driveway and stopped in the courtyard before Anna Merritt's house. It was a good-sized mansion in the French Normandy farmhouse style, with sixteen rooms, garages, an annex for the servants, and surrounding acres of semi-formal gardens that were now mostly in full bloom.

Bill got out of the car and helped Betty out, then swung her about and asked her, "Why did you insist on your car today? I have a perfectly good car of my own."

"Because," she smiled, "I wanted to impress you."

"Okay. Let's go in. Let's hope Anna's in a good mood."

"Oh? You know her that well?"

"Hell, Betty, I've known her all my life. She and the old man are damned good friends. She had almost as much to do with raising me as my own mother."

"Oh, really? The things we learn."

As they were walking toward the house, she asked, "How's your health?"

"Couldn't be better."

"No," she said, "I mean it seriously. A lot of big characters like you aren't really in very good shape."

He had to laugh and squeezed her arm. "Except for the ordinary illnesses of the average juvenile delinquent," he replied, "there has never been anything wrong with me."

"Nothing at all?"

He glanced at her curiously. "You sound as if you're trying to force me to say I'm syphilitic or something. What's with you?"

"Nothing," she chuckled. "Let's just say I'm a bit giddy today."

The butler let them in to the main gallery. Betty told Bill, "You go out to the bathhouse and get into your swimming trunks. I'll meet you at the pool." She left him and went upstairs to the room that was reserved for her exclusive use. She got out of her clothing and into a two-piece swim suit that was not quite a Bikini, yet was not far from it. There was very little cloth over her firm breasts and not much more than that around her hips.

She postured before a full-length mirror, blushed and laughed, and started out of the room.

In the upstairs hallway she ran into Mrs. Merritt. The older woman stopped her and looked her up and down and beamed at her. "God," she whispered, "if only I could still get away with it."

Betty smiled secretly. Mrs. Merritt looked so damned cute. She was wearing gold sandals, with white slacks and a jacket splashed with color designed by the crazy Italian designer Pucci. Her hair was pulled severely behind her head and tied with a chartreuse bow. If one stood a little away she would seem to be eighteen years old.

Betty laughed and said, "You look darling."

Mrs. Merritt laughed with her. "Why, thank you, darling. That is very kind of you. Now, you run along."

"I forgot to tell you, I have a guest. I brought a friend with me."

"Oh, indeed? Well, that is quite all right. Then it will be the three of us. Who is your guest, dear? Someone I know?"

Betty chuckled. "Very much so. I've come with Mr. Kane's son, Bill."

Mrs. Merritt's smile became frozen and a bit twisted. She blinked at Betty and asked hoarsely, "Just whom did you say it was?"

"Bill Kane, Mr. Kane's son."

Mrs. Merritt sucked in her breath and asked, "You know him very well?"

"Yes. We've been going around together now for a little while."

"You—and—and Bill—"

Mrs. Merritt became suddenly pale, her eyes bigger than ever, and she had to lean against the wall for support. Her hands began to tremble. She whispered, "Oh, my God!" Then suddenly she began crying and the tears ran down her cheeks as she covered her face with her hands and sank down to her knees on the carpet.

Betty ran to her, dropped to her knees, and threw her arms about Mrs. Merritt. All she could say was, "What's the matter? My God, what's the matter?"

It was a long while before Mrs. Merritt responded, but at last she looked at Betty and dug her fingers into Betty's shoulders. The two of them got awkwardly to their feet. Betty stared at her and saw there was a nervous tic at the corner of her left eye, her hands were still shaking and her face was so ashen-pale that the deep red of her lips was now grotesque.

Her fingers were still clutching Betty's shoulders. She swallowed and whispered, "Betty, listen to me. Drop Bill Kane as if he had the black plague. Please. Don't ask me why. I can't tell you. But, please believe me."

"But—but—" Then Betty cried out, "Good Lord, what's wrong with him? He seems like the nicest person I've ever known. What is it? Tell me!"

Mrs. Merritt shook her head slowly. "No, dear, I can't. You will just have to take my word for it." Then her eyes seemed to open even wider. Her fingers dug more fiercely into Betty's shoulders. "My dear, tell me the truth. Have you—I mean—have you had any physical relationship—"

Betty shook her head violently. "Of course not. It hasn't gone anywhere near that far."

Mrs. Merritt sighed, almost with every cell of her body. "Thank God for that." Then she shoved herself away from Betty. She was beginning to regain her composure. "Please, dear. Take the word of an older woman who happens to love you. Bill Kane could ruin your future more surely than anything else in this world that could happen to you. I mean every word of it."

Betty said, "This is the second time I've heard the same thing today. Mr. Kane saw me this morning. And he wouldn't tell me what it was, either. Apparently, though, Bill doesn't know a thing about it."

Mrs. Merritt gave her a baffled look, then suddenly understood. She nodded. "That is correct. Bill knows nothing. But you do believe me?"

Betty sighed deeply. "I have to. That wasn't an act you just put on. No actress could be that good. Yes, I believe you. And you won't even hint?"

Mrs. Merritt did not answer the question. She raised her hand to rub her eyes and mumbled, "Now I have a vicious headache. I think I'll go in and lie down. Tell Bill that I am indisposed and that I—ah—well, I probably shall not see him. Good-bye, dear. Next week end, perhaps."

She walked down to the master bedroom at the end of the hallway and disappeared.

Betty went downstairs and walked thoughtfully outside to the pool. Bill was in the pool swimming back and forth. When he saw her, though, he came out of the water in a rush of spray and grinned and whistled loudly. "Man, oh, man," he chuckled, "I knew there was a good body under the clothes you wear, but no one ever warned me that it would be the greatest."

Betty had difficulty returning his smile. She had difficulty doing anything that day—all the life seemed to have been drained out of her. Every time she looked at Bill a knife seemed to be driven through her heart. It had to be some horrible disease. There was no other answer. But what sort of horrible disease could a man have without knowing it? It was puzzling. She decided to consult some doctor and perhaps find out what it was.

She also realized how closely she had courted danger personally that day. She had not really believed Kane at all. But now she could not help but believe him, not after Mrs. Merritt's sudden collapse. Only a fool could doubt her reaction. That complete and unexpected collapse could never have been an act.

Bill soon realized that Betty was more than usually preoccupied that day, and his own spirits were dampened. They lay about the pool and half-dozed in the sun, and in the middle of the afternoon, dressed and took off. They drove south down to Santa Cruz for a sea food dinner in a cliff-hanging restaurant overlooking the ocean. Then they started back to San Francisco on the serpentine Skyline Highway. Betty was still more silent than usual, and Bill became irritated and finally angry. He began driving faster and faster. Betty at last looked up and saw that the lights of other cars coming toward them were much too fast. But it was not the other cars, it was Bill's speed.

She reached around the wheel, turned off the ignition key, and pulled it out of the slot. "Bill," she said, "I have no desire to be mangled or killed because of your stupidity. Now, do you care to drive sanely, or shall I drive?"

He pulled off to the side of the road and sat there quietly for a moment, then glanced at her and said, "Give me the key." She handed it to him, he started the engine again and drove down the highway at a respectable speed.

"Sorry," he said. "I was burning. You've had me all loused up today."

"In what way?"

"Well, you don't laugh, you're distant, and you just don't seem to be with it. Today of all days."

"What's so special about today?"

He glanced at her briefly, then looked ahead and said, "I had intended today to ask you to marry me."

She whispered, "Oh." She sat back and leaned against the door and again a knife was driven through her heart. She stammered, "I—ah—I haven't been—I mean—I've been sort of upset all day. I am sorry, Bill."

"Sure. Aren't we all?" He looked at her again for a moment, turned his eyes back to the road, and said softly, "I might still ask that question."

She placed a hand on his arm gripping the wheel and shook her head. "No, Bill," she said. "Please, don't ask it today. I couldn't take it today."

He shrugged. "Okay. I shouldn't have brought it up at all." He dropped his left hand into the pocket of his coat and felt the tiny velvet case that contained a diamond engagement ring. He stared ahead at the road with eyes that were burning and mumbled, "Some other time then."

"Yes. Some other time."

She felt like crying and looked away from him.

13

SUNDAY night was as bad for Betty as Saturday night had been for Lew Kane. She tossed and turned and slept very little. After the alarm clock rang in the morning she remained in bed for some time staring at the ceiling. What had happened the day before seemed very much out of focus and quite unreal. She tried to tell herself that it was a very bad plot out of a third-rate movie. Yet she could not deny that Kane himself had told her what must have hurt in the telling, and that Anna Merritt had reacted so strongly as to preclude any possibility of fraud. What she had learned had obviously been told to her honestly.

Any association with Bill Kane could be tragic, period.

Intuition told her, It's deeper than something simply physical. It has to be. But what it could be, she had no idea.

She dressed, had breakfast, and made up her mind to be late for work that morning. The hell with the store. She telephoned a friend of hers, got the name of a good doctor, then called his office at nine in the morning. She ran into difficulty when the doctor found out what she wanted. He called on his hospital cases in the mornings, but finally and irritably told her that if she got down to his office immediately he would talk to her. She took a taxi down to 450 Sutter and went straight to his office.

He frowned and glared at her and sat her down, then sat back to listen to her story. She did not attempt too many lies—said it was something that had happened to her—but she did refuse to name names and places, which he did not care about, anyway. She told him the story as straightforwardly as possible.

When she was through he sat back, put his fingertips together in a pyramid, and stared thoughtfully out the window. He was at last interested. Then he swung about to look at her and said, "First off, I would say that somebody is putting you on. They don't want you in the family."

"Yes," she nodded, "I thought that, too. But how do you explain the reaction of the woman, who is no more than a friend of the father involved?"

He squinted at her narrowly. "Couldn't he have called her up and told her how to react? You say they are close friends."

"Oh, definitely so. I thought of that, too. But, believe me, Doctor, no woman could have put on the act she went through without my seeing through it or being at least suspicious of it. What happened to her was very definitely sudden shock and an honest reaction. She wasn't kidding."

He puffed out his cheeks and sighed. "Then we must face the possibility that what these two people told you was the truth." He turned away from her and again stared out the window. "I suppose," he said, "you have been thinking of hemophilia. That is the most commonly known disease of inheritance."

"It has occurred to me, yes. Is it so terrible, Doctor?"

"Well, it is not to be considered lightly. It is almost always hereditary, and it is characterized by a tendency to hemorrhage even from very small cuts and wounds. It is an extremely bad thing for a person to live with. They sometimes bleed to death. However, we have made rapid strides in that field lately, and it is not as tragic any more as it used to be. No, I would say that is not it."

"Why?"

"Because, my dear, no one can have hemophilia without knowing it, and you tell me that this younger son does not know."

She sighed and said, "Yes. Naturally, he would know about hemophilia. How could you hide it from him? What else is there, Doctor?"

"There could also be leprosy."

She shuddered and said, "I thought of that, too."

He said mildly, "Then forget it. Leprosy is not hereditary."

"Oh? I didn't know that." She tilted her head to one side and appraised him, then said sharply, "Doctor, you're beating about the bush."

He smiled at her and nodded. "Yes, I am. I was just wondering when you would be conscious of it. You are a very astute young lady. But have you thought about hereditary or congenital syphilis?"

"What is the difference between the two?"

"Hereditary is naturally passed on from the parents. Congenital is acquired in the womb. It is highly unlikely, however, to think that two brothers, born at different dates, could have acquired syphilis in the womb. So it would have to be hereditary."

She said weakly, "That was the first thing I thought of."

"Yes, I suppose it would be. So let me tell you about syphilis. A person born with it is, more often than not, badly crippled or deformed. On the other hand, it is possible for a person to be born with it and yet just be a carrier, without having it affect him personally at all. I say possible, but I don't say probably. Yet if that were true, and the carrier's parents knew about it, then any doctor would tell them that today the disease can be treated so effectively as to be completely knocked out of the system. In other words, if you knew that such a condition existed, you could most likely get rid of it with proper medication."

He spread his hands palms down on the desk. "So, where does that leave us? It puts us back where we started. It can't be hemophilia because the young man would know about it. Leprosy is out of the question because that cannot be inherited. And it can't be syphilis because the parents would know, even if the young man did not, and it could be medically corrected."

"There is nothing else?"

"To my knowledge as a practicing physician," he said, "which I have been for many years, there is no other horrible disease, of which the carrier would be unaware, that could be transferred to another person, or to their children. In other words, I am unable to answer your big question, except to refer to what I said in the beginning, someone does not want you in the family."

She stared at him and wondered about him. He looked into her eyes and permitted a light smile to tug at his lips. What she could not know about him was that he was a cynic, but also a compassionate man, strangely enough. So now he looked into

Betty's eyes, smiled lightly, and asked himself, Am I God? Let her go to someone else.

Betty walked out of his office more than a little dissatisfied. She was sure the doctor had not actually lied to her, yet she had the feeling he could have been of more help. Instead, he seemed merely to have made up his mind from the beginning—that she was not wanted in the family.

On the other hand, perhaps what was wrong with Bill had nothing to do with disease or anything physical. She thought of that angle and realized again that at no time had Kane or Mrs. Merritt actually mentioned anything about disease. She felt frustrated and defeated, and the more she thought of it the more confused she became. She tried to put the whole thing out of her mind and hurried on to the store, an hour late.

She spent a day of intense harassment. She had hardly stepped onto the floor when she was surrounded with saleswomen, customers, a few angry buyers, and Maloney and Baker. In the midst of it all there was a woman, a Mrs. Ellis, who had a hat and a problem that seemed to take forever to solve.

Betty was hardly home in her apartment that evening when the telephone rang. It was Bill and he was apologetic. "Cookie," he said, "I'm sorry."

"About what, Bill?"

"Well, yesterday was kind of a nothing day. Now I realize I was all wet. I've been thinking about it, and I know you had no reason to be mad at me. It had to be your job. I know how you work under pressure, and I suppose I should understand that you should have at least one day to be preoccupied. That was yesterday, and I'm sorry I got a little out of line."

She smiled and said, "You didn't, really. I just wasn't very good company, and I'm the one who is sorry for that."

He chuckled and said, "Forget it. Look, I would love to see you tonight, but I have a date with Anna Merritt."

She said curiously, "Oh?"

"Uh-huh. Damned if I know what's on her mind, but she called this afternoon and wanted me to have dinner with her and Mr. Klein tonight. So shall I pick you up tomorrow?"

Betty asked curiously, "Mr. Klein? Is that an attorney?"

"Yes. Goldsmith and Klein. Klein has been Anna's attorney for more years than I can remember. A hell of a nice guy. So, I'll be seeing you?"

"Yes, Bill."

She hung up the telephone and sat back, a light smile playing about her lips. How remarkably odd. Goldsmith and Klein. Mr. Klein was Mrs. Merritt's attorney. Goldsmith and Klein had always been Betty's attorneys. Mr. Klein was the one who had always handled her estate. He was the one who still sent her the five hundred dollars a month. And that was odd, too. Because Mrs. Merritt's maiden name was also Parker. Could there be something—? No, no, no! It couldn't be. It was too wild! It was too crazy!

She got up and walked into the kitchen to prepare dinner and found herself not even able to peel a potato. Her hands were shaking and she felt a little sick. She sat down and stared through the kitchen window. Was she imagining things? Was her brain playing tricks on her? She shook her head and tried to think dispassionately. Let me see now. Mrs. Merritt's maiden name was Parker and she had kept it from Betty. So! Mrs. Merritt, shortly after they had come to know each other, had wanted to adopt her. So! Betty's income all of her life had been received through the firm of Goldsmith and Klein. Mr. Klein had been Mrs. Merritt's attorney, "... for more years than I can remember." So! What, in God's name, did it all amount to?

She went back into the bedroom, got undressed, and lay on the bed. As she stared at the ceiling her brain went around and around. No, no, no, no, no! Not what I am thinking. It simply couldn't be. She had a mother and she had a father. They had been killed in Paris and she had been raised on some sort of trust fund. But she had never known her mother or her father. All she knew was what she had been told. But how about the people who had told her? Who were they? Servants and nurse-maids. How would they really know? Wouldn't they only know what they had been told? Of course. Then how did she really know? She faced it, and for the first time in her life realized that there was no way she could really know. Even so, she had lived with it all of her life. It was part of her. It was not too easy to forget or to discard. No, she thought, I'm just dreaming again, just making things up.

She started to get up, but suddenly felt faint and dizzy and lay down again. She had just remembered something—the lock of hair Mrs. Merritt had showed her shortly after they had met. It had nearly matched with her own. She lay on the bed and blinked at the ceiling, and it was a long time before she was able to sit up. Childish thinking, she thought. Damned foolishness. Hell's bells, her mother and father had been killed in Paris and that was the end of the matter. Nevertheless—

When she went to work the following day she was able to put the idea far back in her mind, but not far enough. During that day and the week to follow she quite often found herself standing quietly alone, staring into space and thinking.

Then, on Sunday morning, she realized suddenly that she had not heard from Bill Kane since his Monday night call. That was indeed very strange. Bill had been calling her every night, or every other night at the very least, just to say hello and talk for a while. But now she had not heard from him for almost a whole week—since his Monday night dinner with Mrs. Merritt and Mr. Klein. A slight chill settled in her spine, and she was not able to shake it off.

Betty was anxious to get to work Monday morning. She had to talk to someone. The Big Idea had reached that point where it was necessary for her to have an unbiased opinion. There was only one person she could trust who could possibly come up with an unprejudiced opinion—Joe Haley.

She was at work early Monday morning, but got caught up in a rush of temperamental saleswomen, an angry union agent, Maloney who was upset about some customer who had been brushed off, and an unusual flood of customers. It was almost the noon hour before she was able to call Joe. She asked him to meet her somewhere for lunch.

He laughed and said, "Sure, baby. You take a taxi and I'll take a taxi and we'll meet at Sorrento's. It's a little Italian joint in North Beach—"

"I've been there two or three times."

"Oh? Good. Then you know the place. Meet me there at a quarter to one."

Betty was standing on the sidewalk in front of Sorrento's when Joe got out of his cab. He took her arm and they went inside. It was a very small restaurant on Columbus Avenue, with ivy leaves hanging from the ceiling and in the back was a counter presided over by a grinning spinner of pizza dough. Betty and Joe sat in a booth and ordered.

They chatted about the business and Kane, and the business and Kane again, and then, toward the end of the meal, Betty said, "I have something weird to tell you that's killing me. I hope you don't mind listening?"

"Fire away, cookie. You're the only beautiful doll I know who uses me as a father-confessor. It's so damned unique I'm getting to like it. Shoot."

She told him about Kane's visit and what he had had to say about his son, Bill. Joe stared at her, then burst out laughing and said, "If there is anything at all wrong with Bill Kane then I am a senile cripple. What sort of horseshit is that?"

"All right, now. Listen to the rest of it."

Then she told him about the incident at Mrs. Merritt's home.

This time Joe was thoughtfully silent for a long while, chewing it over in his mind. He said at last, "That is odd. Very odd. And this was right on top of Kane telling you about Bill?"

"Yes. But this was no phony. This was the real thing."

"I'll take your word for it. But hell, Betty, I can't think of anything badly wrong with Bill. He's so damned healthy it's sickening."

"I know. But you haven't heard all of it." She took a deep breath, then let it out slowly and said, "You know my past history. So now let's add up a few facts. I don't truly know who my parents were. I was just told by strangers. I don't truly know how they died, because I was just a baby at the time, and, again, I was told by strangers."

"You said something about some attorneys—"

"That," she almost cried, "is one of the strangest things of all. Now, you just listen. I don't know whether I ever told you, but when I first arrived in San Francisco and hardly knew Mrs. Merritt she wanted to adopt me. I made the tragic mistake of laughing at her—after all, I was a grown adult woman—and she has never asked me again. But bear it in mind."

Joe cocked his head to one side and said with interest, "Go on."

"On another occasion, she brought in a lock of her hair that had been cut when she was a young woman and compared it with mine. It was almost the identical shade of red."

"In other words," Joe smiled, "that flaming red of your hair really is its natural color."

She squared her shoulders and said huffily, "Well, of course."

"Lucky you."

She saw that he had been pulling her leg and laughed, but sobered again almost immediately. She said, "I never knew my parents, Joe, so most of my life I have played a little game with myself of pretending."

He grinned with understanding. "You are the illegitimate

daughter," he chuckled, "of the king and queen of Lower Slobovia. Something like that?"

"Something exactly like that. And now I think I am playing that game again. See what you think of it. Mrs. Merritt's maiden name is Parker, the same as mine, a fact that she never saw fit to mention to me. Shortly after she knew me she wanted to adopt me, a grown woman, mind you, which is more than a little unusual. Then, a week ago I learned something else. The Parker estate, I mean the estate that was left to me, has always been administered by a Mr. Klein of the firm of Goldsmith and Klein, here in San Francisco."

"What about this Mr. Klein?"

"I just learned that he has been Mrs. Merritt's attorney for many, many years." She sat back, then asked, "How does all this add up to you?"

Joe squinted at her and asked, "How do you get along with Mrs. Merritt today?"

"In her home in Woodside she has a room decorated especially for my use. No one else is allowed to use it. Does that answer your question?"

He whistled softly under his breath and looked over her head. He leaned over to finish his lasagna, and Betty had nothing more to say. He called the waitress and ordered two frozen pineapple sherbets and some coffee. He finished his dessert and drank two cups of coffee and had nothing to say. He called the waitress and paid the bill and walked with Betty out to the sidewalk.

Then, for the first time in a long while, he said, "There are a lot of holes in what you have just told me. The Merritts never had any children."

"I know."

"And that story you told me about how you were born and what happened to your parents and how you were raised is pretty damned pat."

"It is the only story I know. Could it be wrong?"

Joe shrugged. "Anything could be wrong. How would you know? You wouldn't know anything for sure until you were seven or eight years old."

"I can think back to five."

"So then five. The really important years are a blank in your mind. Anything could be true, even that you are Mrs. Merritt's illegitimate daughter. That is what you were hinting at, isn't it?"

She nodded, but could not reply. It was too preposterous to get a statement out of her.

Joe said, "Uh-huh. So, all right. There is one way we can put this whole thing at rest pretty damned fast."

She gasped and asked eagerly, "How is that, Joe?"

"Very simple. When Anna married George Merritt she automatically became a VIP. Any move she made from that point on would be in the society columns of the newspapers. So all we have to do is look through the back issues of the papers in 1939 and find out if Mrs. Merritt was in Europe during that year. That should be very easy to do."

Betty thought of it and felt a chill in her spine. She stammered, "I couldn't—I mean—I couldn't do it. Even the idea scares me."

He squeezed her arm. "I'll do it for you."

"But how about Bill?" she cried. "Where does he fit in?"

"I'm damned if I know. That has me baffled, too. But let's take this thing one step at a time. Okay?"

"Oh, yes. And honest, Joe, I am ever so grateful."

He looked down at the lovely female figure at his side and had difficulty suppressing his laughter. No one, absolutely no one, would believe this, that he was actually putting himself out for a beautiful woman with no thought of reward. He hardly believed it himself.

He put her in a taxicab and waved her away, then burst out laughing. But when he got in another cab and sat back in the seat he thought of what he had been told and was again frowning seriously. Very odd. Very odd, indeed.

He wondered if she could really have something.

Joe thought very little of what Betty had told him the rest of that day and the day following. He had his own personal problems, and he was also quite busy. On Wednesday, however, his day off, he called the *San Francisco Chronicle* and inquired about using their back files. He was told that he would find all of them at the city's main library in Civic Center.

Joe had breakfast, then drove downtown to the main library. An elderly woman got him copies of the *Chronicle* for the early months of 1939. Joe sat at a big table and looked through them and suddenly, in March, found what he was after. The fabulous beauty and social leader, Mrs. George Merritt, was throwing a bon voyage party at the Merritt mansion in Hillsborough. All of San Francisco's elite were to be present. She was leaving for an "extensive" tour of Europe.

Joe skipped the following months and got copies of the *Chronicle* for the latter part of August and the early part of September. He found what he wanted almost at once. On September 2, 1939, Mrs. George Merritt had arrived in New York after spending seven months on a Grand Tour of the Continent. There was more to follow, but all Joe cared about were the dates. An important fact, however, was that George Merritt had met her as she disembarked from the *Comte di Savoia* in New York harbor. In other words, Mr. Merritt had not been with her on the Grand Tour.

Joe shoved the papers aside and sat back and stared into space. Betty Parker, he thought, is probably Mrs. Merritt's daughter. It couldn't add up otherwise. It was possible that all the coincidences could spell out something else, but he did not believe it. He accepted the fact almost without question.

In March of 1939 she would probably have been about two months pregnant, and doctors would have confirmed it. It was not George Merritt's child. Otherwise there would have been cause for jubilation. So, she had sneaked away to Europe and disappeared as quickly as possible. She had given birth to the child, put her in the care of someone, made certain continuing arrangements, and returned to America in September—seven months after she had left. How was she to know that during that same month the world would turn upside down because of the madman Adolf Hitler?

Joe went out to his car and sat quietly behind the wheel and thought some more. Mrs. Merritt would have lost touch during the war years, naturally, but as soon as the war ended her first concern would be for the welfare of her illegitimate child. So, what would she do? She would turn for help to the finest attorneys in San Francisco, Goldsmith and Klein. They, in turn, would locate the child and make arrangements to take care of it for the rest of its life.

But what about the story of her life that Betty had grown up with? It was so pat. As a matter of fact, he realized, you couldn't think of a better story to dispose of a child's parents and keep her wandering about Europe without any sort of suspicion concerning her true identity. It had been very artfully accomplished. And then, when she was rather grown up, it had been so easy to bring her to America through the German quota. Very, very pat indeed. He almost admired Mrs. Merritt's ingenuity until he had a hunch that the whole thing was not the thinking of a woman but rather that of a man. And what man would that be? And how would you answer the question of Bill? There was only one answer and that was Lew Kane. I'll be double hogtied and goddamned, he thought.

Kane had been working for the Merritts in 1939. What else was there to answer?

Joe started his car and drove a few blocks up Van Ness to Tommy's Joynt, a very popular restaurant in the heart of automobile row. He picked up a bottle of Heineken's beer at the bar and a hot roast beef sandwich on rye bread at the counter and took them to a table in a far corner of the room. He ate his food and drank his beer and sat back to think.

Every detail of the picture he had in mind dovetailed into place. No exceptions. He had heard somewhere that there was something wrong with George Merritt; he was a homosexual, or a pervert, or he was incapable of having children, or something. Perhaps Anna Merritt had been fed up with him shortly after marrying him. And Kane, at that time, had been working for Merritt and had been a damned handsome man. He and Mrs. Merritt had obviously come together, and she had become pregnant and had gone off to Europe to have the child. So Betty was the daughter of Lew Kane and Anna Merritt. How else could Kane's visit with Betty be explained, and how else could you explain Mrs. Merritt's reaction to Betty's seeing Bill? Betty had no way of knowing it, but she had been seriously dating her own half-brother. No wonder Kane was upset and no wonder Mrs. Merritt had collapsed!

So, he thought, there is no other conclusion. Now what?

Suddenly, another thought stared him in the face. Now he knew how Kane had swung the Merritt-Wilson merger. Of course. It was probably Kane who had had Betty brought to America. Then, after she had completed her education and been seasoned in the department store business, he had hired her for the big Wilson store on Market Street.

He may have been acting in an altruistic manner at that moment, but shortly on or around that time George Merritt had destroyed himself and the widow had been faced with running a large chain of stores, which she probably did not feel up to doing. Very few women did. So she had cast about to sell out and that was when Kane had moved in. It was only a guess, but it was an intelligent one. What else was there to think? Kane had simply used their daughter to blackmail Mrs. Merritt into selling out to him. There was no other answer.

He shook his head and thought, I'll be damned!

Joe was leaving Tommy's Joynt when he almost bumped into Ellen Maloney coming in through the door. She stared at him and gasped, went pale and then blushed. "Well," she whispered, "what—what a pleasure. Joe!"

"How do you do, Mrs. Maloney? I mean, Ellen. What are you doing here?"

She almost dropped her purse, but grabbed it and said, "This is one of my favorite places for luncheon whenever I'm in the city. I dearly love their pastrami sandwiches. Don't you?"

"Uh-huh. Very good with sour pickles. In town shopping?"

"Oh, yes," she laughed. "Window shopping for a new car. Fred always claims that he picks the new car, but I manage to look them over first. Isn't that like a woman?"

"Very much so. Now, if you don't mind—"

She said quickly, "I know you're leaving, but couldn't you come back in and have a beer or coffee with me? We could, well—talk about things."

He glanced at his watch and said, "I'd like to very much, but I have an appointment and I'm already late. Another time, Ellen. And thank you." He walked away as quickly as he could. Half a block away he looked back. She was still standing there staring after him.

He spent the rest of the day driving about thinking, then drove home, took a shower, and changed his clothes. He went down to the dining room and took his place at the head of the table. Mrs. M. alway ate with the family, so that she was seated and also the boys. Then Mary came in and joined them, dressed in something white and shimmering—she was obviously going out somewhere—and took her place at the other end of the table. She nodded and smiled at everyone—except Joe. She ignored him.

Joe looked daggers at her, then cast his smile about the table. The others all looked away. It was obvious to the boys, and had been for some time, that not all was well between their parents. The three of them knew that their mother and father now slept in different rooms, and they also knew that they hardly spoke to each other, except out of necessity. They were both saddened and puzzled. So they sat and were silent—and suffered.

Joe looked at them and knew how they felt, and he cursed under his breath.

Before they had finished dessert, Mary left in a taxicab without saying where she was going. Joe ate along stolidly, staring at the tablecloth. When the meal was through he took the boys to a show in the Richmond District. It was not a bad movie, but no one seemed to enjoy it. On the way home in the Thunderbird Joseph, the six-year-old who was sitting in the back seat, suddenly started crying. He reached forward and placed his arms about his father's neck and said, "Daddy, please." But that was as far as he could go. He did not know what else to say. He sat back in his seat and huddled in a corner. Joe drove on, looking through the windshield and blinking his eyes furiously to hold back the tears that were building up.

He drove home and sent the children to their bedrooms, then he paced the floor of the living room for awhile. He wondered where Mary had gone and if she had come home yet. He went upstairs and paused before the door of the room which he was already referring to in his mind as "Mary's bedroom." He tried the knob and found it unlocked. He looked in the dark room and saw that it was empty. He sighed and turned away and went to his own room.

Mary, at that moment, was sitting in the front row of seats in an empty, gloomy Catholic church. She had been sitting there for four hours and her hands and feet were numb, though she was not aware of it. The flames of many candles flickered in her eyes, but she was staring raptly at the figures of Mary and the Child. She had been occupying that same seat in the church for three and four nights out of every week. She dressed always as if she were going out on a date with someone, but this was her date, the church. She had gone out with Ernie only that once and never with anyone else, except for a luncheon and a dinner with Joe's father. She wanted Joe to think that she was elsewhere.

Her hatred of Joe was now small and temporarily out of the way. She was indulging in the greatest luxury of all, self-hatred. What I did, she thought, has no justification whatever. It was done deliberately and with malice aforethought. She actually framed it in her mind with those words. There was no excuse for her. She was a good, religious Catholic woman, a good wife and a good mother, and she had deliberately betrayed everything in which she believed. She could never expect forgiveness from

God or Christ or anyone else. Which was why she never went to church in the daytime hours. She was afraid she might run into some priest she knew and that she might be led into a confessional. She had no desire to confess. She was unclean and she knew it. There was no room for her in the Kingdom of God. She could never expiate her sin. What she had done was a mortal sin. She could confess and she could tell her beads and spend her hours of penance, and she knew that none of it could cleanse her. There was no hope for her. She blinked her big eyes and two tears cascaded down her cheeks.

Then, for the first time the thought crossed her mind that perhaps Joe's sin was not as vital as her own. She thought of him and how he was. She had heard whispers that he was not all he seemed to be, and that she should be careful of him. And always she had thought of one word—jealousy. No other woman had a husband as beautiful as her own, and they were catty and jealous. But now she knew that some of what she had heard was true. And she thought of Joe again and how he was with other women, always teasing, laughing with them, receiving their adoration as his just due. His manner with women had always been so easy, so casual. Of course. He had them in the palm of his hand and he knew it.

So, all this time he had been playing around. She accepted it as a fact, even though she knew of but one incident. She thought of Joe's nature and faced the illuminating truth that it would not be like him to be any other way. She could not think of him as being anything other than what he was. He was Joe and that was all there was to it. And somehow, intuitively, she knew that he would never change and that she could not expect it of him.

Then she had to face the question, could she live out her life with such a man? She loved him. She admitted that. The children loved him. She knew that well. Even now he had probably taken them out somewhere. He never forgot his family on his days off. And in return? She wavered and fought with herself and tried to doubt his love, but there was no doubt. Joe loved his wife and his family. Of that there could never be a question.

Joe was a good husband and a good father. She was a good wife and a good mother. So then, how did a good wife and a good mother go about blinding herself to the philandering of a good husband and a good father? Oh, God, she groaned, and again she stared at Mary and the Child. Was there ever an answer?

She also had another small worry on her mind that was not yet bothering her too greatly. She had missed her period this month, which was unusual for her, and had gone to her doctor the day before. He had taken tests and had said that he would inform her, though it was still a bit too close to her regular time to be certain. She doubted that she was pregnant, although there was always that possibility. Even so, the thought of Ernie never crossed her mind. Joe would naturally have to be responsible, prior to her terrible sin with Ernie. Her closed Catholic mind would never accept the fact that anyone other than Joe could have impregnated her.

She got up finally to leave the church, hoping that Joe was now home so he would hear her come in.

14

THURSDAY was Joe's late day to go to work, from noon until nine P.M. He slept late that morning, then got into the Thunderbird, crossed the Golden Gate Bridge, and drove slowly about Marin County. He was not thinking of his personal problems. He was thinking of Betty Parker and what to do about the information he had acquired.

There was no doubt in his mind whatever that Anna Merritt was her mother. He would have gambled on that ten-to-one. He was also almost positive that Lew Kane was her father. He would have gambled on that at least two-to-one. So, he told himself, let's accept it as proven.

Where do we go from here?

He did not have to be a genius to know the answer to that one. If he passed on the information in his mind to Betty, he would upset her whole life and probably throw a monkey wrench into a few other lives as well. Mrs. Merritt could probably survive the scandal. After all, she was now a widow. The public exposure of such a thing would hurt her socially, but she would survive. Kane, on the other hand, would not fare so well. He was still married, he had children, and he was juggling a new business that could fail any time he dropped one of the lemons. Kane, therefore, was the one to think about.

What, he thought, do I owe him? Not much, really. He would rather go along with Kane, but he could also do without him.

He had no worries about landing on his feet elsewhere. He might even be better off under some other boss, though he admitted honestly to himself that he doubted it. Anyway, he would not suffer, no matter what happened. Yet he also admitted to himself that he liked Kane and that he had a grudging admiration for the man. He would actually hate to see Kane get hurt, especially if it was through some action of his own. No, he thought, I can't do anything to hurt him.

When he turned back toward the Golden Gate Bridge he had made up his mind. He would tell Betty nothing, at least for the moment. He would sit tight to see what developed, and tell Betty that he was working on it. That should satisfy her, if he made it plausible enough.

When he arrived at work he was a few minutes late and found Betty at her counter. He took her arm and walked her away from the traffic on the floor.

Then he told her, "The key to everything lies in Klein, the attorney."

She asked breathlessly, "How do you mean?"

"Well, you've learned he has been Mrs. Merritt's personal attorney for many years. He has also been your attorney and executor of your trust ever since you can remember. So you put two and two together and decide it comes out four. It's possible you may be right. But everything hinges on Klein."

"No, Joe, no. Klein is just simply something added."

"Nevertheless," he said stubbornly, "he is the key to the whole thing. If you can connect yourself to Mrs. Merritt through Klein, then you have the answer. You see?"

"Oh, yes. Now I see."

"So, okay. So now I have to do a little snooping and see just where Mr. Klein fits in. That won't be easy. You know how attorneys are. But I think I know a way," he lied, "of getting at him. I'll try it out and see what happens and let you know. Okay?"

She was thoughtfully silent for a moment, then she nodded and said, "Anything you say, Joe. You're the only person I can depend on."

"Good. Let's keep it that way. Now, I gotta run. See you later."

He walked away from her and went down to his own floor. When he walked toward his floor-desk he found Fred Maloney waiting for him. He had a carnation in his lapel, but his expression was not as fresh as that of the flower. When he saw Joe, however, he managed a tight smile.

"Hiya, Joe. Thought I'd drop by and tell you how Eric Jeffrey is making out."

"Oh, yeah. The new buyer. Cripes, I haven't even seen him around."

"He's been damned busy. First one in the store every day and the last to leave."

"What's he trying to be, teacher's pet?"

"Not that guy. He isn't put together that way. He's just simply learning the ropes, is all. I got a hunch he's coming along well."

"Good. Glad to hear it." Joe looked out over the floor and saw three salesmen waiting to talk to him, as well as his detail man and a fitter. He looked back at Maloney, impatient to break away and get to work.

Maloney moved a step closer to him. "You know," he said, frowning importantly, "something's been bothering me lately. Maybe you know the answers."

"Like what?"

"Nothing to do with the store, of course. It's just that I've been noticing something within my own set. By that, I mean people of my own age, the fortyish group."

Joe blinked at him. "Oh?"

"Yes. I've noticed a certain restlessness in the wives, a certain distant attitude toward their husbands when they pass that forty mark, a certain—"

Joe laughed and said, "I thought it was the other way around. I thought it was the husbands who figured maybe they'd missed something and started stepping out when they passed forty or fifty."

Maloney shook his head slowly. "Not so much," he said, "I've noticed it especially in the wives. They look at their husbands differently, sometimes almost as if they were strangers. They become peevish and irritable for no reason at all. There's a certain age when they just don't act normal any more." He looked at Joe and asked casually, "Do you know anything about it?"

Joe was about to say something when he realized suddenly that it was Ellen Maloney he was talking about and closed his mouth with an almost audible click of his teeth. He swallowed and looked away for a moment, then laughed heartily, too heartily, and said, "Hell's bells, Fred, you got the wrong boy. What do I know about people in their forties? You know me, the teen-agers delight!"

Fred stared at him, then his shoulders sagged a bit and he looked away. "I guess you're right," he said. "Well, keep the rags moving, pal."

"Will do."

Maloney walked away and took the elevator up to the fourth floor. He was chewing thoughtfully on his lower lip when he walked across the floor toward Betty's counter, which was now becoming known throughout the store as her command post. He looked at Betty, who was shoving papers around, and smiled. "Hi."

She winked at him. "What say, Boss?"

"Not much. Just making the rounds. Anything unusual?"

"Nope. Just had a gal in trying to buy an eighteen-ninety-five skirt with a hundred dollar check. Credit called her bank and found out she didn't even have an account, so Security took over. What is it with people like that, Fred? Why do they think they can get away with it?"

He said tiredly, "People like that, who haven't thought things out very well, are desperate. It's the ones who have thought things out who are the real criminals. I feel sorry for the woman."

"You're a patsy."

"I guess I am, in more ways than one."

Betty wondered why he had made such a remark, then her eye was caught by Kane. He had come out of the corridor leading to the executive offices and was looking anxiously toward the elevators. Then he glanced in Betty's direction, nodded at her, and disappeared down the corridor. Well, she thought, he must be waiting for someone real important.

She listened to Maloney talking store business and small gossip, but she kept her eyes on the elevators. In a minute or so the doors opened and out stepped the long, rangy figure of Bill Kane wearing corduroys, brogans, and a leather coat. He had probably just come from his work. He looked in her direction, and his eyes swung away. For a moment she thought he was going to walk on by, but then he turned on his heel and came to her counter. Fred shook hands with him, then had to hurry away to some other part of the store. Bill looked after him almost wistfully, before turning his attention back to Betty.

He asked foolishly, "How've you been?"

She said coolly, "Well, thank you. I haven't see you in a while."

"Well, no," he said, not looking at her. "I've had work kind of snowball on me lately. At it day and night."

"You could have called."

"I'm sorry, Betty. I've just been so damned busy—when I go home at night I just flop into bed."

Then he looked into her eyes and blinked at her in an odd way, and she sucked in her breath and wondered if "they" had told him she had some horrible disease. God, no! she thought. People didn't do things like that, did they?

Then he suddenly reached across the desk and squeezed her hand, and the look in his eyes was more of an oddity than ever, as if he was trying to project toward her some sort of deep sympathy.

"Have to run," he said crisply. "Dad is waiting for me."

He let go of her hand and walked quickly away, and because his back was toward her she did not see him raise his hand and wipe away a suggestion of mist from his hot eyes.

Bill went directly to his father's office. He opened the door, stepped inside, closed the door behind him, and locked it. Then he dropped into a chair across the big desk from his father and settled back on his spine. He clasped his hands on his knees and looked narrowly at his father, his lower lip protruding slightly. Kane had been watching every move he made. His own eyes clouded and the edges of his lips turned down. The two were remarkably alike, tall, rangy, and lean, with the same eyes and the same set purpose about their thin lips.

Without preamble, Bill said, "You were avoiding me yesterday."

Kane squinted at him and nodded. "Yes," he said, "I was. I knew why you wanted to see me. I had to get my wits together."

Bill looked a bit surprised. "Then Anna must have called you."

"She did, late Monday night. She had a talk with you, I understand."

"Yes. She was scared to death with the inherent danger of the situation between Betty and me. I don't blame her." He said bitterly, "It could almost have been incest." He waited, but as his father had nothing to say he continued, "She came into town, and I had dinner with her and Counselor Klein." He took a deep breath, let it out slowly, and said, "They told me all about Betty."

"I see." Kane swung his swivel chair a quarter turn and stared out the windows. After a silence, he said, "I don't blame her. I was scared, too. You see, I knew that you and Betty were seeing each other. I went to her Sunday—"

Bill interrupted, "Anna told me about that. Now I know what was wrong with Betty that day." He leaned forward angrily and almost shouted, "What the hell did you tell her, that I was syphilitic, or a leper, or something?"

Kane said softly, "Not quite. I just told her that there was a very good reason for her never to see you again. Damn it, Bill," he blurted out, "I didn't know what the devil to do. I was at a loss, yet something had to be done." He looked back at Bill and said, "So now you know she's your half-sister."

"Yes. Anna told me the whole story." He said sternly, "She didn't go into details. Now I'm asking the details of you."

Kane again looked toward the windows and his shoulders sagged. He said weakly, "You're my son. I suppose you have every right. Well, it's all simple enough, human nature being what it is. During those days I was a lot like Joe Haley. I didn't really appreciate your mother at that time, and I must admit I played around. I was then working here at Merritt's and got acquainted with Anna. She was a beautiful woman, she was at loose ends—let's be kind and just say that something was sexually wrong with her husband—so, well, we got together and it happened. That's the story."

Bill snapped at him, "You're hiding a hell of a lot."

Kane said angrily, "And don't expect me to spell it out either. Anyway, when Anna knew she was pregnant something drastic had to be done. Her husband, you see, was sterile. Yet he was exceedingly jealous of Anna. He would have ruined her if he knew her condition. So she took off for the Grand Tour of Europe and he never knew, not at that time, anyway."

Bill said wryly, "I can't picture Anna abandoning a child that way."

Kane roared, "Abandoning! Don't be a damned fool. Betty was never abandoned at any time. When Anna went to Europe she used her old passport with the maiden name of Parker. Then in France, after the baby was born, she staged this phony idea of the parents being killed. It was not really very hard to do, if you have a little money to spend. She returned to America leaving the child in very good hands. Her intention at that time, and mine too, was to wait about a year, then bring the child to America and keep her somewhere close by until she could persuade George to let her adopt the baby. That was the plan. Unfortunately, if Anna told you anything at all, everything went wrong."

"She told me about the French argument over Betty's birthright and the war and all."

"We did the best we could, Bill, believe me. The whole situation was extremely difficult. But we finally did manage to get her to America, and as soon as the time was ripe I got her up here." He bit his lip and said humbly, "I've been trying to treat her like a father ever since. Do you understand?"

"I—I guess so." He, too, said humbly, "You realize what a danger you were running with the two of us? I was attracted to her from the first."

"I know. That's why I had to act when I did. I had a hunch, even then, that it was all going to blow up in my face."

"What do you intend doing about her, Dad?"

Kane shrugged. "The answer, I suppose, is nothing."

"Did you know that I bought a ring for her?"

Kane closed his eyes and groaned, "Oh, God, no. I'm sorry Bill."

"It's all right. It didn't get very far. But what about Mom?"

Kane did not open his eyes. He said thinly, "I hope that nothing will have to be done. I happen to love your mother very much, Bill. Would you willingly do anything to hurt her?"

Bill blinked hotly at his father and said, "Not on your life. There's no reason for her to ever know about it. She'll never get it from me."

Kane looked at his son and a slight smile played about his lips. "Thanks, Bill."

Bill slapped his thighs loudly with the palms of his hands and got to his feet. "So," he said, "that's it. You made a remark that has me puzzled, though. What about George Merritt? Did he ever know?"

Kane nodded. "Yes, he did. When I brought Betty up here from Los Angeles he got a look at her somehow or other, added a few facts together in his mind—he always was suspicious about Anna's European trip, you see—had her investigated; and then he knew. He withdrew as a recluse into the Hillsborough mansion and saw no one. I can only imagine that he felt that Anna had fulfilled her role as a woman, yet he had failed monstrously as a man. So he killed himself. I'm guessing, of course, but it's probably close to the truth."

"So then you moved in on the Merritt chain."

Kane looked sharply at his son. "I don't know exactly how you mean that, but the answer is, in a way, yes." He stood up, too, and teetered from heel to toe. "Now," he asked, "do you condemn me?"

Bill squinted at him and shook his head slowly from side to side. "No, Dad. I've heard before about how you were in the early days. It isn't exactly news to me. I can tell you this, though. As far back as I can remember, to the best of my knowledge, I was raised in a loving family of loving parents."

Kane swallowed hard and after a moment was able to say, "Thanks again. I always did tell Bessie you were the one with the brains."

Bill turned toward the door and unlocked it, then paused for a moment and looked back at his father. "One thing," he said, "does worry me."

"What's that?"

"Well, the rumor is, amongst all your employees, that you brought Betty up here for the big pushover, whenever you were ready."

"Of course, what else could they think? What could anyone think? I'm afraid that couldn't be helped."

"No. How were they to know? But don't you think that maybe Betty thought the same way, too?"

Kane shrugged. "That couldn't be helped, either. But no harm done."

"That's just it, Dad. No harm done as of now. But suppose Betty finds out you are her father? Frankly, I shudder to think of her reaction. So, with that cheery little thought, I'll run along. After all," he said coldly, "you should be sweating, too, like I've been doing. Be seeing you, Dad."

Kane sat and stared at the door that Bill closed after his departure. The little talk with Bill, which he had dreaded facing, had come off quite well. He was relieved. But what the hell had Bill meant by that last crack?

The telephone rang and he picked it up. A store operator informed him that a Mr. John Garfield was calling from New York. Kane's heart skipped a beat. He told the girl to wait a minute, picked up another telephone and told Maxwell Jackson to get into his office fast. The moment Jackson arrived, his eyebrows raised, Kane nodded him into a chair and shoved across the desk a telephone which was connected with his own telephone.

"Just listen," he said, "and keep your mouth shut."

Then he told the girl to put through the New York call and after a moment John Garfield said, "Hello? Mr. Kane? Mr. Lew Kane?"

Kane winked at Jackson and said heartily, "That's right, Mr. Garfield. This is quite a pleasure. I used to know your father many years ago, but I have never had the pleasure of meeting you and your brothers. I trust you are calling to ask some small favor of me here on the Coast. I would be most happy to oblige you. What is it you have in mind?"

Garfield's voice lowered to a slightly more husky level. "That is not exactly it," he said slowly. "For the past few days I have been rather busy with one of your former employees."

Kane said innocently, "Oh?"

"Yes, sir. Mr. Harold Drury, by name. Your former controller. A very fine person, indeed."

"I am in solid agreement with you." Then he said anxiously, "But, my God, I thought he was very well fixed. I had no idea he would be going back to New York looking for a job."

"No, Mr. Kane. Mr. Drury was not back here looking for a job." There was again a faint chuckle as Garfield said, "He was, in fact, offering me something for sale. We just concluded the deal this morning."

"Oh, really? I have no idea—"

Garfield broke in impatiently, "Mr. Kane, my brothers and I have just bought out Mr. Drury's stock in the Merritt-Wilson chain, and I thought you should be the first to know."

Kane closed his eyes and sank his teeth into his lower lip so hard he almost drew blood. He let out a long sigh from the depths of his lungs, then opened his eyes and blinked into space. Garfield was saying something, but Kane could not hear him. There seemed to be a ringing in his ears.

But he had himself under control after a moment and said, "Sorry, Mr. Garfield, the connection went wrong. I haven't been hearing you. Did you just tell me that Drury sold out his stock to you?"

"That is right, sir. We bought him out a hundred percent."

"Hmmmmm. I'll be damned. This is going to take a little while getting used to. Frankly, I'm bowled over."

Garfield said dryly, "I rather figured that. I would feel the same way in your shoes. However, as the old saying goes, business is business. So, Mr. Kane, as soon as possible I shall be coming out to call on you. And, furthermore, considering the block of shares we have bought, I shall expect to be a member of your board of directors."

Kane said vaguely, "I'll be very happy to talk it over with you. But a telephone conversation—"

"Naturally. Very well, Mr. Kane, I shall be seeing you soon."

"Very good, Mr. Garfield. Thanks for calling. Good-bye."

Kane hung up and looked across the desk as Jackson replaced his own telephone in the cradle. Jackson stared at him with astonishment mixed with more than a little perplexity. "The Garfields," he muttered. "Jee-zuss!"

Kane sat back and laced his fingers across his stomach. "Uh-huh."

"But, good God," Jackson exploded, "can't you see what they'll do to you? Can't you see that you're halfway out on your rear-end right now?"

Kane said placidly, "Not so fast. It isn't as tragic as it seems."

Jackson jumped up and started pacing the floor. "The hell it isn't," he barked. "First off, they'll notify the press—"

"Now, Max, that's where you're wrong. They'll do nothing of the kind. They aren't anxious to publicize their new connection with Merritt-Wilson so fast. First, Garfield will come out here and have a look around. He'll bring out some attorneys with him and leave them behind. They'll demand to go over the books, which they can do. The Garfields do not yet have access to our books, so they don't truly know where we stand. But once they get a look they can make up their collective minds. Then, and only then, if they figure everything is solid enough, they will announce their purchase. Or if they don't like what they find, they can quietly sell out Drury's stock, perhaps at a small loss, and wipe it all out on a tax deduction. They don't really stand to lose no matter how you look at it. Anyway, I think that's how they'll go about it."

Jackson stopped pacing, pulled at his lower lip, and stared at Kane. "You may be right. But where does this leave you? That's a high-pressure outfit. They'll skin you alive if they can."

"Thanks for your last words, Max. There's a hell of a lot of meaning in 'if they can.' And I don't think they can."

"Once you got a Garfield on the board of directors—"

"I know exactly what's in your mind. But there isn't going to be any Garfield on the board." He leaned across the desk and said, "I've had a hunch I might expect something like this, so I have already talked it over with our attorneys. As you well know, the Garfields own Westover Mills."

"Sure."

"Which is one of the biggest manufacturers in the country for men's suits. Right?"

"Well, sure—"

"So we don't happen to buy from Westover. We buy from Botany, three G's, and others. In other words, Max, they will try to sit on our board not only as representatives of themselves, the Garfields, but also as owners and representatives of Westover Mills. Under the law I can restrain them from doing that. It all comes under the laws concerning restraint of trade and even has a little something to do with monopolies and overlapping directorships." He smiled again as he said, "Believe me, Max, our attorneys have assured me that no Garfield will ever be seated on the board of directors of Merritt-Wilson. How do you like them apples?" He sat back and laughed deep in his chest.

Jackson was a little slow to follow, but after awhile he, too, began to get the picture and allowed himself a small, somewhat icy smile. "Very good," he said. "Obviously, you have figured this all out beforehand. You even seem to be somewhat pleased. Is it too much to ask why?"

Kane said expansively, "Not at all. I was rather hoping this would happen. You know our situation in New York. It isn't bad and it isn't good. We can live with it, but we will never go anywhere with it." He paused a moment, then said fiercely, "Max, I mean to build the biggest damned specialty chain this country has ever known. That is my ambition. I will never be satisfied with anything less. But as we stand now, we will go no farther than where we are as of this moment. You can't move, you can't grow, and you can't expand without plenty of help from New York. So that is what I am after."

Jackson was again perplexed. "But having the Garfields buy in with you is like inheriting a nest of rattlesnakes."

"No, Max. You're wrong. Everyone in the business knows how badly Garfields want an outlet on the Pacific Coast. So, say the news gets out that they have bought into Merritt-Wilson. Can't you see what that will do to our prestige back east? It will erase every last doubt in anyone's mind concerning our worth." He almost shouted, "Damn it all, Max, it puts us in business!"

Jackson nodded finally, after chewing it over. "Yes, I see what you mean. And if you can keep the Garfields off the board there really isn't very much they can do to you, is there?"

"Not a damned blasted thing. On the board they can ruin me. But if they can't make it on the board, and that I can guarantee, they are completely helpless and have simply played into my hands."

Jackson smiled freely for the first time. "By God, I have to hand it to you. I'd be running scared right now. But you're making it all work in your favor. Say, I'll call the papers first thing in the morning—"

Kane stood up and roared, "You'll do nothing of the kind."

"But you just said—"

"You haven't heard me out. Just think a minute. Why don't we play this hand from strength instead of weakness? We'll just sit tight on our present news and wait to see what happens with Patrick Aloysius Haley. I have a hunch we are getting closer in our views. Anyway, let's assume that the deal for the five new stores goes through with Haley. So we announce that to the press. Then we sit back and wait, and after a week or so we announce the fact that the Garfields have bought in. Don't you see how the picture will look then—as if the Garfields have bought in because we are a strong and moving concern and not as if they have bought in to take us over. Get the picture?"

Jackson said from the bottom of his heart, "You're a genius."

Kane grinned broadly. He dismissed Jackson with an airy wave of his hand. He felt so good, however, that he simply had to tell one other person about what had happened and that other person was, naturally, Jack Harrison. He hoped the old man had not yet gone out for lunch.

He left his office and angled across the hall into Harrison's office. The door was open, and he looked in but saw no one. He was about to back away, when he noticed a shoe standing straight up on its heel behind the desk. He walked curiously about the desk and stared down, wide-eyed, at Jack Harrison.

The old man was lying flat on his back on the floor, his toes straight up in the air. His hands were on his chest and his fingers seemed to be digging into the breastbone. His eyes were wide and protruding, his lips were the color of chalk, his face was without any blood whatever, and his mouth was wide open, gasping for air. He looked at Kane and blinked at him, so that Kane knew he was conscious and that he, Kane, could be seen, but the old man, even though he tried, was incapable of speech.

Kane had a pretty good idea of what was happening. His own face lost its tan and healthy color. He walked to the door, slammed it, and locked it, then returned to Harrison. He bent over and ripped the collar open at Harrison's throat. Then he unbuckled the belt about his waist. The old man was still gasping for breath and each gasp seemed to be his last.

Kane grabbed the telephone on the desk and dialed the number of his personal physician, Dr. Elmo Loper. A nurse answered and Kane spoke to her briefly. In a minute the doctor was on the phone.

"Lew?" he asked. "The nurse says it's an emergency. What's wrong?"

"You're damned right there is. One of my top executives is having what appears to be a heart attack, or a stroke. I'm in his office now. You know the arrangement here on the fourth floor. His office is right next to mine."

Loper said briskly, "I'll have an ambulance there with oxygen equipment within a few minutes. I'll take a taxi and be there as fast as the ambulance."

"Okay." Then Kane's voice became hard, "But hear me out. This man is vital to my plans. I don't want anyone to see him going out."

Loper replied, "We'll take care of that when I get there."

The ambulance arrived in less than five minutes; the doctor immediately after. While the two men in white were putting Harrison on a stretcher, Dr. Loper ripped open his shirt and examined various points of his chest with a stethoscope. The moment he straightened, the other men applied oxygen to the gasping figure. Loper then searched in his satchel and ran two different needles into Harrison's arm.

He told the still white-faced Kane, "One's morphine. You have no idea the pain he's going through. The other is an adrenalin booster. His pulse right now is irregular at somewhere around sixty. Now let's get him to Children's Hospital."

Kane nodded. "Right. And do me a favor, Elmo. Sign him in as a case of acute indigestion, or something of that sort. Okay?"

The doctor's face tightened and he squinted narrowly at Kane and said, "Not okay. What the hell do you think I am, a quack? He gets signed in as a cardiac, period."

As soon as they had gone, Kane sat back in Harrison's chair and buried his face in his hands. Harrison was one of the big cornerstones of the Merritt empire. No store representative on the entire Pacific Coast was better known to all the people who counted in New York than Jack Harrison. Kane almost prayed, God, help the old boy, for my sake.

He heard from Dr. Loper that afternoon and the following day and every day after that. Harrison had been placed in isolation. He was almost constantly on oxygen, and his condition was extremely critical. On Monday Loper informed Kane that Harrison seemed to be improving a bit. "The old bastard is as tough as nails." Then, on Thursday, the doctor called Kane at the store and told him, "He's coming out of it beautifully. Already he's trying to bribe the nurses to smuggle in a bottle. So, if I were you, I'd relax a bit."

Kane breathed fervently, "Thank God."

"However, Lew, I do have some bad news for you. Regardless of how he comes out of this, he will never again show up in his office."

Kane sat back and thought, At least, I can keep the lid on his condition until I can get my own plans across. Thank God for small favors.

15

AFTER talking to the doctor, Kane called Sam Kuller into his office and nodded him into a chair across from the big desk. He told Sam exactly what had happened to Harrison and the doctor's latest prognosis. Sam was considerably surprised. He had believed the rumor Kane himself had spread that the old man was simply suffering a bad case of acute indigestion.

Kane said, "So there it is. Dr. Loper is a damned good man and one of the finest internists in the business. And his word is that Jack will never return again to his office. I accept it."

Sam asked sympathetically, "But he is doing all right?"

"Apparently so. He's yelling for booze, so he must be lucid. But you and I, Sam, have a few facts to face. We must keep the lid on what has actually happened to Jack for a few weeks at least, maybe a month or so. It is vital to me that no one, especially New York, knows what has happened to Jack."

Sam was still not thinking of his own position and nodded solemnly. "I can understand that. The old boy has all the juice back there."

Kane picked up a pencil, tapped it on the desk, and squinted narrowly at Sam. "Haven't you thought yet of what this is going to do to you?" he asked.

Sam blinked at him. "Well, no. I—I—" And then his eyes opened wide.

Kane grinned thinly. "That's right. From now on you are unofficially the chief of merchandising of the whole damned Merritt-Wilson chain. You have now stepped into Jack Harrison's shoes."

Sam gulped and asked, "This is for real?"

Then Kane laughed outright. "That's right."

"But you just said unofficially—"

"Of course. Between the two of us, though, you are now head man. Then, as soon as there is no danger, we will make the official announcement."

Sam let out a long, low sigh, then he, too, was grinning broadly. "Oh, brother! Lew, I'm knocked clean off my feet. I can't begin to tell you—"

Kane said gruffly, "Stow it. You have it coming to you. I can't think of a better man. But the way it was going, you would have had to wait for Jack to retire. So let's just say the process has been speeded up a bit. Spread the word around, which I will do also, that you will be taking over Jack's duties temporarily until he gets back from the hospital. Make sure you put that temporary idea across.

"And stay at your own desk. Make it look as if we're expecting Jack back in his office in a few weeks or so. However—but do this quietly—rifle his desk and files and bone up on everything you can. You know how it is in this business; everybody keeps secrets from everyone else."

"Hell, I do it myself."

"Don't we all! But now I give you free access to everything in Jack's office. One thing more. The only other person who will know about this is Max Jackson." He smiled slightly as he said, "You will be getting a substantial boost in salary, so Max has to know." He stood up and held out his hand. "Okay?"

Sam got up and clasped Kane's hand. Then he wiped his hand across his eyes and said humbly, "You'll never regret this, Lew. That I promise."

Kane walked around the desk and slapped his back and shoved him out of the office. "Hell," he growled, "that I know already. Now let's get hitting that ball, Chief."

Sam went into his office and sat down, but turned away from the others in the room to stare at the wall. He did not want anyone to see the tears in his eyes. He had it made. After all these years, he had reached the highest goal that a man in his position could hope to attain—chief merchandiser of a big chain. There was only one higher position and that was the presidency. Sam knew better than that. He hadn't the temperament for such a position. So, where his personal career was concerned, he was now President of the United States.

He had himself fairly well under control when the telephone rang and he reached for the instrument. It was Fred Maloney wanting to know, "Is Harrison still in the hospital?"

"Yes, he is. Bad stomach."

"It's a wonder he has one at all. But that leaves you as top man. Look, Sam, there's a young lady here who is on the verge of suing us for misrepresentation. I told her I would call the head merchandiser. So, if you don't mind, would you drop down to my office?"

Sam smiled to himself and said, "I'll be down in a minute."

Sam went to the store manager's office on the mezzanine. The door was open, so he walked in. Fred was behind his desk and standing before him was one of God's well-designed creatures in a black sheath dress with a mink stole over her shoulders. Her back was to him and Sam figured she was probably South of Market trying to be Pacific Heights. The latter would never wear a mink stole on such a warm day as this.

Fred looked at him and smiled. "Mr. Kuller," he said, "This young lady has brought back a sports coat her husband recently bought in this store. She says that it was sold to him on the claim that it was one hundred percent virgin wool, whereas she has found that it was mixed wool and not at all as represented. Would you take a look at the coat and care to comment, please?"

Sam stepped forward and at that moment the young woman turned to face him. Sam stared at her and had difficulty to keep from laughing. The young woman was Ida, the prostitute. She, too, blinked at him and her lips twitched with a smile, and it spread to her eyes, but then she was quickly without any expression.

Sam picked the coat up from the desk, turned it inside-out and opened the leaf of the inner pocket. He held it before her and showed her where it was printed, "60 percent virgin wool."

"Now," he asked, "would any salesman try to lie against the printing that is inside this pocket? Or would any court either for that matter? I can only say, madam, that it was your husband who misunderstood."

"Hmmmmm," she said. "We never thought of looking inside that pocket."

"Nice try, anyway."

"Yes, wasn't it? Well, thank you, gentlemen. Good day."

She threw the coat over her arm and stalked regally out of the office. Fred looked admiringly at Sam and told him, "I didn't even think of looking inside that pocket. Thanks for the help."

"No trouble at all."

Sam dashed out of the office and caught Ida waiting for an elevator. "Hi," he said.

She grinned and said, "Hi."

He leaned against the wall and said, "You know, you're getting to be kind of my lucky piece."

She said haughtily, "Leave us not talk professionally, sir. I am not a piece."

He laughed and said, "Nevertheless, you have been around twice now on my lucky days. So, how about tonight?"

She looked regretful. "I'm sorry, but I do have an earlier appointment."

"Which you can't break? How about doubling the fee?"

She stared at him for a long time, then smiled and said, "No doubling. For you, Sam, I'll break the date. Where shall we meet?"

"Well, the way I feel right now, you and I are going first-cabin all night tonight. Meet me on the corner of Kearny and the alley at six thirty. We'll have dinner at the Blue Fox and take off from there. Okay?"

"I can't think of anything nicer." She squeezed his arm and disappeared into a Down elevator.

Sam got into an elevator going up and ran into Joe on his way to the third floor. Joe, however, skipped his floor and went on up to the fourth with Sam. The two of them nodded at Betty, then walked down the corridor toward the executive offices. Joe stopped Sam about halfway down the corridor, where they were alone, and almost pinned the older man back against the wall.

He towered over Sam and glowered down at him as he said, "Okay, now, what's the pitch with Jack Harrison? Let's have it on the line."

My God, Sam wondered, does he have Kane's office bugged? But, no, it couldn't be that. He blinked at Joe and said innocently, "I don't follow you."

"Oh, yes, you do. Look, Sam, I happen to like the old boy. So I dropped by Children's Hospital Saturday and again yesterday to see him. He didn't look like any case of indigestion to me. So I got a little foxy. You know how the nurses keep the charts on the patients out in their hallway offices? Well, I waited until the coast was clear and had a peek in the files. Jack's in that hospital as a cardiac case."

Sam said sarcastically, "Quite a little snooper, aren't you?"

"Oh, come off it, for God's sake. Heart trouble at his age means one thing, he's never coming back to his office."

"Well, now—"

"Let's not have any evasive crap. I know damned well Jack's out for good. So that means one terrific shake-up on the executive level. You'll be coming off as head man. I'll bet on it. But the earthquake will go deeper than that. In other words, dear old buddy, there's going to be an opening in merchandising for some bright-eyed character. Now then, Sam, that's me."

"You think you can skip buying completely?"

"It's been done before."

"As a matter of fact," Sam chuckled, "Kane did it himself."

"Oh, really? Then he should be sympathetic. But you're the really important gun on that level. How would you feel about my stand?"

Sam wished he could be somewhere else at the moment. Whoever was moved into merchandising would be strictly on Kane's say-so. Selections of personnel for merchandising were too important to be made by anyone other than the president himself. It was always that way in the business.

Then he had another thought. The chief merchandiser would naturally exert tremendous influence on any decision Kane would make. So, he thought, that's me, top dog. Let's start thinking and acting like it.

He told Joe, "Let's put it this way. If things come about the way you seem to think, you have my word for it that I am not opposed to you."

Joe shook his head. "It has to be better than that. Be honest,

Sam. If you wouldn't have me in the merchandising offices say so. I can take it. And there'll be no hard feelings. Okay?"

Sam looked away from him and thought a moment, then started chuckling, "You're a bastard. You know that? Damn it all, you do put me on a spot. So, all right, I'll tell you. Just assuming that your suspicions may be correct, you can also assume further that I will definitely request your presence in the inner sanctum and will put in a good word for you. Is that what you want?"

Joe put his hands on Sam's shoulders and squeezed hard. He blinked and said softly, "You're the best, Sam."

Sam rubbed his nose with a thumb, grinned, and walked away.

Joe watched him go and felt very, very good. He, too, knew it would be Kane who would make the final decisions. But knowing that Sam was on his side made the battle seem as if it had been half won before it even started. Would he have something to celebrate tonight! He would get Mary all dolled up— At the thought of Mary his smile faded and disappeared.

He went out on the floor to join Betty at her counter. She was taking a temporary breather, and at the moment no one was very close. She looked about, then asked Joe quickly, "How are things at home?"

He shrugged. "The same. All loused up."

"I've been thinking. Do you mind if I talk honestly?"

"So, all right, I'm a heel."

"No," she smiled. "That isn't it. I was thinking of your wife. She's young, beautiful, healthy, and, I should imagine, still virile."

"Yes, but there's another angle. The Irish are funny people. They seem to enjoy being martyrs. And I think she can make a bigger case out of—"

But then his words came to a dead halt. He was staring at a beautiful young blonde standing before the elevator doors, her back toward him. It must be, he thought. It has to be.

He walked to the young woman, put a hand on her shoulder, spun her about, and found himself looking into Marilyn's eyes. She held his gaze a fraction only, then her eyes turned down. So, he thought, she had seen him and had been deliberately standing with her back to him. Then he remembered that he had been standing at Betty's counter. Marilyn had not been a customer, or he would have seen her walking toward the elevators. In other words, she had arrived where she was from the direction of the executive offices.

"Well," he said, "this is quite a surprise. What are you doing here?"

"I—ah—I was calling on a friend."

The elevator doors opened before them. Joe took Marilyn's arm and guided her inside. When they reached the first floor he still held to her arm. He took her across the floor and out to the sidewalk.

"Now," he asked, "who is your friend?"

She looked up then and into his eyes. "It was a fib," she said. "He isn't a friend. I was calling on my father—Maxwell Jackson."

Joe felt as if he had been slapped in the face as a sudden chill settled in his back. He breathed huskily, "Good God! So he's the one who called my wife. No wonder he knew all about me."

Marilyn nodded and said sympathetically, "I know about his calling your wife. He saw you bring me home and got the license number of your car. There was nothing I could do about that. I am dreadfully sorry."

"Well, I'll be double-damned. Tell me something. Did he ever tell you that I might some day learn his identity?"

"Yes, he did. He said it would be very easy for you to find out. All you had to do was drive by the house and look at the name on the box. Then he said it would be very interesting to see what your reactions would be when you learned that he was the controller of Merritt-Wilson's."

Joe growled, "He wasn't just whistling through his teeth when he said that. It's queer, though, trying to figure out his reasoning. He called my wife deliberately to ruin my life because he figured I had ruined your life. Now, I ask you, how could that be? Every woman gets laid sooner or later, and I have yet to hear of it ruining a woman's life."

Marilyn giggled. "I don't feel very ruined."

"No woman ever does. So what kind of a guy is your father?"

She said soberly, "I don't know, Joe. There's something wrong with him. He scares me at times. He isn't normal. Now, of course, I know why my mother left him."

Joe asked bluntly, "Why?"

"Well, little things. I shouldn't say this about my own father, but I can't help myself. A couple of times, when I was taking a bath, I felt that he was watching me through the keyhole. Then, one night after my experience with you and the doctors, I—well, I got myself boiled and came home real smashed. I guess

I was kind of helpless. So my father got me undressed and put me to bed."

"What's wrong with that?"

Her eyes got big and round as she said, "Well, just about everything. When I say he undressed me, I mean naked. When I woke up in the morning I didn't have a stitch on. Couldn't he at least have left on my panties and a bra?"

He thought of it and shook his head. "He's a queer duck, all right. How much longer are you staying with him?"

"Just another nine or ten days, then I go back east." She said desperately, "I don't know if I can last it out. He is so—so odd."

Joe was thinking, Not just odd, baby; he has incest in mind, or he borders on it. But he said, "I'd try to stick it out if I were you, then forget him in the future. Also, you had better lock your door at night."

"I already do." Her shoulders quivered briefly. "I feel creepy."

"Sure." Then he smiled and asked, "But how have you been enjoying yourself otherwise?"

She shrugged and made a face. "Not much. I've gone to a few dinners with Mother's old friends, but that's it." Then she slanted a mischievous look at him and asked, "Would you take me out tonight?"

"Hell's bells, no! You're jailbait."

"Not any more. I just became eighteen. And I have a profusion of phony indentification cards to use in the bars. Please, Joe."

He slyly looked her wonderfully youthful figure up and down and began to feel a bit of heat in his loins. It had been a long time for him sexually—ever since Mary had banished him.

He nodded and said, "Okay. Meet me across the square at six o'clock, in front of the St. Francis Hotel. I'll get my car and pick you up at the curb."

She laughed. "I'll be there."

She waved her fingers at him and walked away, and he watched the marvelous sway of her buttocks disappearing up the sidewalk, then grinned and shook his head and walked back inside the store.

He went back to his own private jungle, the third floor, and was immediately immersed in work. But as he took care of salesmen and customers and the credit department and wrappers and detail people, his mind was occupied with Marilyn. It was obvious to him that he would be able to spend the night with her. But, as far as he knew, he was the only man she had ever had, and that was not so good on his logbook. Virgins, or recent virgins, usually spelled more trouble than fun. But then he sighed and hoped for the best.

He picked Marilyn up in front of the St. Francis at six and headed for the southern freeway system. As soon as they were out of town and on Bayshore going south Marilyn started talking about her father again. Joe listened and knew more about the man in fifteen minutes than he had ever known before. Maxwell Jackson was definitely a creep. He was obviously sexually enamored of his only daughter, he was jealous of every move she made, and he was not too far removed from committing some act of incest. Marilyn was not too well aware of the latter point, but it was apparent to Joe, and he began worrying about her.

Marilyn dropped her father as a subject, however, as soon as they arrived at La Cabana on El Camino Real just below Palo Alto. The hotel, or motel, or whatever it should be called, had a terraced bar where cocktail waitresses pranced about in long opera hose, deep cleavages, and white wigs. Joe and Marilyn had two drinks in the bar, then went into the dining room for dinner. They had brandy snifters after dinner. Then Joe was suddenly tired of La Cabana, and they took off.

He drove below Palo Alto and checked into a small motel. They went to a rather well furnished combination bedroom-living room. Joe was in no mood even to turn on the lights. He wanted to get undressed at once. Marilyn, however, was suddenly not as bold as she had been. She turned on the lights and made Joe open a bottle of bourbon he had picked up on the way. She gagged and coughed over a drink of straight whiskey, then mixed the next one with considerable water. She sat back and smiled uneasily at Joe and wanted to talk.

Heaven deliver me, he thought. The evening turned out about as badly as he had been afraid it would. Marilyn was not so much interested in sex itself as she was in talking about it. She had given herself to him freely the first time, but that had been premeditated. Now she was a bit afraid, remembering the pain she had experienced.

Joe sat and looked at her and listened to her rambling chatter and occasionally mixed a drink for himself, and finally, when he noticed that it was after midnight, he became completely disgusted with himself. She had lost her physical attraction for him and was simply another giddy eighteen-year-old who would definitely be a lousy lay no matter how he went about it. He sighed and got up and put on his coat.

"Come on, baby," he said, "I'm taking you home. Now."

Joe drove Marilyn home and let her out in front of Jackson's house. She still wanted to talk, but Joe shoved her out of the car, waved to her, and drove away. And again he had to laugh at himself. Never again, he thought. Not that age.

He wondered, however, what it would be like to run into her five years from now, after she had logged a little time.

The following morning Joe parked as usual in the O'Farrell St. garage. He then set out to walk the few blocks to work. He passed Union Square and was turning the corner of Geary and Stockton when he happened to look up and across the street. A young blonde was standing just aside of the entrance to Merritt-Wilson's. Joe frowned and wondered, Marilyn? At this hour? It couldn't be.

He crossed the street and started up the sidewalk. She looked in his direction and saw him and started running toward him. It was Marilyn, but not the well-groomed Marilyn he had known. She was wearing slacks, a baggy sweater, and a cloth coat over her shoulders. Nothing matched. Knowing her good taste, Joe knew immediately that what she was wearing had been thrown on in a hurry. She grabbed his arm and stared into his eyes. Her beautifully coiffed hair was in disarray, she was wearing no makeup, there were still signs of tears on her cheeks, and her eyes were puffed, swollen, and streaked with red. Joe felt a sudden, terrible premonition of something being badly wrong.

"Joe," she gasped. "Oh, my God, Joe."

Joe looked away from her. The people hurrying by on their way to work were staring at them. Joe took Marilyn's arm, walked her to the corner and across the street and into the middle of Union Square where no one was around.

"Now," he said thinly, shaking her arm, "what is it?"

She breathed huskily, "Oh, God, Joe. Oh, God."

He shook her again and asked harshly, "Damn it all, what is it?"

She looked behind her and saw a park bench. She collapsed onto it and buried her face in her hands. Joe sat down slowly at her side and put an arm about her shoulders. "Okay, baby," he said, "you can tell Joe. Your father?"

She nodded violently, her face still buried in her hands.

"He saw me bring you home and threw you out of the house. Right?"

Her face came slowly out of her hands and she stared straight ahead, almost like a sleepwalker. She said softly, "He saw us, yes. But I guess he went back to bed. Then, about an hour ago he came down the hall and banged on my door. It was locked. I wouldn't let him in. He sounded funny and I was afraid of him. He stood out in the hallway yelling that he saw you bring me home and calling me all sorts of vile names. Then—then—he went away for a minute and came back with a heavy iron bookend.

"He beat at the door with the bookend and smashed in the panel. Then he came storming into my room and pulled the covers back from my bed and threw them on the floor. I tried to get away from him, but I wasn't fast enough. He grabbed my nightie and ripped it off of me. All the time he kept calling me the most horrible kinds of names and—and—and telling me what you'd been doing to me."

Joe whispered, "The bastard."

"He was still in his pajamas, but no bottoms. Then suddenly he had me in his arms and was kissing me all over and telling me how he'd always loved me and—and—"

Her head lowered and again she buried her face in her hands. Joe blinked and looked about and did not give a damn how passersby were staring at them. He patted Marilyn's shoulder and waited patiently for her to go on.

At last she did look up and into his eyes and said, "I don't know what he was trying to do, Joe. I just don't know. All I know is that it wasn't right, and I was scared. I was scared to death. I've never been so frightened in my life. And when he tried to get me on the bed I just wouldn't go. I fought back. Once I fell on the floor. When I got up I had that iron bookend in my hand." She put a hand to her mouth and muffled a scream as she said, "I hit him with it, Joe. He came at me and I hit him on the head. Joe," she gasped, "I killed him."

He pulled her into the cradle of his shoulder and hugged her tight and shook his head. "The human animal," he said, "doesn't kill that easily. You probably just knocked him out."

She shook her head and dug her fingers into his knee. "No, Joe. I killed him. I know it. I couldn't feel his pulse, and when I bent over him he had no breath and his face was like chalk. He's dead, I tell you. He's dead."

Joe thought a moment, then asked, "Does anyone else know?" She shook her head. "I came right to you."

Joe got to his feet and lifted Marilyn and said, "Before doing anything, we have to check on your father."

She was afraid to go with him, but he shoved her along without even thinking about it. They crossed the square to Powell Street, where Joe flagged down a taxicab and pushed Marilyn inside. When they arrived at the address, Joe paid off the taxi driver and helped Marilyn across the sidewalk. She had had presence enough of mind to bring along a key and unlocked the front door. They went up the stairs and into a luxurious home, though, to Joe's thinking, a trifle cold. Marilyn led the way down a hallway to her bedroom door. But there she halted and shook her head. Joe looked at the smashed door and went into the room alone.

Jackson was lying in the middle of the floor in the upper part of his pajamas, his groin and stomach and legs grotesquely white. He was, however, propped up on an elbow trying to shake his head. A large pool of blood was on the carpet. Joe heaved a tremendous sigh of relief.

He went back to the hallway and told Marilyn that her father was still very much alive. Marilyn closed her eyes and fainted. Joe caught her and eased her down to the floor. Then he found his way to the master bedroom and into the bathroom where he found a small bottle of spirits of ammonia. He used it first on Marilyn and soon had her sitting up, then went into the bedroom and held it under her father's nose. He, too, was soon sitting up on the floor, holding his head in his hands. Joe got a wet towel and washed off his face and blinked at a deep gash just over Jackson's left temple. Jackson, he was sure, had a fractured skull that needed instant attention.

Joe squatted down and again held the bottle under his nose. Jackson breathed deeply, then jerked his head back and stared at Joe. Joe knew that for the first time Jackson was really seeing him.

"Okay," he said. "How do you feel?"

Jackson stammered, "T—t—terrible."

"No doubt. Now then, you ass-hole, how would you like to go to San Quentin for the attempted rape of your daughter? Do you understand what I just said?"

Jackson took the towel from Joe and held it to his head and

simply stared at him wild-eyed. After awhile Jackson nodded and whispered, "Yes."

"Good. Then we're making contact with each other. Okay. You need a doctor and a hospital and you need them fast. But first of all we need a story. Do you understand that, too?"

Jackson looked beyond him and Joe turned his head. Marilyn was standing in the doorway. Joe turned his attention back to her father.

"We gotta call the police," he said, "and we gotta call for a doctor and an ambulance. But we got a smashed door to think about. People," he said dryly, "just don't like to think of a father trying to rape his own daughter. Maybe somebody else, but not his own child. Am I right?"

Jackson closed his eyes and had nothing to say.

Joe said, "So, here's the story. A sex maniac broke into the house. We don't have to tell them that there was always one in here, do we? I'll jam the lock down at the front door and make that look all right. So, this guy breaks in and finds that iron bookend and smashes down your daughter's door. Naturally, it wakes you up and you come to her rescue. At which point you get your skull busted. But the maniac then panics and runs away. Then your daughter faints, which should allow for some passage of time. When she comes to, she calls the police, and so on. Do you have that right?"

He went to the doorway and took Marilyn's hand and led her down to the front door. He went into the garage and came back with a hammer, which he used to smash the lock on the front door. Then he threw the hammer back into the garage and turned to Marilyn.

He put his hands on her shoulders and told her, "The police are not fools. Even a rookie cop isn't going to believe either of you. But as long as you and your father stick to the story it gives the police something to put on the record, then they can forget it. Understand me?"

She nodded. "What if they should investigate, though?"

Joe smiled thinly. "They won't. They'll put two and two together and probably figure it out. But it comes out domestic to them, and that they would rather not touch. All they want is a story that seems plausible enough and they'll drop the whole business." He sighed again as he said, "Besides, it leaves me out and that's always something to consider. Okay?"

She said weakly, "Yes, Joe."

"Good girl. Now, you go and make your calls. Then give me a call at the store."

"I will."

"So get moving."

He turned her about, slapped her behind, then spun on his heel and walked out the door. He went down Marina Boulevard and turned down the north end of Fillmore. He walked all the way to Chestnut before he was able to pick up a taxicab. As the cab pulled away from the curb Joe saw a police radio car hurrying by followed by an ambulance. At least, Marilyn was able to make the calls. Now to sit back and see what developed.

Marilyn called him at the store a few minutes after three. She had been taken to the hospital with her father, then to a police station. She had then been transferred to the Hall of Justice downtown, where she had been interrogated. After that she had returned to the hospital with the police and finally was dismissed. She had returned to her father's home, gathered her belongings and checked into the Mark Hopkins Hotel.

"It was frightful," she gasped. "No one believed my story at any time. Some of them even laughed at me."

Joe said, "That figures. It wasn't a very good story. But how did you describe the intruder?"

"The first thing that came to my mind—a motorcycle rider, with long sideburns and black leather jacket. You know."

"Uh-huh. And no one believed you?"

"No one. Like you said, though, all I had to do was stick to it. You know what was the biggest weakness?

"The police have never heard of a sex maniac on the prowl after it starts to get light. I thought fast and told them maybe he thought my father had gone to work and was hanging around for that, and they laughed harder than ever." She was silent a moment, then said, "But there's nothing to worry about. The lieutenant told me to hang around a few days until my father's out of danger, then to get out of San Francisco and go back home."

"Excellent advice. One thing more. How badly off is your father?"

"Well, he isn't good. He has a bad frontal lobe fracture, whatever that means. The doctor told me, when I went back to the hospital the second time, that he wasn't in any immediate danger, but that he would be in the hospital for at least a month or more. Then he said it would take him time to convalesce."

Joe mumbled, "Kane's going to love this."

Marilyn asked plaintively, "When am I seeing you again? To-night?"

Joe barked, "Hell, no! You may think you're in the clear, honey, but those cops got an eye on you. I would hate to have them transfer their attention to me. You stay away from me and call again tomorrow. Okay?"

"Well—"

"I'll look forward to hearing from you." He hung up before she could protest.

Then he sat back and worried about a related matter that had suddenly come to his mind. Marilyn's blow had hurt her father badly, but he was apparently not in any great danger. Sooner or later he would be coming back to the store. And when he did come back, who was he going to hate more than any other man in the world?—Joe Haley. Joe had seen him naked and uncovered and knew precisely the kind of man he was. Also, he could never be sure whether or not Joe would say anything. There would be fear of Joe, yes, but hatred would be much greater than fear.

He considered the situation from every angle, but at quitting time had arrived nowhere. After five thirty, and after the outer doors were closed, Joe went to his office and totalled the figures for the day. He had just finished when he felt someone behind him and turned about to face Kane standing in the doorway. Kane was looking worried, but asked him for the final figures. Joe gave them to him and wondered about the unusual procedure.

Kane saw the puzzle in his eyes and said, "Maloney collects the figures and passes them on to Jackson, who then gives them to me. But he hasn't been here today."

"Who hasn't?"

"Jackson. Who else?"

"Oh." Then Joe asked, without thinking, "How is he getting along?"

Kane squinted at him narrowly. "How's who getting along?"

"Mr. Jackson, of course. How is his head—"

Joe's words skidded to a halt and he realized immediately the *faux pas* he had committed. Kane was obviously not aware of anything having happened to Jackson. Now, Joe thought, I've really put my foot in my mouth. And he knew just as quickly that he would have to lie his way out of the situation.

He asked innocently, "Don't you know what happened to Mr. Jackson?"

Kane roared, "No, damn it! I've been calling his house all day, and no answer. Now, just what the hell are you talking about?"

"Well," Joe said, "I overheard two men talking about Mr. Jackson. Seems he got hurt by a prowler, or something, and he's in a hospital."

Kane groaned, "Oh, Good Lord, deliver me. You heard this? Where?"

Joe was about to say he had heard it in the store, but knew that could be tracked down. He thought furiously and replied, "While I was out to lunch. Two plainclothes policemen were at the table next to me."

"How do you know who they were?"

"I know one of them. I've seen him around. I don't know his name, but he's an inspector or something of that sort. Anyway, these men were talking about this accident Mr. Jackson had. Naturally," he said smoothly, "I thought you knew all about it."

"Nothing," Kane moaned. "I know nothing. Tell me about it."

Joe shrugged. "That's about it. It was just casual conversation with them. No details. All I remember is that it had something to do with a prowler attacking Mr. Jackson's daughter and his coming to her defense and getting clobbered. I think he got a nasty skull fracture out of it."

Kane's eyes narrowed another degree. "How come you didn't ask them for details? Jackson, after all, is an important man in this chain."

"Well," Joe said, "I didn't want to butt in, and I thought I would hear all about it back in the store." He said wonderingly, "Now that I think about it, no one has mentioned the incident. And I've been too busy to inquire."

Kane reached for the telephone on the desk as he asked Joe, "What hospital is he in?"

"I don't know. They didn't mention it. Maybe if you called the police department—"

Kane dialed police central and was eventually put through to a Lieutenant Dickerson. Kane explained who he was and the information he wanted.

The lieutenant said, "He has a bad fracture, Mr. Kane. My latest report is that he is under heavy sedation, and no one is allowed to see him for at least the next twenty-four hours."

"Just how bad is the fracture?"

"Bad enough, but not bordering on anything fatal."

"That's good. What hospital is he in?"

"The St. Francis, sir. But, as I said before, you can't see him."

"I know that, but I would like to get more explicit information than you've given me. Now, tell me what happened, if that is permissible."

"No rules against it, Mr. Kane. Let me see now. Oh, yes."

He proceeded to tell Kane what was on his file, which was mostly information that had been given by Marilyn. Kane thought he detected a note of odd uncertainty in the lieutenant's voice, but could not be sure. When he had finished the report, however, the lieutenant asked, "How long has Mr. Jackson been working for you, Mr. Kane?"

"Quite a number of years. Why?"

"And you think you know him pretty well?"

"Yes, I think I do."

"Do you know that Mr. Jackson has a rather questionable police record?"

Kane gasped, "You're kidding."

The lieutenant replied, "I figured you wouldn't know. People rarely do when it comes to this sort of thing. Mr. Kane, there are a few things you should know. Suppose you drop by my office tomorrow about two-thirty."

"Can't you tell me—"

"Not over the telephone, sir. You come by my office tomorrow. I'll see you then. Good-bye."

Kane put the telephone back in its cradle and stared unseeingly into space for a moment. Then he looked at Joe and said, "You're never prepared for that roof to fall on your head. Of all times—!"

The next afternoon he was in the lieutenant's office in the Hall of Justice. There he got the shock of his life. During the past seven years Jackson had been picked up on five different occasions for molesting young girls. On three of the cases the charges had been dropped, probably, the lieutenant hinted, because Jackson had managed to reach the parents and had paid off. The other two cases were too vague to be prosecuted. Nevertheless, the record was there in black and white.

The lieutenant sat back in his swivel chair and told Kane, "I wouldn't be telling you this even now, except for a very good reason. We don't believe the story about the prowler, Mr. Kane. We are willing to go along with it because the daughter is leaving town as soon as her father is out of danger. We are also willing to go along with the story for another reason. If we prosecuted what we think is the truth, it could have a very sad effect on the life of a young girl. We don't want that."

Kane swallowed and asked, "What do you think is the true story?"

The lieutenant's features tightened as he said, "There are some very peculiar people in this world, Mr. Kane. Mr. Jackson is one of them. The story we got from the two of them, but mostly from the girl, has so many holes we could fire a shotgun through them and never hit anything. What we really believe happened is that the father attempted rape on his own daughter and that she was the one who fractured his skull."

Kane pressed his fingers into his eyelids. "Good Lord!"

The lieutenant sighed and shoved himself away from his desk. "I thought you had better know," he said. "Mr. Jackson is not about to change his stripes, believe me. Sooner or later he is going to step into real trouble. So now you know what to expect."

Kane got shakily to his feet. "Thanks," he said. "I can't say that I appreciate what you have told me, but I am grateful."

Kane went back to his office in the store and locked the door. He sat quietly for some time thinking over what he had been told. He knew that when one man exercised judgment over another he could be wrong as often as right. Yet when a man had five identical cases against him, it did represent something within the field of logic. The odds would seem to indicate some sort of guilt. He came to the reluctant conclusion that the police were probably right.

He picked up the telephone and called Fred Maloney. "Come up to my office, please, at once."

When Maloney arrived Kane nodded him into a chair across from the desk and again locked the door. When he dropped into his own chair he stared at Maloney, then asked abruptly, "Can you hold down the controller's job temporarily?"

Maloney chewed at his lower lip, then leaned his elbows on the desk. "What's happened to Jackson?"

"He's in the hospital. A prowler fractured his skull. We're going to be without him for a few months. So, can you hold down the job temporarily?"

Maloney sucked in his breath sharply, then said, "I don't know. As you know, Mr. Kane, every store manager aims for the controller's job. That is the ultimate end. Sure, I've studied for it and worked for it, but I honestly do not know if I'm ready for it. I don't know."

"This is not permanent, you know. I need someone to hold down the spot until Jackson gets back."

"I realize that. Maybe I could do it. I don't know. But what happens to my job as store manager when I step back into it?"

Kane shrugged. "Why should anything happen to it?"

Maloney smiled thinly and explained, "If I take over the controller's job for a few months it means that Chet Baker will be manager of this store for the same number of months. Do you think he is going to relinquish that sort of authority without a struggle when I move back? I'm sorry, Mr. Kane, but I see too many problems in that direction."

Kane asked thinly, "Then you mean you turn me down?"

Maloney shook his head. "No, sir, it doesn't mean that. It just means that I have to do a hell of a lot of thinking. I have a career to consider, Mr. Kane. I don't mean to make a false step that could jeopardize it."

Kane nodded and said more gently, "I can understand that. You will consider it?"

Maloney got to his feet and nodded. "Believe me, sir, I will consider every angle. Do you mind if I take a few days?"

Kane sighed and blew out his breath. "I guess I'd be doing the same in your shoes. Okay. Take a few days and let me know."

Kane sat back after he had gone, laced his fingers together, and began cracking his knuckles. Now what? he thought. Harrison, one of the finest men in the business, was out of commission. Sam could fill his shoes as chief merchandiser, no doubt of that. Sam was a damned capable man. But he could never fill the old man's shoes in other areas where it counted even more. Especially now. That loss had to be made up in some other way. And now Jackson was out right when he, too, was needed most to close the deal with the elder Haley. Maloney might be able to move into his shoes and take care of the books for a few months, but the Haley deal was beyond him.

Kane closed his eyes and his face turned a little gray. Why, he wondered, don't I just give up? I've bitten off more than I can chew, and now it's obvious. But then his eyes opened and he stared at the wall. What would happen if he gave up? He knew the answer to that. Everything he owned was in Merritt-Wilson's. If he quit now he would find himself starting all over again as a salesclerk. Bessie might be able to put up with it, but he knew he couldn't. For him it would be a high dive off the Golden Gate Bridge.

He started to smile thinly, with no humor in his cold gray eyes. So, he thought, I fight as long as I can. There was no other answer.

16

KANE left the store at the closing hour and got his Rolls-Royce out of the garage. He was proceeding west on Geary, just two blocks from Union Square, when he saw Joe Haley walking along the sidewalk in the opposite direction. He remembered that Wednesday was Joe's day off. He rolled down a window, blew the horn loudly, tried to pull over to the curb, and waved frenziedly at Joe.

Joe turned and saw him and returned the wave. He also saw that Kane was trying to get to the curb and that he was waving for Joe to join him. Joe had a sudden hunch why Kane wanted his company, but decided just as suddenly not to join him. If Kane wanted more details concerning the story Joe had told him about Jackson, he would have to wait. Joe needed time to think. He waved and smiled, as if he had misinterpreted Kane's wave, and turned the corner with a sigh of relief. Kane could never catch him now.

He was just turning into the entrance to his garage when he almost bumped into Ellen Maloney coming out of it. "Well," she said, pausing and smiling, "how nice. How are you today?"

He took her hand and returned her smile. "Very well, thank you. And you?"

Her smile faded and she frowned petulantly. "Frankly," she said, "I don't know. I'm on my way to see Fred, if he's still in the store."

Joe glanced at his watch and shook his head. "Store's been closed over half an hour. Security won't let you in. Even Kane would have a hard time getting in once that store is closed. You supposed to meet him?"

"Oh, no. Just the opposite. He doesn't want any part of me tonight."

"I beg your pardon?"

She sighed and explained, "It's all very mysterious. He called home about five and said he was having dinner downtown and would not be home all night. He had something very important to think about and he needed to be alone."

Joe said wryly, "So you rushed right down."

Her eyes opened wide. "Well, wouldn't you? He has never done anything like this before, and it just doesn't make sense."

"Did he give you a reason why he wanted to be alone?"

"No. He just said that something had come up that could be the turning point of his life and he needed to think it out. Then he hung up on me."

Joe thought, Jee-zuss, the eternal female. But then he wondered what could be so important to Fred and almost instantly had the answer. Of course! All store managers aimed ultimately for the controller's job. Fred had obviously been studying in that direction for years. So, as of the moment Merritt-Wilson's was without a controller, and Kane needed someone to fill in. He had undoubtedly offered the job to Fred, but most likely on a temporary basis. Fred would, indeed, have plenty to think about. So would Joe in his shoes.

Joe looked Ellen up and down, at the beautiful legs, at the trim figure that had logged so many pleasant hours, and at the attractive American beauty salon face. So Fred was going to be away all night? He looked into her eyes and saw that the same thought had come to her.

"Well," she said huskily, "I guess I'll have to forget Fred. And here I have a baby-sitter taking care of the children for the whole evening." She laughed nervously. "What a waste."

Joe blinked at her and felt saliva hot in his throat. He thought of Marilyn and the wasted night. He also thought that he needed a woman, and badly, and that something had to break damned soon. Perhaps this was that break.

He asked softly, "Your car in this garage?"

She looked into his eyes and whispered, "Yes."

"Okay. You get in your car and go over the Gate Bridge. About three miles north of San Rafael, on the right side of the road, you'll see a white frame building with a sign reading: LAS CRUCES, Mexican Food. Meet me there. We'll have dinner together." He paused, then added, "Incidentally, there is a small motel just next door."

He watched her as she said, "Yes, Joe." There was no sign of panic.

She met him in front of the restaurant a moment after he had parked. It was twilight and beginning to get dark, but as she joined Joe she looked as if she was stepping out of a closet and walking into sunlight. She was actually radiant and her eyes were shining. What Joe could not know was that he presented a challenge to her in more ways then one. She was afraid that middle age was catching up with her too rapidly, that her figure was failing, that lines were beginning to show in her face, that perhaps her appearance was a bit on the drab side, and that she could never, never ever again arouse a man as good looking as Joe. The fact that he was standing there waiting for her proved her wrong on all points, which was why she was radiant.

She was a bit shy at the dinner table, however. Joe did most of the talking. He did not mind, as he wanted to talk, anyway. It was not often lately that he found himself conversing with a good-looking woman.

It got a bit awkward after dinner, when they were having brandies. Joe knew what was on her mind. She had children to think about and a baby-sitter. She also had to consider the fact that Fred might change his mind about staying out all night and come home when he was least expected. She had many things to think about, so Joe decided to help her out and waste no more time.

They left their cars at the restaurant and walked next door to the motel. It was clean and it was neat, and that was about all that could be said about it. Joe registered as Mr. & Mrs. John Smith, got the key and walked back with Ellen to a fairly large combination sitting room-bedroom. Joe had a bottle of Canadian whiskey and two bottles of seltzer. He got out some ice and mixed drinks and raised his glass in a toast. Ellen looked into his eyes and put her glass aside and moved into his arms. She was warm and responsive and eager, and Joe almost dropped his own glass.

"Okay," he said huskily, "let's get undressed."

Ellen left him and went into the bathroom. Joe turned down all the lights except a small one in one corner. He got undressed and sat on the edge of the bed, sipping at his drink, waiting for Ellen. And as he waited he thought of Fred Maloney. He tried not to think of him, nature had already taken over, but he could not help himself. What, he wondered, has he ever done to me except be a hell of a good guy? Maloney was one of the nicest people he had ever known, and now Joe was about to make a cuckold out of him.

The bathroom door opened and Ellen walked slowly into the room. Joe looked at her naked body in the dim light and caught his breath. My God, he wondered, how did some of these women do it? She had children and she was either nudging forty or a little over it. Yet you would never know looking at her body. Her breasts were still relatively firm, her waist was narrow and sloped beautifully into pear-shaped hips and long, lean legs. She had also let her hair down. In the small light available she seemed to be not beyond her mid-twenties. Cripes, he thought, the greatest wonder of the world, bar none, was the American woman.

She moved toward him and bumped against his knees. He looked her good body up and down and thought of how Fred had looked that same body up and down so many times, and of how he had probably enjoyed that body for so many years and what it meant to him as his wife and the mother of his children, and of how Fred had been talking to him about people in their forties and the very worried look he had, and suddenly he knew he could never possibly do a thing like this to one of the few people in the world he admired and respected. If he destroyed Fred, he would also be destroying himself. But how to get out of it, at this late date? And just as suddenly he knew the answer.

He pulled Ellen down to his lap, but he reached beyond her and found his trousers draped over a chair. He tugged at the belt and finally got it free from the loops. Then he shoved Ellen away and handed her the leather belt and closed her fingers about it. He rolled onto his stomach on the bed, his broad back exposed.

"Beat me," he whispered. "Beat me with the belt. Then you and I can have a ball. Believe me. But beat me with the belt first. I have to have it."

There was a long silence. He could not see her, but he imagined what the expression of her face would be like. After a long time she gasped, "Beat you?"

"That's right. So, okay, I'm a masochist. What's wrong with that? I don't have to beat you. Just do it to me, that's all. Beat my back with the strap until you draw a little blood. Then I'll love you like you've never been loved in your life. But you gotta beat me first. That I must have."

He heard her say faintly, "Oh, my God." Then after a moment, "You're not really serious. This is some kind of a joke."

He raised his voice and cried, "Joke, my ass! Like I said before, I won't hurt you. All I want you to do is beat me." He rolled to an elbow and glanced back at her over a shoulder. She had stepped away from the bed and was staring at the strap in her hand as if it were a rattlesnake about to strike at her. "So," he roared, "use it, damn it!"

She turned her head slowly and looked vaguely into his eyes. "You don't really want me to do this?"

"Goddamn it, Ellen, I wouldn't ask you if I didn't. You don't have to do it too much. Just draw a little blood. I thought I could depend on you."

She sucked in her breath sharply and shook her head. "Oh, no. Not the great lover. Not you. Not Joe Haley."

"Yes, Joe Haley." He said patiently, as if explaining to a child, "We all have our little eccentricities, Ellen. So I like to be beaten. What's so wrong with that? Maybe you like something else. How do I know?"

He reached out then and took the belt from her hand. He spun her about and slapped her viciously across the bottom with the strap. She gasped and smothered a scream and ran for the bathroom. She slammed the door and Joe smiled slightly and sat on the edge of the bed and waited. She dressed herself more quickly than any woman he had ever known and was back in the bedroom in a very few minutes. She could not look at him.

"I'm sorry," she whispered. "I—I can't do it. I just can't do something like that."

He growled angrily, "Then why the hell did you come here with me?"

"Well—I didn't know—it never entered my mind—I'm sorry, Joe."

Then she turned and ran out the front door and closed it. Joe heard her drive away a moment later from the restaurant next door. He heaved a deep sigh and rubbed his hands over his face. He stood up slowly and tiredly and started collecting his own clothes. He began chuckling after a moment. Cripes, he thought, if only Fred knew what I did for him tonight.

Joe saw Fred Friday morning. Fred came onto his floor and went into the little office to check some figures that had been in question. Then he and Joe stood out on the floor and talked shop for a few minutes.

Joe asked him finally, casually, "How's it going Fred, aside from the store, I mean?"

A slight smile tugged at Fred's lips. He was thinking of the night before. In the middle of the night Ellen had come willingly to his bed, the first time that had happened in a long while. She had snuggled against him and kissed him. Then she had whispered in his ear, "Do you know something, darling? You're the nicest man I've ever known." She had then proceeded to make love to him in a way that hadn't happened in many years. Apparently, whatever had been bothering her lately, she had got over it. Thank God!

He looked at Joe and grinned and said, "I have no complaints, my friend. None at all."

Joe returned his grin. "Glad to hear it. Where you heading now?"

Fred's smile faded and he stared seriously at Joe. "Up to see Kane," he replied. "He asked me a question the other day. Today he gets his answer." Then he was smiling again, with confidence. "It's odd," he said, "what a little time will do to a man. Yesterday I would have given Kane one answer. But today I am giving him an answer entirely the opposite. Well, Joe, I'll be seeing you."

Fred walked away from him and wondered what the hell Joe was chuckling about.

It did not take very long. Fred sat on one side of the desk and Kane on the other. Kane watched him levelly, his gray eyes never wavering.

Fred told him, "This bears explanation, Mr. Kane. I want you to know my thinking in the matter."

Kane grunted, "Fire away."

"Okay. I have a career at stake and it's a good one. I like the way it's been going so far and I like the direction. I know, for one thing, I'm a little too loyal to the people under me, but I have never considered that to be a fault."

Kane nodded. "Neither have I. The only way anyone in this business ever gets loyalty is by giving it. So go on from there."

Fred swallowed. Things were going too smoothly. "Yes, sir. I don't say I can hold down Jackson's seat. I have been training and studying for it for years, but whether or not I am ready for it right now I honestly don't know. However, I am willing to give it a whirl."

A smile tugged briefly at Kane's lips. "Good boy."

"But there is something else, Mr. Kane. I have an assistant named Chet Baker who is breathing down the back of my neck."

"So?"

"So this is how it stacks up. I turn my office over to Chet Baker and move out for the next three or four months. And during the time I am gone, believe me, Mr. Kane, Baker is going to do everything he can to consolidate his own position. That's only natural. It's exactly the way I would be doing it, too. But it does put me in a peculiar position. Win, lose, or draw, I will never be able to step back to the position of store manager. Do you understand that?"

Kane frowned and put his fingertips together. "Not exactly."

"It's the kind of man I am, Mr. Kane. I'll take the controller's job, and I'll do my damnedest to do everything you expect of me and maybe a little more. But if Mr. Jackson returns to his post, I will never step back to fight things out with my own assistant."

Kane snorted, "Cripes, Maloney, this is only a temporary arrangement."

Fred shook his head. "Not with me it isn't. This has to be done on my terms, or get yourself another man."

"So just what are your terms?"

"I'll take the controller's job. But, Mr. Kane, I mean to fight to keep it. Which gives you a decision to make. When Mr. Jackson is ready to return you will have to choose between the two of us. If you prefer to have him back, I will simply bow out and go elsewhere."

Kane exploded, "Goddamn it, Maloney, you sound like a sophomore! You got a hell of a good job as store manager. What's wrong with helping me out for a while, then stepping back in your regular job? You're not even used to that job yet. Now you're trying to tell me that you're stepping over eight levels, and you expect me to swallow it."

Fred sighed and sat back in his seat. "Yesterday," he said, "I would not have had this much nerve. But something happened. Today I have it. It's all or nothing, Mr. Kane. For me, that is. If you want me to stay on as store manager, I'll be happy to do it. But if you move me into the controller's job, I am going to do everything in my power to hang onto it. It's up to you."

Kane chewed at his lower lip. There hadn't been time to get an assistant for Jackson and no one else understood the store as well as Maloney. How about the chain, though? What the hell did Maloney know about that? All he knew about was one store. But, no, that was not quite correct. Anyone in the main store had to have his fingers out through the entire chain. He blinked and looked at Maloney again. He started to smile within. Damn it all, he did have guts.

"In other words," he said, "you're putting your career on the line."

Fred thought a moment, then shook his head. "Not quite that bad, sir. If I have to walk out of here, I don't think I will have too much trouble landing on my feet somewhere else."

"Hmmmmm." Kane burst out laughing. "Damn it all, Maloney, but I do have to admire you. Okay. So be it. That's the way we'll work it." But when he stood up to shake hands with Fred he said more soberly, "You realize, of course, that Jackson is one of the best men in the business?"

"I know. That's why I have butterflies in my stomach."

"Okay. Let's see how it works out. And, incidentally, I wish you luck."

Kane watched him walk out through the door, then dropped behind his desk. Funny, he thought, how some things worked out. For two days now he had been wondering if he would be able to take Jackson back when he was well again. What the lieutenant had told him had been troubling his mind sorely. How would he ever again be able to work with a man like that? He closed his eyes briefly. Dear God, he thought, let's hope Maloney pulls the trick.

He had cleaned his desk and was about to go out for lunch when Patrick Aloysius Haley came into his office. The old man squinted at him narrowly, shoved his hat to the back of his head, and leaned over the desk.

"I hear," he growled, "we got troubles."

Kane stared at him. "What sort?"

"Your man, Jackson, is in a hospital."

"Oh, that, yes."

"So now I guess everything blows up in our faces. He was the only one me men were dealing with, you know. What would you know about the deal?"

Kane sat back and stared at him. "Enough, maybe."

"You seen the plans? Do they have your approval?"

Kane shrugged. "They're good enough. I would rather have each store distinctive, but I understand your position. I could go for the plans."

"Well, now, whaddaya know. We gone a long ways, Mr. Kane. So let's you and me wrap it up. I ain't gonna spend more money on this project, that's for sure." He turned away from the desk and walked to the windows. He crossed his hands behind his back and said over his shoulder, "I'm about to make me an offer. You ready?"

Kane took a deep breath and said, "I'm ready."

"Good. This is my offer. I want a basic land rent of a thousand a month on each of the five stores. That's just to keep the wolves from howling. Then, on top of that I want three and a quarter percent off the top." He paused, simply being polite, then asked, "How does that strike you?"

Kane stared at his back and thought, What the hell, the roof's falling in, anyway. But then he realized that the old man was not much of a bargainer. He would go to a certain low point, then he would walk away. Kane wondered what that low point would be. He decided to gamble.

"Mr. Haley," he said, "I am not a horse trader. I believe strictly in figures. They have done pretty well by me so far. I believe that if two men can settle on a certain figure that will make money for each of them there is nothing to argue about."

"That I buy."

"Very good." He crossed his fingers as he said, "But I can't buy your figures. I go for the thousand a month land rent. That I understand. But beyond that I won't go."

Without turning around, Haley asked him, "What will you go for?"

Kane sucked in his stomach tightly and said, "I'll go for three percent off the top after utilities and taxes. Understand me? After utilities and taxes. That's it. If you want it, good, we'll do business and you can start building. Otherwise, no hard feelings."

Haley rocked back and forth on the balls of his feet for a moment, then said softly, "Remember something I told you once?"

"What was that?"

"I said that in the end you and me would settle the whole thing in fifteen minutes."

"I remember."

"It's better than that. We just settled it in less than five." He shook Kane's hand and said, "You got yourself a deal, Mr. Kane. You get your lawyers with my lawyers and they'll draw up the papers. I don't know nothing about these legal matters, and I don't imagine you're much smarter'n me."

Kane asked unbelievingly, "My terms?"

Haley had to laugh. "That's right. Crap, man, ain't nothing wrong with them terms. I've had me men looking into department store leases all over the country. I set me sights high and you knocked me down. Good for you. Now we deal on a legitimate basis. And I got a hunch we'll both make money."

Kane burst out laughing, then brought a bottle of Jack Daniels out of the desk. He poured straight shots for the two of them and they hoisted their glasses to each other. Kane wanted Haley to stay. He wanted to take him out to lunch, to celebrate. Haley shook his head. He had his own celebration in mind—a certain pair of mammary glands of unusual size waiting for him. He shook hands and laughed, slanted his hat on the side of his head, and walked out of the office like a bantam peacock.

Kane thought, Well, I'll be damned. As easy as that.

He picked up the telephone and called Miss Brown, head of advertising. When she was on the wire he told her, "This is a press release for tomorrow. Be sure it hits all the papers. As of now, Miss Brown, Merritt-Wilson is building five new stores in San Rafael, Santa Rosa, San Leandro, North Sacramento, and Vallejo. Construction will begin almost at once. The stores will be built by Mr. Patrick Aloysius Haley, the well-known contractor. You might also mention that this is only the beginning of what will eventually be the biggest specialty chain in America. In addition to that, you might also mention that Mr. Lew Kane is transferring himself from presidency of the concern to chairman of the board."

"Board?" she asked. "What board?"

"There will be one, rest assured. That is all, Miss Brown."

He sat back and smiled at the opposite wall. Butterflies were dancing in his stomach, but he did have some cause for jubilation. Maybe he would be able to see over the horizon, after all. Simply because he was able to announce to the trade that he was building five new stores did not mean he was out of the woods. He had lost two of his best men, one permanently and one temporarily, at least. Making up for that loss was going to be difficult. Yet, business establishments did have a way of going forward regardless of who dropped out. No man was indispensable. Now he would simply sit back and wait for news of the new stores to sink in. Then he would make the announcement about the Garfield's buying into the business. That would be the crucial point. If, after that second announcement, the wholesalers in

New York still refused to go along in a big way on his advertising, he would know he had failed. He would then have to sit back, consolidate what he had, and be content to be a second-rater in the business. He grinned thinly and hoped for the best.

He left his office and went down to the third floor, where he intercepted Joe just as he was going out for lunch. "Come along with me," he said. "Be my guest." Joe cast his eyes to the heavens and sighed and went along with him. Who could refuse the boss?

They went to the Redwood Room in the Clift Hotel and ordered lunch. Joe fidgeted, waiting for the ceiling to fall in, but nothing happened while they were eating. Kane talked about the new stores and about business generally, but had nothing to say of a personal nature. Over their coffees, however, he leaned back in his seat and looked angrily into Joe's eyes.

But he said softly, "So you take me for a boob."

Joe gasped and stared at him. "I take you for what, Mr. Kane?"

"A boob. A big, fat, no-thinking boob. Did you really think I swallowed that story of yours about hearing the inspectors talking about Jackson? Number one, the story was too damned pat. Of all people in the city, you would be the one to overhear such a conversation. Also, I learned a few other things about Jackson from the police. They don't believe there was a prowler that morning. They believe that something occurred between the girl and her father. What is your thinking on the matter?"

Joe called the waiter over and ordered a double straight brandy. When it was delivered he told Kane, "I know that drinking during store hours is against the rules, especially with the boss present, but you'll have to excuse me this once. I need it." He tilted his head back and swallowed the brandy in one gulp. Then he reached quickly for a glass of water and downed that. "Okay," he said. "No more lying. Now you'll get the truth. It isn't very pretty, but that's what you asked for. You prepared?"

Kane nodded. "I can take it."

Joe sat back and thought a moment, then started in the very beginning, how and where he had met Marilyn and what had happened since then. He finished by saying, "She thought she had killed him, you understand. However, we found him alive, though dripping blood from an ugly gash in his head. So, from there on, I took over. I made up the story for her to tell and smashed the lock on the front door and got the hell out of there. That's how it happened."

Kane was thoughtfully silent for a long while, but then he asked, "You're sure what Max had in mind was rape?"

"You have to make up your own mind about that. I'm not about to spell it out for anyone. But, I've been thinking about it ever since. Now I realize that he always has impressed me as some kind of a weirdo."

"I know what you mean. He is not a normal sort of person. Yet I never did wonder about his possible sexual aberrations. Never entered my mind. It should have, I suppose. No family. No real friends. Physically as soft as a jellyfish. Seemingly interested in nothing but money. Hmmmmm. When a man is unnatural in one way, he is usually unnatural in other ways as well. I should have guessed something."

Joe asked bluntly, "What are you going to do about him?"

It was Kane's turn to shrug. "I don't know. I don't really know. As far as I am concerned, business-wise, he is the best around. Yet there is more to consider than that. Maybe if Maloney makes out—"

"Fred?"

"Yes. I'm putting him into Jackson's spot for the time being. That's a hell of a big jump for him to take. Yet, if he shows any inclination to grasp the reins, I might—well, we'll see how it turns out."

"Sure. I wish Maloney luck."

"So do I."

They were walking back to the store when Joe said, "So you and the old man are going to do business? Mind if I ask how badly he's taking you?"

Kane smiled and shook his head. "Not badly. I'm paying through the nose, of course, but not as badly as I expected."

Joe had to laugh. "Hell, Mr. Kane, everyone gets the old man wrong. He's a pushover to do business with."

"I didn't quite find him that easy."

"That's not what I mean. What I mean is that he has one rule he goes by. If there's money in it, he's for it. Naturally, he tries to get more than his due share, but all you have to do is knock him down to that point where he is still making money, and he buys the deal."

"Something like that, I imagine."

As they started through the main doors of the store, Kane looked at Joe and asked coldly, "Incidentally, are you seeing the girl again?"

Joe was silent a moment, then shook his head. "Marilyn? Not the way you're thinking. I shall probably see her before she goes back East, but only to say good-bye."

"Glad to hear it. If I get involved in many more of these things, I think I'll lose my mind."

They started across the main floor of the store and saw Betty Parker come out of an elevator toward them. She looked surprised, but then slowed and smiled at them. Kane glanced at his wristwatch.

"Aren't you a bit late to go out for lunch?"

She nodded. "Marie's in there pitching. I have a legal appointment at two thirty. See you later."

Kane watched her walk on by them and frowned. Legal appointment? What the hell did she mean by that? Joe also watched her go and he, too, was frowning.

17

Betty took a taxicab to the Russ Building on Montgomery Street and went up to the fourteenth floor. She was told to go into Mr. Klein's office, he was expecting her. She went in and shook hands with him and sat on the other side of the broad mahogany desk as he lowered himself slowly and rather painfully to his padded chair. He was in his seventies. Almost as round as he was tall, he had a few pieces of white fuzz on an otherwise bald head, a nose as curved as a hawk's and jowls that hung even with his chin. He should have retired years ago, and knew it, but he could not bring himself to let loose. He was afraid that when he quit he would die, as he had seen happen to so many friends of his.

However, he could still appreciate beauty and beamed at Betty across the desk. "Well, my dear, you look lovelier than ever."

"Thank you, Mr. Klein."

She sat back and regarded him narrowly. She seemed calm and collected, but her heart was pounding rather loudly in her chest. Betty did not know Mr. Klein well. Though he was the testator and guardian of her estate, she had met him only twice before. Both times they had talked about her deceased parents, but Mr. Klein had had very little to say. Now she wanted him to say a great deal.

"Mr. Klein," she said, "I get five hundred a month from my parents' estate, which amounts to six thousand a year. That has been going on for quite some time. I figured it out the other day, and it represents a considerable amount of money that has already been paid out. Yet I have always been led to believe that the estate was rather small."

He shrugged and spread his hands open before him. "Relatively speaking, my dear. It isn't in the millions, believe me. What keeps you going is that the money is well invested."

"I see." Then she asked bluntly, "How long will it last?"

"I don't believe you have anything to worry about for many years to come. Perhaps," he smiled, "not until after you are married."

She asked quickly, "What would marriage have to do with it?"

Klein knew he had made a blunder. She was a sharp woman, and he was not as agile intellectually as he used to be. But he shrugged and said, "Nothing that I know about. It was simply a figure of speech."

"In other words," she said shrewdly, "it could run out one day, and you have no idea when that would happen."

"I didn't say that."

She leaned forward and said, "Mr. Klein, if I have an estate, it has to represent a certain amount of money and a certain number of investments. Now, could you tell me about how much money is invested in my name?"

He pursed his lips and rolled his eyes. Damn it, he thought, now it's happening. He had always known it would happen one day and he had so told the others, but they had not listened to him. She had gone along so far because it was always easier to coast, especially when the money was coming in, but he had always known that there would come a day when she would demand to know. In her shoes, he, too, would have to know, even if it upset the apple cart.

"Offhand," he said, "I don't have the answer for you."

She said slyly, "Then why don't you get it out of your files? It has to be here in the office. All I want is a simple answer."

He rubbed a hand over his mouth and looked her up and down and his own eyes were suddenly as hard and cold as hers. "Young lady," he said, "don't pry."

"Why not?"

"I can't give you a reason. Don't ask me. Just let me tell you that you never had it so good and if you ask too many questions and pry too hard, it may all blow up in your face and you will no longer have that five hundred a month. I would think about it, if I were you. You just don't pick up five hundred a month lying in the streets. Think it over."

"I have thought it over. I can live without that five hundred a month, Mr. Klein. I happen to be very good in my business, and I can always do better than the average. Lately, however, there is something more important to me than that money. You know what it is, too. Do you have anything to say?"

He shook his head, but his eyes evaded hers. "Nothing."

"Very well. Then, as of tomorrow, Mr. Klein, I am hiring a certified public accountant to go through your books and tell me what my so-called estate is all about."

He looked suddenly quite sad as he said, "I wouldn't do that if I were you."

"Because there is no estate?"

"I am not saying. I do have confidences, you know. But I wouldn't do it. Take your five hundred a month and forget it. If you don't—well—you may lose the money and pile much grief upon yourself as well."

Betty sucked in her breath sharply and said, "You just answered one of the big questions in my mind. Now I know there is no estate. Someone is paying me off month by month. And I think I know who it is."

"In that case," he said, "keep it to yourself and say nothing."

She said bitterly, "Mr. Klein, do you know what it is to be raised all your life without any real identity? I have no parents. They're ghosts. I have no relatives. All ghosts. I have nothing to cling to, nothing to grab hold of. I was born in a vacuum, I was raised in a vacuum, and I still live in a vacuum." She said decisively, "Mr. Klein, I mean to bring that to an end. I belong to somebody and I belong somewhere. I don't give a damn what I find out. Do you understand? I don't care if I hurt myself or someone else. I don't even care if I am the only one who knows. But, so help me God, I mean to find out."

He said softly, "I'm sorry for you. The cards are stacked against you. Take the honest and sincere word of an old man, my dear. Whatever you come up with will only hurt very good and very decent people who should not be made to suffer at this late date. Fall in love, my child. Get married. Have children of your own. But, for God's sake, forget what you have in mind."

She sat back and stared at him and then said softly, but flatly, "Anna Merritt is my mother. Will you deny it?"

He was not surprised. He simply asked, "Do you have proof?"

"Enough to satisfy myself. It might not be enough in a court of law, but I believe with a good lawyer it would not be hard to make it stick." She asked again, "Do you deny it?"

"I deny nothing and admit nothing," he sighed.

Betty closed her eyes and clasped her hands tightly in her lap. Her stomach was churning like a Waring Blendor. She had all the answers. Mr. Klein had failed to stop her. Anna Merritt was her mother. There was not the slightest doubt remaining. Now she knew, blindingly, that her mother never had died; that she was very much alive and very close. She groaned inwardly, Oh, God, after all these years. Maybe it would have been better not to know.

She opened her eyes and looked at Mr. Klein, then shoved herself to her feet. She almost whispered, "There really isn't very much more to say, is there?"

"Talk with Mrs. Merritt."

"I mean to. Oh, yes, I do mean to. I guess it is always nice to know that you do have living, breathing people who might belong to you. Good-bye, Mr. Klein, and thank you very much."

She straightened her shoulders as much as possible and walked stiffly out of the office. He watched her go and sat down with a deep frown. She had mentioned nothing about Lew Kane. He wondered why not. Maybe, he thought, her reasoning powers had not yet carried her that far. Cripes, he thought, what a hell of a revelation that's going to be when it happens!

Betty did not go back to work. She could not have gone back to work if her life had depended on it. She took a taxicab and went home. There she threw herself on the bed and buried her face in a pillow and allowed the tears to come, and thought and thought until her mind was spinning like a top.

Anna Merritt is my mother. Anna Merritt is my mother. Anna Merritt—

She rolled to her back and stared at the ceiling. The tears dried and she was no longer crying.

At no time had she ever doubted the story she had been told about her parents' demise. The story had become so firmly embedded in her mind that when she had matured she almost never thought of it. It had been so long ago that it was not worth thinking about. She did, after all, have a life of her own to live, and she lived it. She had not even thought to question the source of her income. It came in regularly, almost like a check from the government. She was used to it. It was part of her daily living. How could you question something that had been going on for years and years, like the tick of a clock?

But now she had asked questions and she had received answers, even though they had been evasive. What had not been said had been as conclusive as though Mr. Klein had spelled it all out for her. She knew the answers. The biggest of all, of course, was that Anna Merritt was her mother. It would take a long time getting used to the fact that she actually had a living mother instead of a dead ghost.

The tears came again and she cried for quite some time. How could Anna—she was now calling her Anna in her mind for the first time—be so cruel, so unfeeling, particularly toward her only child? It was then she sat up on the bed and stared into space. She was Anna's child, but George Merritt had died without a child. She remembered the stories she had heard about him, about his differences, his oddness. She was not his child. Then who—? She gasped and sucked in her breath and suddenly knew the answer.

She thought she screamed aloud, "Oh, my God," but she had not actually voiced a word.

She looked at the clock and saw that it was a few minutes before five thirty. The store was still open. She dialed the number and asked for Mr. Haley on the third floor. In a moment he was on the wire.

"Joe," she said, "you have to do me a big favor. When you leave work, on your way home, I want you to stop by my apartment. I have something to ask you. It's terribly important."

Joe laughed. "Will you have lighted candles and the blinds drawn?"

"Joe," she cried, "this really is important. Please."

He said more soberly, "Okay, carrot-top. You do sound a little exercised. Now, where the devil do you live?"

She told him and he grunted, "Be seeing you," and hung up.

A while later the doorbell rang and Joe was there. He sat down in the kitchen with her and had some cheese and crackers and a straight shot of bourbon; then mixed himself a tall highball. He looked at her seated across the table, watching him anxiously, and chuckled softly to himself.

"What's on your mind?" he asked.

She took a deep breath and told him. She told him about her visit with Klein. Once she cried slightly, and once she broke down completely. Joe watched her narrowly and waited for her to compose herself. When she continued he listened closely. And at last she had finished with Klein.

She looked him in the eyes and said, "That takes care of my mother. Then I wondered about my father and suddenly I knew who it was—Lew Kane."

Joe looked down at the table and shoved some crackers aside. "You're sure about that?"

"Positive. He, after all, is the one who brought me up from Los Angeles. He has always overpaid me. Then there's the thing about his son, Bill, who is undoubtedly my half-brother. It all fits together." She cocked her head on one side and squinted at him and asked, "Don't you think so?"

Joe sighed and raised his eyes from the table to look at her. "Yes," he said, "I do. In fact, I've known it for quite a little while."

She reached across the table and grabbed Joe's hand. "How do you know?"

Joe told her all he knew and tied all the little threads together. There was no longer a doubt in either mind. Suddenly Betty got up and rushed into the bathroom and threw up. When she finally turned about Joe was standing behind her. He had a wet towel in his hands and washed her face.

He said gently, "I know. I know. You were just thinking of the man who is now your father and what you thought about him before—that he was trying to get you into bed with him."

Betty nodded and mumbled miserably, "Yes. Oh, my God, Joe."

"Sure. It was bound to come. But now you can face something else, something bigger. He was acting simply as your father all along."

She whispered, "Yes."

"So, okay, face it. Wipe it out of your mind. Think of the man who is your father, who undoubtedly and obviously loves you. Think of that."

Her shoulders quivered and she chattered, "I will, Joe. I will. Now, if you don't mind, would you please leave me alone?"

Joe grinned, then burst into a laugh. "Who would believe it? Good old Joe Haley, the Boy Scout!"

He turned around and walked away laughing to himself. Betty

turned back to the toilet bowl and started throwing up again. She was thinking of the many nights when she had wondered what it would really be like going to bed with Lew Kane. Perhaps the question had been considered lightly, but it had been considered. And all the time she had been thinking about her own father.

Never, she thought. This I will never get out of my mind.

Betty was back at the store the following morning. She had cried most of the night and her eyes were red, but she had used heavy makeup and no one noticed the difference. At least, no one said anything.

She got quickly back into the tempo and rhythm of her floor and ruled it, as always, with an iron hand. The saleswomen, however, were beginning to appreciate her and the way she ran things. She was rough and she was rugged and she took no back-talk from anyone and she ran things her way, but the salespeople had learned something. She helped their sales. That was really all they cared about. She stopped walk-aways, she helped them make sales to sightseers and shoppers, she saved sales for them that were going down the drain. The floor was coming to have an *esprit de corps* of its own, which it had never had before.

But Betty, herself, was living in a fog. Whenever Kane came by and touched her she cringed. One day Bill came by to call on his father and stopped to talk to Betty. She could not look at him and was almost incapable of conversation. God above, she thought, I have a brother. In fact, I have two brothers. Bill walked away frowning and wondering what was the matter with her.

The rhythm of the store itself continued as usual, but there were a few discordant notes of which Betty was aware. Word had got around that Harrison was not coming back and she was aware, dimly, that there was something dangerous about it. As the days passed word also got around that something was wrong with Mr. Jackson, though he was now home from the hospital, and that there was a possibility he might not come back. That, too, seemed to be dangerous for the firm, even though Mr. Kane seemed to be fairly happy with the way Maloney was taking over the controller's job. Gossip also had it that the five new stores were going to be hard for Mr. Kane to swallow.

Chet Baker was taking over well in his job as temporary

manager, but it was also said that Maloney had refused to step down if Jackson came back. What would he do, look for another job? That wouldn't be good at all. Marie, of course, was getting more difficult than ever, now that she knew Betty had really taken hold, and Betty was wondering how to get rid of her without having her leave the store. You didn't, after all, break another person's rice bowl if it could be helped. Then there was the final word that Joe Haley and his wife were not getting along well lately, and that Betty Parker was the cause of it all.

It was the latter that actually brought Betty out of the fog. The idea was so preposterous that she broke out laughing until she was almost hysterical. She began to look about her with clear eyes, and only then did she really begin to consider her position in relation to the other people involved.

She had no idea how it had happened, but many years ago Lew Kane and Anna Merritt had had an affair. Both had been married to others. But Anna had become pregnant and had been forced to hide it. She had gone to Europe, where she had secretly given birth to Betty Parker. She had then hidden the true facts with the phony story that Betty knew so well. Perhaps she had later intended to bring Betty to America and adopt her. Who would ever know? The war had interfered. Betty had been left pretty much on her own, but with adequate safeguards. At no time had she ever been really abandoned.

Now she was home where she belonged. But did she belong? There was a big doubt about that. She had reconciled herself to the fact that she had parents. She had even gotten over the disgust she felt for herself because of her previous thoughts toward the man who was now her father. She no longer threw up when she thought about it. She could now look upon it dispassionately. But was she really home? That she seriously doubted. Anna had a certain station in society to maintain. Lew Kane had not only society to consider, but his own wife and family as well. There was no way she could claim either as a parent without hurting both. She seemed to be stymied.

The weeks passed and Betty got nowhere with her problem. She even wondered if she had a problem. She was alive, she was young, she was healthy, she was beautiful, many men desired her, and she was financially in very good shape. Where, then, did the problem enter in? Thousands of women her age would like to step into her shoes. Even so, there was a problem. She wanted to claim her parents openly and publicly. It was an ache and a hunger within her. How did one go about such a thing? She had no idea.

She came to work on a Tuesday morning and the outer doors were hardly open when she found herself facing Mrs. Milton Alexander. The older woman was dressed in a suit that cost over three hundred dollars, alligator shoes, an expensive purse, and a hat that cost at least fifty dollars; all of it Merritt-Wilson purchases. She was, indeed, a top customer of the store.

She smiled sweetly at Betty and apologized, "Sorry I haven't been in before, but I have been so busy. Do you have my skirt ready for me?"

Betty excused herself. She went to the tailor shop and came back with the skirt in her hand. "I am sorry, too," she said. "But there wasn't anything we could do until we got your permission."

Mrs. Alexander asked sharply, "What do you mean?"

"Well, Mrs. Alexander, the seams can't be let out as there is no material left, so that leaves one alternative, a gusset on each side."

Mrs. Alexander frowned. "My goodness, I don't know if I would like that. The jacket is very short, you know. Gussets would show."

"Yes, I can't deny that they would. However, it is the only thing that can be done. On the other hand, our seamstresses are very good, and I am sure that they will do their best to hide the gussets. Now, is that what you want?"

Mrs. Alexander rubbed the side of her face with her hand and frowned into space, then sighed and said, "If that is all you can do—"

"I'm afraid so. Would you like me to go ahead with the gussets?"

Mrs. Alexander thought again for a long while, then finally snorted and said, "Very well, young lady. You do what you think is best. I shall drop back in a few days."

Mrs. Alexander had hardly gone when Betty received a call from Susie that she was wanted in Mr. Kane's office. She went down the corridor, walked into his office and sank into a chair. She looked at Kane and thought that if she had deliberately set out to pick a certain man for her father she could not have made a better choice. The idea made her chuckle.

He had really very little to say to her. He looked over some papers on his desk, then raised his eyes to hers and smiled. "The first month," he said, "there was little difference, but ever since then you have shown a steady gain in your department. I realize what you were up against, and I know how hard it has been. Yet you have done extremely well far sooner than I had expected. I would like to compliment you."

She cleared her throat and nodded. "Thanks. I do try."

"No question of that." He sat back then and looked off into space for a moment. "Lately," he said, "things have become a little raunchy around here. So I thought I would take it upon myself to compliment people who have it coming to them. It is a rather sizable group. It includes you and Haley and Sam Kuller—he is doing an excellent job—and Chet Baker, who is taking over very well." He said, more to himself than to her, "Now I understand why Maloney is reluctant to step back, if that becomes necessary. But he is doing quite a job himself. Findex, of course, is always rough, but not for him."

She said sincerely, "I'm glad. Fred Maloney is one of my favorite people. I think perhaps he is a bigger man than you may realize."

He grinned and winked at her. "Slowly but surely, my dear, I'm finding out that I have a lot of pretty wonderful people working in this outfit. I only hope I can stand up and be counted with them."

She had to laugh. "None of us are worrying on that score." She looked at him squarely then and took a deep breath and decided to make the plunge. "In fact," she said, "you are even quite an unusual parent."

Failing to understand her words and believing that she was referring to Bill, he said, "Well, we did get in a bit of an awkward situation—but I see that it has blown over with no harm done on either side."

"No," she said stubbornly, "that isn't what I mean. What I am trying to say is that you are a most unusual father for a certain redheaded young woman to claim as her own."

God, she thought, I said it. I said it out loud. She closed her eyes for a moment and clasped her hands tightly in her lap, then opened her eyes to look at him. His face had gone white, and he was staring at her as if she had dropped a live bomb in his lap. Then he got up and walked beyond her to close the door and lock it. He returned to the desk and sat on the edge of it just before Betty's face. His hands, too, were clasped tightly together. He looked into her eyes and saw what was written there and nodded slowly.

He asked bluntly, "When did you find out?"

She bit her lower lip before replying, "A few weeks ago. I have been suspicious for some time, especially where my mother was concerned—I mean Anna—but the whole thing finally made a complete picture about three weeks ago."

"And you've kept this to yourself during all that time?"

She was about to say that she had, but then she remembered Joe Haley's involvement. "Not exactly," she said. "One other person knows. He found out before I did."

He shook his head back and forth like a wounded animal. Good Lord, he was thinking, another part of the roof has fallen. Would it never end?

He took in a deep breath, exhaled slowly and said, "There is no sense denying it. I have always known you would find out, sooner or later. I imagine you got it through Klein?"

She nodded and whispered, "Yes."

"Of course. I have lived with the fact that one day you would demand to know just how big your so-called estate was supposed to be."

"Incidentally," she asked, "who pays that five hundred a month?"

"Well," he sighed, "at first Anna paid most of it, but as I began doing better financially we split it between us." He asked seriously, "You haven't been unhappy with it, have you?"

She almost laughed, but was not feeling up to it at the moment. What was wrong with him? He was not reacting at all as she had imagined he might. She had even dreamed she would find herself in his arms after only a dozen words or so had been spoken. But he seemed to be tackling the situation like simply another business matter. Her spine stiffened and her eyes narrowed a bit.

"No," she said, "I haven't been unhappy with it. In fact, it has been quite adequate."

He said quickly, "It will continue. It won't be cut off."

Then she really stared at him. For God's sake, what was going on in his mind? Then she understood and almost gasped out loud. He was afraid she might blackmail him if her income was reduced, or cause a scandal, or do something else unpleasant. She had just found a father, and she had also lost him in what might be termed the same breath. She had no idea, of course, of the pressures he was under at the moment, and never thought of them.

She got quickly to her feet and glared at him through tears

forming in her eyes. But she said quietly, "I don't know what to say to you. Maybe I've been without parents too long. Maybe I thought you could have instant love like instant soup, or something of that sort. But I never dreamed that our eventual confrontation would come off this way. I thought—I thought—I guess I thought you would react in a more human way and—"

She brushed the tears from her eyes, walked to the door, and unlocked it. Then she looked back at Kane, and her back was again stiff. "I don't know what I thought," she snapped. "There is one thing I can tell you, though. You have nothing to worry about. As far as I am concerned, the subject is closed."

Kane stared numbly after her as she walked out of the office. He loved her. He loved her very much. But how did you say it? How did you say it and still keep an empire from tumbling about your head? He reached for the telephone and told the store operator to get him a number in Woodside.

Betty walked down the hallway, turned into her own office and got her hat and coat and bag. On her way out she told Marie, "Take over the floor. You'll love it." Then she stepped into an elevator and went down.

She got into a taxicab in front of the store and went directly home. There she got out of her clothes, filled a tub with hot water, and stepped into it. It was the best cure she knew when her nerves were at the breaking point. She settled back and closed her eyes. Her thoughts went racing around and around, making no sense whatever. She stayed in the tub perhaps an hour, then got out and dried herself. It was only a little after noontime, but she dressed in pajamas, wrapped her hair in a scarf and dropped onto the bed to stare at the ceiling. Blackmail, she thought. Good God Almighty!

A bit after three o'clock the doorbell started ringing. She decided to ignore it, but the bell simply would not stop. It kept on ringing as if the party at the other end knew very well she was home. She got up angrily and went into the small hallway to punch the buzzer. She heard the door downstairs open and close, then light footsteps hurrying up the stairs. Puzzled, she opened the door of her apartment and faced Anna Merritt hurrying toward her.

The tears were running unashamedly down Anna's cheeks. She placed both hands on Betty's shoulders and gripped her tightly and cried, "My baby. My own darling baby." Then she pulled her into her arms and whispered in her ear, "Now, my daughter, we can say it out loud. Now we can claim each other."

Betty was not at all prepared for such an emotional outburst and her own nerves were on the verge of breaking, anyway. She, too, broke down and cried. They managed, somehow, to close the door and went into the living room and sank onto the couch, still in each other's arms. Anna was not very coherent, but Betty did manage to learn that Kane had called her and she had come up from Woodside as quickly as possible. Kane had told her everything that had transpired in his office.

Anna finally shoved herself away, dried her tears, and looked at Betty. "Darling," she asked, "do you hate me?"

Betty brushed her own tears away and shook her head. "Of course not. We all make mistakes, and you made a big one. But, at least you have tried to take care of it all your life."

"I tried so hard," Anna gasped, "to get you out of Europe. The moment the war was over I put every wheel I could think of into motion. Nothing worked because of your clouded birth records."

Betty frowned and looked at her almost accusingly. "One thing I don't understand. There was nothing to prevent you from going to Europe. You could at least have visited me."

Anna took her hand and squeezed it. "Impossible. I would have given myself away without even half trying. I couldn't run that risk. Not just for myself alone, but for Lew's sake, too. After all, he does have a family that is very important to him. But now," she cried happily, "we are together at last. You have no idea how happy I am. Honestly, darling, I'm all torn up inside."

"Me, too."

They cried again and hugged each other, then the two of them were talking at once. There was so much to say. Yet it was not quite as strange as it could have been. They had known each other for two years, and they had been quite close for most of that time. They had exchanged confidences and histories and many other things. They knew a great deal about each other. On those points, therefore, there was very little to say.

Though Anna did say, "Now you know why I wanted so badly to adopt you."

"And I put my foot right in it. But do you still feel the same way?"

Anna fairly beamed at her. "There isn't even any use discussing it. I'll call the lawyers and have it arranged as quickly as possible."

"You might raise a few eyebrows, considering my age."

Anna laughed delightedly. "That, my dear, would be the most amusing thing in the world. And I hope they all guess right, that you really are my daughter through some romantic liaison or other. I hope they do."

Betty's chin came up and she said softly, "I hope they do, too. I wouldn't mind at all. I'm proud of my mother."

Anna broke down again and it was some time before she could dry her tears. But then she straightened and told Betty, "Get your things together. You're coming down to Woodside with me. Let's see. Tomorrow is your day off and you don't have to be back to work until Thursday noon."

"I have news for you. I'm not going back ever."

Anna cocked her head to one side and looked at her shrewdly. "Oh, yes, you are," she said. "He is your father and he is a very grand person. I don't pretend to understand his reaction, but there are good and adequate reasons for it. Right now he is the most harassed man you know, fighting for everything in which he believes. You have no idea of the struggles facing him."

"But I faced him and he failed."

Anna said softly, "Listen, please. He took over Merritt's and merged it with Wilson's not just to be a big man here on the Coast. His goal is to be the head of the biggest specialty chain in America. But there is a barrier and a big one. You can't reach the goal he has in mind without the hearty cooperation of the wholesalers in New York. No one can do it. If he fails to get their help, he will remain simply a big fish in a little pond. But if he should force them to come through in New York, he'll be over the top and well on his way."

Betty asked curiously, "What is his position now?"

Anna shrugged. "Hard to tell. When he announced the building of five new stores it did stir some interest in New York. But those hard noses are still waiting to see more. Frankly, I don't know what he can come up with next."

"Doesn't he confide in you?"

"Not so much. When he took over Merritt's it was our agreement that I keep my nose strictly out of the business. So he tells me only what he thinks I should know, and that's not very much. But you do see the position he is in. He is either going to sink or swim, and it won't be very long until he finds out." She got to her feet and pulled Betty up. "Come on. Get dressed and let's go. We have all the time in the world to talk."

They went down the Peninsula in the back seat of the Rolls-Royce, with the window closed between themselves and the chauffeur. Anna laughed and chatted away like a magpie. She stopped talking only when Betty was telling her how she had put together the bits and pieces that were the clues to her parents.

She sighed and said, "How I've wasted time. I could have told you the truth and claimed you as my daughter the moment we met. But I was afraid to. I was afraid of what your reactions would be. So I tried to be devious about it and that didn't work, except that we did remain good friends, thank God. And all the time you were just as anxious to know a mother as I was to know my daughter. Oh, dear. Oh, dear. How we mortals do mess up things."

Betty listened to her chatter and appraised her closely, and a deep warmth crept into her heart. Anna was reacting just as Betty had dreamed a mother should react, loving, tender, gentle, and proud. And Betty felt her own love going out to her. It would take her a long while, she knew, to get used to the fact that she actually had a living mother, but already she felt proud and she felt love. She sighed comfortably and settled back in the seat.

At Woodside, they talked through dinner and the evening, and even when Betty went to bed in her room, Anna came in and got into the other twin bed.

When the lights were out Anna said gently, "You should know about George Merritt."

"If you don't wish to tell—"

"But I do." There was a long silence, then she said, "I don't wish my daughter to brand me as a wanton woman. So it is necessary to know about George." After another silence she continued, "He was a tall, very handsome young man who went in for polo and tennis and all sorts of sports, and the women really swooned over him. When he turned his eyes on me he swept me off my feet. I was the happiest woman on earth."

There was another silence that was longer than the others, and Betty knew that she was crying to herself. But then she said, "On the other hand, I was rather beautiful, if I do say so myself, and I guess I was a rather sexy young lady. At least I had everything needed to be sexy, including the temperament. So I looked forward to the happiest life imaginable with my husband, George Merritt. Then, tragedy struck, as it has a way of doing. George Merritt, to put it bluntly and I hope you forgive me for having to say this, was sadly deficient physiologically in the one member that is most important to a man."

Betty heard her take a deep breath, then she continued, "Believe it or not, I was a virgin, like you. It's something I believe in for a woman. So I was not really aware, at first, of his lack. As our marriage went on, though, I realized that George was getting me excited occasionally, but I was never really satisfied—indeed, I was becoming very frustrated. So, naturally, I started talking with my women friends. You know how it is in the rag-picking business, darling. People are pretty damned frank. And I learned that I was married to some sort of freak. So," she sighed, "George and I had more than our share of blowups after that, and he became vicious. I won't go into that. Suffice it to say, he made my life hell, and I turned against him."

Anna fell silent again, but Betty's curiosity had taken over. She prompted quickly, "And then?"

"Well, that was when I began noticing your father. Whether or not he and Bessie were getting along very well at that time, I don't know. I think, though, that he was very much like Joe Haley. Anyway, I was angry, I was frustrated, I was frightened—you name it. I am not excusing myself. I am simply telling you how it happened." She added lamely, "That's how you were conceived.

"But it couldn't be known, because George's doctor had already told me he was impotent. And how could I divorce him to marry Lew, who was already married and had two young sons? There was also another fact to be considered. George was worth a great deal of money, and I did like having money. I had no desire to lose it. So I made the Grand Tour of Europe, and that is where you were born. I intended bringing you back when you were a year old and adopting you, but Hitler interfered with that. So—well—that's the story."

Betty leaned on an elbow and asked her, "What happened with you and Mr. Merritt? You did stay married to him for quite a number of years."

"Yes. As I say, I liked money, position, social prominence, and so on. So George and I had an agreement. We lived in the same house, and that was as far as it went. I wouldn't even begin to tell you how I spent the next years."

"Wasn't he ever curious about why you went to Europe and why you stayed so long?"

"Oh, naturally. George was no fool. Though nothing was ever

said, he had a pretty good idea of what had taken place. But it was all right with him as long as he didn't have to face any facts. Which happened when you came to this country. Lew called one night to tell me that you were safely in this country and that you were enrolled at UCLA. He should never have called me at home, but he was excited. George overheard the whole conversation on a telephone extension. He then went down to Los Angeles, had you investigated, and followed you around the campus for a few days. Then he came back to Hillsborough and became a recluse, a totally beaten man."

"Why?"

"Because he was finally destroyed as the man he had never been. He had to look at the living, breathing image of me all over again and face the fact that he had not been the one who had conceived you. That was the end of him. And one night, as you probably may have heard, he blew his brains out."

"He sounds terribly weak to me."

"He was. Nature had played a horrible trick on him in the first place, and he was never strong enough to surmount it. However, I could never feel pity for him. He became vicious and took it out on me and everyone else around him. Anyway, darling, that's the whole story. And now, if you don't mind, I am completely exhausted and worn out."

Betty stayed awake for awhile after Anna had gone to sleep. But she, too, had had an exhausting day and was also soon asleep.

They talked throughout the following day and came to two conclusions. First, regardless of what Betty thought of Lew Kane, she would return to work. She had a career to pursue and she was definitely not going to quit and move in with Anna. The latter did not press the point. She knew that Betty was much too vital a person to be content simply with being a wealthy woman's daughter.

The other conclusion was that Anna would expedite the adoption as quickly as possible. Betty was astounded by her own attitude on that point. She fully expected the adoption as her just due. In fact, if the offer had not been made, she would have demanded it. Why? she wondered. Because of the wealth and background involved? She knew that was not it, she was too independent for that, and she soon had the answer. It was simply that she wanted to belong.

They went out to dinner that night to a small but exclusive restaurant on El Camino Real near Atherton, where they dined on snails and frogs' legs. The next morning Betty started back to the city with the chauffeur.

But before Betty left, Anna told her gently, "Naturally, we can't face society with the fact that you truly are my daughter. There are some things one simply cannot do. I don't mind if people guess, and I rather hope they do, but it can't be brought out into the open, as much as I would desire it."

Betty nodded. "I've been thinking of that, too. I agree."

"I'm glad, my dear. So it will have to remain our little secret. But we know, and we know it well. And you and I will never forget it."

Anna hugged her and said, "Naturally, also, one day you will inherit everything I own. There is no other family. I hope that in the future that will compensate you somewhat for the past."

"There is no reason—"

"Hush. I wouldn't have it any other way. You had no way of knowing, of course, but ever since you came to America you have been my sole beneficiary. Now," she laughed, "it won't have to be admitted shamefully after I die that I was a loose woman. Now we can do it simply through adoption."

Betty thought of it on the drive back to the city and was awed by the change in her own dimensions. From a sales person to the heiress of millions in the space of a few days. My God!

Fortunately, she thought, she had a European background and education. It was the first snobbish thought she had ever entertained, and she was not at all aware of it.

18

BETTY changed clothes at home, while the chauffeur waited, then was driven to the store at noontime. She went directly to her office, where she left her hat and purse, and then walked out on the floor—and was immediately swamped. Sales girls swarmed around, customers had to be taken care of, and the telephone rang continuously. The world was back in its proper orbit.

It was perhaps an hour later when Kane approached Betty and leaned over the counter to take her right hand in his hands and squeeze hard. He looked into her eyes and asked, "How do you feel today?"

She returned his gaze and said coolly, "Very well, thanks."

He looked beyond her and saw Marie talking with Miss Snider across the floor. Marie was whispering viciously from the corner of her mouth, "Look at the old coot. Now he even holds her hand in public."

Kane's eyes returned to Betty as he said, "Anna called me while you were on your way to the city this morning. She told me how upset you were over my—ah—reaction. I'm sorry, Betty. I've had so much on my mind lately—"

"It's quite all right."

"I should have told you how proud I am of you as a daughter and as a person."

Betty withdrew her hand and said, "I repeat, it's quite all right."

"No," he said, "it isn't. Maybe I can prove it to you in the future. Meanwhile, you did say something else about another person knowing about your parentage. Do you mind telling me who it is?"

"Not at all. Joe Haley."

His eyes opened a bit wider. "Our Mr. Haley? Well, well. And how does he happen to know about it?"

Betty said stiffly, "When I first became suspicious I needed someone to talk to, someone to set me straight, if I happened to be wrong. I know that Joe is no blabbermouth, so I selected him. He said that he would look into it for me, which he did. He went through the San Francisco newspapers during the year in which I was born. He found items on Anna's Grand Tour. So it was possible that I was correct."

"And Joe told you that?"

"Well, no. He told me nothing. It was not until after my encounter with Mr. Klein, when I satisfied myself that I was correct, that Joe said anything."

"I think I shall have a little talk with him. Be good, my dear."

She said sarcastically, "I do try."

His smile then broke to the surface. "Of course you do."

He went down to the third floor and saw Joe talking with a customer. Kane waited patiently, nothing must ever interfere with a customer, then beckoned to Joe when he was through. The two of them went into Joe's little office and closed the door. Joe wondered what it was all about. He soon found out.

Kane put it all out on the table. When he was through, Joe asked him, "Do you deny any of it, Mr. Kane?"

The older man shook his head slowly. "It's gone beyond the point of denial, Joe. I couldn't deny it now if I wanted to, and I don't. I do happen to love that girl very much."

"It sure puts you on a spot, though."

"I thought that, yes, but now I wonder. Anna is going to adopt Betty. So, the past will be made up to her somehow."

Joe said wistfully, "I wish somebody like that would adopt me."

Kane was beginning to feel rather good and burst out laughing. "Hell's bells," he said. "Your father is probably worth more than Mrs. Merritt. And, from what I understand, you are the sole heir."

Joe frowned. For how long? he wondered. Mary was getting to be almost impossible to live with. She had broken her silence with him a few weeks back and was now talking again. But there was nothing pleasant about anything she had to say. All she did was nag, condemn, and accuse. Even though Joe knew it was impossible, it was almost as if she were pregnant again. That was the way she always was with the onset of pregnancy. He sighed inwardly.

"Of course," he said. "I forgot for a moment."

Kane got to his feet and smiled and said, "Anyway, everything seems to be in pretty safe hands. Neither Anna nor I are about to say anything. I feel confident that Betty knows how to hold her tongue, and from all I understand you have a zipper on your lip yourself."

Joe stood up and returned his smile. "No worries on that score, believe me." Then he chuckled and said, "I always did wonder how you swung the deal on this Merritt chain. Now I have the answer."

"What answer is that?"

"Well, considering everything, of course, all you had to do was put on a little pressure."

Kane burst out laughing again. "You couldn't be more wrong," he said. "The reverse is the truth. It was Anna who put the pressure on me. You see, Joe, she had already changed her will to Betty's name, and she wanted to get out of the business. Yet she wished to leave it in such a way that Betty's interests would be adequately protected. She had faith in me, so she figured I would be the best person to take over. Simple as it may sound, that is how the whole deal was engineered."

"Well, I'll be damned!"

"By the way," Kane said, "I haven't heard anything more about Mr. Jackson's daughter. Do you have any word?"

"Sure. She left for the East a couple of weeks ago. I doubt she will ever be back here again. Do you have any word about Mr. Jackson?"

"Well, in a way. I dropped by his house last Sunday. He couldn't look me in the eyes—not at any time. He knew that I knew, you see. He didn't say, but I have the feeling he is not coming back. That, of course, is something else for you to keep under your hat. You know," he laughed, "I seem to be trusting you more than anyone I've ever known. Well, anyway—I have to get back to my office."

He took the stairs back up to the fourth floor and walked down the corridor to his own office. As he stepped inside he saw a tall young man standing before the windows. He was dressed in a beautifully tailored light brown linen suit, which was a little too cool for San Francisco summers. Otherwise, he was impeccably groomed from head to toe. When he turned to face Kane there was something about him that made Kane tag him as an easterner.

He held out his hand and smiled and said, "Mr. Kane? I am John Garfield, sir. Your secretary was kind enough to allow me to wait in your office."

Kane's stomach flipped over, but he managed to smile and shake hands. "What a pleasure to meet you, Mr. Garfield. Just arrive in the city?"

"Well—ah—no, sir. I've been here a few days checking things over, you might say."

"Of course. Naturally. But sit down. Sit down, please."

Garfield nodded and dropped into the deep leather chair. Kane sank into his own well-worn chair. He shoved cigarettes and cigars across the desk, but Garfield smiled slightly and shook his head. Kane also offered him a drink, but again he smiled and shook his head. His smile was already beginning to irritate Kane. The son-of-a-bitch, he thought. Got the world by the tail, and he knows it. Maybe he's got my tail, too.

Kane mumbled, "I've been waiting to meet you. But I thought you would be out here long before this." He laughed heartily, a little too heartily, and said, "You are one of the principal stockholders, you know."

Garfield said smoothly, "Yes, I know. And I had intended coming out here some weeks back. But then the news reached us that you were expanding by building five more new stores. That, sir, was rather a bombshell."

"Oh, really?"

"Yes." He leaned across the desk and looked into Kane's eyes and suddenly Kane realized he was staring back into two pieces of ice. Then he said coldly, "Do you mind if we drop all the preliminary bullshit, Mr. Kane?"

Kane had to laugh, even though his stomach was still jumping. "You're talking my language, Mr. Garfield. Fire away."

"Very well, sir. My brothers and I simply could not believe the news. But we checked into it and found it was accurate enough."

"Why couldn't you believe it?"

"A very good question. For the simple reason, Mr. Kane, that you don't have the kind of money left to swing that sort of deal. We have good reason to believe that all you have is enough to operate on month to month. So you had to get it elsewhere. Instead of coming out myself, I sent our lawyers out here, and they came back with the answers."

Kane said dryly, "You should have dropped me a letter. You would have had the answer by return mail."

Garfield smiled again, that same smile. "Too bad we didn't think of anything so simple. But we did get the answers. A contractor by the name of Patrick Haley is buying the land and putting up the buildings, for which he will receive a certain percentage off the top."

"Do you find anything wrong with that?"

Garfield's cheeks flushed slightly. "Indeed I do, Mr. Kane. Garfield's has never done business that way. We do all of our own financing all the way."

"Hmmmmm. You are lucky to be able to finance Garfield expansion in that manner. But this is not Garfield's, sir. We are talking about Merritt-Wilson's. You and your brothers, I might remind you, are not in control here. I am. And that is the way I please to finance my own expansion."

Garfield leaned back and pulled at his lower lip while squinting at Kane. "You know, sir, as you said a moment ago, we are principal stockholders. I don't mean to start off the first moment we meet by interfering in your business. I can tell you, though, that we will never hold still for such reckless financing. I can also assure you that the moment I am on the board of directors I shall find ways and means to put a halt to it."

Kane took a deep breath and exhaled slowly. Well, he thought, here we go. Sink or swim.

"I am glad you brought that up," he said.

Garfield smiled sourly, but said sweetly, "There is no way you can stop that, Mr. Kane."

Kane leaned back and said, "Well, now, I don't know. It came to my attention recently that Garfield also owns Westover Mills, one of the biggest makers of men's clothing in the country. Is that correct?"

Garfield nodded proudly and said, "We have our fingers in other enterprises, of course. Yes, we own Westover—lock, stock, and barrel."

Kane chuckled. "So much the better. But Merritt-Wilson's, Mr. Garfield, does not do business with Westover."

Garfield frowned lightly and asked, "So?"

"So what I am trying to say is this. I have no doubt that you have heard of restraint of trade?"

Garfield snapped impatiently, "Oh, now, really."

"But think about it, Mr. Garfield. Think about it for a moment and a great light will dawn. Restraint of trade means exactly that in every court in the land. My attorneys have looked into the matter quite thoroughly. And what they tell me is simple and to the point. If I decide to fight you, which I have, no court I know about will allow you to sit on the board of directors of Merritt-Wilson's."

Garfield's puzzlement was quite apparent. "I don't follow you."

"Then let me spell it out for you, and as you said yourself let's spare the bullshit. If you sit on our board and are also a board member of Westover, you will desire to have the products of Westover used in this chain. That, Mr. Garfield, is purely and simply restraint of trade. All I have to tell any court is that I am afraid of that kind of undue influence, and that I wish to exercise my own option in the products I buy without your restraining hand on the board. Do you follow me?"

"I—ah—"

"No court, Mr. Garfield, will allow it. I assure you of that."

Garfield sank deeply into his chair and pressed his fingertips against his eyelids. At last he dropped his hands, opened his eyes, and stared across the desk at Kane. He was no longer smiling.

He said slowly, "I hadn't even considered that angle."

"But I had and so have my attorneys."

"Mr. Kane, I won't argue the point with you. You do happen to be correct. I admit it. I am also not stupid enough to become angry and make a court case out of it. I am afraid I know even now how that would come out. So what profit would it be for either of us?"

"None."

"I know. This is one of the reasons my brothers trust me. I have never taken the firm into court unnecessarily and unless I knew positively that I could win. I tell you frankly sir, I don't think I could win this one. So," he spread his hands wide, "what do we do now?"

Kane stared at him and the tension went out of his body. He leaned back and roared with laughter. When he was finished he walked around the desk and shook hands with Garfield.

"Son," he said, "you're one of the damnedest characters I've ever met. I've known honest men before, but you top them all."

"Not honesty, sir. Why fight something you can't whip? I know that. You do have good attorneys, and they did come up with an excellent angle. So why should I kick my heels and roll on the floor and froth at the mouth? So, I ask again, where do we go from here?"

"You mean you're really interested?"

"Mr. Kane, we do own a considerable portion of the stock. Naturally, we're interested. Though, at the moment, I can't say which way our direction would lie. Our intent, as you have obviously guessed, was to get onto the board, then see where we could move from there. Our ultimate aim, and I don't think I am telling you anything out of school, was to take over this chain and incorporate it with Garfield's."

"Which is exactly the way I figured."

"Naturally. So you have managed to stymie us. I compliment you. However, there are other angles to consider and, as you are well aware, we will investigate each one. On the other hand, we may be able to save each other a lot of time and money." He creased his trousers with his thumb and forefinger and was silent for a moment, then said, "Is it possible to buy you out?"

Kane shook his head. "Not a chance. I wouldn't even sell at double the going value. I have big things in mind, and I mean to carry them out."

"I see." He looked up and studied the ceiling for a moment, then his eyes returned to Kane's. "Frankly, sir, I don't see how we are ever going to get together. Mind you, now, this is not a threat, but we will fight, of course, to get our way."

"I imagine you will. And I still maintain that I shall prevail in the end. As of this moment that stock you own is worthless to you. If you try to sell it now you will take a hell of a beating."

Garfield regarded him curiously. "Granted. So what do you have in mind?"

"Just an angle that could save you some money. I mean to make this chain grow and make something big of it. In other words, that stock could be worth real money one of these days. So there is another angle to consider. You failed in your first step to get this chain. There is no other large chain in the West that is not already controlled by eastern interests. In other words, as of this moment, your expansion in this direction is thoroughly blocked."

"That could be," then he smiled and added, "but as of this moment only."

"Well, yes. But this is my thought. Why don't you hold onto that stock, then let's see if we can figure out some sort of working affiliation between the two firms. You run your end and I'll run my end, but we could certainly figure out a way to cooperate with each other. What do you think?"

Garfield chuckled and got to his feet. "It is an attractive thought," he said, "but far afield from what we had in mind. I'm afraid not, Mr. Kane."

Kane said, "Just a minute," and decided to play his trump card.

He picked up the telephone and punched the button for Sam Kuller's office. Sam was on the wire after a moment. "Yes, sir?"

"Sam, I have news for you. I want you to get in touch with advertising and have them spread this news to the great American public—Garfield's, Incorporated, has bought twenty percent of the stock of Merritt-Wilson's."

Sam was puzzled as he said, "I know that. You told me before."

"But now I want it known publicly. Have advertising give out press releases, not only here, but on the East Coast as well. Stress the fact that Garfield's has bought in as an investment only. Also, get on the long-distance phone and get in touch with all your contacts in New York and let them know the same thing. Understand?"

"Sure. Will do."

Kane hung up and looked across at Garfield. The younger

man's lips were a thin line. "Mr. Kane," he cried, "you had no right to do that."

"No?"

"Absolutely not. You know goddamned well we did not buy that stock as an investment. We bought it for other purposes entirely different. You have no right at all to send out such a press release."

Kane leaned back and smiled at him, even though his stomach had started flipping again. "I think we have every right," he said. "The purpose for which you bought the stock can no longer be prosecuted. So, from where I sit, you now have an investment instead."

"That's a lie! I shall get in touch with New York at once and have it denied."

"Oh, really? And won't that amuse the trade. Do you know what you would do with such a denial, Mr. Garfield? You would make an asshole of yourself."

Garfield almost shook with anger. "You—you—"

"Uh-huh. You can say anything you like, son, but the fact remains that as far as the trade is concerned you have invested heavily in Merritt-Wilson's, for which," he smiled, "I thank you."

Garfield stomped away from him and walked to the door, but he turned to look back once. Kane thought he detected a slight gleam of admiration in the younger man's eyes. He could not be sure, but he wondered about it.

During the rest of that day, that night, and the following morning, Kane brooded about what Garfield's could possibly do to him. He did not believe he had made an enemy, but, on the other hand, the gage of battle had been cast. And Garfield's was so damned, almighty powerful. Kane knew of no particular weakness that he had at the moment, businesswise, but if one existed Garfield's would find it in time. That was the crux of the whole matter—time. Kane resigned himself to the fact that time was either going to work for him or against him. Either way, it now seemed to be out of his hands.

He sat back and thought of how matters were going in the chain. San Jose, San Mateo, Oakland, and Berkeley were already showing increases, as well as Stonestown and the main store. The others were more than holding their own. Sam Kuller, even though he did not have Jack Harrison's juice in the East, had taken hold well on the local scene. Betty, of course, was doing exceedingly well, as he had expected. Give her time and she would double the output of her floor. Haley, too, was a ball of fire. He had come up with no new innovations lately, yet he always showed a constant increase. The new man, Eric Jeffrey, was already doing better than anyone had ever expected. He had walked around and kept his mouth shut for awhile, but now he had taken control and was doing a job. Fred Maloney was the big surprise. He had jumped eight grades over his head into Jackson's shoes and already acted as if he had been there for years. He was weak on some points, which was to be expected, but he was powerfully strong on others. It might be that he would remain in that slot. There were also no worries concerning Chet Baker. He had his teeth firmly in the job and already had the nerve to demand an assistant. In other words, Kane thought, he had no real worries about the chain itself.

His only worry lay in his plans for the future. In that direction, so far, everything seemed to be shot to hell. Harrison's illness was now known in the East. Already some of the manufacturers had cut their advertising percentage on local ads from twenty to ten percent. He needed at least twenty-five percent to be over the hump, and now he was down to ten. That was very bad. Manufacturers could do about as they pleased when it came to helping local merchants. Kane thought of the system. If, for example, he was running a local ad on Smith's sweaters and Smith paid twenty-five percent of the cost of that ad, it was a big help. Since advertising took such a big cut out of the retail dollar, the percentage with which the manufacturer helped was all-important. Ten percent was practically ruination. He would never go anywhere on that low figure. It was even possible that the manufacturers would refuse to pay any part of his advertising costs, in which case he would stand still the rest of his life. He could almost see that on the horizon.

The building of the five new stores, of course, had stirred them up somewhat in the East. At least, they were talking about him back there. But it had not been sufficient. Now he had used the last of his ammunition—the fact that Garfield's had invested in Merritt-Wilson's. He would just have to sit back and see how that came out. There was nothing else to do.

He left his office and walked to the end of the corridor, then stood there looking out over the fashion floor. Betty was at her counter, talking to Chet Baker. Everyone else seemed gainfully employed. The saleswomen were all busy; even Marie was engaged with a customer. Kane smiled briefly, nodded, and turned away.

Betty had seen him from the corner of her eye, though she had pretended not to. She thought of him briefly as he disappeared back toward his office. She was still angry where he was concerned, and she thought that he was a poor excuse for a father. Imposing, proud, and handsome, yes, but under all that he had been a small man. She turned her attention back to Chet.

He was saying, "I got these tickets from a friend of mine for the Giants and the Pirates. They're right over first base, right over the dugout. The beauty of it, too, it's a double-header this Sunday. How about it, Betty?"

She groaned inwardly. She did like baseball very much, but the thought of sitting through a double-header had her tired already. But she looked at Chet again and appraised him closely. He was a good-looking young man, he was more than presentable, he was always fun to be with, he was obviously going places, and just as obviously he was very much in love with her. Then she looked at him through new eyes, the eyes of an heiress. Even so, he did not suffer too much. Then she thought of him as a husband. Hmmmmm. He still stood up well.

"Okay," she said. "You pick me up at my apartment. But, for God's sake, pack some cold beer. I can't stand that lukewarm stuff at the park."

He chuckled. "I have an ice container at home. Will do. Be seeing you."

He left her, whistling softly to himself, and took the stairs down to the third floor. He had already learned an important fact about the big store that saved him a lot of effort. At least four or five times a day he had to make a complete tour of every department in the store. So, instead of walking up any stairs, he took the elevator to the top floor and started down from there to call at the different departments. He was coasting downhill all the way.

He stopped to see Joe, who was checking some slips at a desk, and asked him, "How goes it?"

Joe shrugged. "Well enough. Looks like we'll make the quota for the day, maybe a little over."

"Good. Any problems?"

"None that I've heard. Just the usual. Say," he asked with sudden interest, "you taking over Maloney's spot permanently?"

Chet had to laugh. "If I do," he said, "I'll be jumping ten years ahead of myself. But I got my fingers crossed."

"Good boy. Keep 'em that way."

Joe watched him walk away and chuckled softly. Things were sure changing fast around the old hay barn. Then he thought of something and dialed his home number on the telephone.

Mrs. M. answered. "Sure," she said, "and this is the Haley residence."

"Hiya, doll-face."

"Oh, you," she giggled.

"Uh-huh. Look, baby, I got a package being delivered at the house today, some new shirts. You gonna be home?"

"Well, I gotta pick the boys up out at the zoo at four thirty, but I'll be home otherwise."

"Good enough. I'd just hate to miss that package. Look for it, huh?"

"I'll be here."

"Okay. See you tonight."

Mrs. M. hung up the phone in the hallway and walked back into the kitchen. Mary was sitting at the enameled table, sipping a glass of milk. She was all dressed to go out. She looked up and asked crossly, "Who was that?"

Mrs. M. answered, "The Mister himself."

"Oh," she snorted, "him! What did he want?"

"Just wanted to know if I'd be here when a package came for him."

Mary snapped, "Clothing, I'll bet. It's always clothes with him. You'd think he was a peacock."

Mrs. M. said lightly, "You never seemed to mind afore."

"Well," she cried, "I do now. Him and his damned fancy clothes." She swallowed the rest of her milk and got to her feet as the outer doorbell rang. "That's the taxi," she said. "I'm going to the doctor's. I'll be back in a couple of hours, anyway. If I'm late, will you put the potatoes on to bake?"

Mrs. M. said patiently, "Yes, ma'am. I always do."

"Oh, for God's sake, don't be flippant with me. Good-bye!"

She went down to the taxi and settled back in the seat as the driver pulled away from the curb. Going to the doctor's, she thought, was a waste of time. She already knew, and definitely, that she was pregnant. No one had to tell her so. Yet it had been over a month since she had been there, and the doctor was probably wondering about her.

Mary went up to the doctor's suite and waited a few minutes in the reception room, then went into the doctor's private office. He got up from his chair and nodded to her, but for the first time since she had known him he was not smiling with pleasure, and he did not offer to shake hands. Mary looked at him curiously as she dropped into a chair across from his desk. Dr. Harding Stone was a man of medium height, who kept his middle-aged figure under control with handball three times a week at the Olympic Club, and kept his flesh looking healthy, in spite of the San Francisco fogs, with a ray lamp at home. He dressed rather shaggily with tweeds, rough shirts, and woollen ties, but managed to look precisely what he was, a prosperous society doctor.

Mary asked, "Well, I suppose you have the results?"

He dropped into his chair and nodded. "Yes, I have. However, it was a little early. If we took tests now, I could be more certain."

"No necessity for that," she snapped. "I know when I'm pregnant. I get mean and nasty, and that's exactly the way I've been feeling the past week or so."

He commented dryly, "So I noticed."

"Well, that's the way I am. I can't help it. Also, my period is as regular as clockwork, and now that's off. We don't need any more tests."

"No, I suppose not. Have you told your husband yet?"

She sighed and shook her head. "Not yet. We—ah—we aren't getting along too well lately. Anyway, I don't start showing for a few more months. I'll tell him then. He can wait."

"Yes, I suppose that would be better." He got out of his chair and walked to the window, looking out over the bay, his back toward her. Then he turned to face her and he was frowning blackly. "Mrs. Haley," he growled, "the child you carry can't possibly be your husband's."

She blinked at him, then burst out laughing. "I assure you," she gasped, "my husband is a very virile man. You've met him. You should know."

"Yes, I have met him. I believe I even know the sort of man he is. But it never entered my mind that you would be that sort, too."

"I don't—I don't—"

"Mrs. Haley, I'm going to violate an oath—it may avert a tragedy. Your husband's doctor happens to be a good friend of mine. We had lunch together yesterday. We got talking about different people, comparing notes, and so on. The names of you and your husband came up in our conversation, and I happened to mention, quite casually, that you were pregnant again. He stared at me and then told me something which, obviously, you have never known."

"What is that?"

He said slowly, emphasizing each word, "I have the misfortune to inform you, Mrs. Haley, that it is impossible for your husband to father a child. Shortly after your last boy was born your husband had himself sterilized to prevent the conception of any more children. It was a successful operation."

Mary said faintly, "I—ah—I don't—"

"He had himself sterilized, Mrs. Haley. He is just as virile as ever, but he is incapable of fathering more babies. Do you understand?"

She gasped, "Not Joe— Not Joe— He's Catholic."

"Apparently, that didn't carry much weight with him. Believe me, Mrs. Haley, he is completely sterile."

She said weakly, "You mean the child is not his?"

"Precisely. It can't be his. You are carrying a child bred and conceived by another man."

Mary stared blankly into space and it was a moment or so before she thought of Ernie Bates. Then she almost fainted. She grasped the edge of the desk with her fingers and her knuckles were white. She felt as if she would throw up, but managed to hold it down. The room spun about and wavered dizzily, then came to rest. She looked at the doctor.

She whispered, "It's not Joe's child."

"No. Can't be."

"There was only one—one other—I was angry—" She shoved herself slowly to her feet, still holding to the desk. She asked weakly, "What am I to do?"

The doctor shrugged. "I'm sorry, but I don't know."

He was afraid she was going to faint and held some smelling salts under her nose, then handed her a glass of water. She drank it down almost in one gulp. Then she picked up her purse and gloves and walked out of the office like a sleepwalker.

She took a taxi to her church and knelt in the front pew and prayed and asked guidance, but her mind remained blank. She looked at the Virgin Mary and thought, My God, I shouldn't be here. I have sinned—and terribly. Now I am to bear the fruits of that sin. I have sinned mortally. I am unclean. I should not be here. Not here. Not in a house of God.

She stumbled out of the church and stopped another taxi a block away. It was getting difficult for her to talk, but she managed to get out her address. The bill for the ride was only $1.40, but she handed the driver a ten dollar bill and walked away. He frowned and wondered if she was drunk.

She dropped her purse and hat and gloves on a chair in the hallway of her home, and walked back into the kitchen. The house was very quiet. She looked at the time and realized that Mrs. M. had probably gone to the zoo to pick up the boys. Thank God, she was alone.

She turned to lean her back against the sink and buried her face in her hands. She was trapped. If she told Joe, she knew what would happen. He would divorce her. A man with Joe's ego and vanity would never be able to live with her and face her day in and day out with the knowledge that the fourth child was not his but another man's. Yet divorce, to her, was a sin as mortal as what she had done. The worst tragedy was that it would break up the family, and that she could never face. Joe would probably take the boys away from her. The courts, once they knew, would undoubtedly back him. To think of losing the boys—!

She broke down then and cried hysterically. She went to her knees on the floor, bent over double, and continued crying. Finally, she straightened up and looked out the window and told herself quietly that she was not fit to be the mother of the boys. The thing that was in her womb prevented it. She opened her mouth and started screaming and pounding viciously at her stomach with her fists. If she could only kill it. Oh, God, if it would only die or go away. How did you get rid of a thing like that?

Then she thought suddenly of Dotty Schroeder. Dotty talked and kidded about her abortionist as other women talked about their doctors or their psychiatrists. She had been married for ten or twelve years, but she made no secret of the fact that she did not want children. Occasionally, though, she or her husband got careless and she had to be aborted.

Mary did not think beyond that point. She had something terrible in her womb, and she had to get rid of it. The fact that

271

she was violating everything she stood for never entered her mind. The THING had to go.

She got out the telephone book, looked up Dotty's number and called her. Dotty was fortunately at home. But when Mary explained what she wanted, Dotty refused to believe her. A good Catholic like Mary? Nonsense. What was another child in her household? Mary pleaded and cajoled and seemed to be getting nowhere. Dotty was sure that it was a rib of some kind.

But when Mary screamed at her, "Goddamn it, you bitch, my husband is sterile! Now, will you tell me who the doctor is?" there was a long silence at the other end of the line.

Then Dotty said softly, "I'll get in touch with the doctor and call you back. Just hang around, dearie. And God help you."

Mary paced the kitchen floor for perhaps twenty minutes before the telephone rang. It was Dotty. She wasted no time with preliminaries. "His name," she said, "is Doctor Chin Lee, a Chinaman. He really is a doctor. And he's very good. However, you'll have to get over to his place right now, because he's leaving tonight for some place or other."

Mary gasped, "I hadn't thought so fast—"

"I'm sorry, but that's the way it is. He says right now or not at all. Frankly, I think he's on the run and I wouldn't bother about him."

"But I have to!"

"Well, in that case—you can try it if you want." She gave Mary an address on Valencia Street in the Mission District and told her, "He says you have to get there right now. But I wouldn't do it, dearie. He's been great with me, but the way he sounds now I think he's on the lam. Know what I mean?"

"I know. But this has to be done. Thanks a lot."

Mary called a taxi. She was going out the door when she remembered and went back to the kitchen to scribble out a note for Mrs. M. "I may not be back for dinner. Go ahead without me. Feed Joe and the boys. See you later. Mary." She left the note on the kitchen table and hurried out the front door.

Mrs. M. read the note when she came home with the boys and shrugged and dismissed it. Later she cooked dinner and was not at all surprised when Joe, also, did not show up. It was perhaps a little after eight o'clock at night when the telephone rang and she answered it. The man on the other end was Lieutenant Halloran of the police force. He asked for Joe Haley, but, upon being informed that he was not at home, asked to whom was he talking? Mrs. M. told him she was the housekeeper. Mr. Halloran asked her a number of questions, then proceeded to tell her that Mrs. Mary Haley was in Children's Hospital and that Mr. Joseph Haley should get there as quickly as he could. Mrs. Haley had had an accident and was in very bad shape.

"My God! Mrs. Haley has three boys. Shouldn't I take them too?"

"Good Lord, no! Keep the boys at home. Don't even tell them anything has happened. There are—well—complications. But you get in touch with Mr. Haley as soon as possible and send him to the hospital."

"Could you tell me—"

"I can tell you nothing, ma'am. Good-bye."

Mrs. M. wrung her hands, then started calling Joe's friends. No one knew where he was. She was trying another possibility when Joe walked in. She grabbed his arm and blurted out what she had learned.

Joe asked immediately, "What sort of accident?"

"The officer didn't say. But he said for you to get to the hospital right away."

"Is she hurt bad?"

"He didn't say that either."

Joe ran out of the house. He got into the Thunderbird and roared across town until he reached the hospital. He ran up the stairs mumbling to himself, God strike me dead. Somehow or other, it's my fault.

19

THE receptionist sent Joe up an elevator to another floor. He walked down the corridor to a nurse's counter and learned that Mary was already in surgery. The nurses would tell him nothing else. He was directed into a small waiting room. He walked in and found Dr. Stone in shirtsleeves, sitting on the edge of a table, nervously puffing cigarettes. There was a young officer in uniform leaning against a wall. There was another man standing at Stone's side, in civilian clothes, but obviously a policeman.

He shook hands with Dr. Stone and was about to start asking

questions, but was abruptly shunted aside. Stone nodded at the man at his side and said, "This is Lieutenant Halloran of the San Francisco Police Department. Better talk with him first. Lieutenant, this is Mr. Haley."

The lieutenant looked coldly at Joe and said with distaste, "Since when does a good Catholic man send a good Catholic woman to an abortionist?"

Joe blinked at him and shook his head. "I don't follow you."

"I guess you're gonna tell me you never heard of Dr. Chin Lee."

"No, I haven't. Who is he?"

The lieutenant's eyes narrowed and some of the ice disappeared in their depths. "You never heard of him?"

Joe shook his head. "Doesn't ring a bell with me at all. What's this all about, anyway? My wife has been in an accident and you start talking about an abortionist." Joe started boiling and growled, "You off your rocker?"

Halloran's eyes narrowed another degree. "Do you know what has happened to your wife?"

"No one has told me anything."

"You don't know she has been messed up a bit having an abortion?"

Joe stared at him, then heaved a big sigh and almost smiled. "Is that what this is all about? You got a woman in surgery you think is my wife? Forget it, officer. It has to be some other woman."

Dr. Stone sighed and said, "It's your wife, Haley. She was found this evening in the apartment of an abortionist. She's in very bad shape."

Joe shook his head. The idea was too wild. "Not Mary," he said.

Halloran was watching him closely and had already made up his mind. He said more gently, "Here's the report, Haley. Your wife was having an abortion in this apartment on Valencia Street. Dr. Chin Lee was the man. Something went wrong. Dr. Stone can explain that better than I can. Anyway, Chin Lee called the police department, gave us the address, and said we'd better pick her up in a hurry. He was already packed to leave the country.

"Needless to say, he was gone by the time we got there. Mrs. Haley was bleeding badly and was delirious. In her purse, however, we found an appointment card with Dr. Stone. So we called him and he had us bring her here to Children's. That's about it. Your wife is in surgery and, from what I understand, it's touch and go." He paused, then asked again, "You never heard of Chin Lee?"

Joe shook his head. He was still half-smiling, though it had become frozen on his face. Not Mary, he was thinking. How could it possibly be Mary? Then he looked at Dr. Stone, and knew that it was Mary. Stone was as pale as a man could get; he was nervous, his eyes would not meet Joe's and the fingers holding a smoldering cigarette were shaking.

Joe asked hoarsely, "It's really Mary?"

Stone bit his lower lip, then said, "It's your wife, Haley."

Joe almost screamed, "Then why the hell aren't you in there with her?"

"Out of my field. This sort of operation is too big for me. Dr. Rasmussen is operating on her right now. He's the best in the business. No worry on that score. I got him right away."

"But what—what—"

"It's hard to explain, I'm afraid. But I'll try. This early in a pregnancy, all the doctor had to do, really, was inflate her womb. However, there was probably some scar tissue left in the womb from the birth of your last son. I thought I had removed it all by electric needle, but there must have been something I overlooked. So, when the womb was inflated, this scar began ripping and the womb burst. It's the first time I've known such a thing to happen in over twenty years, but it happened to your wife. Dr. Chin obviously knew what had happened, but was not equipped to take care of an emergency of that sort. We can all thank him for being decent enough to call the police."

Halloran interjected softly, "We have been trying to nail Chin for years, but could never get anything on him because he has been so good." He shrugged and said, "We'll get him now, though." Then he thought of what he had said and whispered, "Sorry."

Joe looked from one to the other and was again almost inclined to smile. "Can't be my wife," he mumbled. "Can't be Mary."

Stone's back straightened momentarily and he said hoarsely, "I know what you're thinking, Haley. You're incapable of procreation. I happen to know that. It was another man, my boy. She was at my office today, and it came out. It was another man. That's why she went to an abortionist."

Joe walked away from them and dropped to a sofa and stared unseeingly into space. Not Mary. Not the virtuous, Catholic

Mary. To think of her committing adultery was like thinking of himself joining the priesthood. Such things simply did not happen. No one violated character to such an extreme. But then he thought of the ways Mary had taken revenge upon him for some of the minor things that had happened during their years of marriage.

There was no doubting the fact that she was a vengeful person. When she was aroused she could do almost anything. But to go this far? With another man? He thought of what he had done to her and his head lowered and his face sank into his hands. Yes, she was capable of it. He buried the heels of his palms in his eyes, and they were soon wet with tears.

Joe spent the night in the hospital, alone in the waiting room. He learned, a little after midnight, that the operation was concluded and that Dr. Rasmussen had left the hospital. Mrs. Haley was still alive, though very much on the critical list. No, he could not see her. She was in Intensive Care.

Joe went out and bought a bottle of bourbon. Then he went up to the maternity lobby, where he would at least have company and no one would mind seeing him drinking out of a bottle. He started drinking and pacing the floor and thinking.

His brain was racing feverishly. Yet he was not reacting at all as Mary had thought he might. He wondered briefly who the man might be, then dismissed it as unimportant. He didn't really care. He was the one at fault, not the virtuous Mary. She was still a virgin in his eyes.

He was the one who had pushed her to the brink of the abyss and had caused her to commit a sin that was not at all in her nature. He was the one who had committed the grievous fault, not Mary. He had always excused himself because, "That is the way I am." Now he knew that such a simple phrase was not an excuse but an indictment. It would be more proper to say, "I am the way I am because I have never grown up." And now he had to face it.

He faced it all that night and tore himself to pieces over it. So he was a connoisseur of women. Granted. But why continue seeking the fair when the fairest of all was already in your nest? Why bother to caress strange bodies when the most exotic of all was that of your own wife? Further, why cast afield when you hadn't yet plumbed the depths of what was at home? It was all too true. He hadn't grown up, and he knew it.

God, he thought, what have I done?

276

From bachelorhood into marriage he had continued as profligate as ever. Yet he had known Mary and her temper and how vengeful she could be, and he had even known, in the back of his mind, that there would some time be a day of reckoning. That time was now at hand.

Betty Parker found him a little before eight in the morning, half-drunk, his coat off, his collar open, and his sleeves rolled up. She walked to him and pulled him into her arms, hugged him tightly, and pressed her cheek against his. "I'm sorry," she whispered, "so terribly, terribly sorry."

"How," he managed to gasp, "did you know?"

"I was up early this morning. I heard over the newscast that a Mrs. Joseph Haley had had some sort of accident and was at Children's. So I called and talked to a nurse, and here I am. Oh, poor Joe. How is she?"

He couldn't tell her. He simply could not tell her. He put his face in her neck and started crying like a baby.

She was still with him when Drs. Stone and Rasmussen walked into the room. Stone made the introductions. Rasmussen was a roly-poly little man with a pot belly, Santa Claus cheeks, a thick shock of gray hair, and sharp, piercing eyes. He looked Joe up and down and did not particularly like what he saw.

Joe asked anxiously, "How is she?"

Rasmussen shrugged. "Very bad. I just got two hours sleep last night. Even zo, I did better than your vife."

"May I see her?"

He shook his head. "No, I think not. I know the zituation. It is not healthy. I don't know vat you might do. Zo I say no. You go home. Come back later and maybe ve see then."

Joe said flatly, "I'm not leaving here."

Rasmussen looked at him with a little more respect. "Vell, all right. You vait and maybe ve let you see her."

Betty wanted to stay with Joe, but he persuaded her it would be foolish. She kissed his cheek and left the hospital. She was only about half an hour late to work, which, however, was almost unforgivable on a Saturday. Even her own saleswomen glared at her.

She saw Kane that afternoon and told him about the accident. He told her to keep in touch. Later she called the hospital and learned only that Mrs. Haley was still on the critical list. She called again Sunday morning, before breakfast, and was told the same thing. She called the hospital again that afternoon and received the same information. On a sudden hunch, she asked for Joe Haley. After a moment she was talking to a very harassed nurse.

"For God's sake," the nurse pleaded, "get that man out of here. He's driving all of us crazy. No one can get near him. We know what's wrong, of course. Otherwise, we'd be calling the police."

"I'll be there."

Betty got the Jaguar out of the garage and drove to the hospital. She went up to the maternity ward and found Joe sucking on a bottle of bourbon. He was in shirtsleeves, his collar was open, his eyes were bloodshot, there was a black stubble of whiskers on his face, and his clothes were badly soiled. It took no stretch of the imagination to realize that he had not been out of the hospital except to buy booze. He also looked as if he would fall down any moment. He came close to swinging on Betty when she touched his shoulder.

"Please, Joe."

He stared at her and recognized her, then put a hand weakly on her shoulder. She led him out of the room, leaving his jacket somewhere behind. It was almost as if he had been waiting for her to take him away. He got into the right-hand bucket seat of the Jaguar and sat back and closed his eyes.

"She's still the same," he whispered.

"No change?"

"No. She hangs between life and death. No one seems to know anything. You would think doctors would know, wouldn't you?"

"You're tired, Joe. I'm taking you home."

"Okay, I guess. Sure. I can't do any good in the hospital. But, at least, I am close to her there. That's the only reason I stayed."

"Have you had anything to eat?"

He considered the question, then replied, "Not since Friday. It isn't very important. I'm not hungry."

Betty's stomach flipped over as she put the car in gear and pulled away from the curb. Joe's head snapped back and his eyes closed and he was asleep. Betty had a hard time getting him awake in front of his home. She managed it finally and he leaned on her as they went up the stairs. She punched the bell and a red-eyed Mrs. Moriarty helped Betty get Joe inside the house. They could not get him upstairs, however. He turned into the living room, flopped onto an over-sized sofa and was instantly asleep.

Betty told her, "Just let him sleep. I guess that's what he needs more than anything else. Incidentally," she said, holding out her hand, "my name is Betty Parker."

Mrs. M. regarded her beauty suspiciously, but shook hands with her. "I've heard of you," she said. "Mr. Joe holds you in mighty high esteem."

"Well, thank you. I think the same way about him. I'll run along now. I suppose that when he wakes up—"

Mrs. M. smiled thinly. "I'm used to taking care of him, young lady. He'll be fed and shaved and cleaned up."

"Of course. Naturally." Betty glanced at Joe's prone figure, then said, "I'll call tomorrow to see how he is. Good-bye."

She got back to her own apartment just as Chet pulled up in front. She told him where she had been, and he went upstairs with her and waited in the living room as she changed clothes. When she joined Chet, he was frowning.

"I didn't know," he said slowly, "that Haley meant that much to you."

She flared angrily, "Just what the hell do you mean by that?"

He said quickly, "Nothing. Nothing. Believe me."

She glared at him, then decided not to make an issue of it. But she decided against Mario's, just because it happened to be Chet's favorite restaurant. They went to Chinatown and ate at the Imperial Palace instead. It was not a pleasant evening. They broke up early and went home.

She was at work early Monday morning and saw Kane when he came in. He stopped at her desk and told her that he had dropped by Mary Haley's hospital the night before, but had received no encouraging news. He also told Betty that Jack Harrison was leaving the hospital and was going to a nursing home.

"Nine-fifty a month," he whistled. "Imagine that? How they rub it into you today! And who knows how long he'll have to pay that? You know something? I am fast becoming convinced that when a man is dying today he winds up, in the latter few weeks of his life, paying out an entire lifetime's savings to doctors, hospitals, nurses, and so on. No wonder people have nothing to leave to their heirs. The medical society gets it all."

He went on by her and down the corridor to his office. Ten minutes later he was back with a telegram in his hand and a baffled look in his eyes. He handed it to Betty without a word. It was from Paris.

The cablegram read: "JUST MARRIED YVONNE FLAU-BERT. ALSO ACTING HER AGENT SO WILL NO LONGER NEED ALLOWANCE. TELL MOM AND BILL AND WISH ME LUCK. AS EVER. FRANK."

"That," Kane said dryly, "is Frank, your other half-brother."

She lowered the cablegram and said, "Oh?" It was nice to know that her family was enlarging.

"Yes. Now, my dear, who the devil is Yvonne Flaubert? The name is familiar, somehow, but I can't place it."

Betty giggled, "I imagine the last movie you saw starred Mary Pickford."

"Well," he smiled, "not quite that bad. So she's an actress? The name is obviously French."

"Yes. She got her start, however, in German films. She made such a hit that she was brought back to France and England. She is without a doubt the greatest movie star on the European Continent."

"Hmmmm. You don't say. Like the Bardot girl?"

"Well, no. She is young and she is extraordinarily beautiful, but she and Bardot are worlds apart. Miss Flaubert—I guess it's Mrs. Kane now—is a dramatic actress and very, very good. So she is now the wife of your eldest son. Hmmmmm. He must be quite a hunk of man."

Kane nodded. "A lot like Bill. What does he mean by 'her agent'?"

"Lots of movie stars do that when they get married. They make so much money it's ridiculous for the husband to compete with them. So the husband manages her affairs and, I suppose, takes a commission like any other agent." She was silent a moment, then added cuttingly, "Too bad we must keep our little secret. It would be nice to brag that my sister-in-law is the great star, Yvonne Flaubert."

Kane cleared his throat and grumbled, "Yes, yes, of course," and walked quickly away. Betty laughed and thought, I'll cut you down yet, you old goat.

One of the telephones rang and she picked it up to say, "Fashion floor, Miss Parker."

It was Chet who said somberly, "Hi, Betty."

"Oh, Chet."

"Have you heard the news?"

"What news?"

"Mary Haley just died."

To everyone in Merritt-Wilson's, Mary Haley was that paragon of American women, a virtuous wife, a wonderful mother, a dutiful daughter-in-law, a person of charity, not especially bright but beautiful, not especially gifted but religious, not especially anything, really, but astoundingly successful in her field of house-wife. Her death hit the main store as a terrible shock and rever-berated throughout the entire chain.

No one quite understood the "accident," however. The papers merely said she died as the result of peritonitis. Which was true. After peritonitis set in, Dr. Rasmussen had been unable to save her.

Her funeral was tremendous. Patrick Haley, of course, was partly responsible for that. He simply called everyone he had ever done any business with and told them to be at the funeral—or else. Then there were the ordinary Irish, who dearly loved funerals and were out in force. Kane, too, told Joe's friends in the main store that they could take time off to attend the funeral. Lastly, there was Joe's peculiar charm. Even though he was known as one of the liveliest tomcats in the city, very few people felt rancor toward him, and his friendships ranged widely from the tenderloin through North Beach and the Mission District on to Montgomery Street and Telegraph Hill. Joe saw people that day he hadn't seen in years, though he was barely conscious of them.

At the graveside, before the priests took command, Betty was standing far back in the crowd with Anna and Bill and Bessie and Lew Kane. She was watching the broad shoulders of Joe standing by the side of the grave, and her heart was breaking. She knew he had really loved his wife. She also noticed that his head was swivelling about, as if he were looking for someone. He at last turned full about, saw Betty, and walked directly back to her. He placed a hand on her elbow and looked into her eyes. His own eyes were red and swollen.

"Do you mind," he asked, "joining me?"

"Joe," she whispered, "I'm not one of the family. Please."

"I don't give a damn. You're the only honest person I've ever known. When Mary is put in that ground, I want an honest person standing at my side."

"Joe," she whispered again, "it would look very strange."

He blinked back tears as he said, "Did you know that she regained consciousness once before she died? She said something like, 'Now I've atoned for my sins. Now I can meet my God.' Can you imagine a person like Mary worrying about her sins?"

Betty could think of many reasons why any woman would worry about her sins, but she let it go. She simply wondered, and said, "No, I wouldn't."

"She was an honest woman, like you. That's why I want you with me."

Betty was about to protest again, but it did her no good. Joe's fingers closed like a vise about her elbow and he moved her forward through the crowd of curious people. When Betty stood by the side of the grave she looked at the three boys close by. They were just about cried out and were biting their lips and sniffling. Mrs. M. was crying and keening and wailing as if she were in Ireland. Patrick Haley stood to Betty's right, his sparse, thin figure straight and erect, the tears flowing unashamedly down his cheeks. Betty looked up at Joe, who was staring straight ahead into vacancy, and tears also came to her eyes.

And so it was that Mary Haley was given to the earth with a redheaded woman standing by her husband's side and every eye around the grave upon her.

Kane had Betty in his office the following morning. He was furious. "Goddamn it to hell," he roared, "don't you know what it looked like? It was like he was flaunting his mistress at the world, or as if he had already picked out his next wife. Jee-zuss!"

"Please," she said, "I couldn't help myself. There was nothing I could do about it."

"Every goddamned person around that grave was staring at you. And I don't mean they were pleased. They hated you—especially the Irish."

"I'm sorry," she said, "but there was nothing I could do. He had me by the arm and just shoved me up to the grave. I didn't want to, believe me. You were standing there. You heard me arguing with him."

Kane said unreasonably, his face a vivid red, "I don't give a damn. You should have gotten out of it some way."

Then her own temper came to the fore as she cried, "It was unwise of Joe, I know. But I know why he did it—for a really innocent reason. When I think about it now I could cry. But none of those damned hypocrites would understand it, including you."

Kane placed his fists on the desk and glared at her. "You're my daughter," he shouted. "You have to conduct yourself as such. I demand it."

She stared at him open-mouthed, then asked, "Who are you to demand anything of me?"

He roared again, "I'm your father, that's who. I demand and expect a certain mode of conduct from you. And to say that you disappointed me yesterday is the understatement of the year. To see you standing there at the side of that—that goddamned cocksman was too much for me to take. I got sick."

Her own face turned red and she screamed back at him, "Just who are you calling a tomcat? How the devil do you think I got born—an immaculate conception? Who are you to cast the first stone?"

"Well, I—ah—that isn't the point. What I do is my own problem and only I have to pay for it. But what you do is different. I don't want you paying for my sins." He sat down then and buried his face in his hands and said weakly, "All I want for you, Betty, is the best. I was not happy with you yesterday. Seeing you at his side upset me terribly."

Betty stared at his bowed head and asked more gently, "Do you hate him that much?"

"Hate?" he murmured. "I don't hate him at all. My goodness, girl, I happen to like Joe very much. It's just that I know what he is, that's all."

"In fact," she said, "you see yourself all over again."

He was silent for a long while, then he looked up at her and nodded. "I suppose I do. Yes. I've thought of that angle. I managed to straighten out, however. I don't believe he ever will."

"I imagine the same thing was said about you at one time. So, why not give him a chance?"

He shrugged and stared at her, then said, "Look, my dear, I am not worried about Joe Haley. What he does with his life is no concern of mine. But what you do with your life I am very much concerned about. And," he was getting angry again, "I did not like what happened yesterday. Not a damned bit. I absolutely forbid you to even talk with that man again. Do you understand?"

She smiled then and came around the desk and hugged him

and pressed her cheek against his. "Thank God," she whispered, "now I have a father."

Betty was at her counter on Saturday afternoon when she saw Joe step off the elevator and approach her. His hair was combed neatly, he was shaved closely, he was wearing a dark suit, but without an armband (Joe did not believe in the ostentation of wearing his grief on his arm), his face was pale, and his eyes were still not quite clear. He blinked at her and walked uncertainly in her direction.

"You have a place we can talk?" he asked.

"Well," she said, "I do have my own office."

She turned the floor over to Marie and led Joe back to her office, which, at the moment, happened to be empty. She sat behind the desk, but Joe stood looking out the windows, his hands clasped behind his back.

"I understand," he said slowly, "that I owe you a hell of an apology."

"For what, Joe?"

"For what I did to you at the funeral. I have been told by my father and everyone else." He was silent for a moment, then turned toward her and said, "I'm truly sorry, Betty. I just wasn't thinking. All I could see was the most wonderful woman I have ever known having dirt thrown in her face. And all around me were strangers. Even my own father. I needed someone. I needed someone's shoulder to cry on, if you wish to know the truth.

"There was only one person who came to my mind, and I found you and forced you to stand by my side. Isn't that queer? It's the oddest thing I've ever done. But I did it, and I forced shame upon you and apparently I even forced shame on the woman they were burying, which, so help me God, was the last thing in my mind."

She said gently, "I know, Joe. You don't have to apologize to me. I know how you felt at that moment."

"Yes, I believe you do. You're a remarkable redhead, Miss Parker. Very remarkable."

She stopped him as he moved toward the door. "How are the boys?"

He turned and shrugged. "Well as could be expected, I guess. At least, they have Mrs. M., and that's a godsend. She will never take the place of their mother, but she has always been sort of a second mother to them. It does help to soften the blow. She is quite busy with them. School starts next week, you know. Mrs. M. was telling me this morning that she's going to keep the boys so busy until then that they'll drop asleep exhausted every night."

"She's a wise woman."

"Yes, she is, and so are you." He paused, then asked, suddenly, "How are you and Chet getting along?"

She was surprised. "Why, just fine."

"Anything serious?"

"Well, not yet—"

"But he's serious. That's obvious. I imagine he has asked you to marry him, hasn't he?"

It was none of his business, yet she did not hesitate saying, "Yes."

Then he said, deadly serious, "He's not for you, Betty. You need fire and spirit. Think it over. Think it over for at least a year, anyway."

Then he turned and walked out the doorway, and Betty stared after him. Just who did he think he was! Then she realized what he had meant by his last words, "Think it over for at least a year, anyway," and her cheeks flamed as redly as her hair. My God, she gasped, and with his wife just in the grave!

She also learned that afternoon, quite by accident, what had really happened to Mary. Miss Hall had a woman in a fitting room who could not make up her mind between a blue or a green suit of the same style. Miss Hall rolled her eyes and said, "She's been in there half an hour. First she tries on the blue, then she tries on the green. You know the type. Will you talk to her?"

Betty looked into the fitting room and saw that the woman now had on the blue dress. She was in her late fifties, gray-haired, bony and angular, but she had a nice mouth and twinkling eyes. Betty introduced herself and decided to sell her the dress she was wearing. She had only to mention that blue went well with her eyes and that green was a bit passé this season, and the woman's indecision was over with. She thanked Betty most kindly for her help.

Then, as she was taking off the dress, she asked, "Doesn't Mr. Joseph Haley work in this store?"

"Yes. Do you know him?"

"Not really. You see, I'm Doctor Rasmussen's nurse. I was on the case with Mrs. Haley."

"Oh, yes, of course. Tell me, did she have a chance at all?"

The nurse shook her head. "Not really. When peritonitis set in that was the end. She had been pregnant, you see, and—"

Betty swallowed and interrupted with a gasp, "Pregnant?"

"Of course. It wasn't in the newspapers, but everyone knew. She was being aborted when her womb burst, and she was rushed to the hospital." She stared at Betty and saw that she had astounded her. She was an old gossip and was immensely pleased. She blinked innocently and asked, "You didn't know?"

Betty shook her head. The nurse went on talking, but Betty was thinking. Why on God's earth would a woman like Mary Haley ever consider an abortion? She was the kind who wouldn't mind if she had a dozen children. Then, too, there was her religion to consider. Betty was completely baffled.

She left the woman and returned to her counter. Marie came by after a few minutes to complain about some suede suits that had not arrived. "They're advertised in the papers today and they go on sale Monday. How in God's name are we going to mark them if we don't get them before the girls leave for the day? You know damned well they won't do it Monday morning before the sale."

"I've called the basement three times today. Stack tells me they arrived this morning. I'd better go down and get that man moving. You take over."

Betty took the elevator down to the basement and walked back through the semi-gloom to Peter Stack's counter. He leered at her as he saw her coming, his uneven teeth gleaming yellowish in the half light.

"Peter," she said, stopping before him and glaring, "I'm damned mad. You told me three times today that those suede suits would be on my floor in half an hour. What's the problem now?"

"Nothing," he said. "Problem's all over with." He pointed to where some men were opening some big crates. "That's your stuff now. And it really will be on your floor in half an hour."

"What held you up?"

"Third floor, as usual. They got priority in this sweatshop, you know."

Betty sighed. "I know. Always the men first."

"Take it out on Haley, not me. That sonofabitch gets priority in everything. Strictly dynamite, that boy." Then his expression changed and saddened as he said, "Too bad about his wife, huh?"

Betty was still thinking about her and nodded absently, "Very much so."

"I seen her a few times. Strictly gorgeous. Them kids of theirs must be taking it pretty hard. They're all old enough to know and understand."

"Yes, I know. She nearly had a fourth one, too."

"A fourth what?"

"Another child. She died of peritonitis induced by an abortion that went wrong, apparently. That was what killed her."

Stack snickered, then guffawed loudly. "Aw, knock it off. Jee-zuss, I know better than that. She couldn't have been pregnant."

"Why not?"

Stack looked over both shoulders, then whispered to her, "Because it couldn't be done. Maybe you ladies don't know, but all the men in the store know about it. Haley had himself sterilized right after the last boy was born."

Betty blinked at him. "Sterilized?"

"Sure. Told me so himself. That's the reason he plays around the way he does. Can't get in no trouble."

"You must be wrong. I was just talking to the nurse of Dr. Rasmussen, who operated on her. She told me flatly that Mrs. Haley had been pregnant and had been aborted. That was the reason why—"

Her words slid to a halt, and she stared at Stack with wide eyes. His eyes were just as wide and his mouth was hanging open and a bit of color appeared in his cheeks. The two of them had thought of the same thing at precisely the same moment. Betty felt suddenly sick and a little dizzy. If she didn't get out of that basement at once, she was afraid she would faint. She spun about on a heel and walked quickly away.

She did a lifetime of thinking in the two minutes it took her to ride to the fourth floor. Joe had to know. The doctors had to tell him. The police had to tell him. He knew. He was sterile, so he could not conceive a child, yet he knew that his wife had been pregnant and had died of an abortion. My God, she wondered, what must he be going through! Regardless of how religious Mary Haley had been, another man had been involved.

Perhaps—and now Mary was thinking as a woman—it had happened when she had first become angry with Joe. That was probably it. Then, knowing that Joe was sterile (it never entered

287

her mind that Mary would not know), Mary had found herself trapped between the devil and the deep blue sea. How did you explain such a thing to an Irish husband? Maybe Joe knew and had threatened to take the children away from her. But, no, she thought, that couldn't be. She remembered his honest and broken-hearted grief at the grave.

He was blaming himself. There could be no other answer. She remembered many things that Joe had told her about his wife—in particular, that Mary had a temper and was a vengeful woman. Joe, in other words, was blaming her for nothing. She was still a pure, Catholic woman in his mind. He was responsible for everything that had happened, including her pregnancy. Poor Joe, she thought.

Then she thought of how he had been at the funeral and forced herself to think of how she felt about Joe. She liked him very much, she respected him in many ways, and she admired his undoubted talents. Being Joe's wife would be a damned exciting life, no matter from what angle she considered it. However, she would have three boys to raise who were the sons of another woman. And she could have no children of her own. But there could be other compensations. With Joe at her side and Anna's wealth behind her, the sky would be the limit for the two of them. With their combined talents they could even make Lew Kane look like a piker. It was tempting to think about.

But it all came to ashes on one rock. She would never tolerate a man who would cheat on her. Joe had explained it to her more than once, "Every time I see a really beautiful woman I wonder what it would be like to go to bed with her. Then, if the opportunity presents itself, I have to find out." Joe was truly a primitive and he would never change.

Yet there was a danger and she was well aware of it. The man attracted her as no other man ever had in her life. And just suppose he would change because of what had happened to him? Just suppose ...

20

BETTY came to work the following Monday morning feeling very good. She had gone out with Chet Saturday night, wearing her very best formal of chartreuse Chinese silk. He had looked very handsome in his tuxedo. It had been a wonderful dinner at the Palace. Chet had been on cloud eight, and she had enjoyed herself immensely. She had come very, very close to accepting his proposal. After all, how could she do better? Even though she decided to wait, the future seemed to be taking care of itself.

So when she went to work Monday she was feeling good and went about her duties with a faint smile at her lips. She was quite surprised when she saw Kane step out of the elevator with his wife. Bessie had met Betty once only, at the funeral, but she paused to say, "Hello," then went on down the office corridor with her husband. Betty blinked after them. It was the first time she had seen Mrs. Kane in the store.

Bessie was frowning as Kane opened the door to his office and stepped aside. He followed her in and went directly to some drawers in his desk. "Won't take a minute," he said. "Then we'll be on our way."

Patrick Haley had called Kane that morning to say he had the property all sewed up in Santa Rosa as a site for the first of the new stores. Kane was driving up to have a look at it. Bessie was sort of at odds with herself that morning, so he had asked her to come along for the ride and she had accepted. It would get her mind off that "naughty French actress" Frank had married.

Kane found what he wanted in his desk, Jack Harrison's final bill at the hospital, and slipped it into his pocket. He intended dropping by sometime during the day to see Harrison in his new nursing home.

He turned toward Bessie with a grin and saw that she was still frowning thoughtfully. "I don't know," she said. "There's something about that Miss Parker. I felt something strange about her at the funeral, and I felt something strange about her again just now." She gasped and cried, "My God, yes." Her face lit up as if she had turned on a switch. "Now I know. Good Lord, Lew, she's almost the spitting image of Anna Merritt at about the same age! Of course. How stupid of me not to have noticed it before."

He said coolly, "Really? I hadn't noticed."

"Oh, now, come on, Lew." She giggled and said teasingly, "You were pretty sweet on Anna at one time, if my memory hasn't gone bad on me. In fact, that was the only time I came close to losing you."

He came around the desk and took her arm. "We'd better get going. It's a long drive."

"Not any more on that freeway. It hardly takes over an hour. Now, Lew, don't tell me you don't notice the resemblance. You know something? I'll bet you got her there just so she can remind you of your earlier helling days."

All right, he thought. She's going to learn, anyway, and soon. It had better come from me.

"It's funny," he said, "that you should notice the resemblance. Anna is crazy about her."

Then he swallowed hard and said, "In fact, but you have to keep this under your hat, Anna is going to adopt her."

Bessie's eyes opened with mild surprise. "Adopt her? But she's a grown woman."

"I know, but that's how it's going to be. It's in the works now."

Bessie may have been a housewife interested only in her family, but she was not stupid. While they waited for the elevator she studied Betty with the appraisal of a shrewd woman whose mind was racing full speed ahead.

Then she asked softly, "Lew, how old is she, twenty-six?"

He asked irritably, "Why do you say twenty-six in just that way?"

"Because it was twenty-six years ago when Anna made that Grand Tour of Europe, and no one heard from her for months."

"Oh, I see." He wet his lips and said, "Yes, she's twenty-six."

An elevator came and the doors opened, but Bessie grabbed his arm and her fingers bit into his flesh like steel talons. "Let's wait a minute," she said. "I need a longer look at that girl."

There was nothing Kane could do but wait. He looked at Bessie and saw her drinking in Betty's every detail—she missed nothing. Then she turned and looked at her husband and there was a faint mist in her eyes.

"Twenty-six years ago," she whispered. "You and I were having trouble then."

"I know. And I'm sorry for it to this day."

"I know you are, dear. But you were sorry for nothing in those days. I heard plenty of rumors about you and Anna, you know. I loved you, so I ignored the rumors. But you can't forget them, you know."

He said humbly, "I guess not."

Another elevator came and she turned him into it. "This little trip to Santa Rosa," she said, "is just what we need. We have a lot to talk about."

Kane looked back with real distress at Betty, but the elevator doors closed.

Betty watched them go and wondered what would happen if Mrs. Kane found out? She was apparently the one who had to be protected. But it was a question she knew she could never resolve, so she dismissed it from her mind and went back to work.

Kane came back to the store by himself a little after two thirty. He seemed nervous, preoccupied, and depressed. He paused to stare at Betty for a moment, then went on back to his office. In a few minutes he asked Sam Kuller to come into his office. Sam dropped into a chair, in his shirtsleeves as usual, and cocked his head to one side to look at Kane. "So?" he asked.

Kane looked across the desk at Sam. "Anything yet out of New York?"

Sam shrugged. "Nothing."

"Hmmmm. I was rather hoping, after that news release about the Garfields . . . Well, I guess I'm whipped, Sam."

"That's a lot of crap," Sam said angrily. "You're just getting started."

Kane smiled. "As a small merchandiser, yes. With this chain and the way everything stands I can more than hold my own. I don't worry about that. But I was looking beyond, at broader horizons."

Kane shrugged. "So I guess I forget my dreams. I was up to Santa Rosa today, Sam, looking over some of the property Haley bought, the elder Haley, I mean. It's pretty good. He could start construction next week. But Sam," he said, fighting back a desire to start shouting, "I think I had better forget it. I was only using it as a pressure gimmick, anyway."

"You could still use those stores."

"Maybe. But what good will they do? I think I had better cancel out all five of them and forget the whole deal."

Sam blinked at him and felt almost like crying. "I still say you could use those stores."

"Oh, nuts to that. I got a good chain and that's all I got, and that's all I'll ever have—I guess that's all I deserve. Without the New York merchandisers behind me, well—I was shooting at the moon, Sam. I missed. Now I'll pull in my neck and consolidate what I have."

"Maybe if you just grew in a small way, five stores at a time—"

Kane smiled wistfully and shook his head. "It isn't done that way. It's all or nothing in this business. I also had a small crisis in my family today. My wife was mad at me for a little while. You know how she never interferes in my business. But today she got angry and told me that I should get down on my knees and thank God for what I had. Maybe she's right. From now on you are looking at Lew Kane, Esquire, big-time businessman in a small puddle. That's me." He shoved some papers aside and got impatiently to his feet. "That's about it. I just wanted to know if you had anything from New York."

Kane went to stand at the big windows looking out over Union Square. Everything had been so good, so promising—and then the roof had fallen in. First it had been Harrison, then Jackson, then the Garfield intervention, though that hadn't amounted to much, then this last depressing thing about the death of Mary Haley. He seemed to be surrounded by bad luck. And the things he had counted on had come up ashes. He couldn't fight it any longer. Okay, he thought, I'll throw in the towel. Tomorrow I'll call up Patrick Haley and cancel the whole damned business and concentrate on the stores I have and, as Bessie had put it, thank God that I have them. What else was there to do?

He went out to the fourth floor and told Betty glumly, "Get your hat. You're coming with me."

Betty saw that he was very much down in the mouth. She didn't say another word, but went quietly to Marie and told her to take over, then got her hat, purse, and gloves and joined Kane.

They went silently out of the store and to the garage and got silently into the Rolls-Royce. They were driving out Geary when Kane cleared his throat and said, "Bessie knows."

Betty frowned at him. "Knows what?"

"What the hell do you think?" he growled. "There's only one thing she could know that's important—that you're my daughter."

Betty's hand flew to her mouth. "Oh, no!"

"Yes, I'm afraid so. You women have the damnedest talent for going from A to Z and skipping everything else in between. Yet you do come up with the right answers. That's the way Bessie did it. She realized suddenly that you look exactly like Anna, and she put the pieces together from there on—and came up with the right answers. I admitted nothing, but there was no need for me to say anything. She knew."

"Are you positive?"

"Oh, sure. She skirted all around the subject, mind you. She doesn't even like to admit it to herself, but she knows. Frankly, I doubt if she will ever come out flatfooted and tell me what's in her mind, but I know what she's thinking, and I do have to live with it from here on. What I have to live with, of course, I don't know. I suppose it depends on you."

"On me?" she gasped. "Why on me?"

"Because," he said, turning to look at her at last, "she wants me to bring you to dinner at our place tonight, and I couldn't refuse."

"Oh, my God."

"Uh-huh. In spades. Now you just sit tight and think about it."

Kane drove on, then stopped on a wide street before an imposing private residence. "This is it," he said and helped her out of the car. They went up a few stairs and into an entrance hallway that reminded Betty a little of a hospital. Kane said something to the white-haired woman behind the counter, then they went upstairs to an enormous room facing out over the street.

There was a bed just before the windows and in the bed was Jack Harrison. Alongside of him was a stand loaded with books, magazines, and various medicine bottles. There was a color television set facing him and on another table was a radio and an intercommunications system. It was a cheerful room. A young, very good-looking nurse was taking Harrison's temperature. He beamed at Kane and Betty.

"Sit down," he roared. "Sit down anywhere. By God, it's good to see you. I don't get too many visitors. Most people I know real well are dead."

Lew said, "Thanks, Jack. It's good to see you. How do you like this place?"

"Splendid. I've never felt better. Of course," he said, his voice dropping a bit, "I'm paralyzed on my left side, you know. Can't move my arm or leg. But my right side is okay," he added, with what was meant to be a weighted hint, "that's where the telephone is located." He squinted at Kane, then went on, "Service is the best. For once in my life I'm eating regularly, the nurses are beautiful, and," he slowed down, "I've lived beyond my time, anyway."

Kane snorted, "Nonsense. You'll outlive me, you old bastard."

"Maybe I will, at that. Only the good die young." The nurse nodded and left, and Harrison's voice dropped as he asked, "How goes it, Lew?"

Kane settled deeper in his chair and said, "Not good. I made that announcement about expanding with five more stores in the hopes that it would jar them loose in New York. Nothing came of it."

Harrison nodded and had difficulty hiding a smile, though Betty spotted it. She wondered what was in his mind. Kane, however, noticed nothing.

"Then," he continued, "I made the announcement about the Garfields buying in with us as an investment. That hit all the trade papers—even the business section of *The New York Times*. But still not a word out of New York."

Harrison asked innocently, "Have you pressured anywhere?"

Kane barked, "Pressure! How the hell can I pressure those sonsofbitches in New York?"

"You'd be surprised, Lew."

"Aw, forget it. All my dreams are just that, dreams. I made up my mind this morning, Jack, that I would never go any farther than where I am at present. So, okay. It isn't what I want, but I guess I can live with it."

Harrison let his head drop back to the pillows and looked up at the ceiling for a moment. Betty was watching him closely, curiously. He was a good looking old man, even in a hospital bed. His thick hair was pure white and his face was a healthy pink, though his big stomach did make too much of a bulge under the blankets. She thought that he looked like the sort of man she would like as her grandfather. He was thinking no such thoughts about her. He was wondering what it would be like to be in bed with a beautiful redhead like that about forty years back. Heaven, he thought. Pure heaven.

He turned his head then and looked at Kane and his eyes were still twinkling. "I know what you've been doing," he said. "And I know why you've been doing it. So I called Sam day before yesterday and asked him what he knew out of New York and he told me, 'Nothing.' It's about the way I figured it. Both you and Sam make a big mistake, Lew. You think when you drop little bombshells, like you've just done, the New Yorkers will come running to you.

"You and Sam have been underestimating the reaction in New York. You hit home, all right, but then you sit back and expect your lines to be buzzing. Lew, take it from me," he said earnestly, "it doesn't work that way. You have to get on the tails of those bastards. Look at it from their angle. You got a good chain to begin with. Okay, we know the financial structure is weak and so do they. Then suddenly you come out with an expansion of five stores, and they sit back and blink at each other and begin to wonder. Maybe this guy Kane is going places. Then, on top of that, you come out with the Garfield thing and really rock them. As far as they know, at this moment, you could wind up with fifty, sixty, or a hundred stores in your chain. And who wouldn't like to do business with an outfit that size?"

"Look, Jack; it's all water over the dam—"

Harrison said angrily, "You shut up and listen to me, you young whippersnapper. I'm telling you some of the facts of life. So you're doing business with Smith's suits. So you call him up and tell him if he doesn't come through with thirty percent on advertising you're switching to Brown's suits."

"They'd laugh at me."

Harrison's eyebrows arched. "Oh, really?" There was a pad of yellow paper lying on Harrison's lap. He pulled it up and looked at the penciled figures, then turned his attention back to Kane. He was having difficulty controlling his laughter. "I'm still with the firm, you know. You'd better cut me off the payroll pretty damned soon, but I don't think you've done it yet."

"Not yet, no."

"I didn't think so." His eyes returned to the papers and he chuckled and said, "Let's see now. At seven o'clock this morning, which is ten New York time, I called Botany and laid down the law. From now on out they will go for thirty percent of all your local Botany advertising."

Kane stared at him and gasped, "You're pulling my leg."

"Now, then, Stein-Bloch. I called them a few minutes later and they will go for thirty percent from here on out. Now, what's this next one? Oh, yes. Wickshire jackets. That's one of the most conservative houses in the business. They will go for thirty-two and a half percent. Jacobs Robes? Hmmmm. They're good, but not so big. They will carry thirty-five percent. Now, this next one—"

Kane was on his feet staring down at the old man with his eyes open wide. "Jack!" he shouted. "Is this the honest-to-God truth?"

Harrison looked at him and grinned. He said quietly, "Yes, Lew. You know, young man, I still pack a lot of juice back in New York, and I just had a hunch you and Sam were not handling this thing right. So I thought I would see what I could do on my own." His smile faded as he looked directly into Kane's eyes and said soberly, "You're over the hill, boy. Any time a wholesaler will go for anything better than twenty-five percent you got the world by the tail." Then he chuckled again and said, "Give it an extra twist for me, huh?"

Lew Kane walked around the foot of the bed and stood at the windows with his back to them. They could see him rubbing his hands up and down his face. Betty looked at his straight, rigid back and felt like crying. Then she leaned over and squeezed Harrison's arm and said softly, "I love you dearly, old man."

A whimsical smile tugged at his lips as he said, "Forty years ago, young lady, I would be chasing you around the room. You are easily one of the most gorgeous females I have ever seen, and, believe me, I've known my share."

"I'll bet you have, at that. But tell me something. Was it the same with all the wholesalers?"

"Exactly. I put on the screws and they whined and yelled and screamed and pleaded and, in the end, they all came through."

Kane had turned around and asked, "Not even one?"

Harrison growled, "Damn it all, man, how the hell could they turn you down? All they can see is Merritt-Wilson getting bigger and bigger, and if they want you selling their merchandise, they had better get on the ball now. That's all it amounts to. I just applied the necessary pressure, is all."

Kane came to him and sat on the bed. "Jack, as far as I'm concerned, you stay on the payroll for the rest of your life. Just with that telephone, you can do more good than me and the whole organization put together."

Harrison smiled, but shook his head. "Supercargo," he snorted. "That's not for me. You got a good man in Sam. He'll learn the tricks as he goes along. Besides, what the hell could I do with sixty thousand a year? This room, right where I am, is where

I am going to end my life. I know that. And this place costs me a total of nine-fifty a month. That's peanuts, Lew. I got about a half million scattered here and there, and no one to leave it to."

"Merritt-Wilson's has already assumed that nine-fifty a month."

"All right, suit yourself. I guess that's sort of a pension, which I don't mind. I probably deserve it. But what would I do with anything else? Lew, knock me off that payroll the end of this month. I mean it."

Kane looked at him with the adoration of a young boy for his greatest hero. "Jack," he said, "I don't know what to say. I'm all torn up inside. This morning I was a failure. Now there are no limits to my horizons."

Harrison said quietly, "Keep it that way, Lew. I had your same chance when I was much younger than you. I got scared and turned it down. But you don't scare so easy. And, now if you don't mind, I had better get some sleep."

Kane shook his good right arm, and Betty leaned over to kiss his mouth. They started out of the room, but then Harrison called, "Young lady." She came back to the bed. He waited until he saw Kane walking away down the hallway, then he looked into her eyes and whispered, "You're his kid, aren't you?"

She sucked in her breath sharply and asked, "Why do you say that?"

"Hell's bells, young lady, I knew you were Anna's brat the moment I laid eyes on you. Then I got thinking some, and Lew came up on the paternal side. He's quite a man, that father of yours."

Betty swallowed and said timidly, "He has all the marks."

"Uh-huh." His eyes were shining rather brightly as he said, "I got something to tell you I want no one else to know about. I wasn't being so damned altruistic as it may have seemed when I told him to cut me off the payroll. You see, young lady, the doctors give me another three or four weeks to live."

She said from the heart, "Oh, no!"

"Uh-huh. And I know they're right, because I feel it, too. I've never fooled myself about things before, and I don't intend starting at this late age. So now you're wondering why I am telling you. And I don't mind telling you the truth. The one thing I've been missing lately is the company of beautiful women. You do pass a certain age, you know, and suddenly you find the women getting just as old as you are and you wonder where all the beautiful women went. But now, suddenly, I have captured for myself a beautiful woman."

"I don't understand—"

"You will," he chuckled. "I want someone worrying about me, and above anything else I can think of I want a beautiful woman worrying about me. That's you. I'm sorry, but I've elected you, and I want no one else to know about it. This is just between the two of us. Now I can lie here night after night and think of a gorgeous redhead worrying about me—" His eyes closed, his head fell to one side, and he was asleep.

Betty leaned over and softly kissed his cheek. Then she took a lipstick from her purse and wrote on top of the pillow, "I love you," and tiptoed out of the room.

Betty had never seen Kane so excited as when they got in the Rolls. His face was glowing from an inner fire, his eyes were shining brightly, and he used his hands to gesticulate so much that he could hardly drive the car.

"The whole damned Pacific Coast," he cried. "The next store will be opened in Reno, then we'll move into Portland and Willamette, and from there up to Seattle and Yakima, then on back to Missoula, Salt Lake, Denver, and so on."

"How about farther to the east? Chicago and New York?"

"Now," he grinned, "you're teasing me. However," he shrugged, "who knows? Macy's started in New York and wound up in San Francisco. So why shouldn't it be done in reverse? But right now we'll concentrate on the western states. God," he chuckled, "that ever-loving Jack Harrison! Isn't it funny, Betty, just when things are at their lowest ebb you find someone, working behind your back, who pulls all the rabbits out of the hat. Goddamn! Betty," he cried, "I'm over the hill. Do you understand what that means?"

She nodded and smiled. "I have a pretty fair idea."

"Horizons," he laughed. "Horizons in every direction. Now anything is possible. Nothing can stop me. Thank God for Jack Harrison. I hope he lives to be a hundred and ten."

Betty's smile faded and she peered thoughtfully through the windshield.

He took her home and paced the living room floor while she changed her clothes in the bedroom. She left the door partly open so he could keep talking to her, and he did keep talking.

He was so wound up he could not have closed his mouth if he tried.

"You're the only one I can talk to," he said. "I can't talk to Bessie. She wouldn't understand me and couldn't care less."

"Oh, now, please," she called to him. "I am sure she would be interested in any success of yours."

"You don't understand, Betty. Where Bessie is concerned, I am already a success. I was a success the day I married her, and I've never changed in her eyes. I could wind up by buying out Macy's and combining it with Gimbel's, and she would say, 'How nice, dear.'"

Betty had to laugh. "You're kidding."

"No, really. She simply does not give a damn what I do in business. There is only one kind of success to her, and I'm it."

"Sounds to me like she loves you very much."

There was silence for a moment, then he replied, in a lower tone, "Yes, she does. No man in his right mind could doubt that. She loves me very much, and I love her very much. Does that surprise you, considering our own relationship?"

"No, I don't think it does. I can understand it."

"Good. You're a smart girl. But I am a little worried about tonight. She can become shrewish, you know. Goddamn, I would like to get out of this dinner."

"Lew," she said, not at all conscious that she was using his first name, "I have been up against tougher women than her in France and Switzerland and Germany. I am not a bit worried, so you stop worrying."

"Cripes," he laughed, "you're as hard as your old man."

"I didn't go to school just to eat lunch."

She came out of the bedroom in the same outfit she had worn to the first managers' meeting at the store, a simple orange sheath dress with a belt about the waist, a three-quarters length darker orange coat, and a bow in her hair. "How do I look?" she asked, pirouetting before him.

He held her at arm's length and said solemnly, "You know, you really are one of the most beautiful women I've ever seen. What a dirty shame I can't stand on the housetops and shout to the world, 'This is my daughter! Everybody look. This is the honest to God product of my loins.'"

She smiled wryly—she was not sure she liked what he had said—and suggested it was time to leave.

They got in the Rolls and drove off toward Kane's penthouse.

It was just twilight. Betty settled back in the luxurious seat and thought how wonderful it was to be in San Francisco, one of the few great cities in the world she really liked. It was fantasy, of course, but she thought she could smell the crab pots boiling on Fishermen's Wharf, feel the fog pouring in over the sands of the western beaches, hear the clang of the cable car bells, and even smell the spaghetti and pizzas cooking in North Beach. What a wonderful place. And in a few minutes, she thought, it could all erupt in her face in one nasty boil. After all, what did she really know about Bessie Kane?

She was seated with her not much later, on a big sofa, before the big windows looking out over the bay and the Golden Gate. The sun was just sinking over the horizon and the whole sky was gold and pink and blue. Bill Kane was on the other side of the room, his elbow on the mantel over the fireplace, his shrewd eyes closely watching Betty and his mother. Lew Kane was at the bar mixing drinks. He was perspiring a little. He had already told his wife that he had just put over the biggest deal of his life and the only response from her was, "I'm glad, darling. But you always were capable."

Mrs. Kane sat on the sofa turned partly toward Betty, with one pudgy knee up on the cushions. She was watching the younger woman through half-closed lids. Her lips were a bit thinner than usual.

"I understand," she said at last, "that you were raised in Europe."

Betty looked her in the eyes and made no attempt to smile. "Yes," she said, "I was. I came to this country after my second year of college."

"You like it here?"

"Very much so. It's like returning home, you know. After all, my parents were American."

"Oh, yes. I heard something about that. Didn't they have an accident, or something?"

Betty said bluntly, "So I was told."

"Hmmmmm? Oh, I see. You were told. Yes, of course. I don't imagine you ever knew them."

"No. I was informed about them only through nursemaids. I always had to take the word of others, you see. But I did believe them."

Bessie caught her breath and asked a leading question, "But since then—?"

300

Betty looked her squarely in the eyes and said, "Whoever my parents were, Mrs. Kane, I had nothing to do with bringing them together, I had nothing to do with what we might call their fancy for each other, and I certainly, God knows, had no say over my birth. At no time did I ever have any control over what eventually became my presence here on earth."

Bessie swallowed and changed her tack quickly, "I understand Anna Merritt is going to adopt you."

"Yes, she is. If I ever asked for a mother, it would be Anna Merritt. I love her. I believe she loves me. We seem to have a lot in common."

Bessie knew that she was getting out of her depth, but she persisted, "You do, at that. You're so remarkably alike."

"I know. That is what drew us together in the first place. She seems to think that I am her image at that same age."

"Yes, you are. Very much so."

"I'm glad. Because, you see, she is still a remarkably beautiful woman, and I hope I can carry it as well at her age."

Kane arrived at that moment with the drinks. He was sweating more profusely than ever. He raised his glass and said, "Cheers, everyone," but Bessie was paying no attention to him.

Bessie was saying to Betty, "Mrs. Merritt, you know, is worth millions of dollars. Which would, of course, make you quite an heiress. So don't you think it a little odd of Anna to adopt a grown woman as her daughter just because you two seem to resemble each other?"

Betty smiled for the first time. "No," she said, "I don't think it so odd. Love is a peculiar thing, Mrs. Kane." She looked for a long moment at Kane, then back at Bessie. "A few months ago," she said, "I would have denied that I would give my love to anyone unless they fought for it and won it, let's say, on the field of combat. Yet, recently, I have had to change my mind. I have met a few people I have come to love in the briefest sort of time, with no challenge and no combat. I love them simply because they are what they are, and I am what I am. For example, I love your husband."

Bessie drew in her breath sharply, but Betty continued unperturbed, "Mr. Kane, regardless of what our relationship may or may not be, or what you might think it is, is my idea of everything that a true gentleman should be. I would almost give my right arm to tell the world that a man such as Mr. Kane is my father. The same goes for Mrs. Merritt, as I explained before.

I would love to be able to say that Mrs. Merritt is my mother. And your son, Bill. If I were ever given a choice to pick out my own brother I would put Bill's name at the top of the list. But, you see, I can't do any of these things. Yet I do love them. Mrs. Kane, is there anything wrong in how a person loves?" Then she asked slowly, "Can you deny me the love I have for these three people?"

Bessie looked at her and slowly her eyes swung away until she was looking down at the floor. Then she looked out over the darkness that was settling on the bay and coughed. Kane turned on a lamp in a far corner, which did very little to illuminate the room. Bill stood where he was, watching the two of them.

Bessie's eyes came slowly back to Betty and she said, "I can never deny love, my dear. I'm not thinking of myself, mind you, but a situation does exist here that could be dangerous."

Betty placed a hand gently on her arm and said, "Not through me. On the records, Mrs. Kane, my parents died in an accident right after I was born. Let us leave it that way. All I am concerned about right now is a few people I happen to have fallen in love with. And I intend to go on loving them. You don't really mind, do you?"

Bessie looked into her eyes for a long, long while, then she suddenly gasped and kissed Betty on her cheek. "You know," she said, "you are the damnedest young lady I have ever encountered. I don't think I have ever known anyone quite like you. You must come from very good stock." Then she looked at her husband and said, "Lew, would you mind carving the roast?"

Kane blinked and nodded and went to the table.

Bill left his position at the fireplace and approached the sofa. He leaned over Betty, a tight grin splitting his face. "You," he said, "are a phenomenon. There is only one thing that's wrong. I wish things were the way they were before. I would marry you in one minute flat. But now, well, I guess I just have to sit back and be proud of you."

"There is a deeper love, you know."

"I'm beginning to find that out." He looked at his mother and said, "Open your heart, Mom. Here is a gal so damned easy to love it's ridiculous."

Bessie squinted at Betty and nodded. "We'll see. Time always tells."

The four of them sat down at the table, and though the food

was excellent Kane did a very bad carving job. His carving hand was shaking a bit.

Kane was passing the plates about when the doorbell rang. He excused himself and disappeared into the entranceway of the penthouse. The three left at the table could hear his conversation without even trying to listen.

Kane said heartily, "Well, Joe, hello. How are you?"

Joe Haley replied, "Not too bad, Mr. Kane. I tried to call you all day at the store but couldn't get you. So I thought I'd drop by your place and tell you not to expect me back to work for at least a couple of weeks."

"For God's sake, Joe, that's understood. It never entered my mind that you would be back for some time. Look, have you had dinner?"

"No, sir."

"We have an excellent roast of beef. Come on and help us finish it."

"Thanks, Mr. Kane, but no. I'm not fit company for anyone right now."

"Betty is here."

There was a long silence, then Joe said, "Well, if you really don't mind, I would like to join you at dinner."

He and Kane came walking into the dining room and Betty's eyes narrowed as she appraised Joe. He was dressed beautifully, as usual, in a dark brown gabardine suit, an off-yellow shirt and brown tie, and very thin, lightweight oxfords obviously from Italy. He shook hands all around and smiled at Betty and pulled up a chair to sit at her side. Bessie went into the kitchen and brought back a plate and some cutlery for him. Joe looked at the roast and sniffed it and said, "Smells good. Maybe I do have an appetite, after all."

Betty sighed and sat back in her chair. She was thinking, He haunts me. His face was haggard and lined and pale, his eyes were bloodshot, his hands were shaking a bit—he had probably been drinking too much the past few days. Betty was wondering, What did you do with a man like him? You could study about the primitive American Indians. You could study about the natives of the Amazon River. You could study about primitive peoples anywhere, and maybe you might learn something. Maybe you might learn how to handle and cope with a primitive person. That was what it would take, of course. And then when you learned, you would have to tighten the screws. She had the guts for that. She knew it. She closed her eyes and thought, Poor Chet.

Then she also thought, as had so many women before her through the centuries, I am probably the one person in this world who can keep him in line.

Epilogue

THE doors of the big store were hardly open the following day when an older, well-groomed woman approached Betty's counter. Betty thought she recognized her and the thin smile she was wearing. Trouble, she thought. Then the woman smiled sweetly and said, "I am Mrs. Milton Alexander. Do you remember me? I left a skirt here?"

Betty remembered instantly, and her stomach sank. She was supposed to have had the seamstress put gussets in the woman's skirt and had forgotten completely about it.

She decided to be honest and said, "Yes, I do remember you, very well. Unfortunately, Mrs. Alexander, I owe you an apology. We were supposed to put gussets in the skirt. Wasn't that it?"

Mrs. Alexander's eyes narrowed, "Yes, indeed. Is the skirt ready?"

Betty sighed and said, "I'm sorry, but the answer is no. I am afraid I forgot all about it."

The older woman was suddenly frigid. She looked at Betty icily and said, "You mean to tell me that after all the months that skirt has been in here you still have done nothing about it? That is hard to believe."

"Mrs. Alexander, believe me, I am personally responsible for the oversight. I am terribly, terribly sorry, but I forgot all about it."

Mrs. Alexander's head went back and she stared at Betty. "Young lady, who is the president of this firm?"

"Mr. Kane. Mr. Lew Kane."

She said frostily, "I saw the manager once before, if you remember, but obviously I didn't go high enough. I suppose if one wants anything done around here one must see the president himself. Where could I find him, please?"

Betty nodded beyond her and said wearily, "Just down that corridor behind you, the last office. But, really, Mrs. Alexander, I am sorry."

The other woman snorted and turned on her heel and disappeared down the corridor. Betty thought suddenly, Aw, the hell with you. Why should I bother?

Mrs. Alexander came back about fifteen minutes later, glared at Betty, and went down in an elevator. She had hardly gone when Kane came walking out of the corridor and leaned his elbows on Betty's counter.

"Okay," he smiled, "what was that all about?"

"Well," Betty said, "it really is my fault. She brought this skirt in months ago, part of a suit. It had been let out from an eight to a ten and there was no material left to let out any further. She had obviously put on weight and there was nothing that could be done about the skirt. Last time she was in, however, we decided to put in gussets and she approved. And I, like a ninny, forgot all about it. So the skirt still sits in the tailor shop."

Kane chuckled and said, "Get on it, Betty. And have that skirt ready by four o'clock, because that is when she's coming back for it."

Betty shrugged. "Will do. Actually," she added, "we probably owe it to her. I was the one who goofed, after all."

She went into the tailor shop, dug out the skirt, and showed it to the head seamstress, who looked at Betty and shook her head. "We can't put gussets in this," she said. "There is no material like it in the store. Ask Heiner about it. She's the buyer who bought these suits, I remember."

Betty took the skirt and went down to Miss Heiner's office. She examined it, thought a moment, and then said, "Out of the question. You can't get this material. We bought these suits from a local outfit, Jacob Wolfgang. He's gone out of business."

"You're sure?"

"Absolutely."

Betty carried the skirt down to Kane's office and told him what she had learned. "All right," he said, "offer to give her another suit at the same price."

Betty shook her head. "I don't think it will work. This skirt has now become a challenge with her."

Kane thought a moment, then found the telephone number of Jacob Wolfgang and put through a call. In a moment he was explaining his difficulties to the manufacturer.

Wolfgang asked him, "Can you describe the material?"

Kane described the material exactly. Wolfgang thought a moment, then said, "Yes, I think there was a bolt or so of that stuff left. But it's in the warehouse at Fourth and Harrison."

"Good. I'll meet you down there."

"Oh, now, wait a minute, Mr. Kane. I would do anything in the world to oblige you, you understand that, but I haven't been in that warehouse in months and where we would even begin to look I don't know."

Kane made a snap decision. "It's worth a hundred dollars to me if you find the material."

There was a short silence, then Wolfgang said, "I'll meet you at the warehouse." He gave Kane the address and hung up.

Kane winked at Betty. "I'll get you off the hook. Don't worry about it."

Kane took a taxi to Fourth and Harrison and arrived at almost the same time as Wolfgang. They went into the gloomy warehouse and Wolfgang switched on the lights. He examined the skirt that Kane had brought with him and then started looking along the dozens and dozens of dusty shelves. They spent an hour and the search appeared fruitless. Then, as they were about to leave, Wolfgang thought of one last place, and there was a bolt of the material. He handed it to Kane and Kane gave him a hundred dollar bill.

Wolfgang sighed and said, "A hundred or not, Mr. Kane, I wouldn't do this for anyone in the world except you."

"Naturally. Because one day you may be back in business again. Thanks, anyway."

Kane left him and took another taxi back to the store. There he picked up Betty and walked with her into the tailor shop. He handed the skirt and the bolt of material to the head seamstress. "Now," he said, "put in the gussets."

She examined the material and the skirt, then looked at Betty. Distress flags were flying in her eyes. "Miss Parker," she whispered, "you can't do it. It's impossible to match this plaid where it won't show. I remember this suit. The jacket is very short. Any gusset, no matter how well you do it, is going to show. And I know Mrs. Alexander. She would never be happy with it."

Kane snorted with exasperation, "Then what the hell can we do?"

The woman thought a moment, then looked slyly at Kane. "There's only one thing we can do. Give me three hours and I'll build her another skirt."

"You mean a new one?"

"That's right, Mr. Kane. However, as you well know, under the union rules, we are not supposed—"

Kane cut her off by digging into his wallet and handing her a twenty dollar bill. "Pretend the union doesn't exist for the next few hours"

She tucked the bill into her bra and grinned and said, "Come back in three hours."

When Mrs. Alexander returned a few minutes after four o'clock Betty was ready for her. The new skirt was laid out across the counter and Betty was smiling broadly. "Well, Mrs. Alexander," she said, "I am sure that now you will find everything eminently satisfactory. Would you care to try on the skirt?"

The older woman said huffily, "Indeed, I would. Give it to me, please."

When she came back with the skirt over her arm, Kane came down the corridor and joined them. She stared at him for a long while, as if he had just committed some crime, then glared at Betty.

"Young lady," she said, "There are no gussets in this skirt."

"Yes, ma'am. I know."

"Yet it fits perfectly."

"I am very glad."

"Which, of course, brings us back to the beginning. When I brought this skirt in here some months ago I told you then that letting it out should be a very simple job."

"Mrs. Alexander, if you please—"

"Oh, no," she snorted, "you don't sweet-talk me. You have done exactly what I told you to do in the first place. Which certainly proves my point."

"If you will listen, please—"

The older woman was smiling bitter-sweetly. "I don't care to listen to you," she snapped. "I have never been so fed-up with a store in my life. I don't ever intend coming back here again. Please cancel my account."

She spun away from them, walked to the elevators, and disappeared between softly closing doors. Betty stared after her and did not know whether to laugh or cry. Then she turned and looked at Kane.

He was watching her with one eyebrow cocked high, then suddenly he burst out laughing. He put an arm about Betty's shoulder and said, "Honey, you can't win 'em all."

DISCARD